Between Friends

"Kitt delve[s] into issues of interracial ...onships and biracial children with great sensitivity and understanding."
—*Publishers Weekly*

"...ning opening scene that is so terrifyingly ...l it will send shudders through most ...rs. . . . Tense, thoughtful, and sensual."
—*Library Journal*

Significant Others

"Her finest work to date. I loved it. I highly recommend it."
—Heather Graham

The Color of Love

"...oving. . . . Kitt does an incredible job ...ring both characters' reservations about having an interracial relationship."
—*USA Today*

Praise for the r

Close

"Sandra Kitt is a mas
—Eric J

"A bold and imaginat
keep readers t
—E. L

"With insight and se
explores the comple
across the color line. E
realistic and beautifu
has written a
—Valerie V

"A riveting drama of i
the gritty urban politi
a heartwarming love
—Eva

Famil

"*Family Affairs* celebrate
family and the hea
—Jayne A

"Kitt provides . . . unus
to her widely di
—*Publish*

"Nobody does family dran
—*Roman*

"
relati

"A stu
re
read

"N
expl

SHE'S THE ONE

Sandra Kitt

A SIGNET BOOK

SIGNET
Published by New American Library, a division of
Penguin Putnam Inc., 375 Hudson Street,
New York, New York 10014, U.S.A.
Penguin Books Ltd, 27 Wrights Lane,
London W8 5TZ, England
Penguin Books Australia Ltd, Ringwood,
Victoria, Australia
Penguin Books Canada Ltd, 10 Alcorn Avenue,
Toronto, Ontario, Canada M4V 3B2
Penguin Books (N.Z.) Ltd, 182–190 Wairau Road,
Auckland 10, New Zealand

Penguin Books Ltd, Registered Offices:
Harmondsworth, Middlesex, England

First published by Signet, an imprint of New American Library,
a division of Penguin Putnam Inc.

ISBN 0-7394-1996-x

REGISTERED TRADEMARK—MARCA REGISTRADA

Printed in the United States of America

For Gail Starkey

"The making of friends who are real friends is the best token we have of a [person's] success in life."
—EDWARD EVERETT HALE

Thank you for your unwavering support and understanding.

Also to:

Betts Staeck, Patterson Riley, and L. Mike Harrison, for being wonderful role models.

ACKNOWLEDGMENTS

My sincere thanks to the following people, who were generous with both their time and expertise:

Diane Gilroy, of the Association of Children's Services in New York City, who navigated me through the myriad of details about this agency created for the care and protection of children.

Laura Kapnick, Director of Library Services at CBS Network offices in New York. I appreciated the tour and the sharing of perspective from one of my professional colleagues.

Kenneth M. Stanley for his insights on jazz.

Captain Don Ubell of Engine Company 52 in Riverdale, where I live. I not only had a chance to interview Captain Ubell but watched him with his team in action as they left me in mid-question to respond to a real alarm!

Daniel Keane, Ladder 1, New York City Fire Department, for providing me with the inside details and many terrific anecdotes about being a fireman. His E-mails were great!

Lorinda Klein, Director of Public Affairs at Bellevue Hospital, who arranged for me to tour the City Morgue with morgue manager Felix Velazquez.

And finally, to Chief Fire Marshall Louis F. Garcia, who brought the heroism to life with stories from his career with the Fire Department.

You all made the research not only informative, but fun.

Chapter One

Stacy was scared.

She didn't want Marcus to find her. She didn't want to have to try and say no to him again. Just saying no had never worked before, anyway. He'd always managed to convince her that things would change and that he really did love her. That he would stay out of trouble and away from other women. That he would do the right thing and not take his bad luck and failures out on her and Jade. But he was always breaking his promises. Sooner or later, something would set him off. Then they'd have to move. She'd have to find another job, make up stories, tell more lies.

She didn't want to live that way. She wanted a better life. For herself. For their daughter, Jade. She could do it. She'd learned to manage without Marcus since he'd been sent up. She had her own apartment, friends, a job. She didn't need him anymore.

And he'd never wanted Jade.

She surfaced from the subway on Chambers Street and looked around to get her bearings. All the courts were down here in Lower Manhattan. City Hall, One Police Plaza, and even the FBI were within walking distance . . . and not one of them could do a thing to help her. She'd tried. Once she'd even told the police about things Marcus had done that they didn't know about. But she couldn't give them proof. He'd threatened her so many times. She complained. It's a domestic matter, she'd been told. One of these days he would hurt her seriously. She didn't want him to do that to Jade. Get a restraining order, they'd advised. Move.

She was tired of running.

Stacy glanced around the crowded downtown street. Paranoid, she scanned all the people around her. What if Marcus had already started to follow her? What if he knew where she'd moved? Stupid. Sure, he already knows, *she thought wildly. Hadn't his crony, HoJo, tracked her down to tell her that Marcus had made parole?*

She crossed the street and headed west, dodging the cabs and delivery trucks, the town cars and all the traffic flooding the narrow streets, flowing on and off the Brooklyn Bridge. Someone blew a horn. She ignored the angry blast and accompanying obscenities even though her heart lurched with adrenaline as she reached the sidewalk. She rechecked her watch. She had less than five minutes to make it to the office of Protective Services.

She picked up her pace, reached the next crossing. She stepped off the curb. Someone yelled, shouted, "Watch out." She turned her head. A monster on wheels barreled down on her, blasting and snorting. She froze. There was no place to go and no time to move.

The impact tossed her into the air, her body loose-limbed and out of control. Her arms flailed. She dropped her purse. Her shoes came off. She landed on the street, her head bouncing against the cement until she was senseless and numb.

She couldn't move.

She made a feeble attempt to lever herself up. People were speaking words that made no sense. "I'm okay," she wanted to say, but she couldn't breathe. She had no idea how much time had passed, but she knew it was running out. She would never make it.

She collapsed back to the ground, hurting everywhere. Her eyes fluttered open to see strangers surrounding her, hiding the sky and blocking out the daylight. Her gaze roamed around the blurring, out-of-focus faces filled with horror, regret . . . and pity. She sighed in finality; she couldn't possibly get to Protective Services now.

She couldn't keep her eyes open any longer, and they drifted shut.

Suddenly she felt a little bit better. Flashing through her consciousness were years of memories. Things she'd forgotten. Things she didn't want to remember. Fast-forwarding through all her mistakes. The only thing she'd ever done right was Jade.

She couldn't hear the voices now. Everything was fading away. She didn't even hurt anymore. Maybe she'd just lie here a few more minutes. Then she would have the strength to get up and go home to Brooklyn. She had friends there. People who would help her. She wouldn't worry about Marcus anymore.

Everything would be okay.

Everything . . .

"Hold the doors, please," Deanna Lindsay called out, picking up her pace as she hurried to catch the elevator. She was discouraged from jogging in her two-inch pumps by the slick faux-marble floor of the television network's lobby.

"Don't run, I've got it," a male voice called out.

Deanna reached the door and pushed in behind several other passengers. She expertly finger-combed her short, full hairstyle, which the brisk March wind had blown apart. She had lightened her hair with henna, and the reddish glint helped define her own toffee-colored complexion. In a narrow metallic frame around the elevator door, she caught a partial and distorted image of herself. She absently adjusted the bright tangerine Pashmina shawl tied around her shoulders over her taupe winter coat. She wore her favorite gold loop earrings, but wondered if her teardrop pearl pair would have been a better choice with this outfit.

"Hi, Norman. Thanks for holding the door," she said to the man who acknowledged her with a smiling nod. She caught her bag as the strap slid from her shoulder to the crook of her elbow. "Sorry . . ." she murmured when the bag swung into a black woman standing next to her.

"That's okay," the woman responded.

Deanna glanced at the woman quickly again and recognized her as the ninth-floor receptionist. Gloria . . . she didn't know the last name. Deanna smiled politely, murmuring good morning, and turned to face the door.

"You know, you're the last of a dying breed, Deanna."

Deanna looked inquiringly at Norman, who worked in the network PR office, a few floors below her own department.

"Am I? Why do you say that?"

He pointed to her feet. "I thought all you modern women had given up on high heels. Sneakers are the universal footwear, and they're a lot more comfortable."

"You're absolutely right," Deanna agreed. "But Reeboks don't go with my suit. Anyway, I'm not a jockette. I'm a thirty-something middle manager." Norman laughed. "And heels make me look taller."

"What about dress-down Fridays? Don't you take a break then?"

"Sneakers are fine for sports, but not the boardroom. I have to at least look like I'm in charge."

There was some chuckling behind her and Deanna hazarded another glance at Gloria. She found the woman's eyes sparkling with amusement and realized that Gloria was wearing sneakers.

"So you think not wearing sneakers means you'll be treated better?" Norman continued to bait her.

"Probably not," Deanna conceded with a shrug. "But I dress for the position I want, not the one I have."

"Oh, really? So, what position do you want? CEO, I suppose."

"Goddess," Deanna said with a straight face, eliciting laughter from the other occupants.

"No chance of that around here," Gloria remarked.

"You never know." Deanna shook her head. "I have God on my side. *She* would approve."

Everyone was still laughing when the elevator stopped on four, and Norman got off with a cheerful wave. The door closed and the elevator continued its ascent. After a moment Gloria spoke up.

"Hmpf!" she said. "They're never going to put a black woman in charge of anything around here 'cept for administrative assistants."

"There are plenty of black writers and anchors," Deanna replied. "I'm the manager of the Information Center."

"Is that what you do?" Gloria peered at Deanna with a skeptical frown. "Someone told me you're just a librarian."

Deanna could hear the derision in Gloria's tone, as if a librarian was some sort of lower form of animal life. It was particularly irritating coming from someone who was not required to have more than a high school diploma for her job.

The elevator came to the next stop and Deanna and Gloria disembarked. Deanna continued down the adjacent hallway to the Information Center.

The lights were on when she quietly entered. She glanced at the clock. Eight-fifteen. She did a sweeping visual inventory of the circulation desk, and the row of stacks beyond. She could see nothing out of the ordinary. And yet . . .

"Good morning," Deanna called out, loud enough to be heard, and calm enough not to sound wary or suspicious.

For another moment everything was still. Then a figure emerged from behind a cabinet just outside of Deanna's office. Deanna thought it might be Stephen Adler, her administrative assistant. But the person coming forward was Nancy Kramer. She held several folders and loose papers close to her chest.

"Hi, Ms. Lindsay."

"Nancy . . ." Deanna kept the surprise from her tone. She glanced beyond the younger woman toward her office, wondering if her door was still closed and locked. Then she brought her attention back to Nancy's face, carefully watching her expression. "What are you doing here so early?"

Nancy's dark brown eyes blinked, and her gaze didn't hold Deanna's for more than a few seconds.

"Trying to finish up some work. I didn't think there'd be a problem with me coming in before the center was open."

Deanna studied her for a moment. Nancy Kramer had been in the department for several months. She came with excellent recommendations and impressive schooling, and she was generally a good worker.

But Deanna didn't approve of her staff working extra hours without her knowledge.

"There wouldn't have been a problem if you'd told me first. Just what is it that has to get done before nine o'clock in the morning that couldn't wait until you came in at your normal time?"

Nancy smiled vacantly in return, peering at Deanna through her glasses with an expression that might be fear, shyness, or predictable employee jitters when talking to her boss.

"Well, I like to make sure I don't fall behind. Especially when I have to take time to help out Ruth or Marianne. They get so busy, and I want to help as much as I can. I feel so lucky to be here."

Deanna listened patiently to the wide-eyed compliment, raising her brows. "I appreciate your initiative, but I'd rather that you ask first. Ruth has experience, and she's the senior reference librarian. She understands the office routine and who's responsible for what. When she's unavailable, you can ask me."

Nancy nodded. Her dark hair, cut in a short pageboy, swung against her cheeks. "Of course. I just want to do a good job, and I notice that sometimes I'm here alone. That's okay, isn't it? I wouldn't want to get Ruth or Marianne in trouble for being away from the library. They've been so helpful."

"We have a pretty relaxed office," Deanna replied. "As long as the work gets done, I have no complaints. Just make sure to log in all reference requests, and indicate when and who answers them."

Eagerly Nancy held up pages of a printout. "I have some I'm working on right now. And I noticed there are some books that haven't been catalogued yet, so I thought I'd do those."

Deanna nodded and began walking toward her office, key in hand. "Yes, thank you. But it could have waited until regular hours."

In her office Deanna put her coat away. She sat, slipping her feet out of her shoes as she booted up her computer. Waiting to log on, she looked over her calendar of appointments and meetings for the day. She put her phone on the speaker system and listened to voice mail messages as she simultaneously opened her E-mail box on her screen. There were thirty-two messages. Patiently, Deanna began to read . . .

"Good morning."

A cup of fresh coffee appeared near her right hand as she expertly worked the keyboard and mouse.

Deanna glanced at her watch. Nine o'clock already. "Good morning, Stephen . . . thanks. You're a saint."

"The next time you get bent out of shape because I screwed up on something, I'm going to remind you that you said that," Stephen Adler said.

Deanna arched a brow and shook her head. "Won't do you any good. Your slate is wiped clean at five o'clock this afternoon. Is that your phone ringing?"

"It's Ruth's," he said, leafing through envelopes and messages in Deanna's out box. "I'll send this file upstairs. What are you doing here so early?"

"What I'm always doing when I get here early. Trying to catch up on my work."

"You worry too much," Stephen murmured.

"Easy for you to say. You don't have to deal with the anchors and writers when they're on deadline. What I want to know is, how could you schedule me for three meetings today?" Deanna asked, frowning at the screen as she efficiently deleted several messages she didn't need to read. "How am I supposed to get work done?"

"My rule of thumb is, *I* never say no to the head of the department when he wants to see you. And don't try to do everything yourself. Delegate. That's why you're a manager."

"You're too smart for your own good," Deanna replied good-naturedly. "Maybe I should fire you."

"No, you won't," he responded confidently. "I'm probably the best assistant you've ever had, and you know you can count on me not to bullshit you. Besides, I know the filing system. You get rid of me and you'll never find half of your important files."

Deanna laughed. "You know, I only let you think you're in charge," she responded, as he too laughed and retreated to answer his ringing phone.

Deanna idly considered once again Nancy Kramer's very early presence in the office. She appreciated that Nancy was being conscientious, but she wanted the work to get done during normal business hours. She decided to make that point at the next departmental meeting.

On the other hand, if Nancy was making some headway in the continuing backlog of monographs waiting to be catalogued, Deanna was inclined to forgive the overzealousness. Richard Peyton, her boyfriend of two years, would tell her she should be glad she had people working for her who didn't need to be drop-kicked to get them motivated. Deanna grimaced. She'd have to chastise him for a typical male sports analogy when she met him for lunch later. He was leaving on a business trip the next morning, and this would be their last chance to get together until he returned.

Her telephone rang. "This is Deanna," she answered.

"Hi. This is Barbara Cook, Sylvia Day's producer."

"What can I do for you, Barbara?"

"We're working on a segment for *Your Health* that will air on the *News at Noon*. On health and exercise. How we've become a nation addicted to overindulgence and instant gratification."

"Oh . . . you mean we're all getting fatter." Deanna smiled.

"Except for you. You're the envy of most of the women on staff."

"I didn't know I was being watched. Instead of concentrating on those of us who overeat, why don't you do something on why there are still people in America who go hungry?"

"Good thought, but not light enough for lunchtime news . . ."

"No pun intended . . ." Deanna interjected wryly.

"I'll keep it in mind for another story."

"I'm afraid to ask when you need this," Deanna said, writing down the inquiry and checking her watch.

"Any chance of getting it by E-mail within the hour?"

"Will do."

As Deanna hung up, Stephen appeared in her door.

"It's Bellevue Hospital on the line."

Deanna frowned. "Bellevue? What do they want?"

"Actually, it's the medical examiner. He wants to talk with you."

Deanna's gaze sharpened. "Isn't that like . . . the morgue? Are you serious?"

"As a heart attack."

"Stephen, I hate it when you . . ."

"Sorry. The morgue is located at Bellevue Hospital. Want me to put the call through or have him call back?"

"He wouldn't tell you what this is about?"

"Nope. Just that it was important that he talk with you as soon as possible."

"All right," Deanna said, racking her brain as to why the M.E. would want to speak with her. As it was, she'd never known that the morgue was part of one of the city's largest and oldest hospitals. It made sense. Like one-stop shopping, Deanna thought irreverently. She picked up the phone.

"Hello. Can I help you?"

"I hope so," a raspy male voice began. "This is Dr. Marvin Gavin. I'm the medical examiner for the city morgue. Are you Deanna Lindsay?"

"Yes. Are you sure you want to talk with me? Is this a reference question?"

"Well, in a way it is. I'm looking for anyone who may have known a woman by the name of Stacy Lowell."

Deanna thought for a moment. "Stacy Lowell . . . I don't think so."

"Are you sure? Perhaps this is someone you used to know. Maybe from another job, or you went to school together . . ."

Deanna rifled through her memory, but nothing immediately emerged as a possibility. "No, I'm sorry. It doesn't sound familiar at all. Why do you need to know?"

"Unfortunately Ms. Lowell is now in temporary residence here. I have information that she might have known you. We found your business card in her wallet. On the back is what appears to be a home phone number. I thought it might be yours, but when I tried calling, someone Spanish answered."

"That was probably my old number," Deanna supplied. "I moved about five years ago. But I never knew a Stacy . . ."

She stopped suddenly. Instantly an image came to mind of a woman she hadn't seen in years. How could she have forgotten Stacy?

She'd been very young. Sweet and petite. A runaway who was over her head in the fast-paced and often unwelcoming life of New York City.

"This woman you have?" Deanna asked. "What happened to her?"

"Stacy Lowell was killed two days ago, the victim of vehicular homicide. A traffic accident. So far, the police and my office have been unable to locate any family who can positively identify her. They ran what information they found about her in the local papers, figuring maybe someone who knew her would recognize the description . . ."

As he talked, bits and pieces of memory came back to Deanna. And with them came a recollection of the circumstances around which she and a woman named Stacy had once known each other.

Stacy's last name wasn't Lowell then. Nonetheless, Deanna couldn't help a sudden sickening suspicion that she and Dr. Gavin were talking about the same woman.

"Stacy is dead," Deanna said, more to herself than to Dr. Gavin.

"Sounds like you might have known her after all. Will you help?" Dr. Gavin asked.

"What do you want me to do?"

"I'd like you to come to the morgue and identify the body."

"Maybe it's not the Stacy that I knew," Deanna said.

"Can you describe the woman you remember?"

Deanna closed her eyes and rubbed her forehead. "She was small. On the short side. She had blond hair and hazel eyes."

"Can you recall any particular distinguishing marks?"

"Not really. Stacy seemed very . . . wholesome. Sort of Midwest. I used to tease her about it. That is, if we're talking about the same woman. I hope not."

"Well, the woman we have here also has a faint scar across her right forearm."

Deanna's stomach seemed to somersault. "Oh, no . . ." She rested her forehead in her hand. She remembered a scar. She knew what it was from.

"Bingo?" Dr. Gavin asked hopefully.

Deanna still hesitated. She felt pulled back through a time warp. Her stomach muscles contracted again as the exact details of what had brought her and Stacy together were resurrected from her past. And what had eventually sent them on their separate ways.

"Ms. Lindsay?" the doctor prompted when Deanna remained silent. "Does any of this sound familiar yet?"

"Yes, it does. I mean, yes. I did know someone named Stacy."

"Good. Would you mind coming in?"

She sat with her eyes closed, processing the doctor's words, taking in the possibility that the Stacy she had known was dead. She felt sad and guilty because she hadn't stayed in touch. Stacy had been a troubled young woman who struggled not only to make sense of life, but also to survive it.

Deanna said in a soft but firm voice, "It sounds like you have more than enough information. Maybe you can check with Social Security or someplace like that. I just don't think I want to see her like . . . that."

"I understand. Believe me, Ms. Lindsay, we're trying everything. Right now you're the best lead we have. You may have known the deceased before she changed names. Your identification might help the authorities locate next-of-kin. It won't take long. Perhaps half an hour of your time. Can I see you sometime today?"

"You mean . . . come to the morgue?"

"That's right. We brought the deceased here after she expired at the scene of the accident."

Deanna sighed and sat back in her chair, fishing around beneath her desk for her shoes. She slipped her feet back into them and stood up, anxious to end the call and get back on familiar ground. She needed to walk around a bit and catch her breath. ". . . expired at the scene . . ." She was having a hard time with the concept of Stacy being dead.

"I don't know . . ."

Dr. Gavin sighed audibly on the line. "Let me tell you what will happen if no one comes forward to identify or claim her. We'll have to keep Ms. Lowell's body here and continue our search, perhaps for several months, hoping that her family will be notified somehow, sooner or later. Maybe someone will try to call or visit and discover she's no longer at her apartment, or even alive. Maybe someone will pick up on our notification in the daily papers. But it's a long shot and it means waiting. And the longer we wait, the slimmer the chances are of anyone coming forward. We'd prefer not to have to bury her as an a.k.a., or worst-case scenario, a Jane Doe.

"I know I'm asking a lot. Unfortunately my business is dead people. It's *never* a happy occasion. But someone has to do the job. And the woman we have here known as Stacy Lowell deserves a little dignity, don't you agree?"

Deanna winced. How could she not? She and Stacy had met under unfortunate circumstances more than six years ago. Deanna didn't necessarily want to be reminded of that time.

She caught sight of Stephen in her doorway, miming the time on his watch. Deanna resolutely shut down her memory banks and gestured that she'd be only a few more minutes.

"Dr. Gavin, I have to go. I'm late for a meeting."

"Does that mean no, I can't talk you into helping us?"

Deanna felt the guilt she'd tried to keep at bay sneaking up her back and arms in a chill. "You say it will only take a few minutes?"

"Absolutely."

"Do I have to see everything . . . ?"

"Just the face. Unless you remember some particular body marking, like the scar I mentioned, or a mole. Does that sound okay?"

"All right," Deanna murmured finally. "Tell me where I have to go."

Deanna finished her call and sat quietly. *Stacy is dead,* she told herself several times, as if trying to take in the news. She had no doubt that this was the same Stacy she'd known not so many years ago. Her business card in Stacy's wallet, found at the scene of the accident, was proof enough. But why was Stacy using a different last name? And why couldn't the authorities find records for any such person?

Deanna picked up her phone and dialed. The phone was answered on the first ring.

"Peyton, Securities," came the quick, businesslike response.

"Hi, Richard, it's me."

"Hi, me," he replied, his tone warming. "We're still on for lunch, if that's why you're calling. I thought maybe we'd meet at Bice. That's about equal distance between your office and mine . . ."

"I'm calling because I can't make it."

"Another hot story to fact-check? That's why we had to cancel on Monday."

"No, it's not about work this time."

There was a pause. "You sound more upset than busy. What's wrong? Are you okay?"

Deanna was about to say that she was when she realized she wasn't. She seemed to be experiencing a delayed response to the news of Stacy's death.

"Well . . . I'm a little stunned. I just got a call from the medical examiner's office. They want me to come down to identify a body."

"A bo— Not someone in your family?"

"No, thank God. Someone I used to know a number of years ago. My business card was found in her purse. It's complicated, Richard. They can't find her family, and she's using a different name than when I knew her."

"Sounds like she was hiding. Maybe she doesn't want her family to be found. Maybe it's a different person."

"Maybe, but I still think I'd better go down. I thought I'd use my lunch hour."

"I could come with you. I've never been to the morgue."

"I don't think this is meant to be a social visit."

Richard chuckled. "I'm just teasing. The morgue is not on my list of tourist attractions. Seriously, if you want me to come with you . . ."

"Thanks, but I just want to get it over with. I'll be okay. I just wanted to let you know. Sorry to disappoint you about lunch."

"How about tonight?"

"Aren't you leaving for Paris in the morning?"

"I am. But I can stay over and have breakfast with you before heading to the airport."

Deanna smiled and finally began to relax. "I like that idea."

"I'll pick you up at work around six-thirty . . ."

She was stunned by the evidence of poverty, defeat, loneliness, and broken lives.

Deanna could count on one hand the number of times she'd been to a hospital, and those had been considerably different facilities than Bellevue, with its lack of warmth and Grand Central Station atmosphere.

The hospital lobby was crowded with infants and toddlers, dragged along like little rag dolls by young mothers who were barely more than children themselves. Deanna was both fascinated and dismayed by the steady stream of people coming and going, wondering if regular trips to the hospital and social service agencies were considered opportunities for socializing.

She'd been told that Bellevue was a place that functioned by volume, and she could see that business was brisk. There was evidence that far too many teenage girls and young women came here to give birth. Too many men with gunshot and stab wounds, broken bones, or ulcerous limbs. Or they were amputees, victims of lost body parts and failed dreams. Far too many men and women in advanced stages of poor health or alcoholism.

She had a horrible thought that they all came here just to die. Or, perhaps like Stacy, came already dead.

She waited by the security desk for someone from the medical examiner's office to escort her downstairs. In her professional ensemble she was so out of place as to draw the open gazes of people wandering by with expressions that said, "What are you doing here?"

She was asking herself the same thing.

"Ms. Lindsay?"

"Yes," Deanna said, startled. She pivoted sharply to face a youngish man.

He was thin and pale with straight dark hair and a receding hairline. Behind his glasses she saw kind eyes. She wondered why that surprised her. He extended his hand to her.

"I'm Dr. Gavin. Come this way, please." He indicated the bank of eight elevators just behind him. "I'm glad you could make it," he added as they waited for a car.

Deanna smiled, not sure how to respond. "Glad to be here" didn't seem appropriate. Twice before leaving her office she'd debated changing her mind. Not because she didn't want to help the medical examiner but because she would then have to accept the tragedy of what had happened to Stacy. She'd hoped that things would work out better for her. Stacy had deserved a chance at happiness.

The elevator arrived and they got on. Despite the large group of people waiting for elevators, she and the medical examiner were the only two headed for the lower level.

"Sorry I had to keep you waiting," Dr. Gavin said. "Someone else came in unexpectedly."

"To view a body?" Deanna asked.

He raised his brows. "It *was* the body. Died at another hospital during the night. We do all the city autopsies here."

When the elevator stopped and the doors opened, the doctor stepped out and headed down a hallway, Deanna following closely behind.

The first thing she noticed was the silence.

The second was that the movies had scripted it all wrong.

She had expected far worse than a nondescript maze of corridors that led to a series of closed, unmarked doors. There was no hallway furniture and no hotel artwork on the walls. This was not a place meant for people to wait.

The lighting was fluorescent, cool and oppressive. There was no one lurking around who looked particularly nocturnal . . . like vampires in a dark and silent kingdom. Her imagination had most definitely gotten the better of her.

"I just want to assure you, Ms. Lindsay, that we try to make this procedure as quick and comfortable as we can."

"I'm very glad to hear that," Deanna said dryly. "Is it going to be cold in the refrigerator room?"

"The refrigerator room?"

"Where you keep the bodies."

Dr. Gavin laughed out loud. "That's fiction. You're not going to have to stand in a cold dark room while a refrigerator tray is pulled out with a corpse on it." He finished on a chuckle, shaking his head. "It makes for great drama, but we don't do it that way. By law we have to perform an autopsy, so you won't actually be seeing Ms. Lowell's body. It will be shrouded. You'll see only her face."

He stopped at the only open door in the hallway. "Ernesto, Ms. Lindsay is here to see unit 53. Do you have the paperwork ready?"

"Right here," a voice responded.

A short Hispanic man exited the office, followed by two uniformed police officers. Without acknowledging Deanna, the man proceeded down a hallway.

"Ernesto is the morgue manager," the doctor explained as they all trailed behind him. She could hear the two officers comparing their duty assignments for the afternoon. Deanna felt chilled, as much by their indifference as by her own nervousness.

They all came to a stop outside a closed door.

"Ms. Lindsay, if you'd wait here for a moment, I'm going to have the officers go in first. They have to verify that the deceased is the same person they came upon at the scene of the accident, the one whose description they entered into the police report. That's done to establish consistency in the chain of custody."

"Okay," Deanna nodded, glad that she wouldn't have to be first.

The two officers accompanied the manager and the doctor inside, and the door closed behind them.

As she stood alone in the hallway, Deanna felt a strange sense of déjà vu. Not about where she was, but because of an intriguing similarity to another institutional place that also, in a way, was about life and death. Back then, there had also been the foreboding tension of waiting. Anticipating. She glanced around the quiet hallway. It was lit like the place where she'd met Stacy, but that first environment was calculated to put people at ease.

Deanna heard the elevator doors open and footsteps. A black man came around the corner, moving toward her with restrained grace. He didn't seem surprised to see her. His steady gaze made a thorough assessment of her, making her feel uncomfortable and a little defensive. She didn't think he was hospital personnel, but he moved with the confidence of someone who knew what he was looking for.

"The office is that way." She pointed helpfully.

"I know."

He stopped just a few feet away, openly staring at her, yet she was sure she'd never seen him before. He was tall and dark. His expression was serious, his full mouth pursed slightly, and a muscle tightened reflexively in his jaw. But it was his eyes that held Deanna's attention. Incredibly direct. Knowing. Suspicious.

"Deanna Lindsay," he said.

Deanna nodded, surprised. "How did you know my name?"

"I'm Patterson Temple."

His three-quarter-length black leather coat opened to reveal dark blue gabardine work pants and a shirt of the same color. He didn't seem to bow to fashion, having neither a pierced earlobe nor gold chains nor silver slave bracelets. His close-cut hair had a tight wave.

"Do I know you?"

"We've never met, if that's what you mean. I heard about you."

His voice was deeper than a tenor, but not really a baritone, with inflections that indicated a black working-class background and an easy cadence that suggested someone who wasn't given to hurrying. His gaze was bold, making her think that this man was capable of seeing more than she might want him to.

She raised her chin a fraction. "From whom?"

"Dr. Gavin."

Deanna was becoming irritated and hoped it showed in her expression. His didn't change at all. He regarded her with a wariness that she felt was totally unjustified. "Why would Dr. Gavin tell you about me? What's your part in this?"

He shrugged, putting his hands in the pockets of his leather coat. "Same as you."

He was good-looking enough, despite his in-your-face persona. His jaw and chin were square, giving the lower half of his face a look of strength and determination. His neatly trimmed mustache continued around his mouth and chin in an attractive Vandyke. It emphasized the shape of his lips and gave his brown face a sensual masculinity. She wondered how often he played on that, and whether he was going to try it with her.

She wasn't the least bit interested.

"Are you here to identify Stacy, too?" Deanna asked.

"I'm here to see if you and I agree that the woman they have is Stacy Lowell."

"I didn't know Stacy as Lowell."

"That's what the doc said. But you probably met her before I did."

"'I haven't seen her in years. I sort of lost touch with her."

"The doc was able to find you through her, so you didn't really lose touch."

"My business card was found on her," Deanna murmured, glancing away. "I was surprised she still had it.'' Actually, she realized, it was none of his business how well she knew Stacy.

He paced in front of her, glancing around the corridor. ''On the other hand, maybe we're talking about two different women.''

''You think so?''

He stopped to regard her again. ''Yes, I do.'' He boldly let his gaze move over her in a critical assessment. ''You don't look like the kind of woman Stacy would be friends with.''

The implication annoyed Deanna and she struck back. ''Quite frankly, you don't seem her type either,'' she said tartly.

Patterson Temple raised his brows at her tone, but otherwise showed no reaction.

Their sparring ended when the door to the viewing room opened and three men exited. As the two police officers walked past Deanna, one of them said flippantly, ''Your turn.''

Dr. Gavin nodded to Patterson, shaking his hand. ''Mr. Temple? Thanks for coming in.''

''No problem.''

''You've been here before, I take it?''

''A couple of times. Part of the job.''

Deanna listened to the brief exchange, curious about Patterson's cryptic response.

''The officers have confirmed that the deceased is the same victim from the vehicular accident. If you'll step inside, please . . . If you two don't mind, I'll take you both in together. That should speed this up a bit. Do you know each other?''

''Now we do,'' Patterson responded wryly.

Deanna heard the note of derision in his voice. She glanced pointedly at her watch.

''Okay, let's do it,'' the medical examiner said and

held the door open. Both men waited politely for her to move first. Deanna appreciated the courtesy, but this was one of those times when she would have been happy to enter last. Nevertheless, she went through the door with a confident step and her head up, but her stomach muscles began to knot in apprehension.

It was a very small room. One table and two chairs were squeezed into the space. One wall had a Plexiglas window. On the other side of the window were drawn pink venetian blinds. Deanna stared at them, wondering, why pink? She pressed her hands together. They were ice-cold. Ernesto, the morgue manager, spread some forms on the table and left the room.

She heard Patterson Temple enter, and although there was room for him to stand next to her, Deanna felt him take a position behind her and to her left. The doctor stayed near the door.

This is it, she thought, taking a deep breath and holding it.

"Now, when you're ready I'll signal the technician to open the blinds. Take as much time as you need to make a clear identification. I'll ask you some questions, you sign the affidavit, and then it's done. Okay?"

Deanna let out her breath. "Okay."

She waited, staring at the pink Pepto Bismol blinds. They made her stomach feel funny. Chills ran along her arms. She anchored her hands on the strap of her shoulder bag.

"It's your call," Patterson said behind her.

She couldn't help cutting him a look before facing forward and bracing herself. "I'm ready," she said.

Dr. Gavin dimmed the lights. Deanna was aware

of Patterson Temple behind her, though he made no sound.

She closed her eyes. Faintly she heard the blinds being pulled open.

She waited a long moment before opening her eyes again. She allowed her attention to settle on the still form.

A woman's face was swathed in a stark white hospital sheet that emphasized the gray pallor of the skin. The face showed evidence of several minor bruises and contusions, but was still remarkably youthful. To Deanna the face seemed infused with an innocence that she remembered. To her naked eye, Stacy had hardly changed at all from when Deanna had first met her, when Stacy was a very young seventeen.

She looked peaceful. Serene. Not at all like that time when they'd both been scared and unsure. Deanna recalled telling Stacy that they would both survive, mostly because Deanna had needed to believe it herself. They had passed through that time together holding on to each other. Being brave together. But there were also funny moments. They had offered to each other the only thing that they could at the time, the assurance that if one of them was ever in need, the other would be there.

This was *not* what Deanna had had in mind.

It was too late to conjecture, to second-guess, to wish anything different from what it was. She was too late to be of any real help to Stacy, who now lay still and beyond need. Asleep and at peace, forever . . .

Chapter Two

"I appreciate your cooperation, Ms. Lindsay, Mr. Temple. I know this was difficult, but now we can move on and try to locate Stacy's family. Are you okay, Ms. Lindsay?" Dr. Gavin asked, frowning. She was standing with one arm held against her midriff, and a hand pressed to her mouth and chin. Her eyes were closed.

"I guess I should have advised you not to come alone. Everyone has a different reaction to this experience. Ms. Lindsay?"

"I'm fine," she murmured through her fingers.

"Are you sure?"

Deanna blinked. Patterson Temple was watching her closely. She drew in a deep breath, moistened her lips, and nodded. Dr. Gavin retrieved the documents from the table.

"If you'll both just sign these for me. They verify that you've been a witness to the viewing of one deceased Caucasian female listed and positively ID'd as Stacy Lowell."

Deanna took the form Dr. Gavin handed her. Without reading it, she quickly signed her name in the space indicated, her handwriting shaky.

Patterson Temple did the same. Paperwork in hand, the M.E. said, "I told you about the scar tissue on Stacy's forearm. It's not all that old. Does either of you have any idea what it's from?"

Deanna wasn't about to enlighten him, certainly not in front of Patterson Temple. It hardly mattered now whether Stacy had scars, moles, or birthmarks. Patterson Temple spoke up behind her when all she did was shake her head.

"No idea. If that's all the questions, doc . . .

"For now. I know where to find you both."

As they left the viewing room, Deanna was grateful for the slight chill of the hallway. She stopped to inhale a lungful of soothing air, hoping it would also cool her insides.

That was a mistake. Nausea immediately churned her stomach.

She wasn't sure if she said or did anything in particular that caused Patterson Temple to close a strong hand around her upper arm. Deanna's instinctive reaction was to pull free, avoiding such familiarity. Instead, she found that she needed the support. She began to feel hot all over.

A phone rang. Ernesto stuck his head out of his office.

"It's for you, doc . . ."

"I'll be right there. I'll leave you both here. Thanks for coming." Dr. Gavin hurried off.

Deanna tried to swallow, determined to overcome the stifling wave of heat, but she knew she was going to choke instead.

"I . . I think . . ." she managed to whisper.

"I know. This way."

Patterson Temple started walking down the corridor with her in tow.

She let herself be led as if she were tethered to a safety line. He stopped in front of the door marked

LADIES and rushed them both inside. She felt the uncontrollable contractions beginning to twist in her stomach, the taste of bile pungent and sour in her throat. She wasn't going to be able to keep it down.

In panic, she fought to hold on. She didn't want to give Patterson Temple the opportunity of seeing her embarrass herself by freaking out over the sight of a corpse. The fact that he seemed to be unfazed only made Deanna angrier. Not with him but with herself. She'd hoped to show a little more cool, a lot more stamina, and a bit more grace. Instead, he was going to think her a weak sistah.

He tried to direct her to a vacant stall, but she pulled free and headed for the nearest sink. He reached past her head to turn on the water. As she began to gag, he left her.

Patterson stepped back into the corridor. He had no desire to hang around while Deanna Lindsay was sick to her stomach. He wasn't surprised, though. He'd been expecting it. Deanna Lindsay didn't strike him as the kind of woman who came in touch with the tough side of life, of police reports and car accidents and dead bodies. He was only surprised she'd held it together until the doctor left them.

Stubborn, he thought. Has to be in control. Doesn't want to look bad .. or ruin her clothes. Served her right, acting like she was doing somebody a favor by showing up.

He began to pace outside the door, trying to shake off his annoyance. He didn't know why Deanna Lindsay rubbed him the wrong way. Maybe because he'd seen at once that she was going to pay him no mind after he introduced himself. Like he wasn't someone she wanted to know.

Now he was damned curious. How the hell did someone like her, black *and* boojee and with attitude, get to know someone like Stacy Lowell? At least the Stacy he used to know. Stacy had been only twenty-four or twenty-five when she died, and Patterson figured Deanna Lindsay was probably ten years older, although she looked younger.

He heard the water being turned off in the bathroom. So she was okay. There didn't seem to be any reason for him to hang around and he was about to leave when he realized she wasn't coming out. He tilted his head close to the door and listened. It was quiet on the other side. He raised his hand, poised to knock and call her name, when he heard slow footsteps.

He was standing against the wall and out of her line of vision when Deanna appeared. He stood watching her without alerting her to his presence. She was still wiping her hands on a paper towel, then using it to dab at her forehead. She had reapplied her lipstick, retied the bright scarf around her throat. He had a chance now to take a good look at her before leaving with the memory of her cool gaze and lofty air.

He liked her hair. She wore very little makeup, so that you hardly noticed it. She wore one pearl ring on her right hand, nothing on the left. So, she wasn't married. That didn't surprise him either. Miss Thang was proper. Upscale. And probably high-maintenance. Not a lot of brothers could live up to that.

He allowed that she was an attractive woman. Classy and pulled together. In fact, Deanna Lindsay had all the makings of a Buppie, the classic thirty-something upwardly mobile educated single black urban professional. Too rich for his blood. A little too full of herself.

But he also saw something more. Vulnerability. It was what had struck him when he'd first spotted her. She was subdued and pensive now. In the aftermath of seeing Stacy's body, her face had softened and relaxed. In fact, she seemed not only dazed, but hurt. He didn't get why.

She sighed and thrust the used paper towel into the pocket of her coat. That was when he moved.

Realizing that she wasn't alone, Deanna turned to face him. "I thought you'd be gone by now," she said, her expression guarded.

"That what you were hoping?"

"It's what I expected," she corrected. But she didn't question why he was still there.

"Feel better?" he asked.

She hid her surprise at the question, moistened her lips, and nodded, averting her gaze as she began to button her coat.

"I guess I wasn't prepared for what it was going to be like, seeing someone dead like that. Not one of my finer moments," she said.

"Could have been worse."

"I shouldn't complain."

"That's right. Stacy is the one who's dead."

She felt chastened. She was *never* going to forget how Stacy had looked. She glanced around the bare hallway.

"This is it, then? I tell them that it was Stacy Lowell in there, they mark it on some piece of paper, and everybody goes home?"

"What did you expect?"

"I don't know. It seemed so businesslike. I guess

I thought there would be . . . something more . . ." She shrugged.

"Like when someone you love passes away?"

She looked to see if he was being sarcastic. "Yes, that's right."

"We're here," Patterson said, pointing back and forth between them. "Someone else'll show up. Family."

"You know that for a fact? That she has family?" Deanna began walking slowly to the elevator. He fell into step beside her.

"Yeah, I know that," he said. "I mean, everybody's got family, right? I just don't know who they are or where they live. I *know* they don't know she ended up here." He noticed that she still looked queasy. "Come on, let's get out of here," he said, letting her enter the elevator ahead of him.

Deanna was glad to be headed back up to the main floor. They didn't talk on the short ride, but she was aware of his close scrutiny. Did he think she was going to faint or get sick again? Was he staring out of curiosity, concern . . . or disappointment? No . . . it wasn't concern, she decided.

The truth was, something about him made her a little uncomfortable. She was put out by him, felt he was somehow making fun of her. On the other hand, he hadn't given her any reason to think highly of him, either. She stared at his left hand. It hung at his side, strong and very large. Working hands . . . calloused but clean. Deanna's attention darted to his face. He was still watching her. She glanced away.

When the elevator door opened, noise and activity rushed in. They stopped in the middle of the lobby with hospital personnel, visitors and police swarming all around them.

"Where are you headed?" he asked.

"To my office. I told them I might be late getting back from lunch."

"As long as your office already knows you're going to be late, let's get some fresh air. Maybe go someplace to talk."

"What about?" she asked cautiously.

"Stacy."

She shook her head sadly. "What's there to talk about?"

"I get the feeling that the Stacy you knew and the Stacy I knew were two different people."

"Why do you say that?"

He spread his hands. "I base that on the kind of people I knew she knew. Somebody like you doesn't compute."

She bristled under his assumption that he knew or understood anything about her.

"What are you suggesting? That I . . ."

He held up his hand. "Okay, hold it. Back it up. All I'm saying is maybe you don't know what went on in her life. How long has it been since you were in touch?"

"It's been a long time. Almost seven years."

"Aren't you curious? Interested?"

It irritated her that Patterson Temple could be right. Of course she was curious. She suspected there was a lot he could tell her.

She looked at her watch. "Half an hour. Then I have to go."

They left the hospital to find that there were several dozen people gathered outside the building around the plaza.

"There's a little coffee shop on the corner . . ." he began.

Deanna made a face. "No, thanks. I couldn't eat a thing."

"You don't really eat there. You have coffee and you sit and talk."

"They can't stay in business just selling coffee," she countered, distracted by the interplay of people around them.

"They do takeout. Fat sandwiches, good burgers. The chili's not bad."

She glanced up at him. "How much time do you spend down here?"

"More than I want to," he admitted.

She could tell from the dark glare in his eyes that today was one of the times when he wished he didn't have to be there. She was intrigued by his answer, but didn't pursue it. "I don't think so."

"Fine. Let's sit over there. It's warm enough."

He steered her to one of the mesh benches a short distance from the entrance. It was the first week of March, but it wasn't really cold. Deanna sat down, while he stopped at a vendor cart and ordered coffee, black with no sugar. She crossed her arms and legs and absently watched him chat with the vendor as he waited for his order to be filled.

She frowned pensively, wondering what his story was. Patterson Temple was tall but not really big, although he seemed to fill up a space and was hard to ignore. And yet, there was something about him that came across as very physical. Very male. He looked like the kind of man who would bogart his way into a woman's life, as her brother would say, who was capable of using equal degrees of subtle persuasion and sensual intimidation.

His speech hinted at the black dialect of the streets, the tone informal, the words round and slow. He had her on that. She had been raised to speak proper English. Only her brother, Tate, know how to switch back and forth so that he could fit in wherever he went.

Deanna didn't realize she was staring until Patterson Temple returned to stand directly in front of her. She watched him consider her for a silent moment, and then he held out a Styrofoam cup. She accepted the offering.

"It's tea," he said.

"Thanks," she said, letting the heat of the cup warm her hands. "How do you know I even like tea?"

He sat next to her, bending forward to brace his elbows on his knees. "Doesn't matter. It'll make you feel better."

He peeled back a portion of the plastic top and took a swallow of his coffee. Deanna was amazed that he didn't find it too hot. He came across as if nothing ever really fazed him.

"What kind of work do you do?" she asked.

He took several more swallows and idly watched the pedestrian traffic in and out of Bellevue before saying, "I work for the city."

"Civil service?" she responded, not surprised. Sanitation, maybe. Or the MTA.

"Fire Department."

"Oh . . ."

He turned his head to stare at her. "Oh?"

She blinked and gave her attention to prying off the lid of the tea. Steam wafted against her face. "I didn't mean it that way."

"Yeah, you did. You don't even know what it is I do."

He sounded testy. Deanna was tempted to issue a

comeback, but decided it wasn't worth it. At least he was employed.

"How did you know Stacy?" he asked.

She didn't know what to say. Almost any response would give away more information than she wanted to reveal. She carefully sipped the hot tea, thought about his question, and felt herself being dragged back through time. Already she was recalling the person, the place . . . and the regrets. Patterson Temple's question was more complicated than he realized.

"Stacy was looking for a job, and a place to live. She was pretty new to the city and things . . . ah . . . weren't going so well for her."

"She worked with you?" he asked, sounding incredulous.

"No. Actually . . . Stacy lived with me." He was still staring at her. "For less than a month. Then she got her own place."

"She never mentioned that," he said reflectively.

"Maybe she forgot about it. Maybe it didn't matter. Maybe she didn't want anybody to know." She avoided his gaze.

"That's it?"

"That's it."

"You mean . . . there's more to the story but you're not telling, right?"

"Whatever."

"Stacy's gone," he reminded her.

"I know that. But *I'm* still here, and that period of *my* life, not just Stacy's, I consider personal." He turned away, not pursuing the point. "Your turn," she pressed. "How did *you* meet her? Was she a friend?"

He arched a brow. He knew what she was hinting at. He'd never been interested in Stacy that way. Not because she was white, but because she was so needy and confused. Way too young. It would have been taking advantage of her. Other people had already done that. Methodically, he began to crush the empty coffee cup between his fingers, folding it in half.

"The truth is, Stacy was a friend of my grandmother's. I knew her only because of Betts."

"Your grandmother?" Deanna repeated, surprised.

"They met at the supermarket in the neighborhood. Stacy was on line with a cart of food she couldn't pay for. My grandmother gave her money. They became friends. Stacy would do anything for Betts."

"That was very nice of your grandmother."

"That's the way Betts is. She'd give away her last dime if she thought you needed it more than she did."

"Betts . . ." Deanna tested. "I like that."

"They got to be pretty tight. After Jade was born, Betts did a lot of baby-sitting so Stacy could work."

Deanna looked sharply at him and her entire body stiffened. "Jade?"

"Didn't you know Stacy had a daughter?"

She looked squarely at him. "No, I . . . I didn't. I . . . Where is she?"

"With my grandmother. Betts was baby-sitting Jade the day Stacy was killed. Stacy brought her over after school and said she had to get into Manhattan to take care of something. We don't know what except Betts said Stacy seemed pretty upset at the time. She was supposed to be back around six or six-thirty. When she didn't show up or call by ten, Betts phoned me. She was afraid that something had happened. She was right. I checked with some friends I have in the police department and with EMS and found out about the accident."

Deanna couldn't focus on his words. Why hadn't Stacy ever told her about her baby? Especially since they'd both agonized together about having a baby, or getting an abortion. Either decision was going to affect them for the rest of their lives.

"How old is Jade?" Deanna asked Patterson.

"Six, I think. I know she had a birthday last December. The day after Christmas."

Deanna didn't need to do the math. Stacy had been three months pregnant when they'd met. She'd said she wasn't ready to have a baby. She couldn't afford to support one. But she'd apparently changed her mind. She'd had a little girl named Jade. Deanna couldn't help but wonder where *she* would be right now if she'd done the same thing.

"Hey, Pat. What are you doing in Manhattan? You know somebody in the burn center?"

"Hey, Michelle . . . Keisha." He stood to face the two black female police officers. "Not today," he replied. "I had to check out someone at the morgue."

"No one close to you, I hope," one of the women said.

Deanna studied the two officers, who were dressed in padded uniforms and laden with equipment. A very unbecoming outfit, she thought. She had never felt particularly confident in the abilities of female cops, even though she understood that they'd gone through the training and were deemed qualified to serve and protect.

The one who was engaging Patterson Temple in conversation was attractive, petite and forthright, with a cool look in her eyes. The other was overweight with a bad hair weave. Both spared Deanna only passing glances.

"An accident victim," Patterson said, without elaborating.

Deanna wondered how he could be so unemotional about someone he'd known and liked.

The petite officer grinned coyly at him.

"So when are we going to try out Sweetwater's?"

"You asking me out?" he responded. "Why don't you come hear *me* play some night?"

Deanna listened to the banter with its flirtatious overtones. She stood up and walked to the garbage to throw out the half-finished cup of tea.

"I thought you were gonna call *me*," the woman challenged.

"And have your man come after me? I don't play that," he said easily.

Deanna looked at them once more and found the two women glancing at her, as if Patterson Temple were explaining who she was. Her annoyance increased. She didn't need to be explained. The women finally moved on. He made his way back to where she stood. He moved with the athletic grace of someone who didn't let anything rush him. She made a point of glancing at her watch.

"I really have to go," she announced when he reached her.

"So do I. Where's your office?"

"Eighth Avenue near Fifty-sixth. I'll catch a cab."

"I'll drop you off. I'm parked around the corner."

"That's okay, I'll—"

"No trouble."

Reluctantly, she fell into step next to him. They reached his car, a black Jeep that she had to stretch to climb into in her high heels. She tugged her dress down and rearranged herself in the seat, aware that Patterson was openly watching. She ignored him. They exchanged next to no conversation on the way uptown. Her thoughts were keeping her busy. Yes, her relationship with Stacy had been short, but Patterson Temple had suggested that maybe she hadn't known Stacy well at all. She was feeling heavy with the weight of what she now knew about Stacy's decision to have her baby . . . and her own not to. She was feeling stunned and sad that Stacy was dead . . . and she had left behind a little girl named Jade.

"Where do you work?" Patterson suddenly asked.

"At one of the network stations."

"You a reporter or something?"

"I'm the manager of the research library and video archives."

"You're a librarian?" he asked for clarification.

"Information specialist," she said haughtily.

"Nice, easy job. You read books all day, right?"

She cut him an impatient glance. "Librarians are too busy to sit around reading all day. The job is more complicated than that." She paused. "At least you pronounced it correctly."

"When I was a kid I used to say 'liberry.' Then the teacher would say, 'What kind of berry is that, Mr. Temple?' " He imitated a female voice and laughed.

Deanna thought the anecdote was cute, but she didn't let him know it.

They pulled to the curb in front of her building. Deanna reached for the door handle and turned to face him.

"I appreciate the ride."

He acknowledged her thanks with a nod.

"And I want to thank you for helping me back at the morgue. You know, when I . . ."

"You're welcome."

Deanna still hesitated. "Does Jade realize that . . . that . . ."

"Her mother is dead?" He inhaled and exhaled deeply. "Betts told her that her mother went away for a while. Jade is waiting for her to come home. I think it's going to get tricky in the next few days. Betts is on it. I know she'll tell Jade when the time's right."

"What about Jade's father?"

Patterson shifted restlessly in his seat. "He's out of the picture."

"Well, do you know where he is?"

He stared at her pointedly, flexing the muscle in his jaw. "I said, he's out of the picture."

He hadn't really answered her question. Or maybe he was just telling her to mind her own business.

"What's going to happen now?" she asked.

"About what?"

"About Stacy. About her daughter."

"The morgue will keep Stacy's body while the police search for her family. I don't know for how long. Someone has to take Jade. But it's not your problem, right?"

Deanna didn't know if that was a criticism or just an observation. Patterson Temple seemed to be baiting her. She already knew he probably didn't think much of her. But that was okay. He wasn't on her A list, either. Something about his remark bothered her, however, and she didn't know how to answer. So she said nothing.

"Good-bye," she said with finality.

She got out of the car and closed the door, walking

briskly to dispel the disquiet that Patterson Temple's comment had created in her.

"Betts?"

Patterson walked in the front door of the small wood-frame Brooklyn house, closing it behind him. He turned back to peer through the shade of the living room window at the man striding away. Something about him was vaguely familiar, but Patterson quickly gave up trying to figure out why. Automatically he wiped his boots on the inside mat. It was a carpet remnant in dark green placed atop the actual carpeting of the same color to prevent a worn spot from developing.

Patterson took off his leather coat and hung it in the minuscule foyer closet. He knew better than to throw it over the arm of a chair or to hang it on the banister pole with its knobbed top, like he used to do as a kid. Betts believed in a place for everything and everything in its place, and woe be it to anybody who did otherwise. Not in *her* house.

The house seemed empty, but he knew his grandmother was around somewhere, since the interior was overly warm, a sure sign that she'd been in the kitchen cooking up more food than she needed. He smelled garlic and paprika, and cinnamon from something baking.

He crossed the living room with its doily-adorned furniture and profusion of plants. Past the gallery of photographs on the end tables and TV. Almost all were of him, from infancy to manhood. Special-occasion pictures—his high school graduation, his induction into the navy, and his commission from the fire department—were lined up along a shelf in a breakfront cabinet next to a mismatched assortment of other heirlooms and treasures. As much as Patterson disliked the display, he knew better than to suggest that the pictures be put away. To him they were an embarrassment, but to Betts they were a testimony to the survival and perseverance of her grandchild.

He heard the low volume of a radio tuned to an independent gospel program. She also favored some of the Southern broadcasts of white televangelists. "'The word of God is true no matter who's telling you," she would say.

He reached the kitchen doorway and leaned in. Something was steaming in a pot on a top burner, and fresh okra was draining in a colander in the sink. There were books and papers all over the table. He leaned over the kitchen sink to push aside the curtains and look out into the backyard. But it was past dusk and he would have been surprised if he'd found Betts out there, even though she was devoted to her garden.

"That you, Pat?"

He turned at Betts's voice coming from somewhere above him. He heard slow footsteps on the stairs.

"Yeah. I'm in the kitchen."

"Well, have a seat. I'll get there when I get there."

Patterson peeked into the pot. Neck bones were stewing in broth. He looked in the ancient bread box and found three leftover sweet potato biscuits. He helped himself to one, biting into it with relish and squishing out some of the soft center filling.

"Ummmmm. I love you, Betts."

A diminutive figure finally entered the kitchen. "Whew . . . Lord have mercy," she sighed, shaking her head and breathing heavily from the exertion of coming down the stairs.

She swatted Patterson on his thigh as she squeezed by him in the confined space. Her head, which barely reached Patterson's chest, was crowned by silver hair styled in a short and youthful bob. Despite her complaints of age and resignation to her passing at any moment, Bettina Butler was quick and surprisingly agile.

"Move out the way now, let me check my pot."

Patterson obligingly stepped aside as his grandmother lifted the lid and tested the meat with a two-pronged fork.

"Few more minutes . . ." She craned her neck to gaze up at her grandson. "You staying for dinner?"

He finished the biscuit, licking the remains of the custard center off his thumb and dusting his large hands together. "Not tonight. Just thought I'd check in."

She scoffed at his concern. "Now you know there was no need to come all this way just for that." She glared at him over the rim of her glasses, through eyes that were playful and bright despite the corneal rings that were evidence of developing cataracts. "Mr. Stanley's coming over. You ain't afraid to trust him alone with your nana?"

Patterson shook his head. He leaned against a counter edge and thrust his hands into the pockets of his slacks. "I'm not worried about Mr. Stanley, old lady. It's you I gotta watch. That poor man don't know what he's got himself into."

Bettina Butler cackled in delight. "Now don't you go thinkin' just 'cause I'm old I forget how to carry on some."

Patterson frowned at her but chuckled quietly. "You're going to give Mr. Stanley a heart attack." She laughed merrily at his comment.

"You okay here? How's it going?" he asked.

She grimaced and waved her hands dismissively at him. "Honey, I'm always fine."

"Somebody come to fix that vent for the dryer in the basement?" he asked.

Betts frowned at him. "What are you talking about?"

"I saw someone walking away from the house as I drove up. Looked like he was just leaving."

She shook her head and averted her gaze. "Nobody come to fix nothing. That vent is still broke."

Patterson considered his grandmother. It was not often that she'd ever kept information from him, or told him a half-truth, but he'd learned to tell when she did. He tilted his head to the side.

"Who was he, Betts?"

"I already told you . . ."

"Was it Marcus?"

Betts immediately looked resigned, and sighed. "I didn't tell him a thing, Pat. He came looking for Stacy, and I told him I hadn't seen her lately." She stared pointedly at Patterson and added quietly, "That's the truth, ain't it?"

Patterson began to pace the small kitchen. "I thought I recognized him. He was still outside when I drove up. So, he's out of jail."

"The day after Stacy died. I was hoping he'd forget about that child. He's bad news, and I know Stacy wished she'd never met him," Betts said fervently.

"She's dead. It doesn't matter anymore. He must not know if he's going around the neighborhood looking for her."

"Well, it ain't gonna take him long to figure it out."

"Did he ask about Jade?"

"Not a word, thank God. I always told Stacy, Marcus don't care for a soul but hisself. I sure hope he don't come back."

"Where's Jade?"

Betts took off her glasses and let them hang by the cord around her neck. "Upstairs asleep."

Patterson picked up on his grandmother's tone. "She okay?"

Betts at first muttered something unintelligible, then began a halfhearted attempt to sort the papers on the kitchen table. Finally she stopped and sat down, looking at her grandson.

"I figured it was time that Jade knew about her mama. She had to be told. She was askin' a lot of questions. You know, like how come she can't go back to school, and how come she was staying with me instead of in her own place? When was her mama coming back to get her?"

"Oh, man . . ." Patterson sighed.

"So I called up Pastor McDaniels and asked her to come on over, and she did. We sat Jade down and tried to explain what had happened to her mama."

Patterson rubbed thoughtfully at his chin and crossed his arms over his chest. "So, how did she take the news?"

Betts reached out and clasped his arm. "Remember when I had to tell you your own mama had died? You was younger than Jade."

"Yeah, I remember."

"Darlin', you didn't say a word for three days after that. Then for two days you kept telling me you was going home anyway. You could take care of yourself."

"I did, eh?"

Betts chuckled. "On top of that you told me you

didn't like grits for breakfast, and you were *not* going to church school on Sunday."

Patterson grinned. He remembered that part, too.

"You were a fresh little thing. But you were *my* baby. I let you fuss, but you got over it real quick. Well, that's where Jade is at. She'll be all right. She cried herself to sleep after what me and Pastor McDaniels told her. Just wore herself out."

"Maybe she's too much for you. I don't think you should keep her."

"Pat," she interrupted patiently, "the child hasn't been born that I can't handle. Now I may have to move slow, but I do move. She's just confused and scared. Who can blame her?"

"I know how much you liked Stacy, and I know you don't think Jade is going to be a lot of trouble, but I worry about you."

Betts smiled at him affectionately. "I know you do, darlin'. I'll let you know when I've had enough. Jade can stay with me as long as she wants. I won't let her go with her daddy. That good-for-nothin' . . ." She stopped and closed her eyes, raising a hand heavenward. "Forgive me, Lord. I know I shouldn't speak ill of those who don't know no better."

"Let's wait a few days and see what happens. The police will probably give Jade's information over to Children's Services."

"Is that like foster care?" Betts asked.

"That's part of it. If no family comes forward, Jade could end up in their jurisdiction."

"Well, I sure hope that won't happen. In the meantime, Jade stays right here with me. Are you sure you don't want something to eat? It's getting late. I thought I'd hear from you before now."

"Got a full alarm in the afternoon. By the time we

got back to the station I was pretty whipped. And there was a lot of paperwork."

"Nobody hurt, I hope."

"The building was empty."

"Praise be to God," Betts murmured.

"Looked like arson, but I don't think there was much insurance value on the property. It must have been drugs or a revenge thing."

Betts's aged brown face, remarkably free of lines, was wreathed in worry. "Patterson, now I want you to be careful out there . . ."

He took one large step to cross the kitchen and kissed her cheek. "Always."

"Now, tell me about this morning, when you went to see Stacy."

"You don't want to know what it was like."

"Lord, child . . . I've looked on dead folks before. I want to know about that woman you mentioned. The one that the police found who was Stacy's friend. Did she show up?"

Patterson kept his face blank and stared across the kitchen at the opposite wall. He saw that the kitchen clock had stopped. He would have to remember to replace the batteries. He cut a sideways glance at Betts. There was no getting around having to tell her.

"Yeah, she was there."

Betts was waiting for more, leaning forward. "What happened?"

"She threw up," he said with a straight face.

"She—" Then it fully registered and Betts laughed. "Not used to seeing dead people, I guess."

"I think there's a lot of things she's not used to."

Betts stared speculatively at Patterson. "That sounds like you didn't think much of her."

He shrugged. "It's not about what I think, Betts.

She doesn't seem like the kind who would be friends with Stacy. They don't have anything in common. She wasn't all that interested in what Stacy's life was like."

"Did she tell you that?"

"No, but I could tell."

Betts made a sound of impatience and stood up again. She took clean plates from the cupboard and set them on the table.

"Then you don't know for sure. Could be you caught her off guard, or she's scared, too. You know, not everybody's as brave as you are," she said dryly as she turned off the flame under the stewpot.

"I'm telling you she doesn't want to be bothered. She's a library manager or something in midtown. Came dressed like she was going to a press conference," he added, unable to keep the derision from his tone.

"Oh, yeah?" Betts forked the meat from the pot into a shallow bowl. "Nothing wrong with that. Did you tell her about the child?"

"Yeah, I told her. She didn't know that Stacy had a kid, but she didn't ask any questions about her, so she probably doesn't care what happens to Jade."

"Now, Pat, don't be so hard on her," Betts cautioned. "Sounds like she's just busy with her own life. Independent. Not like some of these black women looking for a man to take care of them. You know the kind I mean. Get pregnant with anybody's baby thinking that'll make a man stay. Not everybody's cut out to be 'round kids. Lord knows, they can wear you out and drive you to drink. I'll tell you about it sometime," she finished on a soft laugh, twisting to glance meaningfully at him.

"Betts, I know you liked Stacy and you like Jade, but . . ."

"You think I'm too old, but I'm *not* turning that child over to the city. Now, I know you thought this woman who knew Stacy would offer to help, but you don't know anything about her. Maybe she has kids of her own. Maybe she just can't."

Betts finally turned to fully face her grandson, wiping her hands on a dish towel. She was serious as she came forward and touched his arm, staring up into his determined countenance.

"Let me tell you something else, darlin'—and I don't mean to rub salt in your wounds—but your attitude toward this woman sounds to me like the pot calling the kettle black."

"Meaning?"

"You sound mighty put out 'cause you think she don't care about Jade. But when are you going to own up to your *own* child? When are you going to do something about that?"

Patterson met his grandmother's gaze and wasn't the least bit offended. She'd made her point and he couldn't fault her.

"That's different. I didn't have anything to do with what happened back then."

"You sure did," Betts countered.

"I mean, I didn't even know I had a kid."

"Patterson, you know now. You have a choice now. Ain't that right?"

His jaw tightened with unresolved anger and the demons of regret. He stared blankly ahead before conceding his grandmother's words with a nod.

"Right . . ."

* * *

Deanna hadn't gotten much sleep again and had left Richard's bed to be alone. She was haunted by more than just Stacy's face in death.

She was also remembering Stacy as she had been in life, a life that had not been very kind to her. Stacy had never quite learned the art of taking care of herself. She had been young. Pretty. White. She had blond hair and hazel eyes, those attributes by which women were assured of having more fun. But Stacy had been too insecure to trade on her looks, and they had mostly just gotten her into trouble, made her an easy mark.

She and Stacy had been bound together through mutual experience and shared pain. Through secrets and promises.

Since she'd had to identify Stacy at the morgue yesterday, a Pandora's box of memories had spilled out. Deanna knew they would all have to be looked at again before she could put them away for good.

"Deanna?" She heard Richard's voice from the other room.

"I'm in the kitchen," she responded calmly.

She wrapped her hands around the mug, hot from the tea she'd poured but had yet to drink, and was reminded of when Patterson Temple had gotten her tea. How clever of him to know, Deanna mused, that tea would stop her from getting sick again. Belatedly she also accepted that the gesture had been thoughtful.

She heard the rustle of bed linens and a stifled yawn. She heard the early-morning crack of joints, and Richard's bare footsteps coming from the bedroom and down the hallway as he sought her out. When he appeared he had nothing on. Though he worked at staying in excellent physical condition, he wasn't obsessive about it. He was the only man she'd ever been with who slept naked, and Deanna had always found that sexy and bold. She herself resorted to a cute mini shift after making love with him, when modesty was irrelevant and after the fact.

His slightly olive skin made the dark thatch of curly chest hair seem that much darker and thicker. The hair on his head was tousled. He kissed the top of Deanna's head, caressed her shoulder and the side of her neck.

"What's going on?" he asked, taking another seat at the table and reaching for her tea. He drank half of it in two swallows.

"I'm sorry I woke you. Nothing's going on." Deanna shrugged, even though she was nervously pulling at her hair.

Richard reached out for her hand, kissed the palm, and held on as he stared at her.

"You know, one of the things that attracted me to you was your smile. You look so happy when you smile. The other thing is that you can't lie convincingly. I can count on one hand the number of women I've known . . . maybe since I was *ten*"—she chuckled—"that I can say that about. So don't try to tell me nothing's going on. Maybe I can help. It's not me, is it?"

Deanna smiled warmly at Richard, squeezing his hand. She reached out with her feet beneath the table to stroke his hairy leg. "No, it's not you."

"Fine. So, is it you?"

She frowned in confusion. "I don't know what you mean."

He looked closely at her, his thumb stroking her wrist. "Are you pregnant?"

Deanna was so stunned she couldn't say anything.

She just stared at him, knowing her eyes were wide. "No," she responded emphatically.

Of course she wasn't pregnant, but it was as if Richard had read into her emotions and memories about the time when she had been.

"You can tell me if you are, and we can do something about it," Richard said.

Deanna knew he was trying to be kind and understanding . . . and honest. But the thought of having to make that decision again sent a wave of chilling anxiety through her. She shook her head in a short, tense movement.

"I . . . I'm not. I know how you feel about that. I certainly don't want to have a baby if . . ."

If what? she wondered suddenly.

A lot of things. If she and Richard weren't serious about each other. If they weren't committed to a future together. If he hadn't changed his mind about not wanting kids.

She took a deep breath to calm herself before he read more than she wanted him to. "I'm not pregnant, Richard. I'm *very* careful about that."

He smiled slowly, pleased with Deanna's answer.

"Maybe you're still freaked out about that visit to the morgue. Look, it's over now. I'm sorry it was an old acquaintance, but these things happen," Richard said. "She's at peace now. You can say a prayer and let her go."

Deanna nodded, her head bowed. She didn't want Richard to see how his words were having an effect on her. Instead of being able to let go, as he suggested, Deanna knew she was slowly beginning to embrace the memory of Stacy, albeit against her will.

"You're right."

He stood up, holding her hand, and gently pulled her to her feet and into his arms. She went willingly.

"I'm flying to Paris today and I won't see you for almost a week. Send me off with a smile." He tilted up her chin and kissed her.

She'd always been impressed and pleased by how sensitive Richard was to her feelings. He cared. And as long as they were both in agreement and he was right . . . everything was fine.

Deanna let him soothe her, desperately needing the reassurance and affirmation of his touch and his affection. Hand in hand they silently returned to his bedroom. Wordlessly Richard guided her back beneath the sheets, which had grown cool in their absence. His body heat quickly warmed her up.

She hoped to find oblivion in his kisses and caresses. It came in the delirious abandon with which they connected to each other's bodies. It was exhilarating and breathless and sweet.

And it was brief.

It did not have the effect that Deanna, at least, was hoping for. It did not vanquish her memories, or absolve her of guilt for the decisions she'd made. It only made clear in a strange way that she and Stacy had unfinished business.

Chapter Three

Deanna closed her eyes and rubbed her forehead. As usual she had kicked off one shoe, and her leg was curled beneath her on her executive-style chair. On her desk was what remained of her lunch—most of an overstuffed chicken salad sandwich with a slice of kosher pickle and a handful of potato chips. She'd taken only a few bites before realizing that the food made her feel queasy.

Deanna methodically began to rewrap the sandwich. Maybe she would finish it later, or take it home for an easy dinner. But she suspected she was going to throw it away.

She was annoyed by the waste and her lack of focus ever since the morning when she was called down to the city morgue. Her conversation with Richard the previous morning notwithstanding, she was behaving almost as if she was pregnant. The butterflies in her stomach, the thought of food making her nauseous.

"What is your problem?" she muttered to herself.

There was a knock on her office door.

"Yes, come in."

"You *are* in here," Stephen said, as if he had been slighted by not being informed. "I thought you were at lunch." He stepped halfway in, holding mail and packages under one arm.

"I *am* at lunch. I just decided to eat in," Deanna said flatly. She shoved the wrapped sandwich back into the brown delivery bag and put it in her out box. On her next trip to the copy room she would take it to the staff lounge refrigerator.

"Just wanted to be alone?" Stephen inquired.

She glanced at him with raised brows. "Why did you ask that?"

"You seem distracted. Not really here. The news desk called for some graphics, but I thought Ruth could handle it."

She smiled thinly, searched for her shoe and wiggled her foot back into it as she stood up. "I appreciate your getting on top of that, but my personal life does not take precedence. I should have been told about the call from Matt and his team."

"I don't want to be nosy, but—"

"There's nothing wrong, Stephen. And, no, Richard and I didn't have a fight."

"Okay, I'll back off. But if there's anything I can do . . ." He let the sentence hang.

"Like?" she prompted, eyeing him with a frown, coming to meet him near the door.

"Make sure you know how everything is going here. You know . . . the time sheets are getting signed okay, and supplies are being ordered, and the staff are all working their little hearts out."

"Thanks. I appreciate that you've been keeping tabs on some of these things for me. Ruth is working with Marianne on a special project archiving materials from the public affairs office." She held out her hand for the mail. "How's Nancy?"

Stephen gave her the small pile of envelopes marked Confidential or Personal, and one Fed Ex. "Well . . . she's doing her work . . ."

Deanna began to leaf through the envelopes, studying the return addresses. She cast Stephen a curious glance. "I hear a 'but' coming. What are you trying to tell me?"

"Maybe she's just trying to prove herself, but she's sort of . . . into everything. And she asks a lot of questions, about staff and who's who, and what goes on. She seems real interested in who the top bosses are and who makes the decisions and has the power."

"Well, that's easy. I do. At least here. Anyplace else is not her concern. You can answer these." Deanna returned several letters to Stephen. "I think I like the fact that Nancy doesn't wait to be told that something has to be done. She just does it."

Stephen grimaced, his expression and body language showing his skepticism. "Yeah, but . . . it makes everyone else look bad. Like we're not doing our jobs."

Deanna grinned at him. "Then you should take that as a warning. Everyone is being watched and I'm the only one you have to worry about pleasing. I feel Nancy is enthusiastic about the job. Right now I see that as a plus, unless it proves otherwise."

"Keep your eyes open," he said significantly, and turned to leave.

Deanna thoughtfully watched his retreating back before putting the mail on her desk. Sitting on the corner, she pulled the tab on the Fed Ex envelope and extracted a wad of documents paper-clipped at the top. She scanned them quickly, then, stunned, started again at the beginning.

After the first sentence her attention was caught completely. By the end of the third sentence, where the document talked about "legal obligations to a minor" and "temporary guardianship" and "hearing to determine parenting arrangements," Deanna's heart was thumping with disbelief and anxiety.

"What . . . what is this?" Deanna whispered to herself.

She began reading yet again, the declaration from the Board of Education that she had been named in official school documents as guardian of one Jade Taylor Lowell, age six, in the event that the child's mother, Stacy Lowell, became incapacitated or in some other way unable to care for her daughter.

Deanna read the cover letter over and over until finally the message sank in. And with it came not so much panic as an intense disorientation. For a moment her mind was blank. She had no idea what to think, how to feel. She reached around to her desk for her phone and swiftly entered a number.

"This is Joy," came the crisp response.

"Oh, I'm so glad you're there. It's me."

"Hey, Dee. What's the matter? You sound very agitated."

"Joy, you will never believe what's going on. I just got a letter from the Board of Ed . . ."

"What about?"

"I've just been informed that I have been named the guardian of a six-year-old child."

"Guardian . . ." Joy said with disbelief. "For whose child?"

Deanna took a deep breath and got her emotions under control. It was a long story, and she didn't know where to begin. Joy was one of only two other people who knew about her abortion seven years ago. The other person was her sister, Carla. And she hadn't told either very much about Stacy. That was part of the unspoken promise, part of their pact.

"You remember me telling you a little about Stacy."

"Oh. She's the one who was killed?"

"That's right."

"Okay, what's the rest of the story?" Joy asked. "What's this about being a guardian?"

The story poured out of Deanna in disjointed pieces. Joy interrupted frequently to ask questions or throw in a legal comment, which, as a lawyer, she was wont to do even in social settings.

"All right," Joy finally said, "I think I get the gist of this. I'm sorry about what happened to Stacy. I recall that you liked her a lot."

"Yes, I did," Deanna confessed. Her other line rang. "Joy, hold on. My assistant is ringing." Deanna put Joy on hold and pressed the button for Stephen. "Stephen, I'm on a . . ."

"I know, but this caller says it's urgent."

"Who is it?" she asked impatiently. She was afraid she would lose Joy, who would think nothing of disconnecting if she was kept waiting longer than she wanted to be.

"Patterson Temple."

"Take his number. I can't talk now, and I'll try to get back to him. Better yet, find out what he wants," Deanna instructed, quickly hitting her Hold button. "Joy, are you still there?"

"Yes, but I can't talk much longer. Any chance you know how to reach Stacy's family?"

"No. Stacy never wanted to talk about where she was from. I sort of guessed there was probably abuse at home and no one who she felt would protect her. She was a runaway."

"How old was she when you met?"

"Seventeen or eighteen. She looked a lot younger,

which was probably one of the things that got her into trouble."

Joy sighed. "Okay, look . . . I have to take a deposition in a case. Why don't you fax me those documents and I'll take a look at them. Child welfare is not my thing, but I can at least advise you. Quick question—have you ever met Stacy's child?"

"No, I haven't. I didn't even know she had a child, a little girl. I had no idea that she would change her mind abut her abortion."

"It happens."

"I know," Deanna murmured.

"Another thing. Do you have any interest at all in complying with Stacy's wishes?"

Deanna's immediate instinct was to say no. Her life was just as she liked it. Busy and fulfilling. She had her independence and a boyfriend who admired her and found her desirable. She could do anything she wanted without answering to anyone—and she had studied and worked hard to be able to make that statement. Her plans had never included children, and marriage was a low priority right now.

"I . . . I don't know how I feel about that, Joy."

"Do you know of someone else you could suggest? Someone that maybe Stacy would approve of?"

"There is this man named Patterson Temple."

"Who's he?"

"A fireman. He seems to have known her pretty well. He was at the morgue with me. Joy, it was horrible . . ."

"I don't want to know. Is this Patterson someone who liked Stacy or was he just sleeping with her?"

"I don't think it was that kind of relationship. Patterson is black."

"So? All men do it the same. You and I both know that." Joy chuckled.

"Actually, it's not him so much I'm thinking of, but his grandmother. Stacy left Jade with her just before she was killed."

"Okay, this is good. You have an alternative to suggest if you want to. What else does that letter say?"

Deanna quickly scanned the page. "It says . . . there's someone I should contact for an appointment. They would like to interview me, and they've suggested that a caseworker from Administration for Children's Services be assigned to Jade."

"Is that the child's name? Pretty. Go ahead and call. Let them interview you."

"Can you be there?" Deanna asked anxiously.

"It depends on when. If I have to be at a hearing or in court, you'll have to go alone. But I don't think you'll need me there. Listen to what they have to say. Find out what's involved with being a guardian. And then tell them what you want to do. Simple."

Simple.

Already Deanna knew it was anything but that. Joy's assurance actually did little to assuage her dilemma.

"What do you think will happen to her?" Deanna asked.

"To the child? I don't know. But don't worry about it. Someone will take care of her. It's not your problem."

Deanna nodded, deep in thought. That was the same thing Patterson Temple had said to her.

And she still wasn't sure it was true.

* * *

Deanna opened her purse to look for her cell phone. She was ten minutes early for her appointment at the Administration for Children's Services offices, an appointment that she'd not been looking forward to since getting their letter three days ago. She used the time to check in with Stephen and her staff. She answered several minor questions and gave two directives before disconnecting.

"Mrs. Levine will be with you in a minute," the receptionist said pleasantly to Deanna.

She nodded, and absently began to look around the nondescript office, with its combination of factory-reproduced framed art of flowers and children. Also posted were statements and declarations from the federal or state government.

Her cellular began a muffled ring from her purse, and Deanna reached for the unit again as the receptionist reappeared to indicate that Mrs. Levine was ready to see her. Deanna held up a finger for time as she answered the call.

"Hello?"

"Hi. Where are you? I called your office and your assistant said you wouldn't be in until maybe lunchtime."

Deanna stood up, trying to gather her belongings and talk at the same time. "Hi, Mom. I can't talk now. I'm about to go into a meeting."

"Well, you said you had something to talk to me about," Faith Lindsay reminded her daughter.

Deanna trailed slowly behind the receptionist, who was leading her through a maze of office cubicles to a formal office with a door.

"I know, but I can't do it now. Let me call you back tonight . . ."

"Dee, I don't know if I'll be home. I may get together with Branca and Francie tonight. We were thinking of meeting for dinner."

"Mom, I really have to go. I'll call you. 'Bye."

Deanna folded the phone and turned it off before putting it away.

"Sorry," she murmured to the waiting woman, as she was ushered into the office.

"I'm Ida Levine. Have a seat," the woman behind the desk introduced herself, as she reached to shake Deanna's hand. She indicated a chair.

Deanna took her seat, relaxing as she assessed the middle-aged woman.

"I understand you were surprised to learn you'd been named guardian in the case of Jade Lowell. Can you tell me a little about your knowledge of and relationship with Jade's mother?"

Deanna explained that she and Stacy had known each other only a short time and that they hadn't been in touch in nearly seven years. Deanna also confessed that until Stacy's death, she had had no knowledge of Jade.

"Well, given the circumstances, can you explain why Stacy might have named you guardian of her child? She didn't put down any family members, and as I understand it, the authorities are having trouble determining if she even has family."

"I know. I can only think that . . . Well, Stacy and I really bonded when we did know each other. We were both going through a bad time, and we sort of helped each other through it."

Mrs. Levine sat staring at Deanna as she listened, and Deanna knew that she was being assessed as well. But she wasn't going to suggest that her relationship with Stacy had been more than it was. They had been two women from vastly different backgrounds who needed to hold on to each other to survive a crisis.

"The situation is rather unusual," Mrs. Levine said as she read the documents in front of her. "Stacy Lowell, as she's called in records, was willing to give you a huge responsibility, and you two didn't even keep in touch. That says quite a lot about her trust in you, Ms. Lindsay. She obviously thought very highly of you. How does that make you feel?"

Deanna shifted in her chair and took a deep breath. "Unworthy."

Mrs. Levine smiled warmly. "The bigger issue, of course, is whether you want the responsibility. Technically, if someone is named as guardian the way Stacy has named you on her daughter's school records, the authorities abide by it without question. However, we're told that Lowell was probably not Stacy's legal name. Therefore, there's the question of whether family, assuming she has any, has been notified about Jade's existence and Stacy's death. That's why we've been brought into the case. There's an official police report stating that Stacy's next of kin is unknown.

"And there's the question of Jade's father . . ." She leafed through several more sheets of paper. "Did you know he has a criminal record?"

Deanna shook her head. "I'm sorry. I don't know anything about him."

"Well, his name is Marcus Lowell. He's been arrested and convicted a number of times, mostly for nonviolent crimes. He's not mentioned at all in Jade's school records. But we found a former employer of Stacy's, and her work record lists Marcus as her husband. That was about five years ago.

"There's no information that Marcus Lowell has

been present in Stacy and Jade's family life. Actually, he could very well have been in jail much of the time. His history doesn't suggest that he's a desirable parent. That's the only potential problem I can see, however. He is the child's natural father, and he does have rights. He could come forward to request that Jade be turned over to him. His criminal record may not be compelling enough of a reason to say no."

Deanna leaned forward anxiously. "Mrs. Levine, I have to ask a question. What does it mean, to be named a guardian?"

Ida Levine sat back in her chair, crossed her legs, and removed her glasses. "It means that you agree to assume responsibility for the day-to-day care of the child. You provide Jade with a home, see that she attends school, continue to be in contact with her caseworker. Basically, you're raising her. It could only be temporary. That's for you to decide. If the authorities locate Stacy's family, they may want to make a claim for custody. They have the right to do so. On the other hand, if there is no one else, you, in essence, become the parent. At least until a court hearing determines otherwise."

Deanna felt a flood of sensations wash over her. Everything from fear to disbelief to surprise . . . to excitement. She was overwhelmed. There was another fundamental question she wanted to ask. Was she, a black woman, the best guardian for a white child? But then, if Jade had no one else, perhaps it was a moot point.

She thought of all the ways in which her life would be affected by a child. What about her work hours? What about Jade's schooling? What about money and medical treatments, and doing things with her, all of which would have a vast impact on her own activities—going away for weekends, lectures and plays, eating out? Richard?

It made her head spin to think of all the ways her routine would change. Was she willing to make those adjustments?

"How do you feel about taking care of a child who, by your own admission, is a total stranger to you?" Mrs. Levine asked.

"I . . . I don't know. I mean, I believe I'm capable of taking care of her, but I'm not sure it's the best thing. That is . . . I'm not really prepared, and . . ." Deanna pressed her temples with her fingertips and shook her head at the sudden mind-boggling details that were occurring to her second by second. "There's just so much to consider."

"I know. Just because you're named doesn't mean you have to do this. Jade can be placed in foster care. If need be, she could eventually be put up for adoption."

Deanna didn't know where the impulse came from, but she found herself shaking her head. "No, that's unacceptable." She realized that Mrs. Levine was watching her with raised brows. "I can't let that happen to Stacy's child. That would be like giving her up to a . . . a . . . a stranger."

"You mean, like yourself?" Mrs. Levine said quietly.

Deanna just stared at her.

"Look, of course I'm not going to try and talk you into anything, but the fact that Stacy named you should count for something. I wish you'd at least think about it. I believe you'd do a terrific job. I see from the answers on this questionnaire that you're from the New York area, you live on the

Upper West Side of Manhattan, you have an interesting job . . . and, by the way, I think Logan Jeffries, the anchor on the ten o'clock news, is gorgeous." Deanna grinned. "I also see that you're thirty-four, never married, no kids." She glanced speculatively at Deanna.

"That's right," Deanna said, feeling slightly defensive. "I have a fulfilling life. Marriage and children just haven't happened."

"You're young. There's still time," Mrs. Levine said.

Deanna didn't answer.

"I can't see any reason on paper at least, why you shouldn't go ahead and become Jade Lowell's guardian. I'm satisfied with your credentials and your situation at work. If you want to proceed what I would do next is ask to see where you live. ACS would like to make sure that there is adequate space for the child, that she has a place to sleep—that sort of thing."

"When do you want to do that?" Deanna asked, mentally reviewing the state of her apartment and what needed to be arranged if she were to accommodate Jade.

"We'd like to get Jade settled and stabilized in a new home environment as soon as possible," Mrs. Levine said. "Can the caseworker come tomorrow?"

"Sure, that's fine," Deanna agreed, feeling as though the decision had already been made for her.

"You can stop the process anytime you decide you're not interested," Ida Levine told her. "Would you like to continue?"

Deanna swallowed and clasped her hands together. "Yes," she answered.

* * *

"You agreed to *what*?" Joy asked in disbelief.

"I haven't committed to anything yet. I simply said it was okay for them to come and see where I live," Deanna explained over her cellular as she thrust several bills into the cab driver's hand and waited for her receipt.

"Dee, why did you do that if you have no intention of taking that child?"

"I didn't say I wouldn't," Deanna defended, knowing that she sounded conflicted and contradictory. She climbed out of the cab and slammed the door harder than was necessary. She was annoyed at being questioned. And she was annoyed by her own ambivalence. "The truth is, I was a bit ticked off by the question of whether I can provide a suitable home for Jade. How dare they imply that it might not be good enough?"

Joy chuckled. "Girl, you sound like you don't know what you want."

"I don't!" Deanna said forcefully, as she headed toward the entrance of her office building.

She acknowledged several people she knew with a nod or a brief wave. She was about to dismiss the tall black man standing just to the right of the revolving doors as a delivery person or a studio technician because he was dressed in dark blue pants and shirt, and open jacket. She suddenly realized it was Patterson Temple.

"Joy . . ."

"I think you'd be making a mistake taking that child. I can tell you from personal experience that it's hard. Single women don't get nearly enough credit for being able to do what we do. And you've never even been interested in having kids."

"Joy, I have to go. I just got to the station and . . . I . . . I see someone I probably should talk with."

"All right, fine. Don't forget our manicure appointment at six-thirty."

"I won't."

"And dinner. I don't want to go to Jezebel's again. Too far on the West Side."

"Fine. See you later." Holding the phone in her hand, she stood regarding Patterson with curiosity and wariness. He was both taller and older—more mature—than she remembered. It was evident in the way he carried himself and the way he responded to what was going on around him. Perhaps the Vandyke beard was what gave him that air.

His scrutiny made her uncomfortable, and she couldn't help but feel he was finding fault with her.

"Are you waiting to see me?" Deanna asked.

He jerked his head toward the lobby. "They said you'd be back any minute. I've used up most of my lunch break waiting."

"Sorry. You should have called."

"I did. I got your secretary and he took my number. He said you'd get back to me. I waited," he said stiffly.

He *is* annoyed, Deanna realized. "Why did you need to speak to me?"

"Betts got a call from ACS and Jade's school. She's going to be turned over to someone else. They told her it was because Stacy wanted it that way, if anything happened to her. Do you know anything about that?"

Deanna heard more than just aggravation in his tone. She heard concern for his grandmother's feelings.

"As a matter of fact, I do. I'm the one Stacy named as Jade's guardian."

He looked genuinely surprised. And skeptical. "You?"

"Well, you don't have to make it sound like it's a stupid idea," Deanna said dryly. "I knew nothing about it until three days ago when I got a letter from the ACS office. That's where I'm coming from now. They wanted to interview me."

He looked her up and down, and shook his head—as if to say he couldn't credit that she, of all people, would become Jade's caretaker.

"There must be a mistake. I think Jade is better off with my grandmother. But she's too old to take care of a six-year-old kid. Jade would wear her out in no time."

Deanna felt relieved that he said it so she wouldn't have to. ACS was well aware, and impressed, with what Bettina Butler had done for Jade since her mother died. But they were clear that they were concerned as much for Betts as they were for Jade's welfare.

"I'm sorry," Deanna said sincerely. "I sense that your grandmother and Jade are very fond of each other."

He inhaled deeply and looked around, struggling with his feelings and the way things were going to be. "Nothing's changed. They're still close." He gazed squarely at her. "Look, I don't believe you really want to take care of Jade. I don't think she fits into your lifestyle."

She bristled. "What do you know about my lifestyle?"

"It doesn't include kids. Or a husband. I bet you keep an appointment book 'cause you're so busy . . ."

"Palm Pilot," she shot back.

"Do you even know how to cook?"

She shrugged. "Doesn't matter. I'm not inviting you to dinner anytime soon."

He scowled at her. "I'm serious. We're talking about a kid who just lost her mother and is pretty scared. She doesn't need someone who has to check to make sure she has time for her."

"I don't think I want to hear any more," Deanna said, stepping around him and heading for the revolving door into the building. "If it makes you feel better, I haven't decided if I'm going to take Jade or not. Despite what you think of me, I know I can do a good job."

Patterson Temple narrowed his gaze. "Jade is not a job. She's a six-year-old kid." He turned and walked away.

Deanna felt the sting of his doubt and his dislike of her. Maybe he was right. Was she taking Jade's situation seriously enough? Was she being arrogant and cavalier? Should she even consider taking on such a huge responsibility?

She was surprised when Patterson suddenly stopped and turned back. Slowly and reluctantly, he retraced his steps until he stood before her again.

"Another thing. There's going to be a funeral service for Stacy."

"She won't be buried in Potter's Field, will she?" she questioned with dismay.

"No. Someplace in New Jersey. Betts got permission to sign for Stacy's remains. She's going to have a proper burial."

"That's good," she said. "How . . ."

"Betts took up a collection at her church and around the neighborhood." Deanna immediately reached for her wallet. He touched her arm to stop her. "It's done. The service is Saturday morning, uptown."

"But I'd like to contribute something."

"You can send flowers if you want."

Deanna didn't respond. Flowers seemed inadequate.

"Where is the service?"

He gave her the address and time.

"I'm glad," she commented softly. "But I'm so sorry that this even has to be done. I wish things had worked out better for Stacy."

"One good thing happened to her," he responded, just as softly. "She had Jade." As abruptly as before, he walked away.

Pensive, Deanna entered the lobby. She was still deep in thought a few minutes later, waiting for the elevator, when she heard her name being called.

"Hey, Deanna. Thanks for the report. We were able to use about half of what you compiled."

Deanna smiled at the balding, bespectackled man who joined her. "Hi, Matt. What report?"

"You know, the thing about new research in spinal injuries where the doctors think that they may be able to regenerate nerves to quadriplegic patients so they might walk again someday."

They both got on the elevator. She looked at him, puzzled. "How did you get that report? I haven't finished doing the literature search in the medical database."

Matt shrugged. "I got it. Hand-delivered."

"Really?"

"You know, you should just accept the credit and let it go." He chuckled. "The on-air reporter was so grateful he was willing to give you almost anything. Aim big. Want to be president of the network?"

"Two extra weeks' vacation." Deanna smiled at him, and he laughed. "Matt, would you happen to remember exactly who delivered that report from the library?"

He thought a moment. "Someone named Nancy. Nice lady. Very helpful. Looked like a librarian . . ."

Deanna swatted his arm as he left the elevator on the seventh floor, laughing. But she was only mildly amused.

"I knew I should have gone with you to that interview," Joy said. "I can't believe you're really thinking of taking that child. What are you going to do with her?" she asked, lifting a hand to examine the fresh coat of nail polish. She began to blow gently across the tips as the manicurist worked on her other hand.

Deanna tried not to let Joy get to her. She'd already had to endure Patterson Temple's criticism. She couldn't seem to shake the memory of their encounter. Deanna inspected the bottles of available color and picked one for her own newly shaped and buffed nails.

"Maybe this isn't going to be a big deal," she said with more confidence than she actually felt. "Mrs. Levine at ACS said the situation will be considered temporary. Everyone is still trying to locate Stacy's family. It might not take that long."

From her treatment table next to Deanna's, Joy shot her an indulgent grimace. "And what are you going to do if it goes on for months?"

"I don't know. Maybe they'll have to place Jade in

another home. But we don't know if it will come to that."

"Fool," Joy said airily. "She's not like a bag of chips you can return because you discover they're stale."

"Thanks for the vote of confidence. I'm just realistic enough to consider that if I take Jade, it might not work out between me and her."

"Girl, are you *not* the same sister who told me once if not a dozen times that you weren't interested in having kids?"

"I haven't changed my mind," Deanna said, glancing at Joy. "Anyway, I never said I don't *like* kids, or that I break out in hives if I'm anywhere near them. You've seen me with your son his whole life."

"I know you treat Devon like a crown prince, but that's only 'cause you can send him back home to me after you've spoiled him."

"You're lucky," Deanna said warmly. "Devon is so sweet. Handsome and talented . . ."

"Just like his mother, thank you."

"And his father," Deanna reminded her.

"Ummm," Joy murmured quietly.

Deanna waited a moment. "Still think about Bradley?"

"Ummm."

Deanna believed that Joy was too attractive, bright, and fun to be with for there not to be another love in her life sooner or later. When she was ready. She was slender, with wonderful style and grace. If not model beautiful, then pretty close to it. Which Deanna was sure contributed to her success as a labor attorney, especially doing arbitration, settlement negotiations, and court trials. She'd seen Joy in action in social settings; she could walk into a place and stop everything cold . . . and never notice. She was also quick and smart, and when people engaged her in conversation, they were surprised by her thoughtful intelligence and sense of humor. Men in particular sat up and paid attention. For now, she didn't notice that, either. Her husband's death so young, from complications due to childhood-onset diabetes, had stunned them all. But Joy was the one woman whom Deanna believed was made for marriage.

"I still think Jade would be better off with someone else. No offense," Joy said calmly.

"She's been with Patterson Temple's grandmother, who was thought to be too old."

"Patterson Temple again. Who is this guy?" Joy asked.

Deanna made a sound of aggravation with her tongue against her teeth, even as her stomach twisted at the memory of their face-off. He seemed to have a knack for striking her nerves with a directness that wouldn't have been at all effective if deep down inside she didn't think there might be some truth in his assessment of her.

"Don't even get me started," Deanna mumbled.

"I want to know more about him."

"No, you don't."

"Well, he keeps popping up here, there, and everywhere in this story about Stacy and her daughter. What does he look like?"

"I didn't notice."

"I don't believe you. He must be cute."

The manicurist indicated that she was finished and placed Joy's hands in a contraption meant to speed up the drying process.

"He's annoying," Deanna finally said. "He had the nerve to tell me he wasn't impressed because I said I might take Jade. He questioned my motives."

Joy didn't respond as she stood up and reached into her pocket for the tip she had handy for the manicurist. She used her palm to smooth out the lines of her skirt and then carefully buttoned the matching jacket.

"You're not going to like this, Dee, but I think he's right."

For all of Betts's words of enthusiasm that she believed Deanna and Jade would be fine together, Patterson was not so sure. Maybe he wasn't being fair. Deanna was tough, strong. He hated to admit it, but he liked that she would square off with him. He suspected that beneath her cultivated confidence was a softer side. At the morgue, he'd caught a glimpse of how vulnerable she could be. Maybe she could find time in her life for a little girl who needed her, after all. But he doubted it.

A black woman raising kids alone was no big thing. Even other folks' kids. Betts had done it. But she'd done it in this community of other women, where everybody watched out for everybody else's kids. Like that African saying that it takes a village to raise a child.

Deanna Lindsay didn't strike him as being tribal.

"You asleep?" A female voice intruded on his thoughts.

He lay quiet. He didn't feel like talking.

"Pat?" the feminine voice asked again.

He stared at the ceiling, an arm bent behind his head. He hoped his silence would discourage any more questions, but Eleanor had more than one way to get his attention, and she was not exactly the subtle type.

Patterson felt her roll in the bed toward him. Her body heat combined with his made him feel stifled and confined. He realized he should have left sooner and gone on home to his own bed. He'd never meant for this to become a routine. Go out for dinner and end up in bed. He didn't like being locked in. He never made any promises.

But Eleanor was never very good at taking no for an answer. Her intention now was not to get close or to cuddle, both of which were foreign to her, anyway.

Patterson honestly did not want to make love again. He was too caught up in the revelation that he couldn't just dismiss Deanna Lindsay. He didn't like her acting as if she thought he was somehow beneath her. He didn't like that she made him feel he lacked something essential to be taken seriously by her. She wasn't coy, and maybe that threw him off. Deanna Lindsay didn't play games.

He felt Eleanor trail her fingertips lightly over his torso, teasing his nipples and then gliding down to his navel. His stomach muscles contracted involuntarily. He closed his eyes as her sorcery began to work.

But he was still distracted. He was not finished with trying to figure out Deanna Lindsay. And he hadn't even begun to come up with why he'd want to.

He groaned at the coiling tension. Eleanor had always known how to push his buttons. Before long she'd succeeded in capturing more than his undivided attention. He gave in to her teasing and her success at making him hard.

Nonetheless, the last thoughts he had before finally falling to sleep were not the feel-good stuff that comes after sex. Or any attempt to reconcile his doubts and feelings about Eleanor. It was wondering if he had more in common with Deanna Lindsay than he wanted to admit.

Chapter Four

Ida Levine rose and came around her desk to stand facing Deanna. "Are you ready to meet Jade?"

Deanna stood slowly as well. This was it. She was about to meet six-year-old Jade Taylor Lowell. Despite Joy's best efforts to talk her out of it, she had agreed to become Jade's guardian for an undetermined length of time.

She should be able to respond to the question confidently. But she couldn't. Instead, her mind reviewed through reason after reason as to why her decision was a mistake. Nevertheless, she said, "Yes, I'm ready."

Mrs. Levine beamed. "I'm so pleased. The agency couldn't have asked for a better caretaker for Jade. Jade's caseworker, Marilyn Phillips, is available to help you anytime. Attorney Joy Harding spoke very highly of you, as did the director of the women's center where you volunteer. I also called Patterson Temple for a reference."

Deanna looked sharply at Mrs. Levine. "Really? May I ask why?"

"Mrs. Butler, who you know was caring for Jade, said that Mr. Temple had met you. He's a well-respected city employee, and I wanted his feedback."

Deanna couldn't imagine what Patterson would

have told the ACS. She half expected to hear a laundry list of complaints and objections, and was surprised when none were forthcoming. Instead, Mrs. Levine gestured toward the door.

"Have you told Jade about me?" Deanna asked as they walked through the labyrinth of corridors connecting dozens of office cubicles.

"She knows that she's going to be living with you in Manhattan and that she'll be attending a new school. You realize that's another big adjustment, especially since she's coming in halfway through the school year."

"I've already been in touch with the Board of Education, and they're arranging the transfer of Jade's records to the elementary school in my neighborhood," Deanna said. "They told me to bring her in Monday to register. Does Jade know who I am?"

"She knows your name. She was told that her mother especially wanted you to take care of her." They boarded the elevator outside the agency offices and took it up one floor.

"How did she react?" Deanna asked.

"She wanted to know why her mother never told her about you before. Why you never came to visit them."

"Good questions," Deanna murmured wryly.

They exited the elevator and walked into a large, brightly lit playroom, outfitted to appeal to children. The walls were covered with cartoon characters and movie screen heroes. There were children-size furniture, cases filled with books, games and puzzles, and lots of toys. Half a dozen children played together while a woman moderated. From a connecting room could be heard the hyper voices and action of a TV program.

Deanna looked at all the children in the play group, but there was no six-year-old girl among them.

"Theresa, where are Marilyn and Jade?" Mrs. Levine asked the moderator.

The woman pointed. "In the TV room, watching *Pinocchio*."

"I know you're a little nervous," Mrs. Levine said quietly, "but remember that you have to set the tone. She has to be able to count on you, and know that everything is going to be all right. Just be yourself."

"I will," Deanna said as they approached the open door.

A large-screen TV occupied one corner of the room. Jade's caseworker, Marilyn Phillips, who had visited Deanna's apartment the day before, was seated in one of the few small chairs. The four children present were sprawled on the carpeted floor, staring raptly at the video. One boy and three girls. One of the girls had tan skin and a riot of curly light brown hair streaked with blond highlights. Another little girl was blond, her hair pulled back into a ponytail. The last girl was black.

Deanna stared at the blond-haired girl, willing her to turn around. Stacy had had blond hair.

"Marilyn?" Mrs. Levine called quietly.

Marilyn Phillips stood to meet them. She was a black woman, about forty, with a kind face. The little girl with the blond ponytail looked over her shoulder at the strangers.

Deanna smiled nervously. The girl was pretty, with a small face and inquisitive gray eyes.

"Hi, Deanna. It's nice to see you again," Marilyn said, pulling Deanna's attention away from the girl.

"Can we take Jade and Deanna into your office?" Mrs. Levine asked.

"Certainly. Jade, there's someone I'd like you to meet. Will you come with me, please?"

Deanna continued to watch the blond girl, trying to determine if there was a resemblance to Stacy. By now the other children had become distracted by the adult voices, and all turned as Jade's name was called out. To Deanna's surprise, the girl with the tight curls stood as Marilyn held out her hand.

"Jade," Marilyn said, "this is Deanna Lindsay. She's here to meet you, and she's going to be your guardian."

Deanna knew that Ida Levine was waiting for her reaction. She knew she was staring in stunned surprise, but she couldn't find her voice. Her gaze traveled over the little girl and settled on her hair. Not just very curly but slightly kinky. She was a beautiful child, Deanna thought, with caramel-colored skin. It was obvious that Jade Taylor Lowell was *not* white.

Deanna looked toward Marilyn Phillips and Ida Levine, who were apparently waiting for her to say something. She cleared her throat. "Hello, Jade. I'm very happy to meet you."

Jade slowly and surreptitiously gazed at Deanna from startling seafoam-green eyes.

"Let's go into my office," Marilyn said, leading the way.

Deanna let Jade and Marilyn walk ahead of her, while she tried to process this unexpected twist. She hoped she didn't appear as dazed as she felt. She tried to recall those brief six weeks with Stacy. Had Stacy ever said anything about her man? Deanna couldn't remember.

She wondered if Jade's paternity was the reason

why Stacy had been so ambivalent about whether or not to have her child. Nevertheless, at some point she'd made up her mind not to abort her baby.

"I'm sorry you don't know who I am, Jade. I'm sure it's confusing, isn't it?" Deanna said. Jade stared out the window. Deanna tried again. "I'd really like us to become friends. Your mother and I used to be friends. That's why she wanted you to stay with me."

"I want to stay here," Jade said in a barely audible voice.

Deanna's stomach sank as her anxiety rose. She'd not given much thought to the possibility that Jade might not *want* to stay with her. She saw that being responsible for the child was going to be more than just providing a place to live. She was going to have to earn Jade's trust. And she was terrified.

"Here we are," Deanna said smoothly, unlocking her apartment door. "Come on in."

She stood to one side, holding the door as Marilyn Phillips urged Jade inside. The little girl did as she was directed, looking furtively around as she entered. Marilyn came in behind her, pulling a child's blue, yellow, and red suitcase on wheels.

When they were all crowded into the small foyer, Deanna closed the door. Now that she was back on home turf, she felt slightly relieved, still nervous but back in control.

She took off her coat and hung it in a nearby closet. "Let me take your coat, Jade," Deanna said, holding out her hand.

Jade shook her head and made no move to unzip her bright red jacket. On her back was a knapsack in the shape of a turtle, and she held on to the straps, as if she was afraid someone would try to take it from her.

Marilyn smiled at Deanna. "That's a good idea. I want to take off my coat." She did so, passed it to Deanna, and then turned to Jade. "Come on, hon. Let's take your coat off and you'll be more comfortable."

Jade shook her head again. "I don't want to."

"How would you like to see where you're going to sleep? You have your very own bedroom," Deanna offered.

"That sounds wonderful," Marilyn said cheerfully. "I'd like to see it, Jade. Let's go together."

Reluctantly, Jade followed the two women down a hallway.

"Here we are," Deanna said, walking into the room and waiting for Jade and Marilyn to join her.

Deanna had made the second of two bedrooms in her co-op apartment into a combination office and guest room. Although not a large room, it held a desk on which were a closed laptop computer, reference books, a lamp, and a laser printer. Next to the window was a bookcase. Deanna had consolidated her own things to fit into the top three shelves, leaving the lower three empty for Jade. The bottom shelf had two large pull-out baskets that normally held vertical files. She'd removed their contents so they could be used for Jade's clothing. Deanna was glad that a window guard had already been installed by the building management, several years earlier. There was an overstuffed chair that pulled out into a single bed. Deanna had already prepared the bed with a set of sheets printed with Disney characters from *The Jungle Book*. Next to the pull-out bed was a stool from her kitchen to serve as a nightstand. It held a small lamp shaped like a crescent moon.

"What a nice room for you, Jade," Marilyn said.

"Would you like to take off your knapsack?" Deanna asked again.

Jade looked around the room as if it contained a trap. "No," she responded in a tiny voice and began to back out.

"What am I going to do?" Deanna whispered to Marilyn as they followed Jade to the living room.

"Just keep emphasizing that this is where she's going to live. The sooner Jade realizes that, the quicker she'll accept it and settle down. It's better that I don't stay very long."

"I don't want to force Jade to do anything she doesn't want. I don't want her to . . . dislike me," Deanna said quietly.

"It's not a question of forcing her, Deanna. Jade may not like it at first, but she'll discover by herself that she's going to be okay with you. Don't worry if she cries. That's one of the few ways children have of expressing their feelings. They're all different. We've placed some children who accept change quickly, but others take a longer time."

Deanna had the suspicion that Jade might fall into the latter category. She was sitting on the edge of a sofa cushion, her coat and backpack still on. But she was also examining one of three teddy bears that Deanna had collected over the years and kept on the sofa.

"What a cute teddy, Jade," Marilyn said.

Deanna took her cue from the caseworker's comment. She decided to sit next to Jade on the sofa. But not too close.

"That's my favorite teddy bear, too," she said to

Jade. She didn't wait for a reply. "I got the teddy bear you're holding from some friends, when I was fourteen. I was in the hospital and they came to visit me."

Jade turned the bear in her hand upside down, squeezed it, examined the little knit sweater which had the colors and look of an American flag.

"How come you had to go to the hospital?" she asked in a sweet voice.

Deanna gently rubbed the ear of the stuffed animal. "I had to have an operation. I had my appendix removed, and my friends brought me this teddy bear."

Jade gathered the toy against her chest in a hug, and then laid it on her lap. "I had to go to the hospital when I was little."

Deanna looked at Marilyn, puzzled, but could see that the caseworker didn't know what Jade was talking about.

"Really? How come?" Deanna asked.

Jade lowered her head until her mouth was pulled into the opening of her coat. "'Cause I fell off the Jungle Jim in the park and I was bleeding. But I didn't get a teddy bear."

"I'm so sorry," Deanna crooned.

Jade poked a finger into the stomach of the second teddy bear. "Who gave you this one?"

Deanna grinned. "An old boyfriend. When I first started college."

Jade pointed to the last of the teddy bears. "And this one?"

"That belonged to my younger brother, Tate. He was going to throw it out when he was about twelve, and I asked if I could have it."

Marilyn Phillips asked a few more simple questions of Jade, who gradually became less skittish. For each bright answer or unsolicited comment, however, there were moments of sullen silence, and Jade still would not take off her knapsack and coat.

After a while Deanna suggested that they eat something. She left Jade with Marilyn and went to the kitchen to quickly put out the makings for sandwiches and a plate of cookies she'd prepared that morning. As she was pouring apple juice for Jade and heating water for tea for herself and Marilyn, the telephone rang.

"Hello?" She placed the cordless phone between her ear and shoulder as she walked about the kitchen.

"It's Stephen."

"Oh, Stephen . . . I can't talk right now. Is everything okay?"

"Pretty much. I gave out the assignments you wanted me to. I know you won't be in until next Monday, but we have a bit of a problem."

'What is it?"

"Ruth's husband had a mild stroke this morning, and she had to leave. She'll probably be out for a while. Maybe a week. That leaves the reference desk uncovered."

"Put Nancy there. And have Marianne help out in the afternoon when it gets the busiest. I'll make more adjustments if I need to."

"Got it. If there's anything I can do . . ."

"Nope. I'll call you later. Thanks, Stephen."

By the time Deanna finished the call, Marilyn had Jade seated at the small dining table and was handing her a sandwich. Deanna was glad to see that Jade had a healthy appetite but was dismayed that even while eating the child kept her coat on.

After they'd eaten, Jade asked to go to the bathroom. It was then that Marilyn was finally able to persuade her that she had to take off the knapsack and jacket in order to slide her arms out of her overalls. Deanna offered to show her where the bathroom was, but Jade marched off alone.

"I'm going to get ready to leave," Marilyn said, opening the foyer closet and removing her coat. "You have my office and home phone numbers. Call me anytime if you need to."

"What if she starts crying?" Deanna asked.

"Just be patient and stay calm. Remember, Jade is going to depend on you and you have to be in charge."

It was on the tip of Deanna's tongue to ask the caseworker to stay a little longer, but Jade was returning from the bathroom. She went straight for her knapsack and pulled it on, but Deanna, at Marilyn's suggestion, had already put away her coat. When Jade realized that Marilyn was leaving, her eyes brightened in distress and her bottom lip quivered. She raced to the door.

"I want to go, too," she began to whine. "Where's my coat?"

Marilyn stooped to speak directly to her. Deanna could do nothing but stand by and watch the poignant good-bye.

"Jade, you have to stay here now. You can't come with me."

"I don't want to stay."

"Don't be frightened," Deanna said fervently, her throat tightening. "You're going to be fine with me. I promise."

Jade began to cry, reaching out for Marilyn, who

hugged her briefly and then pulled away. She, too, made promises: to call, to come to see her.

Deanna could only stare at the child, convinced that she was Jade's worst nightmare. She came out of her paralysis and went to hold Jade to prevent her from following Marilyn out the door. Jade began to struggle. Deanna was afraid to force the little girl to obey. Afraid that Jade would dislike her even more if she did.

"You going to be okay?" Marilyn asked from the doorway.

"Yes, yes." Deanna nodded quickly, holding the twisting child and awkwardly waving a hand for the caseworker to leave. When the door closed, Deanna continued to hold Jade for a moment longer. Her nerves jangling from the child's plaintive crying, Deanna maneuvered herself within reach of the door and bolted the high Medco lock, which was out of the reach of small hands . . . and attempts to escape.

Deanna finally released Jade, only to have her fly at her, attempting to physically shove Deanna aside to reach the door.

"Jade, it's all right," Deanna said.

Her voice wavered as she realized how much tension she herself was experiencing. But she couldn't let herself lose control.

"I know you're scared, sweetheart. So am I," Deanna confessed, her voice high. She put her arm around the now hysterical and screaming child. "Honey . . ."

Jade broke away, running to grab her brightly colored child's suitcase, which contained everything she owned in the world. Pathetically, she began dragging the case to the door, knocking to the floor the teddy bear she'd held so carefully before, bumping against an end table and causing a white vase with dried flowers to topple over. It crashed to the floor and broke into several pieces. Again Jade tried to push Deanna out of the way. When that didn't work, Jade let go of the suitcase and began hitting Deanna with her fists.

Deanna was stunned by the attack, caught off guard by the little girl's fright and rage. The blows did not hurt Deanna physically at all, but Jade's singleminded determination pierced Deanna's heart and soul. She stood silently and absorbed the punches, but already the child was weakening, emotional exhaustion depleting her energy.

Failing to get past Deanna to the door, Jade turned and ran through the apartment, her knapsack bobbing up and down comically on her back, her wild curly hair bouncing about her small face. She went from room to room, seeking another way of escape. Deanna let her go, knowing there was no other exit. Finally Jade came back into the living room. Her crying had become sobs, coughing and hiccups. Balefully, standing defeated as she swayed, she regarded Deanna. Slowly Deanna held out her hands.

"Come here. Let's take off your backpack."

"No!" Jade screamed pitifully.

Deanna sighed and let her hands drop. She lowered herself to the edge of her leather club chair and looked with empathy at the little girl.

"I'm so sorry," Deanna said quietly, even though she knew that Jade would not understand what she was sorry about.

It was just that Patterson Temple was right. It was Jade who had lost everything.

The phone rang, but Deanna ignored it. She couldn't allow herself to be distracted. Jade needed her full attention right now, for as long as it took to make her feel better. The phone eventually stopped ringing and the answering machine clicked on.

Jade leaned her head wearily against the arm of the sofa. "I don't want to stay heeeeeere."

She sobbed. And sobbed.

All Deanna could do was sit and watch, every now and then speaking softly and soothingly. Over and over again letting Jade know she didn't have to be afraid, even as it seemed to her that the child's heart was breaking.

The phone rang again. Deanna let it ring.

"Why don't you answer?" Jade screamed, her face flushed.

"It's not important," Deanna said.

"What . . . what if it's . . . Mrs. Phillips? Maybe . . . she's coming . . . back for me," Jade hiccuped.

"I don't think so. Not tonight, honey."

As if her last possible hope had been taken away, Jade slid, defeated, to the floor with her head against the sofa cushions and continued her inconsolable tears. Eventually she seemed to run out of energy and tears. Coughing, she climbed onto the sofa, all the while keeping her eyes on Deanna, as if she expected her to turn into the bogeyman. She wiped her wet face with the back of her hand. Her eyes drooped, her chest heaving with the contractions in her throat. Finally, she keeled over to lie on the sofa, her legs still hanging over the edge. In less than ten seconds Jade Lowell had fallen asleep, her turtle-shaped knapsack still strapped to her back.

Deanna sat and stared. It was a long while before she could let go of the tension that had kept her body tightly wound. She eased back into the chair and just watched the little girl, turned instantly from a whirling dervish into a sleeping angel.

So much for thinking that this was going to be easy, Deanna thought ruefully.

She wondered if maybe Joy and Richard were right. Even Patterson Temple had somehow known she was ill-prepared for a child. Strangely, of the two men, she felt Patterson Temple's lack of faith most of all.

Moving quietly, Deanna put to rights the small disasters around the living room. She threw away the broken vase, carried Jade's suitcase to her room. She quickly unpacked the little girl's meager belongings. Then she returned to the kitchen to clean up. When at last she sat down with a much-needed cup of tea, she found and examined two badly broken fingernails, noticed a button missing on her suit jacket, and saw thin scratches on the back of her left hand. From the pocket of her jacket, she removed the card with Marilyn Phillips's home phone. It was a life preserver Deanna could grab hold of . . . if she needed to. It was also a reminder of her own inexperience and shortcomings. For her own sake she was going to try her best not to find reason to call Jade's caseworker.

Deanna returned to the living room and watched as Jade slept. She was such a pretty child. Deanna remained curious about Jade's paternity. She frowned as her mind drifted back to how she and Stacy had first met.

Stacy had been from a low-income family somewhere in the Midwest. Deanna had figured out that Stacy had run away from home and was finding life in New York hard. She had only a high school education and no skills. She was also almost three months pregnant.

So was Deanna.

And they'd both decided to have abortions.

They'd been placed together in the same dressing room, where they'd removed all of their clothing and jewelry, and been given thin blue cotton gowns and oversized paper slippers. Joy had accompanied Deanna to the clinic because the clinic counselors had recommended that someone be available to take her home. Stacy had come alone.

She and Stacy had sat silently together, each waiting to be called to be prepped for the procedure. Deanna didn't pay much attention to the young girl, too angry with herself for having been careless with a man she hardly knew, and now forced to make a decision she didn't want to make.

She had not told her mother, terrified of her reaction. She'd never told the man she'd slept with . . . a man she'd met at a conference in another city, a man she'd slept with after a business reception and amorous flirting and too much to drink. Had he taken advantage of her? Or was she solely responsible for consenting to sex without thought or protection? The distinctions hadn't been clear even then. The result was an unwanted pregnancy.

She was not ready to have a baby. But it was more than that. Deanna had decided when she was fifteen years old that she didn't want to have kids. Perhaps having been the oldest she'd done too much babysitting, or felt too often as if she and her siblings were a chore to her mother.

Getting an abortion had seemed the only practical solution. But it hadn't been easy.

"Are you going to do it?"

Deanna remembered it was Stacy who had spoken first.

"What?" Deanna asked.

"Do you think God is going to punish us if we do this?"

"I don't know," Deanna had replied, "but I'm not changing my mind."

"Does your baby's father want you to do it?"

Deanna finally looked closely at her, hearing the serious doubts and the sincere fears in the girl's voice. Deanna was not given to discussing her personal business with strangers, but she could see that Stacy needed to talk to someone.

"The . . . father," Deanna said with difficulty, "doesn't know about it. It was an accident. I . . . wasn't careful."

"I don't mind so much. I want to have a baby. Then I'll have someone to love me."

"What about your baby's father?" Deanna asked.

The girl hugged herself, rocking back and forth, shaking her head. "He doesn't know. I'm . . . afraid to tell him. I'm afraid he'll be so mad he'll send me away. I don't have any place else to go."

"What about your family?"

"I can't go home. I ran away, and I can't go back."

"It doesn't sound like you're going to be able to take care of a baby. Maybe an abortion is the best thing right now. You can always have kids later. You have time. Didn't you talk to the counselor? They won't let you do it unless you're absolutely sure."

"I was sure yesterday. Now, I don't know. But I don't want to lose Marcus."

Deanna became impatient. "Doesn't sound like he's worth it. If you want to keep your baby you may have to cut this guy loose. You can live without him."

"You sound so smart," the teenager said. "I wish I wasn't so afraid."

"It's okay to be afraid," Deanna told her. "I'm afraid too. But I know this is the right thing for me to do."

The door opened and a nurse stood with a record folder in her hand.

"Deanna Lindsay?"

Deanna stood up. "That's me."

"We're ready for you. This way . . ."

Deanna nodded as she headed for the door. She was briefly stopped by the girl.

"My name is Stacy."

"Hi, Stacy. I hope it works out for you."

When Deanna sleepily opened her eyes sometime later, she lay still and cautiously placed her hands on her abdomen. It felt different there. Flat. And empty. A little achy soreness in her groin . . . and a pad between her legs. She sighed deeply with relief, and for the first time since she suspected she was pregnant, she felt she was finally back on track with her life. She could put this behind her. But she also felt ashamed, and very sad.

She glanced over at the other two beds in the recovery room and found them empty. She wondered about Stacy. She had seemed very confused, but Deanna knew that at seventeen or eighteen, Stacy probably wasn't ready for the responsibility of a child. She closed her eyes and thought, *It's over.* But then she thought of her mother, who'd had three children and raised them in what became a difficult marriage. She thought of her sister Carla, who'd married an older man who could take care of her. She'd never thought either her mother's or sister's options were very appealing. She told herself she would never marry out of fear, or have kids out of loneliness, or just because it was an accident.

But she hadn't expected that the change in her body would trigger a new awareness in her heart and mind. That she would realize how everything she did was tied to her soul. The aborted fetus was little more than tissue and membrane. But suddenly she felt as if she had gotten rid of part of herself.

Deanna was suddenly grateful to be all alone in that sterile, plain room so that she could quietly cry and no one would know.

Deanna decided Jade would be more comfortable in bed. Perhaps she would sleep the rest of the night, and things would be different in the morning.

Carefully she pulled Jade's left arm out of the strap of her backpack. She sat on the coffee table, shifting and rolling Jade's body to the right, so she could remove the backpack and set it on the floor. She put her arm around Jade and the child's head rolled against her as she lifted Jade to her chest. The completely limp body was warm, and surprisingly light.

Deanna carried Jade to the small bedroom, thankful now that she'd had the foresight to prepare the bed in advance. She put Jade down and began to undress her, leaving on her panties and a long-sleeved striped T-shirt. She covered the sleeping child, who had remained asleep throughout the process and, leaving the lamp on as a night-light, left the room.

In the kitchen Deanna listened to her phone messages. One was from Marilyn Phillips, the other from Richard. Deanna wasn't up to talking to either of them at the moment. Instead, she sat at the kitchen table and called Joy.

"Girl, I was waiting to hear from you. What happened today?"

Deanna realized it was a relief to be able to talk about how traumatic the afternoon had been. She mentioned her discovery and her response to the fact that the little girl was biracial.

"Really? You didn't know that before?"

"It was never mentioned, and there were two people who could have told me before I met her. The woman at ACS and Patterson Temple."

"Why wouldn't anyone say something about that?"

"Well . . . is it that important? Does anyone need to make an issue of it? It's just that there's almost no information about her background. Nothing about her family.

"And you never knew anything about this?"

"Why should I have known? When Stacy talked about her boyfriend, it was just some guy named Marcus."

"So tell me about her. What's she like?"

Deanna reflected back on the afternoon, trying to find any moment when she could get a clear impression that wasn't overshadowed by Jade's great emotional distress.

"Joy, she's beautiful."

"I bet."

"She's got a head full of kinky blond hair that's all over the place, and pretty green eyes. She's very articulate . . . and she has a very healthy pair of lungs. You should have heard the way she cried and carried on when the caseworker left after we got to my apartment."

"Was she awful?" Joy asked.

"No, not awful. Just . . . heartbroken and scared," Deanna concluded.

"When do I get to meet her?"

"I don't know. Right now, she doesn't want to stay with me."

"Sounds like you have your hands full. Maybe you should reconsider."

"There's no need. I'm going to keep her."

After Deanna ended her conversation with Joy, there didn't seem to be anything else to do and it was getting late. She decided that a good night's sleep might help. She was going to need to be rested for whatever the next day would bring for her and Jade.

In bed she tried to review all the materials she'd gotten from ACS about taking care of a child, about how to get help if needed. A crash course in parenting.

Deanna began to piece together all the information she'd learned over the years from her mother, her sister, and Joy. She could be like her mother, who had raised three kids to be educated, useful citizens and decent people, but who'd treated being a parent like being an executive. There was also Carla, whose two boys were the center of her life, and Joy, who'd wanted more children but who'd lost her husband after having only a son. And there was Stacy, who'd left a little girl who belonged nowhere and to no one.

In the middle of the night Deanna heard Jade crying. She quickly pushed back the covers and got out of bed. In the dark she crossed the hallway to the other room. She'd left the door ajar and could clearly hear Jade's quiet sobs.

"Mommy . . . Mommy," she called plaintively.

Deanna came into the room, murmuring softly. "It's okay, honey. You're not alone."

"I'm scared . . ."

"Of the dark? I left the light on for you. See?" Deanna murmured, pointing to the lamp.

Jade glanced indifferently at the whimsical light, as she sat up, tangled in the bed linens. "No . . . I don't want to stay here alone."

"I'm here. My bedroom is just across from yours."

"I'm scared," Jade continued.

Deanna thought a moment. She pulled the covers away and motioned for Jade to get out of bed. "Okay, come with me," she said, reaching out a hand. To her surprise, Jade took it.

Deanna led Jade into her bedroom and helped her into the queen-size bed, covering her up again.

"I'll be right back."

Deanna made her way to the living room and found the teddy bears. She brought all three to the room and tucked them under the covers with Jade before slipping into the other side of the bed.

"Feel better?" Deanna asked.

"Ummm-hmmm."

"Good."

"Am I going to stay here?" Jade asked in a sleepy voice.

"Just for tonight, so you won't feel all alone," Deanna whispered.

"Are you scared of the dark?" Jade asked.

"Sometimes," Deanna admitted.

"I wish my mommy was here," Jade mumbled, falling peacefully back to sleep.

"I wish my mommy was here, too," Deanna murmured wryly.

Chapter Five

Deanna picked up the intercom phone hanging on the wall next to the door.

"Yes?"

"Morning, Ms. Lindsay. Your mother is on her way up."

"Thanks, Julio."

In the five minutes she had before her mother reached her apartment, Deanna flew back to her bedroom to finish dressing. She pulled on her favorite yellow crewneck and jeans. Hastily she finger-combed her short hair while glaring into the mirror at the dark smudges under her eyes. She hadn't bothered with a shower, and she wasn't feeling particularly rested. In less than twenty-four hours, she was both feeling and seeing the effects of having Jade Lowell come to live with her.

The bell rang, and Deanna hurried to open the door. "Hi, Mom," she said.

Faith Lindsay stood on the threshold with an expression of controlled impatience. She frowned, taken aback by her daughter's appearance. "Dee, what in the world is the matter with you? You look terrible."

"I didn't sleep well last night. Come on in," Deanna answered, closing the door behind her. "You look great. I love that coat."

"You've seen this before," Faith said. She had the regal carriage of someone used to receiving deference and respect, and not wasting her time.

She handed Deanna her coat, and a hint of L'air du Temps wafted through the room. Beneath it she wore stylish black slacks that emphasized her slim figure, a mauve silk shell, and a deep purple front-zippered jacket. Her short brushed hairdo was expertly colored to hide the gray. It made her look, without exaggeration, at least fifteen years younger than her fifty-eight years. Simple gold jewelry and beautifully cared-for hands added to the illusion.

"I can't stay long," Faith said, looking around the living room. "Dee, what is all this about some child you're taking care of?"

Deanna gestured for her mother to accompany her to the kitchen. She pointed to a carafe on the counter. "I just finished brewing some coffee. Want some?"

"What I *want* is to know about this child," Faith said, sitting at the small table.

"That's what I want to talk to you about," Deanna began. She poured two mugs of coffee and placed one in front of her mother. Then she sat down opposite her, unsure where to begin.

Faith leaned forward. "Okay, I'm listening. You nearly scared me to death, calling at midnight to say you had to see me this morning."

"Well . . . it's complicated," Deanna finally admitted. She carefully gave her mother an edited version of how she had become temporary guardian to Stacy's daughter.

She'd never told her mother about her abortion, and she didn't plan to do so now. Perhaps she was afraid of admitting that she'd been so stupid. Or maybe she was just afraid of seeing the disappointment in her mother's eyes. Her parents hadn't raised their three kids to be irresponsible.

"I don't understand how you met anyone like this young girl," Faith said when Deanna had finished.

Deanna squirmed in her chair. "That's not important right now. The thing is, Stacy and I did . . . bond. She trusted me and she needed me," she said, neglecting to mention that in her own way, she had needed Stacy too.

"And you're telling me you actually agreed to do this? To take in somebody's child and care for her? Dee, you must be out of your mind. What do you know about taking care of children?"

Deanna felt a rush of heat to her face, the parental judgment rolling over her, making her feel small and inadequate. As attractive as her mother was, she could also be aloof and unsympathetic. She held people to her own personal standards, standards that Deanna, as a child, had found impossible to meet. Yet her mother's irritating attributes disguised considerable strengths, such as common sense and self-sufficiency. Her opinions were dependable, consistent. As much as Deanna might not want to admit it, her mother was rarely wrong.

"Obviously I don't know anything about children," Deanna responded dryly. "I thought it wasn't going to be a big deal to take care of one little girl. But after what went on here last night, I realize there's much more to know, so much that's expected of me. Where do I begin?"

Faith sat listening intently and thoughtfully. She put her cup down and stood up.

"Show her to me," she said imperially, waiting for Deanna to lead the way.

They went to Deanna's bedroom. Jade was still fast

asleep, lying on a diagonal across the bed. One teddy bear was under her stomach, another on the floor, the other hidden somewhere in the linens. Her hair was flattened and matted.

Faith stared at the sleeping child for a full minute. "What's her name?"

"Jade."

"Jade," Faith repeated, making a face.

Deanna pulled her mother out of the room, not wanting to wake Jade just yet. They returned to the kitchen.

"When we got here yesterday she wouldn't let me come near her. After the caseworker left, she cried and screamed. I made up my second bedroom for her, but she woke up in the middle of the night in a strange bed, scared and alone, so I let her sleep with me.

"She has almost no clothes. I don't know anything about her, what she's used to. She hasn't eaten since yesterday afternoon, and when she does wake up . . ." Deanna shrugged, as if to ask, "What then?"

"Her name is Jade?" Faith shook her head. "You young women and these silly names. Well, at least she's not Ta Kee Sha," Faith said with exaggerated derision.

"I think Jade is a pretty name. It's the color of her eyes."

"She's half black, isn't she?"

"I think so. Unfortunately, no one seems to know much about her father. Who he is or where he is." Deanna deliberately didn't mention his criminal record.

Faith finished her coffee and stared into the empty cup, a bemused expression on her face. "Well . . . now I've heard just about everything. So, what are you going to do? I'm sure you know you can't keep that child. How are you going to work? What about school and clothes and everything else involved? Besides, this Stacy person does not sound like she came from a good family, especially if no one can even find them. Heaven only knows what that child is really like, and what kind of habits she has. After what went on here last night I don't think you should get involved."

Deanna was hurt that her mother had so little confidence in her. While she was willing to admit she was rocky on the methodology of handling a six-year-old, she wasn't ready to throw in the towel. She'd hoped for a different response. Support would have been nice. Praise even better.

"Mom, I'm going to keep her," she said.

"Do you have any idea what you're letting yourself in for?"

"I'm beginning to. And I'd like your help. Jade's confused and I'm scared. What if she won't stop crying?"

"You want me to give you a crash course in being a mother and raising a child? In twenty-five words or less? It took me three children to figure it out, Deanna. There are no shortcuts. But let me tell you this much—it is *not* easy."

"What's so hard about it?"

"You never know what to expect. It's the surprises that do you in."

"When I was little you always seemed so tough on us."

Faith didn't meet her daughter's gaze, as she formulated a reply. Finally, she shook her head and said, "Raising kids is a lot of work."

"Did you like being a mother?"

"Liking it had nothing to do with anything. It's what I had to do. I got married, I had kids, I raised them. None of you ended up in jail, and I didn't go out of my mind. I'm not surprised that Carla married young. Forget about Tate for a while. He's having too much fun being a womanizer," she observed. "I know you've never been interested in having children, and that's just as well, since I didn't much like it when you took up with Richard."

"Richard is a wonderful man. Why don't you like him?"

"I don't know. Maybe because he's white. Maybe because I know you're sleeping with the man and I don't think he intends to marry you. Maybe because I can't imagine him as the father of any of my grandkids."

"Maybe I don't want him to marry me," Deanna said.

"That's even worse."

Deanna listened to her mother's criticisms, feeling an old resentment surfacing, wanting to use it as a weapon against Faith's parental superiority.

"Richard and I get along together and he treats me well. He just happens to be white."

"Does that mean you don't think a black man is going to treat you right?"

"It doesn't mean anything except that I'm involved with Richard. He could have been a black man with the same qualities, but he isn't, okay?"

"Well, I always say people have to make their own mistakes and learn the hard way."

"Is that what happened with you and Daddy? You figured you'd made a mistake?"

Faith turned sharply on Deanna. "My marriage to

your father is *not* on the table for discussion. Don't be disrespectful."

"Neither is my personal life, and I'd like the same respect for my decisions," Deanna cautioned, getting up to pour more coffee for both of them, using the chore as a calming distraction.

Faith Lindsay did not acquiesce, nor did she apologize. She calmly watched her daughter, not the least fazed by her firmness. "Dee, I'm just being realistic. It seems to be the thing these days to cross the color line and all that. Just like a fad. You get a little education and forget all about your history."

"Mom, this is getting way off the point. I didn't ask you what you think of Richard. I need some advice about how to handle Jade Lowell."

Faith's head turned toward the other room. Deanna heard a tiny whimper. "Sounds like your houseguest is awake. You better go see after her."

Deanna took a deep breath and pulled back her shoulders before she made her way to the bedroom. Jade was sitting up, tangled in the blanket. Her hair was standing out every which way, but she also looked absolutely adorable. Deanna sat carefully on the edge of the bed and smiled brightly into the little girl's pale green eyes.

"Well, good morning, sleepyhead."

"I'm not a sleepyhead," Jade mumbled in her tiny voice, scrubbing at her face and still keeping a wary eye on Deanna.

"Oh, I'm sorry. Maybe you're a pudding face."

Jade ducked her head even more, but not before Deanna detected the hint of a smile.

"I'm *not* a pudding face."

"Well, what should I call you?" Deanna asked carefully.

Jade looked as if she was considering her options, eyeing Deanna as if trying to determine whether she was friend or foe.

"Jade."

Deanna gasped as if in surprise. "Jade! What a beautiful name!"

Watching Deanna closely, Jade nervously rolled her hands in the blanket.

"What's your name?"

"You can call me Deanna . . ."

At that moment the telephone rang. Deanna debated for only a second about the choice between letting it ring and being distracted from the first tentative communication she'd had with the little girl that wasn't punctuated by her tears.

"I'll get it," Faith called out from the kitchen.

Jade looked bewildered. "Who's that?"

"That's my mother."

Jade's face suddenly began to screw up in pain. "I want *my* mommy."

Deanna forced herself not to pull the little girl into a comforting hug. "I know you do, sweetheart. Do you know your mommy asked me to take very special care of you? But you have to help, okay?"

"Dee, it's Richard on the line," Faith called out.

"Tell him I'll call him later."

By the time Deanna had helped Jade out from under the covers, Faith appeared in the doorway.

"Hello. You must be Jade. I'm Faith, Deanna's mother," she said, her voice even and calm. "I bet you would like to use the bathroom. Are you hungry?"

Deanna's jaw dropped as Jade scrambled off the bed and allowed Faith to lead her to the bathroom, while talking about Pokémon and glasses of chocolate milk—one of which Deanna had never heard of and the other of which she didn't have in her kitchen. There was no sound of Jade crying. Deanna took the opportunity to make her bed, a chore she was compulsive about. For the moment, she was relieved to have her mother run interference with Jade. Deanna had other things on her mind, not the least of which was the viewing and funeral for Stacy to be held early that afternoon.

She put together the pull-out bed in Jade's room, then got clothing for her to wear. After Jade's traumatic first night, Deanna wondered if seeing her mother's coffin wouldn't be too much for her to handle. And how, she thought helplessly, do you explain to a child what a funeral means?

When Deanna returned to the kitchen, she found her mother leaning against a counter sipping another cup of coffee. Jade was seated on a high stool next to her, devouring two slices of melted Brie on toast, a banana, and a glass of what looked like milk. A neat trick, since Deanna didn't have any in her refrigerator. Deanna pointed to the glass.

"Where did that come from?"

Faith shrugged. She took another swallow of coffee, then poured the rest into the sink. "I used your half-and-half, added water and a spoonful of sugar. You know you can't continue to feed her that way," she said, as she lightly touched the little girl's hair before turning to walk out of the kitchen.

"Where are you going?" Satisfied that Jade was preoccupied with eating, Deanna followed her mother to the foyer.

"I have some errands to run."

"Mom, what I really need to know is . . . what should I do? What if Jade goes on another crying jag? What if—"

"Dee, the truth is she's going to do a lot of things that are going to get on your nerves, scare the hell out of you, and make you wish you'd never seen her." She took her coat out of the closet and put it on, all the while looking at her daughter skeptically. "I personally think you're in way over your head. Children do not come with instructions and an on/off switch. They can find more ways to aggravate you than you can imagine."

"Thanks for the vote of confidence. You make me sound like an idiot. Or at least like I'm so selfish I'm virtually useless in a situation like this."

"Not useless," Faith disagreed. "Just way out of your territory. You were never interested in having kids. I remember you telling me that before you'd even started college, and I had no reason to doubt you. As a matter of fact, it was probably a smart decision."

Deanna glanced away briefly, knowing it was best not to say anything on that score.

"Anyway, if you wanted kids you would have had some by now . . . with or without marriage. You're thirty-five years old, so if you're going to change your mind you better do it soon."

"I'm thirty-four," Deanna corrected quietly.

"I don't agree with women who think a child doesn't need a father. I'm glad my kids were almost grown before your father and I divorced."

Faith got her purse and reached for the doorknob. She stood thoughtfully for a brief moment, then turned back to her daughter. "I just want to say something about my marriage to your father . . ."

Deanna shook her head. "I didn't mean to be rude before. You don't owe me an explanation."

"You're right, I don't. What I'm doing is making

a confession," Faith said earnestly. "Dee, if I had to do it over again, I *never* would have gotten married. You might not want to know this, but I also never would have had kids. But my kids are the best thing that came out of my marriage to your father."

Deanna was stunned and could do no more than stare at her mother. She'd been aware of the tension that had existed between her parents, at least since she was thirteen or so, but she'd never guessed her mother felt it was all a mistake.

Faith Lindsay had never been shy about saying how she'd put aside her plans to become a lawyer when she'd married. She'd finally enrolled in law school before the divorce was final and for the last five years had worked part-time for a prominent judge. Her confession explained a lot to Deanna about her parents' relationship that she'd never understood while growing up. It explained even more about her mother.

Faith opened the door. "Now, listen to me. That child in there has lost her mother. She's going to hurt for a long while. Keep that in mind, Dee, but don't forget that you're in charge and she has to listen to you. Don't let her gain the upper hand or she'll make your life miserable. Tell her no when you have to, and mean it. Buy some food she can eat, not the stuff you live on. And get her some clothes. Put her on a schedule and set limits. I know you think I was tough and mean when you kids were little. You're going to find out why soon enough. There's more, but I don't want to scare you to death," Faith said dryly, stepping into the hallway. "Good-bye, Jade," she called out, heading for the elevator.

"'Bye," Jade shouted from the kitchen.

The exchange made Deanna smile. "Thank you. Thanks for stopping by."

"There's something else."

"I know. Don't forget I'm not her mother."

"Oh, don't worry," Faith called as she entered the empty elevator. "She's going to keep reminding you that you're not. You wait and see. What I was going to say is, you better be careful because you and I know that child is black. But *she* doesn't know that. Yet."

"Jade, do you have your sneakers on yet? Jade?"

When there was no answer, Deanna left her bedroom, where she'd just changed from jeans into slim stretch pants.

"Jade?"

Deanna peaked into the other bedroom but found it empty. She walked down the short hallway into the living room. Jade was trying to reach a crystal dish on a bookshelf three feet above her head.

"Jade, don't! What do you think you're doing?" Deanna shouted.

The little girl jerked around. "You scared me." Her voice was quavering and tremulous. "I was just getting some candy . . ."

Deanna pulled Jade's arm, forcing the child to jump from where she was perched on the sofa cushion to the floor. "You can't have candy this early in the morning. You didn't ask if you could have any, and you're *not* supposed to stand on furniture. You could have hurt yourself."

Jade stood with her head lowered, pouting as Deanna continued to chastise her.

"I asked you to finish putting your sneakers on

and to let me comb your hair. I need to do some grocery shopping, and we need to figure out . . ."

Deanna stopped when she heard a high-pitched sound coming from the child. A closer look at Jade's face confirmed that she was starting to cry.

"Jade—" Deanna touched her shoulder. Jade shrunk against the wall like a cornered animal.

"You . . . scared . . . meeee!" Jade wailed, her small face distorted.

Deanna sat down heavily on the sofa and turned to the little girl, who stared at her as if she were a monster. "I'm sorry. I didn't mean to, hon. I think I scared me, too," she said in a tired voice. "Come here . . ."

Jade resisted, shaking her head and crying even harder. "I don't like you. I want to go home. I want to go home!"

"I just want to show you what's in the dish, Jade. Don't you want to see?"

Deanna waited patiently. Jade stepped cautiously forward, her green eyes swimming with tears that rolled piteously down her cheeks. Deanna retrieved the dish.

"See. They're not real candy. They're just glass." She lifted one of the pieces. Instantly fascinated, Jade came close enough to peer into the dish.

"Go ahead. You can hold it."

Jade sniffed and took the glass ball, turning it over and over with her small fingers. Deanna sat still as the girl inadvertently leaned against her legs.

"It's pretty," Jade said, using the back of one hand to wipe her face. "Where did you get it? At a store?"

"Actually, they were a gift." Deanna put the glass piece with the others in the bowl and got up to return it to its place on the shelf. "See, I put it up there so it wouldn't get broken by mistake. I was afraid you'd get hurt if it fell on you. That's why I yelled."

Jade stared warily at Deanna. "Do I have to go to the bathroom?"

Deanna was confused. "Go to the bathroom? What do you mean?"

"My mommy makes me go to the bathroom and stay there when she gets mad at me."

Deanna put her arm around the small, thin body, and although there was a momentary resistance, Jade allowed the contact, letting herself be drawn closer to Deanna.

"No. I'm not going to make you go to the bathroom, hon. Why don't you and I talk about a few house rules? Can we do that?"

Jade nodded, settling against Deanna's arm.

"Good. Now, first of all, you don't stand on the furniture. That's a no-no. You don't reach for things off the bookcases or shelves without first asking permission and making sure I've said it's okay to touch."

Jade pointed to the twenty-seven-inch TV on a console with the DVD player on a shelf below. "Can I watch TV?"

"Absolutely," Deanna said, glad that she could finally say yes to something. She certainly didn't want the little girl to feel completely restricted. After all, this was to be her home too. "I'll show you how to use the remote."

"Do you have *The Little Mermaid*?"

"No, I'm afraid not. But I think I have *101 Dalmatians*, and maybe we can rent some more at the video store."

Deanna was grateful that the crisis had passed. She watched Jade's small, pretty features, and it seemed to her that the little girl adapted fairly quickly to whatever she was told. She realized that Jade was giving her the benefit of the doubt. It was a revelation to Deanna that what she said and did mattered. But if Jade was going to accept her, they needed to talk about Stacy. The little girl needed to know that Deanna was not trying to replace her mother.

Deanna smiled warmly at Jade, pleased when she permitted her to smooth and stroke her soft, curly hair. "I know you miss your mother a lot. I don't blame you."

"Betts told me my mommy is never coming home again. Is that true?"

"Yes, it is, hon. That's why you're staying with me. So I can take care of you."

"Oh," Jade murmured thoughtfully. She glanced up at Deanna. "You're not going to be my new mother, are you?"

The question caught Deanna off guard. She hadn't expected it so quickly. "No, I'm not."

"You don't look like my mother," Jade observed, patting Deanna's cheek.

"That's true. Does that bother you?"

Jade lowered her gaze. She shrugged and shook her head. "No. It's okay."

"Good. And one more thing."

Jade looked up questioningly. "What?"

"I'd like us to be friends. I know this is all very strange to you, and you don't know me. It's very strange for me, too. Maybe you and I can help each other out. When I do something wrong, you tell me and I promise to listen and do better. But you also have to listen to me when I tell you something. Now, does that sound fair?"

"I guess so," Jade mumbled.

"We'll work on it together. Put your shoes on. We're going to the supermarket to buy some food. What do you like best for breakfast?"

"Honey Bunches of Oats," Jade said clearly.

"Okay." Deanna nodded. She hadn't heard of any such thing, but she would certainly try to get some.

"What do you eat for breakfast?" Jade asked.

Deanna, who usually ate nothing, knew it would be a mistake to say so. She wanted to establish some kind of healthy routine. "Oh, sometimes a piece of toast and coffee."

"Mommy says breakfast is the most important meal of the day, 'cause you never know when you're going to eat again."

Deanna was touched by Jade's guileless comment. She had a vision of Stacy living in near poverty, struggling to support herself and her daughter. "Your mother was absolutely right."

"You can have some of my cereal if you like. I don't mind."

Deanna smiled warmly at the earnest expression on Jade's face. "That's very kind of you. I think your mother would be very proud of you."

"Do you think she knows where I am? What if she tries to find me and can't? Can we leave a night-light on for her in my room?"

Deanna pushed the product label on Jade's T-shirt back inside the garment. She wished life could be so simple. Just leave a light on and you could find your way in the dark and always be safe. She didn't know how to explain to a six-year-old child that it wasn't a question of her mother's being lost, but of her having gone to an entirely new place.

"I think that's a very good idea," she responded.

* * *

Deanna rushed herself and Jade into the foyer of the funeral parlor, collapsing her umbrella and shaking off the excess rain before closing the door.

"What is this place?" Jade asked, looking around the dimly lit entrance.

"Don't you remember we talked this morning about the special service for your mother?"

"When we say a prayer for her."

"That's right," Deanna confirmed.

Nevertheless, she was still cautious and watchful, not sure how much Jade really understood about the ritual.

The funeral home was small and simple. There was a display panel that referred to Stacy Lowell's ceremony as a "Coming Home" service. A reference, Deanna knew, not to the sad ending of death and decay but to the joyous journey home to God. It was a charming, feel-good point of view, she thought, but it didn't change the grim reality. She was glad that she'd not been to many of these services herself. She could count her experiences on one hand: a classmate in college during her junior year had died of an embolism, a coworker at one of her first professional jobs had had breast cancer, and her own father had dropped dead ten years earlier of a massive heart attack. Deanna found it interesting that death could bring people who were total strangers together like nothing else could.

She led Jade to a room in which a canned organ interlude could be heard. Next to the door was a podium with a guest book on it, and Deanna stopped to sign it. She saw only half a dozen names there, among them Bettina Butler and Patterson Temple. She glanced down at the little girl.

"Do you know how to write your name?" Jade

nodded. "Then you should sign the guest book so everyone will know you were here today."

"Okay," Jade said.

She took the pen that Deanna handed her and stood on her tiptoes, stretching toward the open book.

"I can't reach it."

"Here, let me help you," Deanna offered.

Bending her knee and bracing it against the front of the podium, she lifted Jade and held her steady so she could carefully write her name. Then she sat Jade back on her own feet. Also on the podium was a box containing laminated cards that had a picture of clouds with the sun shining through them on one side and on the other a prayer dedicated to Stacy's passing, her name, and the date. Deanna took a card and put it carefully in her purse. One day she would give it to Jade.

They entered the small viewing chapel. Near an altar to the left was an open wooden casket with flowers displayed around it. Recalling her own response at the morgue just ten days ago, Deanna faltered. She didn't know if it was wise to let Jade see her mother's body.

Deanna turned to stop Jade, but the little girl ran into the chapel—not toward the coffin as Deanna had feared but toward an elderly woman seated alone, whose face lit up with a smile when she spotted the little girl. She opened her arms and Jade rushed right into them, to be enveloped in a warm hug.

"Betts!" Jade squealed.

"Oh, bless your heart. Hello, darlin'. How's my sweet girl? It's so good to see you."

Deanna approached slowly.

"I'm going to a funeral for my mommy," she heard Jade saying in a tone of surprising acceptance.

"I know, darlin'," Betts crooned, petting the child and kissing her cheeks, straightening the fastener that held a thick lock of hair off her forehead. "Now, who brought you here today?"

Jade, half leaning and half sitting on Betts's lap, pointed a finger at Deanna. "She did. She's taking care of me at her house."

Bettina Butler tilted her head to peer at Deanna through her glasses. Deanna smiled, waiting out the inspection. She judged the small brown-skinned gray-haired woman to be in her seventies.

"Hi. I'm Deanna Lindsay, Jade's guardian."

Betts nodded and returned Deanna's smile, all the while studying her. "I'm Bettina Butler."

Jade shook her head. "No, you're Betts."

Bettina laughed lightly, bouncing Jade on her knee. "That's right, I'm Betts. Nice to meet you, Deanna. Pat told me about you."

"Really?" Deanna was tempted to ask what he'd said.

"I recall Stacy mentioned you to me some time back. She hadn't seen you for a while before she died."

"That's right. I'm sorry we never got to see each other again."

"Ain't that the truth," Betts agreed. "But I trust the good Lord knows what he's doing."

"There aren't many people here, are there?" Deanna counted less than a dozen people, including herself, Betts, and Jade.

"No, there sure ain't. But don't you worry. Folks who care will come. Except for *him*," she said, indicating with a nod of her head a grizzled-looking man who was sitting in the rear. "Just wanted to get out of the rain, I bet."

"Who's that?" Jade asked, pointing to an older woman who sat reading a newspaper near the door.

"I don't know, darlin'. Mr. Hawthorne, the funeral director, says she comes to everybody's services, even if she don't know them," Betts said in a low voice.

"Where's Patterson?" Jade asked.

Yes, where is he? Deanna added silently, keeping her own curiosity under wraps. Ever since getting Jade and herself ready to come to the service, she'd been thinking about seeing him again. She'd already begun to brace herself for the contention that existed between them.

"Right here, Jade."

Deanna turned abruptly at his voice. He approached from the front hall, dressed in dark slacks and a coordinated dark shirt with its mandarin collar buttoned to his throat, but without a tie. A sports jacket made him seem more formally dressed than he really was.

"Patterson!" Jade said with excitement, scrambling off Betts's lap and racing to meet him.

"Lord, you'd think Santa Claus had just arrived." Betts chuckled as Patterson bent to scoop Jade into his arms.

Deanna noted with some surprise that there was an easy bond between them. Jade seemed even smaller, held against his chest. He looked not only relaxed but different from the man she'd met twice and who hadn't left her with a particularly favorable impression. He and Jade were having a quiet little conversation; he seemed to hang on her every word.

"You met my grandson last week, isn't that right?" Betts asked Deanna.

For a second Deanna was tempted to say no, that

the man she'd met and this one showing such gentleness and affection toward Jade were not the same. As he came to a stop next to her and met her gaze, his eyes seemed to hold hers with equal caution. But there was no point in letting Bettina Bulter know what she thought of her grandson.

"Ms. Lindsay," Patterson murmured in greeting.

"You can call her Deanna, like I do," Jade said with authority.

"Yes, please," Deanna confirmed.

Patterson accepted her permission with a nod.

He was prepared to remain annoyed with Deanna Lindsay, but seeing her again made him reconsider. He had to admit his reasons for disliking her were pretty shallow. While Betts had been upset to have Jade removed from her care, even he knew it was better for the little girl to be with a younger guardian. What had bothered him was that Deanna had been so smug about it. He just hoped, for Jade's sake, that she knew what she was doing.

Patterson had been with the funeral director in the office, going over final plans and directions for driving to the cemetery. Although he hadn't seen Deanna and Jade arrive, he had clearly recognized their voices. His attention had been drawn to their brief exchange before they'd come into the chapel, and he couldn't help but admire the patience and responsiveness he'd heard as Deanna had spoken with Jade.

Still, he scanned her face, looking for any signs of a high-and-mighty attitude. What he detected was more uncertainty than aloofness. She was dressed less formally than when he'd seen her before. That made a difference, he decided. Black slacks and a turtleneck sweater, a yellow-gold blazer under a black leather jacket that brushed her thighs.

"There's my mommy," Jade suddenly cried, squirming to be let down.

Patterson set her on her feet and looked at Deanna. "Has she been up to the front yet?"

"No, I wasn't sure what to . . . you know . . . whether Jade should . . ."

"Let her see her mama," Betts said. "Let her say good-bye."

Deanna still questioned the wisdom of having a small child look on her mother in death, but she acquiesced.

"Come on, Jade." Deanna held out her hand. "Let's go up together." After a moment's hesitation, Jade slipped her smaller hand into Deanna's.

They approached the open casket together. Only when they stopped before it did Deanna realize that Patterson had joined them. Jade stepped onto the velvet prayer bench and stared into the casket for a long moment. Deanna glanced over her shoulder at Patterson, who was waiting solemnly.

"She's wearing a dress," Jade said.

"Betts picked it out," Patterson told her.

Jade cautiously stroked her mother's cheek. "She looks like she's sleeping," Jade whispered.

"Yes, she does. Would you like to say a prayer for her?" Deanna asked. Jade nodded. "Do you know the Lord's Prayer?" Again Jade nodded. "Good. Let's say it together."

Deanna felt awkward as she and Jade began reciting the prayer, and she was surprised when Patterson joined in, his deep voice soothing. When they finished, the organ music paused before starting again with a hymn that indicated the service was about to begin. Patterson turned to retrace his steps and take a seat. Jade went with him. But Deanna continued to stare into the casket at Stacy, knowing this would be her last opportunity to express what she had been feeling ever since she'd received that phone call from Dr. Gavin. This was her last time to reflect on their brief friendship and what it had meant to both of them.

"I never forgot you, Stacy," she said in a very low voice. "I always wondered if you'd gone back to your family after all. I never knew about your baby. Jade is . . . she's beautiful." The organ music grew louder. Someone coughed behind her. She leaned forward slightly and whispered. "I'll take care of her. I feel like I've failed you somehow, but I promise I won't fail Jade. Good-bye. Safe journey . . ."

Deanna was caught off guard when she realized she was on the verge of tears. The traffic accident aside, she felt deeply that she should have done more for Stacy. Maybe she couldn't ever make up for what they'd both been through, but she knew a second chance when she saw one.

Marcus Lowell stood at the chapel entrance until the music started, and the minister began walking up the aisle to the open coffin. Everybody was waiting for that woman to sit down. *She must be crazy,* he thought, *standing up there talking to a dead woman.* He'd come first thing that morning to check Stacy out. She was dead, all right. Too bad. He liked her better than any of his other bitches, even though she was white.

When his man HoJo told him Stacy had clocked out, he thought, *For fucking real*? He wasn't sure he believed it. It would be just like her to try and get over on him. Like he was too stupid to see through her petty ante shit to get away. He'd always been able to find her before. Or she would just come back on her own. It wasn't like she was gonna run home, especially after what she said her stepfather did to her.

Man, I'd have cut his fucking dick off, he thought in derision. He'd even said he'd do it for her. But she never would tell where she was from anyhow.

The crazy woman finally sat down, and Marcus looked around again, but he couldn't see the kid. She had to be here, 'cause that old bitch that used to watch her was here. She was always giving him lip about how come he couldn't do right for his own child. What the fuck did she know? He gave money to Stacy when he had it. He coulda just as easily put her ass out on the street, back where he'd found her at Port Authority, especially after she went ahead and had the kid. Everybody was on his case 'cause she come out looking so damned white.

Besides, he had to make money. And he had to stay out of sight of the cops, 'cause they was always jacking him up. He wasn't gonna forget that his bitch had turned him in to the cops, either. Given him up. Good thing she went and got herself killed. *Else he'd a had to put a serious hurtin' on her ass.* Three fucking years . . . man, he should of been out way before now. It was all Stacy's fault.

"Hey, Marcus, come on, man. It's rainin'." A stocky black man stood outside in the funeral home's deserted entryway, whispering through the partially opened door. "Let's get the fuck outta here. You seen your lady's dead. I hate funeral homes."

Marcus mouthed impatiently to his bud, HoJo, "Shut the fuck up. I told you I gotta take care of something."

"Calvin ain't gonna wait if we get to that store

late. We can knock it off just when they close, 'cause no one'll be inside. Come on. You the one said you needed money."

"Wait outside. I ain't finished yet." Marcus ignored his friend, knowing that HoJo would do what he was told. He stepped into the chapel and took a seat in the back, way to the left. There weren't all that many people anyway.

The minister started the service. Nobody here knew him except for the old lady and the tall dude. Her grandson or something like that. Marcus looked at his watch, a nice one he'd lifted from some old guy, and wondered how long this bull was going to take. He wanted to get to the kid. She might be worth something.

Deanna thought the brief service very moving. The minister emphasized that Stacy had finished her journey and completed the work God intended for her here on earth. Betts had been right about more people showing up. Mostly Stacy's neighbors, a few friends from the video store where she'd worked. No one else.

When the service was over, Deanna watched the few mourners file past the casket once more. One man remained seated alone in the back, his head lowered, and Deanna wondered if, like the dozing neighborhood drunk, he'd only wanted to come in out of the rain.

She wasn't sure what was supposed to happen next. She stood to one side, watching as Patterson spoke quietly to the funeral director. She was impressed with his calm authority, covertly watching him as he greeted some of Stacy's neighbors, answered questions, dealt with the minister. He was unobtrusive, letting Betts accept people's expressions of sorrow. They clucked and crooned over Jade, who, unsure what the sadness was about, remained silent, staying close to Betts, as if Betts and Patterson were her real family.

Deanna felt useless and left out.

Patterson began to walk toward the entryway. Deanna got up to follow. "Patterson, wait a minute . . ."

He turned to her, appearing distracted.

"I can see you have a lot to do, but . . . I was just wondering what will happen now. Should I stay with Jade, or leave before the casket is put in the hearse?"

Patterson relaxed. "I guess I didn't tell you the plans."

"No, you didn't," she said, without any note of accusation.

"Jade is the only real family Stacy has here, so I told the director not to bother with a limousine. I'll follow the hearse to the cemetery with Betts, Jade, and you, if you want to come. You don't have to. I can make sure Jade gets back to you later."

Deanna felt hurt, as if she wasn't really wanted. As if he didn't care one way or the other whether she came along. Then she wondered why she'd let him get to her. "I think it's best if I stay with Jade. I'll come. If you don't mind," she forced herself to add.

Patterson watched her thoughtfully. She didn't appear to be spoiling for an argument, or trying to be condescending. He realized that he still had a tendency to be on guard around her.

"We're leaving soon," he said, then walked away.

Deanna sighed and turned back to what remained of the gathering. Betts was talking to the minister, who had removed his robes and was gathering his prayer books, ready to leave for the cemetery. The casket had been closed and the flowers removed through a barely noticeable door to the immediate left. But Deanna didn't see Jade.

Worried, she finally spotted her with the man who'd been sitting alone in the back of the chapel. He was hunched down, holding her by her shoulders as he talked. Jade seemed reluctant to be near him. Deanna had thought he was a stranger, all alone in the back, but he might have known Stacy. As she came closer, he stood, taking Jade by the hand.

"Excuse me," Deanna called, hurrying toward them. The man appeared not to have heard, but Jade glanced over her shoulder, her eyes wide with confusion.

"Wait a minute," Deanna said, only a few paces from them now. "Who are you? Where do you think you're going with her?"

He stopped. "This ain't none of your business. Jade's coming with me."

"No, she isn't," Deanna said, maneuvering herself so he couldn't walk out. "Who are you?"

"He says he's my daddy," Jade told Deanna quietly, glancing at him warily.

Deanna's mouth dropped open.

He was a black man, several years younger than herself, and only a few inches taller. He was thin and wiry, dressed in designer street clothes, but not the oversized, baggy style of hip-hop. He was good-looking, and even a casual glance showed some resemblance between him and his daughter.

Deanna came out of her stupor when she heard Betts's voice. Despite her age, the older woman hurried to reach them.

"Marcus, you have no business here. What you want with that child? Jade, come on here to Betts."

"She's my kid," Marcus announced in a cocky manner, holding firmly to Jade. "I just want to talk to her."

"You ain't never paid your daughter no mind, and you never treated Stacy right. So forgive me if I don't believe you."

"You can't stop me if I want to take her."

"Well, I can," Deanna spoke up firmly.

Marcus gave her a scathing glance. "Who the fuck are you?"

"That's Deanna," Jade answered helpfully.

Deanna faced Marcus squarely, not intimidated by his punk attitude or his foul mouth. "I'm Jade's guardian. She's living with me and I'm responsible for her. I was a friend of Stacy's."

"Bullshit."

"Lord have mercy," Betts lamented at Marcus's disregard of the occasion, the place, and good manners.

"Only reason why you got her is 'cause the city is paying you. Jade belongs to me. That money is mine."

"I'm not getting paid," Deanna said hotly.

"Don't bother trying to explain," Patterson said, appearing in the chapel door behind Deanna.

She felt relieved that he'd finally returned. Immediately she saw a change in Marcus, who released Jade. Deanna pulled the child close to her.

"Pat, he tried to walk out the door with Jade," Betts informed her grandson.

Patterson touched Deanna's shoulder, gently shifting her to the side so he could face Marcus. Marcus never moved. It was clear that he wasn't afraid of Patterson, but he was also no physical match for him.

"Get out."

Marcus snickered. "I ain't going nowhere 'til I'm ready. You can't do a damn thing to me, either."

Deanna urged Jade to go to Betts, who eased her away from Marcus and his public display of bad behavior.

"I don't plan to." Patterson stayed calm. "But let me tell you this. Jade isn't going with you. You're going to stay away from her. And if I *ever* catch you anywhere around her again, I won't bother asking you to leave."

Deanna held her breath. The minister, hearing the raised voices, came toward them holding his hands out in a calming manner. Deanna knew the minister's heart was in the right place, wanting peace and conciliation, but she was well aware that it wasn't going to happen between Marcus and Patterson.

Marcus looked at the minister and shrugged, clearly realizing he was outnumbered. He jabbed a finger in the air at Patterson and moved to leave. "This ain't even none of your business. Just remember. I can see Jade any time I want."

He pushed his way out the door, leaving them all silenced.

Patterson looked to find Betts hugging and whispering to Jade, distracting her with a piece of mint candy from her purse. He glanced at Deanna and found her a little angry, but steady. He nodded his approval of how she'd handled herself.

"Do you think he means it?" Deanna asked.

"I doubt it. Jade isn't any use to him."

But he wouldn't put it past Marcus to figure something out.

Chapter Six

Patterson listened to the chatter and boisterous laughter of his five-man engine team as they removed their bunker gear, consisting of heavy fire-resistant overalls and boots, and changed into civvies. They were returning from the weekly scheduled practice drill conducted with other truck and engine companies. Some of his men hadn't taken the drill seriously enough, either during the actual practice or now that it was over and they'd been warned of what could happen in a real emergency.

"The guys from Ladder seventeen are pussies, man. Do you see how they punked out on that last exercise?" Eddie chortled.

"Yeah, but they got on your ass fast enough after you dropped the line. *Nobody* drops the line, Eddie. 'Cept rookies." C.B. pointed an accusing finger.

"I didn't drop it. I told you, my man Danny pulled the sucker out of my hand."

"Man, if you can't hold on to something that's bigger than your dick, you're in trouble," Billy piped up.

Still joking, the men shuffled into the equipment room, stowing their coats and helmets on the proper shelf with the inset shields on the front that indicated their individual rank within the company facing out. Eddie, on the losing end of the debate, looked around for someone to support his claim that the fumble was not entirely his fault.

"Hey, Captain. You saw the whole thing, right? Did I blow the routine? We didn't lose any points, did we?"

Patterson sat on the end of a bench, bent over as he unlatched the last fasteners on his massive boots. He sat up and used the toe of one boot to lever against the heel of the other until he pulled his foot free, then glanced briefly at the young man who stood next to him.

"Let's just say it's a good thing it wasn't for real. You're not supposed to fumble the line. At least you get to do it over without anybody getting hurt or property destroyed," Patterson said, standing up and moving his boots to their storage place.

There was cackling from several of the other guys and one pointed at Eddie in triumph, having proved his point.

"Won't happen when it's real, Captain," Eddie said, accepting the judgment against him as he moved to his locker. "At least I made up the points and we still came out ahead. We still kicked ass!"

With the exuberance of invincible young jocks, the rest of the men agreed on that part of it.

Patterson glanced over his shoulder at the men as they teased and dogged each other to decompress, no one wanting to admit that there was pressure to get it right. He pulled out a pair of street boots and closed his locker door.

"Hey, listen up," he called. "How many times do I have to tell you, this isn't a contest of us against the other companies?"

No one was listening. They were all too high on

their perceived victory. He shook his head in resignation.

"Hey, Pat . . . there's some kid out here looking for you," Gary, the house watch attendant, shouted from the door.

"Who is it?"

"Didn't say. Just wanted to know if this was your company and if you were here. I told him yeah, that we just got back in and you might not be able to see him. Thought I'd check."

Patterson moved to a board where the assignment sheets were posted. "Did he say what he wanted? I go off in an hour."

"I'll check," Gary said, disappearing.

Patterson marked the time of return to the station house, then reminded his men that there was some housekeeping to take care of in the apparatus room. Still ragging each other, the men split up to do their chores.

Gary returned, calling out, "Forget it, Pat . . ."

"Forget what?" Patterson had reached the door of his office. The telephone was ringing.

"About that kid. He's gone."

"Thanks." Patterson leaned over his desk to pick up the phone. "Temple, Engine Forty-seven,"

"Hi . . . this is Deanna."

It took a fast second for the name to register. Recognition was followed by surprise, and finally by a combination of wariness and tension. It had been exactly a week since he'd seen Deanna at Stacy's funeral, although, to his annoyance, she had crossed his mind once or twice in between. He didn't particularly want to be around her. For some unknown reason, she seemed to catch him at his worst. Like last week after the funeral, when they were all headed for the cemetery.

He'd felt the need to keep his distance. He was afraid he'd do or say something that would give her reason to ridicule him. She was too classy for his taste. So he'd been standoffish during the drive and at the grave site and even afterward, when she had reluctantly accepted his offer to drop her and Jade in Manhattan. He'd been distant and cool toward her. And he couldn't seem to help it.

"Deanna Lindsay," he repeated. He perched on the edge of his desk. "Giving up?"

"I know you expect me to fall flat on my face, but I'm not going to. I certainly wouldn't call you if I'd changed my mind," she said breezily.

He couldn't help grinning. "So you survived the first week and you're calling to brag about it, right?"

"I don't think anything I do or say could impress you. Why would I bother?"

Patterson had to allow that she wasn't far off the mark. "Okay then, to what do I owe this honor?" he said dryly.

Deanna sighed. "I wish there was someone else I could call rather than bother you. I know you're busy. And you've done more than anyone could expect for Jade, but . . . it's Saturday and the Administration for Children's Services is closed."

"What do you want with ACS?"

"I need to find out how I can get into Stacy's apartment. Jade needs her things. Clothes mostly, but she might have books or toys . . ."

Patterson would bet that none of the bureaucrats had thought about that ten days ago while they were running around trying to figure out what to do with Jade.

"ACS can't help you with that."

"They can't?" Deanna asked in surprise. "Then what should I do? Is there someone else I could call? Maybe Marilyn Phillips, Jade's caseworker?"

"This isn't her territory, either."

"Oh, great," Deanna muttered in exasperation.

Patterson slid off the edge of his desk. He realized that Deanna had a legitimate concern. "If you want to get into the apartment I can probably help you," he said, deciding to make up for his bad behavior of the previous weekend. The fact that Betts had picked up on his off mood had bothered him. If there was one person on God's earth he never wanted to disappoint, it was his grandmother.

"I wouldn't want to put you out."

He could hear the hesitation in her voice. "You won't. I know the super of the building. He liked Stacy and Jade. He'll want to help."

"You mean, I don't need special permission from anyone, or some official paper from the city?"

"None of that," he said smoothly.

"Fine. When can I do this?"

He looked at his watch. "I get off duty in about forty-five minutes. Can you get here by then? I was headed home to Brooklyn so I'll take you. Stacy didn't live far from Betts."

"That's perfect. I'll have to bring Jade with me."

"That's fine."

"Do you think that's a good idea?"

"What do you mean?"

"Well . . . it's where she used to live with her mother. It was her home. I just wonder if, you know, she's going to get upset and start crying again, or want to stay there."

He hadn't thought of that. "Just come to the firehouse. It's on West Eighty-third Street. We'll work it out when you get here."

He got off the phone and took a moment to sit and think. He hadn't expected Deanna to phone. He'd been wondering how he was going to check on Jade without having to call *her*. Not for his sake, but for Betts's.

Even now, after he'd already offered to help, he wasn't so sure it was a good idea.

It had annoyed him to find out that Deanna lived in Lincoln Square, right opposite the Metropolitan Opera House. Rich folks lived around there. Mostly rich *white* folks, the kind who had another house somewhere else. The kind who ate out a lot, had season tickets to this or that, and gave to charities that did for the poor black kids of New York City. They were the kind of people who wanted you to know they were do-right folks. 'Course, they put their name on everything so you wouldn't forget. That's who Deanna Lindsay reminded him of. Only younger. Only black. *Almost* black.

He remembered how on the ride back to Brooklyn after the funeral Betts had gone on about how pretty Deanna was, and how nice she talked, like she spoke a foreign language fluently. No slang. No black English. When he got right down to it, he and Deanna weren't even on the same page.

Restless, Patterson left his office and busied himself with making sure his crew had finished their work as scheduled. An hour later he clocked out.

He was marking time with a few of the men standing outside the station house when he saw a cab double-park across the street. As Deanna emerged, he saw that she was dressed down again. Her hair was loose around her face, not stiff with sprays or streaked with color.

She glanced his way and seemed to identify him among the others, although she didn't acknowledge him by either word or gesture.

As the cab pulled away, he spotted Jade. The moment she saw him, she pulled her hand away from Deanna's and broke into a run.

"Patterson!" Jade squealed.

"Jade, wait a minute! Be careful," Deanna called, throwing a frightened glance up the one-way street to check for oncoming traffic.

Patterson moved halfway into the street and stooped to take the little girl's impact as she barreled into him. He lifted her off the ground briefly with a hug and placed her on the curb. "Hey, little girl. How've you been?"

"Fine." Jade tugged at his arm. "We're going to my house to get my things."

"I know," Patterson confirmed, glancing at Deanna and wondering what she'd told Jade about the outing.

"Patterson is going to drive us out to Brooklyn," Deanna told her. "I appreciate it," she said to him.

He turned away. "My car is over here."

He pointed to the Jeep Cherokee parked down the block, an official NYFD parking permit in the windshield. He unlocked the passenger side so that Deanna could get in, and he put Jade in the backseat behind her with the seat belt secured.

"I'll be right back. I'm just going to tell the next shift officer that I'm leaving."

From her vantage point Deanna could watch his movements and what was going on just inside the firehouse entrance. He was clearly giving instructions to several men and spoke a while with one in particular. She'd never given much thought to civil-servant jobs, always thinking of them as suitable for people who didn't have the skills or education to do anything else. On the other hand, she really didn't know much about what Patterson did. The other men were white, except for one who appeared to be Hispanic. Patterson was the only black person there . . . and he seemed to be in charge.

Each time she was in his company, Deanna was unsure what to expect. The blunt and annoying stranger who'd been so aloof after the funeral, or the thoughtful man who cared so much for Jade. Not all that long ago she would have dismissed him without a second thought. A fireman? Please. But now it wasn't easy to get Patterson Temple out of her mind. Watching him as he returned to his car wearing civilian clothes, the leather coat she'd first seen him in, dark glasses, and a black NYFD baseball cap, Deanna was having second thoughts.

During the drive to Brooklyn he turned on the car radio—not to black R and B or rap but to jazz. Conversation consisted mostly of Jade's incessant questions and Patterson's quick replies. He was incredible with Jade. He only spoke to Deanna when she asked a specific question.

"Patterson has one of those," Jade observed at one point.

"One of what?" Deanna asked.

"Like on the radio. He's a magician. He has a guitar."

"Musician," he corrected.

Deanna looked at him inquiringly, but he didn't elaborate.

"I'm going to get one and Patterson's going to

teach me to play it. Maybe I'm going to play in his band, too."

"You have a band?" Deanna asked, interested.

He looked at her quickly, then turned back to the road. "Just a bunch of guys I know. We get together and practice."

"You play guitar?" she persisted.

"I taught myself to play when I was sixteen. Does that count?"

"I wasn't suggesting anything," Deanna defended herself calmly. She let a few moments of silence pass between them. "Where do you live?" she asked instead, as they came off the Brooklyn Bridge and onto Flatbush Avenue.

"North end of Park Slope, near Park Place."

"Really? That's a nice neighborhood."

"You didn't think I'd live in a nice neighborhood?"

"I didn't say that. I only meant that I know Park Slope is very upscale. It's . . ." She stopped. He was right. She was judging him.

"Up near Lincoln Center, now that's an expensive neighborhood. What should I think about that?"

She chortled. "That I'm lucky I can afford it."

"See, for me luck had nothing to do with it. I made a smart decision. I bought a run-down brownstone that took four years of my life to make livable. I have the first floor and the ground floor. I lease out the top two. Pays for my mortgage."

She needed a moment to process the information. "You . . . own the whole house?"

"It's a waste of money to rent. You don't build up any equity that way."

Deanna felt like shaking her head to clear it. In just three sentences he'd managed to shift the paradigm into which she'd so nicely fit him. He had intentionally put her in her place. Reluctantly, she admitted to herself that she deserved it.

"Jade, who's your best friend?" Patterson asked now.

"Hmmm . . . Michelle. She lives in my building on the fifth floor, and she has roller blades. My mommy won't get me them 'cause she says I'll hurt myself."

Deanna listened as Jade referred to Stacy in the present tense. She had to accept that it was going to take a little time for Jade to understand that her mother was permanently gone. At only six it was a big concept to grasp.

"How would you like to visit Michelle while me and Deanna get your stuff from the old apartment?" Patterson asked.

"I want to come with you," Jade complained.

Deanna half turned in her seat. "Honey, we're only going to be gone for a short time. It's not going to be much fun. The apartment is going to be very dark and . . . and we're not even sure we can get in."

Jade pouted.

"Tell you what," Patterson said. "After Deanna and I finish, I'll take you to Chuck E. Cheese."

"Okay. Can you find my rabbit? His name is Oliver."

"You have a rabbit?" Deanna asked.

"It's not a *real* rabbit. Just a stuffed one. And I want my yellow boots . . ."

They were soon rounding the traffic circle at Grand Army Plaza and getting on Eastern Parkway and to the Crown Heights section where Stacy had lived. Patterson parked the jeep, and they headed for a building near the corner of St. John's Place.

It was perhaps fifty or sixty years old, constructed of red brick and without a front stoop. Once in the entry Patterson had Jade ring the bell of her friend Michelle's apartment.

"How do you know anyone will be home?" Deanna asked.

"People with no money hang around their neighborhoods on the weekends."

Sure enough, someone answered the lobby bell and Patterson explained through the intercom who he was and what he wanted. Without hesitation, the woman he spoke to said she would be happy to watch Jade. Michelle had been asking for her, in fact. She buzzed them into the building, but Patterson had a key in hand nevertheless.

"How come you have a key?" Deanna asked.

He led the way to the elevator. "I told you. I know the super."

Deanna wasn't sure that explained very much, but she let it go.

They took the elevator to the fifth floor, left Jade visiting her friend, and descended to the third. When they got off, Patterson turned right at the end of the hallway. There was some sort of official notice glued to the door. Before Deanna had a chance to read it, Patterson produced another key and began unlocking the door.

"Wait a minute," Deanna said, touching his arm to point out the sign. "I don't think we're supposed to go in. This sign says—"

"I know what it says," Patterson responded, opening the door, "but I have the key, the door is open, and we can go in. Do you want to or not?"

Deanna didn't like it that he was leaving it up to her. "I need to find Jade's things, but I really feel like . . . this is illegal or something."

"That's one way of looking at it," Patterson said,

his impatience showing. "You need to get into the apartment. I got you into the apartment. We can leave if you want. But then you'll have to go to court to get in the *legal* way. What do you want to do?"

She scowled at him. "I didn't expect you to break the law to help me out."

"You don't understand how things work in the city. You call half a dozen agencies and ask can you get into the apartment. They're going to ask who you are. Why do you have to get into somebody's home? We're talking maybe five, six weeks before you get an answer. Then they tell you no. With no reason. Make up your mind. What do you want to do?"

She hesitated, frankly nervous that they might get caught. She licked her lips, then reluctantly nodded. "Okay, let's do it. It's not like I'm going to steal anything."

Patterson's mouth twisted in amusement. "No . . . but this *is* breaking and entering."

Having said that, he walked through the open door.

It was a mostly tidy three-room apartment with functional but not stylish furnishings. Almost no natural light came in through the windows, so Patterson turned on a ceiling light. Children's things were scattered everywhere. Despite the worthiness of her mission, Deanna had a terrible feeling about invading someone's personal territory, even though that someone was dead. She stood there, indecisive, afraid to touch or disturb anything.

"Do you know what you want to get?" Patterson asked.

"Jade's clothes. She needs things for school. Maybe some of her toys and things she likes. Oliver," she remembered.

He nodded with a wry grin. "We better not leave without him."

They walked through the apartment, deciding what to take, noting evidence that someone else had been there since Stacy's death.

"The police," he suggested. "They would be looking for anything they could use to help find Stacy's family."

"What about Marcus? Do you think he was here too?"

"Probably. If Stacy had anything of real value, it's gone."

Deanna began the uncomfortable task of looking through the closets and dresser drawers while Patterson searched for something to put everything in. He found a canvas duffel bag in the closet and a leather tote hanging from a doorknob.

In the bedroom Deanna located the yellow boots Jade had mentioned. She also found sneakers but no real shoes. She grabbed another jacket and several accessories.

Patterson stuck his head in the door as she stood contemplating a small pile of costume jewelry that had been emptied from a box onto the top of the chest of drawers.

"I found Oliver," he said.

"Oh, good," Deanna said in relief. She went back to staring at the items.

"Look, you better take whatever you feel Jade should have from here," Patterson said, watching her expression. "Go through everything. You won't get a second chance."

"But what if—"

"We'll worry about that if it happens," Patterson

said, forestalling her worry about the right or wrong of what they were doing.

Yet he admired Deanna's scruples. He knew too many people who, under the circumstances, wouldn't have given a second thought to helping themselves.

In the end Deanna took very little belonging to Jade. The clothes were cheap and poorly made, bought for fashion rather than durability. She packed a few toys and books. And she took the jewelry box, Jade's only legacy from her mother.

Patterson had far fewer qualms than Deanna and searched for things like bank books, money, legal documents. He found nothing.

In less than an hour they were done. They put everything into his car.

"Thank you," Deanna said.

Patterson closed the hatch. "No problem. But if I were you, I wouldn't mention how you got those things, understand?" She nodded. "You had no choice."

"Yes, I did. But like you said, it would have taken too long."

Patterson crossed his arms over his chest. "Frankly, I didn't think you had the guts to take Jade on. I guess I owe you an apology."

"Yes, you do," Deanna said tartly. "And if you're making one now, I'll take it."

Unexpectedly, Patterson broke into a loud laugh. Deanna caught herself staring. He had perfect teeth, and a beautiful smile. An all-out laugh that came from his stomach. He grinned and shook his head.

"Hold on a minute. I don't take back *everything* I said."

"No?"

"No," he responded emphatically.

"I didn't think so," Deanna answered, arching a brow. "Neither do I."

He stroked the hair on his chin. "Fair enough. He had an odd speculation in his gaze, as if he were sizing her up again. "How did it go last week?"

"Okay. I enrolled Jade at school and met with Marilyn Phillips. She gave me some documents to ensure that I have temporary legal guardianship."

"So it's official? Are you sorry you took her?"

"I refuse to answer on the grounds that—"

"No, I'm serious."

She spoke as seriously as he had. "There are moments when I wonder. She wakes up in the middle of the night crying. I don't know what to say to make it better. She can be stubborn, and sometimes she won't listen to what I tell her. She still misses her mother, and I feel so helpless," she continued as they headed back into the building to pick up Jade.

He nodded in understanding. "She cried when Betts had to tell her about the accident. Don't take it personally."

"How did Jade come to be with your grandmother?"

"Betts was baby-sitting the day Stacy got killed. Stacy just showed up, asked if she could leave Jade for a few hours. Said she had something real important to take care of in Manhattan. I think it had something to do with Marcus getting out of jail sooner than she'd counted on. When we heard that Stacy was dead, Betts just kept Jade until we knew what was going on."

"And your grandmother didn't mind?"

Patterson looked squarely at her. "Why would she? Betts liked Stacy. She's crazy about Jade. Treats her like she's her own great-grandchild." He added in a sudden reflective note. "Betts believes in helping folks who need it."

Unlike you, Deanna could almost hear him thinking.

"Is that why you became a fireman? Because she taught you about reaching out to people?"

Patterson looked mildly amused. "I'm a fireman because it's a good job. It pays well and has great benefits."

Deanna sighed. He seemed smart and intelligent. She couldn't imagine why he'd settled for being a fireman. He didn't come across as some guy without ambition or talent, nor did he exhibit the swagger that some black men assumed—as if they were poised for a fight, with smart-mouth answers to everything. The kind of black man who always had something nasty to say about any woman who wouldn't give him the time of day.

Patterson Temple didn't fit that mold.

They'd reached the fifth-floor apartment, and Jade rejoined them.

"We found Oliver!" Deanna announced.

"You did?" Jade's eyes glowed with excitement. "Well, where is he?"

"In my car," Patterson answered.

Her face brightened even more. "Are we going to Betts's house now?"

Patterson addressed Deanna across Jade's head. "Do you want to see her? You can stay for dinner. Betts won't mind."

"Please." Jade danced up and down, making her curly hair bounce.

Deanna pressed gently on Jade's shoulder. "We can't go today, Jade. You and I have to unpack all your things, and figure out where to put Oliver."

"I want to see Betts," Jade began to plead.

"No big deal." Patterson tweaked one of her springy curls. "Maybe you can come next week."

Jade's face fell. Deanna crouched to her level. "I think it would be a nice thing to give Betts a present to thank her for taking care of you when she did. What would you like to get her?"

Jade's attention was immediately captured, and she stood thinking about it. "I don't know."

"How about a plant?" Patterson suggested. "She has a garden out back of the house."

"That's a great idea." Deanna shot a grateful nod to him. "Maybe you can help Betts put it in the ground and it will grow and get flowers." She saw the interest in Jade's eyes. "But first you and I will have to go shopping."

"Now?"

Patterson shook his head. "Like Deanna says, you have other things to do."

They left the building. Both knew that it was the last time either of them, or Jade, would be returning there. Deanna glanced up the street.

"Let me see if I can get a cab."

"I'll drive you home," Patterson interrupted.

"No. I appreciate the offer, but you just finished working, and you're almost home. We'll be fine."

"I don't mind . . ."

I know, she thought, bemused, but stood her ground.

"I thought you were going to take us to Chuck E. Cheese," Jade reminded him.

"Jade, I'm sorry, but Deanna's right. It's getting late. So how about I take you some other time?"

"We'll go to McDonald's tonight as a treat when we get home," Deanna added. "How's that?"

Jade approved. Patterson flagged down a gypsy cab and negotiated a flat fee for the ride into Manhattan. He transferred Jade's belongings to the cab's trunk but carefully pulled the brown stuffed rabbit out of the tote and handed it to Jade, who clutched the toy joyfully.

Deanna stood behind the open car door and smiled tentatively at Patterson. "Thanks for your help today. It would have been hard trying to get in without . . . you know . . . what we did," she said.

He merely nodded, continuing to look closely at her. "Call if you need help with anything else."

"Thanks for the offer. I think we'll be okay."

"When do you want me to pick you up next Sunday?"

"For what?"

"For dinner at Betts's with Jade."

"Oh . . ."

"Jade's looking forward to it." To his surprise, he realized he was, too.

"Why don't we talk at the end of the week?"

"Fine." He squatted down in front of Jade. "Gotta go."

She put her arm around Patterson's neck and gave him a big hug. " 'Bye. Oliver says 'bye, too."

He hugged her back and released her with a kiss on her forehead. "Take care and mind Deanna. I'm going to be real mad if I find out you gave her a hard time, you hear?"

"I will." Jade nodded.

Patterson stood watching until the cab disappeared, wondering how it had ever come to this. That he was becoming an accomplice in the care of a six-year-old kid. That he was helping a woman who, under any other circumstance, would probably have nothing to do with him. And vice versa.

Patterson realized that if it wasn't for Jade, he wouldn't stand a snowball's chance in hell of ever meeting someone like Deanna Lindsay. Now that he had, he was also wondering if he could rise to the challenge of separating the real woman from the one he'd expected. Could he stop thinking of her as better than himself? Could he stop seeing himself as less?

Deanna looked at the time and realized that the day was gone. She had yet to pick up her dry cleaning, and she'd missed an appointment with her hair stylist. She paid the cab driver and thanked her doorman, who had come out to help with the two bags of stuff taken from Stacy's apartment.

"That guy is here looking for you," her doorman said, as they followed him into the lobby.

"What guy?" Deanna asked, although Patterson was the first person who came to mind.

"The one that I see you with sometimes."

"Deanna . . ."

She turned at the sound of Richard's voice. He was walking across the lobby toward them. She smiled brightly, realizing that she hadn't seen him in more than two weeks. The last time she'd even spoken to him, he'd just returned from Europe and Jade had already moved in with her. It seemed like such a long time ago, given everything that had happened since then.

"Hi. I'm so surprised to see you," Deanna said when he stopped before her. She self-consciously reviewed her appearance and was annoyed that she hadn't bothered with any makeup and had done nothing with her hair that morning.

Richard was dressed just as casually, in jeans, boots, a black crew sweater, and a leather aviation jacket. He returned her smile and kissed her cheek, then spread his arms.

"What happened?"

"What do you mean?"

"I waited for you on the corner of Sixth Avenue. We were going to the antique mall, remember? We made the arrangement a few weeks back." He cast his glance at Jade, who stood silently appraising him. "Hey," he said to her but gave his attention back to Deanna.

Deanna gasped. "Oh, Richard. I'm sorry, I did forget. You should have called to remind me. I couldn't have made it anyway. I had Jade and there was so much I had to do today . . ."

He watched as the doorman placed the bags by the elevator. "What's all that? Where are you just coming from?"

"We saw Patterson," Jade volunteered. She held up her rabbit. "He found Oliver for me."

Deanna intervened, drawing Richard's puzzled attention. "Richard, this is Jade Lowell. I told you all about what happened to her mother."

"Hello, Jade. I'm Richard. It's nice to meet you." He looked at Deanna. "She's very pretty."

"I'm sorry I forgot about today."

"I was worried. I called and left messages. I figured you were running late or got held up somewhere."

"I had to get out to where Jade used to live with her mother. We're just getting back."

"Why didn't you tell me? I would have been happy to take you."

Deanna had to consider her response. The truth

was, it had never entered her mind to ask Richard. That she had called Patterson first did not escape her.

"I'm still getting used to this," she said, glancing down at Jade, who was distracted by a cocker spaniel being walked by its owner. "Things need to be done that I never thought of, and . . ."

"More responsibility than you thought?" Richard asked astutely.

"Yes," Deanna admitted, then frowned at him. "What did you do when I didn't show up?"

"I went to the show anyway. I had no other plans but to spend the day with you. And the night . . ."

Deanna put her arm around Jade's shoulder. "I think we're going to have to make it another time," she murmured.

He held her gaze. "We haven't spent any time together since the morning after you got that call to come to the city morgue."

"I know. But this . . . new development was completely unexpected, Richard."

"You could have said no."

"I'm glad I didn't."

He nodded and pursed his lips. "So, now what happens?"

"We're going to McDonald's for dinner," Jade said.

Richard chuckled in disbelief, his gaze on Deanna. "McDonald's? You hate fast-food restaurants."

"It's only this once. I'll have a salad or something."

"Patterson was going to take us to Chuck E. Cheese, but then he couldn't," Jade said to Richard.

"Chuck E. Cheese?" he asked blankly.

Deanna laughed at Richard's expression. "Exactly."

"Deanna, I'm hungry," Jade murmured, hugging Oliver.

"I know. We're leaving now."

"And who's Patterson?" Richard asked.

Deanna fumbled for a second, and Jade spoke first. "He's my friend."

"Oh." Richard nodded. "A friend of yours, too?" he asked Deanna.

"No. He was acquainted with Jade's mother and offered to help this afternoon."

"I wish you'd called and told me."

"Richard, I'm sorry. It's just that—"

"Okay, don't worry about it. Things happen. Can I join you for dinner, Jade?"

Jade glanced at Deanna for guidance.

"I think that would be very nice. Richard is a . . . a friend of mine."

"Okay, you can come."

"Thanks. We'll take my car. I'm over here," he said, guiding them back outside and pointing to the parked BMW.

Deanna excused herself for a quick moment to ask the doorman to hold the bags until she returned. By the time she got to Richard's car he'd already settled Jade in the backseat.

"Don't forget the seat belt," she said to him before getting into the passenger seat.

"Sorry about that. I'm not used to watching after kids."

"Patterson's car is bigger than yours," Jade piped up from behind them as Richard pulled into traffic.

At the first traffic light Richard reached out to take Deanna's hand. She grasped his and smiled at him. Now that she was seeing him again, she realized she missed the comfortable routine they'd developed over the past two years. She regretted that it wasn't going to be possible to be with him that night. She was pleased to see that he shared her disappointment.

"I want to hear what it's been like taking care of her," he said. "And I want you to tell me all about this guy Patterson."

"That's her, right?"

"Yeah, that's her," Marcus responded, standing outside of the fast-food restaurant and closely watching the woman who'd mouthed off to him at Stacy's funeral. "Talkin' to some white guy. That's my kid. That's Jade."

"So what are we followin' the bitch for?" HoJo asked impatiently, keeping half an eye peeled for the cops.

"I told you. I just want to check her out. She got in my face and pissed me off. I don't like that shit."

"She's just, like, taking care of her, ain't that what you said?"

"Yeah, but she's gettin' money for doing it, man. That ain't right. That money belongs to me. She's my kid. Stacy was *my* woman."

"What the fuck, Marcus? That money ain't gonna amount to shit. It's chump change. I already told you I know how we can get some serious money. I know this bitch that works at this check-cashing place on Amsterdam. I can get her to help us set it up, man."

Marcus cut HoJo a look of disgust. "I ain't risking the joint again for that. It ain't worth it."

"Come on, man, let's get the fuck out of here."

"Chill," Marcus ordered. "I'm trying to think how to play this."

"Look, if you want her just take her. She's your kid, like you say."

Marcus nodded, motioning HoJo back into the

shadows, watching the white guy, Jade, and the woman get into a swank BMW. He knew she was connected. He knew she already had money.

"I don't want the kid, man. I just want to use her to get all kinds of shit from the city for free. They'll think they're helping me take care of her. Money. A place to live."

"Yeah? *Then* what you gonna do with her?" HoJo asked.

Marcus turned away as the luxury car drove off. "Don't worry about that."

Chapter Seven

Deanna sighed as she read the next E-mail message, by her count the eighteenth. She had twice as many waiting to be opened. After a quick scan of the subject box and first sentence of the text she decided to print out a copy and read it later. Maybe during lunch. Maybe during her subway ride home from work.

She looked at the time and gave up all hope of finishing before the start of the Monday staff meeting in fifteen minutes. Then the phone rang. When Stephen didn't pick up after the second ring, Deanna snatched up the receiver.

"This is Deanna."

"I thought you said you'd call me over the weekend."

"Joy, I'm really busy right now. Can I—"

"No, 'cause you can't be trusted to call like you said you would."

"Well, I'm sorry, but there was a lot going on this past weekend. I've a meeting in a few minutes, and I'm going crazy . . ."

"Just a quick minute."

"Joy . . ."

"How's motherhood?"

"It's . . . been a real adjustment." Deanna sighed

again. She deleted two more E-mail messages. "I'm trying to be patient and understanding because of what Jade's been through . . . and my house is a mess . . ." Deanna heard Joy's sultry chuckle on the line. "What's so funny about that?"

"That isn't mirth you're hearing, girl, it's recognition. People forgot to tell you about the other things that come with having kids. They're a lot of work."

"You don't feel that way about your son, do you? He's a nice boy, and he's going to be a fabulous man."

"I hope so, Dee. I think so, too. But what you see are the results of a lot of agonizing decisions and discipline, worry and love. It's nonstop. You can't let your guard down for a moment. You hope your child turns out all right, but you just never know. I sure wish his father was alive to see him."

"I had the strangest conversation with my mother about having me, Carla, and Tate," Deanna said. "She practically admitted she didn't really want children."

"I can understand that. I think one of the real joys and fears of having kids is knowing you're totally responsible for another human being. And there is absolutely nothing in the world like getting a hug and a kiss from your child and him saying 'I love you, Mommy,' and you know it's for real."

Deanna found herself not only lulled, but persuaded by Joy's description of motherhood. She didn't make it sound easy, but she did make it sound wonderful. Those were the experiences she'd given up more than seven years ago.

There was a soft knock on Deanna's office door.

"Joy, hold on a minute." She covered the mouthpiece. "Stephen, come in."

The door opened, and a man cautiously stuck his head into the office. "Sorry, it's not Stephen."

Deanna was surprised to see her boss. "Oh, hi, Peter. Do you need me or can someone on the floor help you?"

"I'd better talk to you. I'll wait until you're finished with the call." He backed out of the office and closed the door again.

"Joy, I really do have to go. My boss is waiting to talk with me, and I have a meeting."

"I called for another reason. What time are we supposed to be at Regina's on Saturday?"

Deanna gasped. "Oh, my God . . . I forgot all about Regina's brunch."

"But you're still coming, right?"

"I don't know. I have Jade to think about."

Joy chuckled. "Well, let me or Regina know."

Deanna got off the phone and hurried out of her office. She nearly collided with Stephen in the corridor.

"Five minutes," he said, stepping aside as she walked past him.

"Thanks, Stephen. I'll be right there."

Deanna found Peter Byrne, research department director, waiting by the reference desk, casually reading the titles of newly catalogued books.

"Peter. You wanted to see me?"

"I know you have a staff meeting in a few minutes, but I wanted to ask you about the research the news director received last week. It was on the U.S. attorney general and problem cases over the past ten years."

Deanna frowned. "I don't remember that request. They asked me to do it?"

"Actually, Matt Wolff E-mailed me and I E-mailed the reference desk, asking you to sign off on the final report. I take it this is the first you've heard of it?" he said, extending several sheets of paper to her.

Deanna hesitated. "Whose name is on the report?"

"Nancy Kramer."

"I wasn't in last week, Peter. I took some annual leave time. Was there a problem with what you received back?" She scanned the pages.

"Well, the research didn't quite address the question, and it had at least one glaring error—Ruby Ridge was omitted."

"I take full responsibility for not making sure this work was done correctly."

"I know your work, Deanna. This wasn't it. I just want to be sure that this is an exception, not the norm. The good news is that the research wasn't needed for broadcast. The VP is giving a talk at a national conference and wanted to use these cases as examples of selective distribution of information to the public, how it skewers people's perception of the truth."

"When is his speech?"

"He's flying to Chicago on Thursday and the conference is Friday afternoon."

Deanna thought quickly. "Good, there's plenty of time," she said. "I'll get right on it after my staff meeting. I'll have something for you by late this afternoon."

Peter looked pleased. "Great. Sorry I had to dump this on you at the eleventh hour."

"No problem. Consider it done." She watched him walk off.

As Deanna entered the conference room, Stephen passed her several pink message slips. One was from a sportswriter, another from a segment producer of one of the newsmagazine shows, and the last was from her mother. They would all have to wait.

Deanna took her seat at the head of the table. The meeting was routine and went smoothly, but Deanna found herself distracted as she mentally reviewed her conversation with Peter. She carefully watched Nancy Kramer, not sure what she was looking for. Guilt. Guile. Innocence. It bothered her that something so basic had been so mishandled. It bothered her even more that Nancy seemed to be developing a penchant for ignoring directions and making up her own rules. Deanna didn't object to her taking initiative, but she *did* mind insubordination.

She would get back to Nancy later. The thing to do now was complete the report in a timely fashion.

Late in the afternoon Deanna was feeling pleased and relieved when she printed out the last pages of the report on the AG's office for Peter Bryne. Keeping a hard copy for her records, she E-mailed him the research along with an attached file of some of the text materials she had downloaded from the Internet.

Deanna stretched her back and stifled a yawn. "Not so bad," she murmured in satisfaction.

"I'm going," Stephen announced.

"What time is it?"

"It's almost six. Do you know where your children are?" he asked in a TV announcer's voice, imitating the well-known commercial.

He was gone before he could see the horrified expression on Deanna's face.

"Where's Deanna?" Jade asked in a small voice.

"She's on her way right now," Patterson said, playfully shaking one of her legs as she sat next to him on a hall bench of the elementary school.

"We're the last ones here."

"Mrs. Carlton, the secretary, is still here. See, the light is on in her office. And Joan, the music teacher, is still here. You're not scared, are you?"

"No," Jade said, although her voice indicated otherwise. She glanced up at him. "What if I have to stay here the whole night by myself?"

"That's not going to happen, Jade. Deanna will be here. She just called. She's on the way. I bet she couldn't catch a cab."

Patterson glanced down at her small, worried face. She was tired, her eyelids droopy. She let out a deep yawn and rubbed her eyes. He couldn't help feeling annoyed. Deanna had messed up, and the little girl was frightened. But he was also concerned. Everything else considered, Deanna had proved that she wasn't irresponsible.

"I'm hungry," Jade murmured.

"Yeah, me, too," Patterson nodded, staring down the corridor toward the front door. It was already dark outside. He could see people passing in either direction toward Broadway, or Columbus Avenue.

"I want to go home . . ."

He saw that Jade was on the verge of sleep, her head falling to one side until it rested against his arm. Patterson was afraid of making any sudden moves that might scare or hurt her even as he was awed by her unconscious trust in him. It was a sweet feeling. Still, it made him feel more regret than he wanted. He'd always felt a certain guilty ambivalence about his affection for Jade. A relationship with someone else's child instead of his own. The kind of relationship he couldn't have with his own son, whom he'd never met. A long time ago he'd accepted that he'd missed his one chance at being a father.

He'd given up his right to claim possession because of his pride and his ego.

The door swished open. Patterson looked up. For a split second he didn't identify the woman who'd just walked in as Deanna Lindsay, but as an attractive black woman in a hurry, rushing forward with an expression of both fear and contrition. She was out of breath, her hair tousled by a spring wind that had pushed it back from her face. Most of her lipstick had been bitten off and her coat was unbuttoned, flapping against her legs.

She slowed when she recognized him, breathing deeply as she tried to pull herself together.

"She's okay," Patterson said calmly. "She just fell asleep."

Deanna nodded. She bent and gently shook the little girl.

"Jade, wake up." She lifted Jade's head from Patterson's arm. "Jade, honey . . ."

Jade dragged her eyes open. "Where were you?" she asked in a small, accusing voice.

Deanna sat on the other side of Jade and brushed her hand over her hair. "I bet you thought I forgot about you," she tried to tease, avoiding Patterson's penetrating gaze.

"Everybody went home and I was all by myself," Jade told her.

"I'm sorry I was so late," Deanna apologized to Patterson. "I'm glad I was able to reach you."

He turned slowly so that Jade would be forced to sit up. "No problem. My shift starts at nine."

Deanna encouraged Jade to stand as the little girl struggled to wake up. "Come on. Let's get you home."

"She said she's hungry."

"I'll get some quick takeout from the Chinese place in my neighborhood, and just get her into bed. Chicken with broccoli is probably the most nutritious . . ."

Patterson let out a deep chuckle as he stood and watched Deanna maneuver Jade's arms into her jacket. He picked up Jade's turtle knapsack from the floor. "It's not going to matter, and it's not going to hurt her."

"You're probably right. Come on, honey," Deanna said. "I better let the secretary in the office know that I'm here. I'm sure she stayed late because of me. Wait here with Patterson, okay?"

"Okay," Jade murmured.

Patterson and Jade began walking slowly toward the entrance. By the time they'd reached the door, Deanna was already half running to catch up to them.

"They said you gave your number as a backup contact for the record and wondered if it was okay with me," she said.

"That's right. You have a problem with that?" Patterson asked as they walked out.

"It's not fair to keep bothering you this way."

"I'll let you know when it's not fair and when I don't want to be bothered."

"I hope I didn't interfere with your plans."

"Man, you *are* feeling guilty, aren't you? The way I figure it, we stand at love right now."

She was confused. "You mean like in tennis?"

He gave her a lopsided grin and raised his eyebrows. "Yeah, that's right. We're even."

"Are we going?" Jade complained.

Deanna transferred her attention away from the teasing speculation in Patterson's eyes. "Yes, hon.

We're going to stop and get something to eat before we go home."

"Can Patterson come with us?"

Deanna stole a quick look at him.

"Maybe next time," he said. "I have to take care of something before heading off to work. Can I give you a lift?"

Deanna shook her head, aware that he'd been far too accommodating already. There was something a bit off-putting about being in debt to Patterson Temple, she decided. She would have felt much better if the situation were reversed.

"Thanks, but no. We're going to walk over to Broadway and take a cab."

"Fine. Are we still on for Sunday?"

She'd thought he was just being polite when he'd extended the invitation. But apparently Patterson never said anything he didn't mean.

"I guess so. Jade likes your grandmother. She's looking forward to seeing her."

"So, how will you get all the way out to Brooklyn where she lives?"

"A cab or the subway."

Patterson laughed with a shake of his head. "You're stubborn, too. Why don't you just ask if I can take you and Jade?"

"Like I said, I don't want to be a bother."

"You mean you don't want to owe me anything," he said astutely. "I'll call before I come by to pick you up. About eleven."

"Patterson, I can—"

"See you on Sunday."

"'Bye," Jade said, reaching up to him for a hug and kiss.

He obliged her, then faced Deanna and was surprised when she suddenly stuck out her hand to him. Patterson looked at it for a moment before finally accepting it, squeezing it gently as she shook his. Her hand felt small and delicate, though her grip was firm. The skin was smooth and very soft, and a little cool from the night air.

"Thank you, Patterson."

"For what?"

She shrugged, somewhat embarrassed. "For coming to the rescue. I mean it. And for not giving me a hard time about being late."

He liked it that Deanna wasn't afraid to look him in the eye. That she was neither intimidated by him nor coy. That she could say she was sorry . . . and he believed her.

"You forgot about her, didn't you?" he asked softly so that Jade couldn't hear.

"I didn't mean to. I'm . . . ashamed to admit it, but something came up at work and I got busy."

Patterson knew it would be easy to say something cutting. Instead, he nodded, accepting Deanna's apology at face value.

"Could be worse," he said.

"How?"

"What if you didn't show up at all? What if you hadn't taken her in the first place?"

She shook her head in confusion. "No . . . I don't think I really had an option."

"Yeah, you did. I think you made the right choice. I'll see you on Sunday."

With a quick good night to Jade, Patterson walked back to his car. Deanna was left with the feeling that she still had something to prove to him. She'd always been self-confident, not afraid to take chances or try something new. She didn't mind so much being wrong if something didn't work out. After all, everyone makes mistakes. But she didn't want to look foolish. She didn't want to seem careless.

She was suddenly aware that she never used to analyze her life, or agonize over her decisions. She'd never needed to. But now, she realized, she didn't want Patterson Temple to be right in thinking less of her.

Patterson wasn't sure what he was actually witnessing late the next afternoon as he approached Eleanor Kennedy's office and saw her with another black man. Either a colleague talking serious business with her . . . or two lovers whispering secrets. Either way, his first reaction was mild curiosity. The second was that he was probably right about something he'd been suspecting for months.

Eleanor was playing him.

If not with this particular man, then with someone just like him.

Based on what he was witnessing, Patterson suspected that Eleanor might also be ready to call it quits. If she thought he was going to be jealous and call this brother out, she was wrong.

The man talking to her was younger, closer to Eleanor's own age. Clean-shaven, dressed in a well-cut suit, he was packaged for success, and for claiming rights he hadn't yet earned.

When Patterson had first met Eleanor, he'd gotten the same look she was now sharing with this new man. A slow and intense focus on him, bold with interest and sexual heat. Patterson had met her challenge and accepted the invitation. Now he could tell that she'd put the same welcome mat out again, even though she already had a guest in the house. Himself.

All he felt, though, was relief that his decision to end their relationship would not break her heart.

When Eleanor became aware of his presence, Patterson didn't see anything that looked like concern, guilt, or even surprise on her face. She barely broke stride in her conversation with the other man.

What bothered Patterson even more than her attitude was that her companion, taking his signals from Eleanor, didn't acknowledge his presence either. It became a question of who would blink first, and Patterson was determined it wouldn't be him. In reality the wait was long enough for Patterson to get the message, whether or not that was her intention.

Eleanor was a good-looking woman. She dressed in clothes meant to draw attention to certain generous areas of her body. She moved with calculated grace, which to men made her memorable and to women a danger. She was definitely of the Miss Thang breed of women, a different class altogether from someone like Deanna Lindsay, who had finesse and style.

Nevertheless, Patterson would bet that Deanna and Eleanor had one thing in common. Both were more interested in *what* a man was than in *who* he was. When Eleanor finally met his gaze, it was with a smile Patterson knew was no longer for him alone.

"John Nettleton, let me introduce you to Patterson Temple."

The man put out his hand readily enough as his eyes sized up his competition. "Temple," John nodded.

"John is the director of youth services in Westchester County," Eleanor explained in a tone that made the title seem exalted.

John raised his brows. "Not the entire county, just one of the districts."

"Still very impressive. We need more of *us* in those positions. Patterson is a fireman," Eleanor added flatly.

John made some noncommittal sound, raising his brows even higher.

"John is on a task force from the governor's office," Eleanor purred.

"Another task force," Patterson observed. "On what?"

"We're looking into whether or not various cities in the state are providing enough outreach services for disadvantaged teens. So . . . you're a fireman."

"That's right," Patterson said, and left it at that. "Am I interrupting?"

"We're done," John answered for Eleanor, checking the time. "I have a train to catch. Eleanor, thanks for everything." He took her hand, clasping it in both of his. "Good to see you again. I'll tell the committee what you're recommending. And I'll tell them you should be on the committee."

Eleanor smiled at him. "That's so nice of you."

He waved good-bye and left. Eleanor turned to Patterson.

"You didn't have to be rude to him, Pat. You barely talked to him."

"You didn't have to be so rude to *me*. You acted like my showing up was bad timing."

"All I did was introduce you."

Patterson's jaw flexed. "Yeah, making it sound like compared to the brother I don't measure up."

Eleanor sucked her teeth impatiently. She pivoted

to enter a partitioned area that was her office. Her coworkers had left for the day, and she wasted no time on niceties.

"Well, you *could* do better for yourself."

Patterson remained standing, not bothering to sit in the extra chair placed in the already crowded cubicle. No matter how hard Eleanor tried, she could not make it into the office space it was never intended to be. He shoved his hands into the pockets of his slacks.

"I'm doing fine where I am. My shift starts at nine," he reminded her.

"You know, if you're going to be so sensitive about what you do, maybe you should do something else. I don't understand why you don't take the test for fire marshal."

"I like being *right there* to help people. I don't want to sit in an office all day pushing paper and sucking up to brass."

Eleanor looked annoyed. "It was a waste of my time to try to get you to move into management. You could have retired from the department in five years with a great benefit package. Instead, you want to ride those goddamn fire trucks like you're a little boy or something."

"I'm much more effective on the front lines. I'm good at what I do."

"All right, all right—let's not fight about it, okay?" She glared at him. "You have a chip on your shoulder this evening. What happened to you?"

The question brought him up short. He suspected that if he thought about it, it wouldn't take much to come up with a short list. Or one name—Deanna.

"Probably," he answered, "the same thing that's happened with you."

Eleanor ignored him as she got her purse from a desk drawer and began checking the contents to make sure she had everything. "I don't know what you mean."

"Let's go out to eat like we planned. We can talk about it then."

She gave him a look. "Well, I don't want to go if you're in a bad mood."

"Suit yourself. We'll discuss it here. You and me. It's not working. So, let's cut our losses and move on."

"Who are you, to cut me loose? You have some nerve! I was the one who thought you had more going for you than some of these sorry-assed black men who don't want to do shit with their lives. I was the one who tried to get you to better yourself."

He raised a brow. "Sorry I'm not good enough for you."

"And that band you got isn't going to amount to anything. Nobody's going to pay money to hear a bunch of amateur firemen who think they can play music."

Patterson stared at her in fascination. He'd never before focused on the fact that Eleanor was motivated only by superficial ideas of status and class. She clearly didn't believe in sacrifice, or in doing something for nothing.

Eleanor had made him comfortable for a long time. She hadn't been his ideal, but she had been what he thought he deserved. Now he realized that wasn't the same as what he might want.

"You think you deserve better than what I have to offer?" she asked.

"Now we agree on something."

Eleanor looked dumbfounded. Patterson suddenly

realized that he'd been playing it safe in his relationship with her. If her expectations hadn't been met in the time they'd known each other, neither had his. Perhaps he'd been afraid to venture into unknown territory, try something different, take a chance and find someone new. He was reminded of Deanna's bold acceptance of the situation with Jade. In the face of all the odds and her lack of experience, she'd been willing to take a chance. Maybe she had more courage than he did. Maybe he could learn something from her.

Eleanor couldn't compete with that.

"Deanna . . ."

She stopped in the middle of picking up wet towels and little-girl clothes and glanced over her shoulder. Jade was standing on the bathroom threshold. Her Spice Girls nightshirt was a little too small, and she held her stuffed rabbit, Oliver, by the ears, his body hanging limp at her side.

"How come you're still awake?" Deanna asked. "I thought you were sound asleep."

Jade shrugged. "I can't."

Deanna sat down on the side of the tub. "How come?"

Jade hugged the stuffed toy to her chest. "I don't like it in there by myself."

"You mean in the other bed?" Jade nodded. "What if I stay there with you until you fall asleep? Maybe that would help. Okay?"

"Okay."

Deanna hastily stuffed the wet towels and Jade's clothing into the hamper. She'd hoped to take a nice hot bath herself, but realized that it was already late and maybe she'd do better taking a shower in the morning. Except that she hated morning showers.

She steered Jade back into the small bedroom. Jade got under the comforter while Deanna sat on the edge, tenderly tucking the covers around her.

"How was school today?"

"Okay," Jade murmured. "I don't like some of the other kids."

"You don't? Why?"

" 'Cause they call me names."

Deanna frowned. "What kind of names?"

"The black kids call me black. But I'm not like them."

Deanna studied the small upturned face. She gently stroked Jade's soft hair, looking into her appealing green eyes.

"Honey, that's not a bad name. I'm called black, too."

"But I don't look like you."

Deanna thought of what she could say to explain race to a child who was half white and half black. Her skin was fair, a creamy peach, her curly hair as blond as her mother's. But the hint of her father's features in her face and body were a clear indicator to most folks that Jade was biracial. How could she tell a child that in the world she would grow up in she would have to choose one side or the other? Not for herself, but for everyone else. For all of Jade's exotic beauty, Deanna was just beginning to get a glimpse into how complicated her life could become.

"Of course we don't look alike, hon. It doesn't matter. It's only important that you understand you're just as special as anyone else in school."

Deanna was concerned that Stacy had apparently made no attempt to teach her daughter how she was different and why. It was the reason Jade couldn't understand why her classmates were treating her so harshly. Differences made people uncomfortable. She didn't want Jade to be made a target by the other kids. Deanna knew she needed to speak with Jade's teacher.

"We'll talk about it another time," she promised. "You don't have any homework, do you?"

Jade looked puzzled. "What's homework?"

"Maybe you're too young for that. Do you know how to read?"

"A little. My mommy used to read to me sometimes."

"Did you like that?"

"Yeah. And she used to make all the funny sounds in the book, too."

Deanna smiled. She was pleased that Jade remembered the details of her life with her mother. She was equally pleased that the mention of those times didn't immediately send Jade into an emotional tailspin. As a matter of fact, except for minor tearful moments, the child had settled down. It occurred to Deanna how very brave Jade was. Given all that had happened and all that she had already been through, she seemed to have adjusted quickly to a situation beyond her control.

She tried to smooth back the unruly tendrils of hair around Jade's face that had escaped the gathered bunch behind each ear.

"What else did you and your mother do together?" Deanna asked quietly, looking for any signs that talking about her mother was too upsetting for Jade.

Jade was silent for a moment, rolling her eyes toward the ceiling. "One time we went ice skating in Central Park. That was fun." She giggled. "Mommy fell down, but I didn't."

"Ice skating," Deanna repeated in surprise. She

hadn't been ice skating since she was twelve or so. "Did you like that?"

Jade nodded. "And another time we went to the zoo and I saw all the baby animals." She wrinkled her nose. "It smelled inside the cages."

Deanna chuckled. She'd thought so too when she was little. "Did your mother ever take you to the Thanksgiving Day parade?"

"I can't remember."

"My sister and brother and I could never get our mother to take us to see the parade. I always wanted to go when I was your age," she reminisced.

Jade reached out to play with the silver beaded bracelet Deanna was wearing. "Do you have a daddy?"

"I did, but he . . . died," Deanna said carefully. "Just like your mother has died."

"Oh. Does died mean I won't ever see mommy again?"

"I'm afraid so."

Jade silently continued her examination of the bracelet. "I have a daddy."

"I know, sweetie." Deanna hesitated. "Would you like to see him again?"

"He scares me," she admitted.

Deanna heard the reluctance in the child's confession.

"Why, sweetheart?"

"Because he's mean." She rubbed her eyes. "Can you read me a story?"

"Well, I don't have any children's books, but I could make up one. Would you like that?"

"Yeah," Jade murmured, resting her head against Deanna's arm.

Deanna suddenly felt an incredible sense of responsibility. She lifted her arm to encourage Jade to rest against her side. It came to her forcefully that not until that instant had she really understood what it meant for this child to depend on her. Deanna was filled with an overpowering desire to protect her. To try and do what was best.

She didn't fool herself into believing for a moment that Jade could erase the sacrifice she'd made more than seven years ago. Yet Deanna did recognize that in a strange way, this was a chance to find out what it might have been like if she had let herself become a mother.

Deanna remembered her amazement at the warmth and energy of her lively, active nephews whenever they'd hold still long enough for her to give them a hug or a playful wrestle. But Tyler and Cody had parents, grandparents. A home. For all intents and purposes, Jade Lowell only had her.

Deanna found a comfortable position and began. "This is a story about a mouse who lives in a house where the only thing to eat is cheese. The problem is, cheese makes him sneeze . . ."

Jade giggled and snuggled closer.

Encouraged, Deanna went with whatever came into her head. She spun off a wild and nonsensical tale, all the more fantastic because she gave the mouse a royal name and title, with human attributes and emotions. She stopped at one point, unsure how the story was going to end.

"I'm sorry I don't have any pictures to show you," Deanna said.

She got no answer from Jade, and when she bent to look into the child's face, she saw that Jade had fallen sound asleep. Deanna didn't move right away, afraid that she might wake the child.

Afraid to let go of the feeling of being needed.

Chapter Eight

Reaching across Bettina Butler's kitchen sink, Deanna pulled back the sheer curtains to peer into the backyard. It wasn't as big as the one behind the house where she'd grown up, but it was lovely. What Patterson's grandmother had managed to accomplish in the small space put her own mother's attempts at gardening to shame.

Crocuses and daffodils dotted the flower beds, the first blooms of spring. Deanna recognized the early leaves of climbing clematis along the back fence and pachysandra and hostas beneath the low branches of an apple tree. In a few weeks, the smell of lilacs would surround the back porch.

Betts was sitting in a lawn chair, her forearms braced on her thighs as she instructed Jade on how to dig a hole. The small azalea they'd brought for Betts seemed puny and inadequate compared to the careful variety in Betts's garden, but Betts had exclaimed and carried on as if she'd been given a rare and delicate orchid. Jade had beamed with pride and pleasure.

They'd arrived shortly after Betts had come home from church. She'd still been outside on this mild April afternoon chatting with her neighbors.

Betts lived in a predominately black neighborhood

in Bedford Stuyvesant. Her house was small, with no driveway, and only five feet of space separated it from the houses on either side. On the trip there, Patterson had spoken of his childhood home with great affection. Perhaps it couldn't compare with the suburban grace of where Deanna had grown up in Montclair, New Jersey, but she realized that Patterson hadn't missed out on anything. Money couldn't buy what he had been given by his grandmother. It was the same love and affection that Betts now showered on Jade as they worked together to plant the azalea.

"Why don't you go out and join them?" Patterson's voice came from behind Deanna. He'd been upstairs repairing a leak in his grandmother's bath. He put down the pail and wrench he was carrying and moved to stand next to her at the sink.

" 'Fraid of getting your clothes dirty?" he teased.

"I don't have a green thumb." She held hers up.

He chuckled. "That's no excuse."

"I think it's better for them to have time together. Your grandmother is wonderful with Jade."

Patterson looked out the window. She could smell the freshness of his pullover sweater and feel the heat of his body as his chest brushed her shoulder.

"You saying you're not good with Jade?" he asked before turning on the faucet.

She watched him wash his hands as she crossed to the stove to put a little distance between them. She stirred the lima beans, simmering in a buttery sauce, as Betts had asked her to do. The smell evoked memories of her own grandmother, and she fleetingly recalled family gatherings in Virginia with the kind of Southern foods that her own mother had been raised on.

"I'm not saying that," she answered. "It's just—I had to yell at her this morning because she spilled her milk on the sofa. Then she wouldn't get dressed."

He grabbed a dish towel and dried his hands. "So?"

"I worry that I'm being too hard on her. Especially after everything she's been through."

Patterson looked thoughtful for a moment. "That doesn't mean you can let her get away with doing whatever she wants. Doesn't mean you don't care, either. Betts can be tough when she has to, but mostly she's nice to everybody. She likes to say that all God's children need love."

He opened the refrigerator and took out a can of soda.

"You say that like you don't buy it," she observed.

Patterson popped the tab on the can. He held it up to her as an offering. Deanna declined. Shrugging, he took a long swallow and studied her. She was pulled together in slim jeans and a crisp white blouse that contrasted with her smooth brown complexion. He took another swallow, conceding to himself that she didn't *have* to work at looking good.

"Let's just say," he said, "I don't always meet the kind of people that Betts or God says are deserving of help."

She was tempted to ask him if that included her, but decided he would likely say it did just to aggravate her.

"Did it ever occur to you that maybe it's not that other people are not deserving? That maybe *you're* being too hard?"

He took another drink from the can before responding. "No."

Deanna couldn't help chuckling and shaking her

head at his audacity. "Betts must have had her hands full raising you. I saw all the pictures in the living room. Are the boy and girl in the photos your sister and brother?"

"No, there's just me."

Deanna lifted the lid off a pot of steaming white rice. She used a two-pronged fork to fluff it while casting Patterson a curious glance.

"So your grandmother raised you alone."

Patterson shifted restlessly. "What you really want to know is, 'Who are my parents, and where are they?' "

"And the answer is?" she asked without hesitation. When Patterson didn't respond right away, she turned in curiosity. "Are you going to tell me?" He was swirling the contents of the soda can. He met her gaze.

"My mother died of lupus when I was five. Then I came to live with Betts. That's my mother's picture in the living room."

"What about the boy with her?"

"My uncle William. He was killed when I was fifteen, shot to death during an argument."

He stopped there, waiting for her reaction. There was none as far as he could tell. Maybe she didn't know what to say. Patterson would bet that Deanna had no personal experience with the kind of violence and misfortune he had seen or known for most of his life.

"What about your father?" she asked.

Patterson moved about the kitchen. "My father left my mother and me when she started to get sick."

"You never saw him again?"

"Maybe half a dozen times. I haven't seen him in fifteen years." His tone was challenging.

Deanna didn't ask any more questions, although she was fascinated by the details of his life. So much drama. So much tragedy and death. Had that contributed to his seemingly unemotional response to Stacy's death?

"I'm sorry," Deanna said awkwardly.

"What are you sorry for?"

"Why are you so defensive? I'm sorry because you lost your mother at such a very young age. You and Jade have that in common, don't you? Maybe that's why you seem to understand what she's going through."

Patterson set the can on the countertop. "Maybe. Life happens. Things go wrong. People die. You deal with it." He picked up the wrench and pail from the floor. "I'm going down to the basement with this stuff. I'll be back."

Deanna felt frustrated as he disappeared through a door between the kitchen and living room. Patterson could be difficult and judgmental. But he could also be kind and funny. And she was more and more curious about him.

The back door opened and Jade burst in, carrying the plastic pot, which now held a seedling.

"Look what Betts gave me," she cried.

She was filthy, having managed to get dirt all over her face and in her hair.

"Now, don't forget what I told you 'bout taking care of that," Betts said, entering behind Jade. She closed the door and patted Jade's shoulder affectionately as she headed for the sink.

"I won't." Jade nodded solemnly. "Look, Deanna."

"That's pretty. What is it?" Deanna asked as Jade shoved the plant under her nose to smell.

"It's a little piece of mint," Betts said, washing her

hands before checking the stove. "It'll grow anyplace and it's tough." She glanced over at Jade and inclined her head a little. "Give her something to put her mind to and not think about you-know-what," Betts finished.

Jade began to shake the pot. Dirt dropped onto the floor.

"Jade, be careful." Deanna grabbed her hand. "You're making a mess. Put that by the door, and let's get you cleaned up."

She directed Jade to the bathroom, then squatted down to wipe up the dirt with a damp paper towel.

"Now that's a good idea." Betts nodded approvingly. "Darlin', I forgot all about the cheese biscuits. Everything is right there on the counter. Can you throw them together for me? Won't take but a few minutes in the oven."

Deanna threw the used towel in the trash. "I'm sorry but I don't know how to make biscuits."

Betts looked more amused than surprised. "You know how to cook at all?"

"Of course, but not . . . not . . ."

"None of this old-time country food," Betts guessed, chuckling.

"My mother never taught me. Frankly, I'm not sure *she* knew how. We ate differently when I was growing up."

Betts sighed. "I bet you one of them that likes . . . what you call it? With the raw fish?"

"Sushi," Deanna filled in.

Betts shook her head, as if to ask, "What is the world coming to?" "I'll have Pat do the biscuits. Where your folks from?"

"My father was from California. My mother was born in Virginia."

"Well . . . it takes all kinds. We're going to sit down and eat as soon as Mr. Stanley gets here."

"Well, here he is, so let's eat!" a raspy male voice announced.

An older man entered the kitchen. He was dressed in his Sunday best, complete with a buttoned-up vest and a bow tie. He wasn't as tall as she was, Deanna noted, but he was taller than Betts. His brown cheeks were peppered with freckles and he was virtually bald. Thick glasses gave his eyes the over-large brightness of an inquisitive child.

"I let myself in," he said with a smile.

"Mr. Stanley, I wondered when you was going to get here," Betts said.

"Now you know I gots to be dead to miss your fine cooking, Miss Betts. Afternoon," he said, nodding to Deanna.

Deanna smiled at him, but her attention was suddenly caught by the sound of music coming from the living room. Not Betts's radio gospel station with the wailing of church choirs but the gentle plucking of a guitar. Curiosity moved her to the living room entrance and she gazed in. Patterson was sitting on an ottoman, one long leg stretched out and the other bent at the knee to provide a resting place for his instrument. His fingers played over the metal strings as he fashioned a soft melody.

Deanna recalled that Patterson had said he played guitar, and Jade had mentioned his band. She'd thought it was a hobby of some kind, but his skill and talent went far beyond that of a simple pastime.

He played beautifully.

The piece was melancholy and dreamy. Sort of jazzy and slow. He was playing from the heart. She wanted to stay and listen. Even more than that, she wanted to watch him as he was playing.

Betts called to her, and she reluctantly stepped back inside the kitchen.

"Deanna, that's Mr. Stanley," Betts said. The man held out a wrinkled hand.

"I'm sorry," she said, "my hands are . . ."

"That don't matter. A little dirt never hurt." He laughed cheerfully.

Still distracted by Patterson's music, Deanna hastily wiped her right hand on a towel and shook the gentleman's hand.

"Girl, I told you to watch this food. This macaroni and cheese needed a little more milk," Betts said, checking on a bubbling casserole.

Deanna felt as if she were being chastised by her own mother. "I'm sorry. I couldn't tell."

"You sure better marry a man who can cook or has a lot of money," Betts teased. "Never heard of no black woman who can't cook."

"That's Patterson," Jade exclaimed, returning from the bathroom and disappearing just as quickly into the living room.

The heat in the kitchen became stifling to Deanna, but Betts never broke her stride or a sweat as she continued to monitor half a dozen simmering pots and pans. At the same time she held a conversation with Mr. Stanley and made sure Deanna did nothing to ruin Sunday dinner.

Holding a roasting pan by two bright potholders, Betts set her pork tenderloin on a rattan trivet on the counter. She reached for a carving knife in a utility drawer as Jade ran in, holding up a little plastic triangle.

"Look what Patterson gave me."

"Why, isn't that nice," Betts crooned. "What is it, darlin'?"

"I don't know," Jade admitted, looking at the piece.

"It's a pick," Deanna said. "You use it to play the guitar."

"Like this," Jade said, miming strumming across the strings.

"That's right." Deanna nodded. "It's very small, so don't lose it."

Jade put it in her pocket.

"Hello, little miss." Mr. Stanley smiled at Jade.

"Hello," Jade murmured shyly. "Who are you?"

"Jade, don't be rude," Deanna whispered.

"I'm a friend of the family. I'm Mr. Stanley. And who might you be?"

"I'm a friend of the family, too," Jade announced. "What's your first name?"

"Stanley."

She looked confused and wrinkled her nose. "Your name is Mr. Stanley Stanley? That's silly." She giggled.

Betts chuckled quietly to herself. "Ain't it the truth? Pat!" she called out. "It's time to cut the meat."

"Jade . . ." Deanna warned again. She heard the music stop and a few moments later, Patterson entered the room.

"Is your name Jade?" Mr. Stanley asked. Jade bobbed her head. "That's very pretty. Do you know that Jade is a precious stone? Just like the color of your eyes."

"Tell Mr. Stanley what your mother called you," Patterson suggested, reaching for the platter of meat and the carving knife.

"My mommy said I had cat eyes. But she's dead," Jade said.

Patterson began to cut the meat. Mr. Stanley and Betts exchanged quick glances. Deanna waited for what Jade would say next.

"I'm very sorry to hear that," Mr. Stanley said kindly.

"That's okay. I think God needed her to be in heaven with Him. That's what Betts told me."

"That's right, darlin'."

"Can I help?" Deanna asked, to turn the conversation.

"You sure can," Betts said. "Set the table for me, please." She opened a cabinet and pointed to the china she wanted Deanna to use. "The plates are right in here."

Even Mr. Stanley helped with preparations, taking the ice bucket from the top of the refrigerator and filling it with cubes from the freezer.

"I can help, too," Jade offered.

"Here, darlin'. Put one of these at each plate on the table." Betts opened a drawer beneath the china cabinet, pulled out cloth napkins, and handed them to Jade.

Deanna and Jade followed Betts into the dining room, which wasn't much bigger than the kitchen. There was barely room to move around the table as they bumped into, squeezed by, and maneuvered around each other.

The tight quarters would have driven her mother crazy, Deanna thought ruefully. Faith would have said that she had nothing in common with Bettina Butler, or Mr. Stanley, or Patterson. She would not have been comfortable in Betts's modest little house in the low end of a middle-income community in

Brooklyn. She would have noted the differences and exalted herself above these people.

Deanna had never known anyone like Patterson and Betts. There was something southern, warm, and very quaint about being with them.

"Jade, do Betts a favor and go tell Pat and Mr. Stanley we're sitting down now," Betts said.

"Okay," Jade said, happily running to the kitchen.

"She looks like she's doing fine," Betts commented to Deanna as soon as Jade was out of sight. "I knew she'd come around." She peered at Deanna. "What about you?"

Deanna shrugged. "I'm okay."

She decided not to tell Betts about the half dozen ways in which her normal activities had been thrown off track. There was no way she could justify comparing the necessities of taking care of Jade to missed gym classes or canceled dates. If she did, she was afraid she'd come across as petty and selfish when all she was really acknowledging was the very thing that Faith had warned her about. Life had changed. Her time wasn't her own anymore.

She wondered if she would ever go back to being the person she used to be before Jade. Or if she'd want to.

"Jade is a sweetheart, but you can't let that child run you ragged."

"Am I looking tired?" Deanna asked ruefully.

"No more than anybody else raising kids. You hear from those people looking for her mama's family?"

"No. To tell the truth, I'd almost forgotten. Things will change if they do find relatives."

Betts sighed and shook her head. "It's whatever God wants it to be, child." She glanced covertly at Deanna. "Do you belong to a church?"

"No, I don't," she admitted. "I'm what you call a lapsed Christian who goes mostly on holidays, for weddings . . ."

"Somebody's death or a baby's christening," Betts nodded. "I wondered if Jade was in Sunday school, is why I'm asking."

"No, she's not. I never even thought about it. What if Stacy was Catholic or Jewish?"

"I don't think the good Lord is going to ask. Don't worry about it. I guess right now you have enough on your hands."

Jade returned to the dining room with Mr. Stanley and Patterson in tow. Patterson carried the platter of meat in one hand and a napkin-lined basket piled with steaming biscuits in the other. Quickly, other bowls and plates of food appeared, along with an old-fashioned pitcher of iced tea. Deanna bit her tongue, about to ask Betts where she kept her wineglasses. She doubted that Bettina Butler owned any.

Everyone took their seats as Betts indicated their places at the table. Deanna found herself between Mr. Stanley and Jade, opposite Patterson and Betts. She caught Patterson looking at her and saw interest and speculation. For once she sensed she'd done something that met with his approval. She found herself automatically smiling before averting her gaze. She was about to reach for the bowl of lima beans when Betts said quietly, "Let us join hands and say grace."

Embarrassed, Deanna pulled her hands back and, following Betts and Patterson's example, clasped hands with Jade and Mr. Stanley, completing the small circle. They were now an instant family temporarily joined.

"Jade, can you remember what I taught you when you stayed with me?" Betts asked.

"I think so," Jade said. "You have to close your eyes now," she instructed Deanna, squeezing her own shut.

Deanna did as she was told. Jade's voice was sweet and earnest. " 'God is good, God is great, and we thank Him for our food.' "

"Amen," everyone chorused in unison.

"Well, that's the last one," Deanna said, wiping the bottom of the saucepan and passing it to Betts to put away.

"Thank you, darlin'. I sure appreciate your help."

"Have you thought about getting a dishwasher?" Deanna suggested.

"Baagghh!" Betts said dismissively. "I don't need no dishwasher. Use my own two hands. Did fine all my life. Besides, mostly it's just me I'm cookin' for. Pat cleans up if he comes over."

Deanna smiled. "I'm surprised."

"No need to be. I taught Pat to take care of himself. I told him, don't be expecting some woman to do everything for you now. Know how to do it yourself."

"Very wise," Deanna said. "I wish my mother had taught my brother that. Tate's idea of helping is not to leave any food on his plate."

Betts laughed merrily. "Lord, child . . . ain't that something." She sat down at the kitchen table and patted the chair next to her.

From the living room, Deanna could hear Patterson playing "Three Blind Mice" on the guitar, and Jade's high-pitched laughter caused her to grin to herself. Jade's simple happiness was infectious. In addition to Patterson's musical recital, Mr. Stanley had set the

TV on a preseason baseball game. All the sounds and voices and quiet laughter made Deanna feel lazy—and content. She kicked off a shoe and curled her leg under her on her seat.

"I was very fond of Stacy," Betts began, "but, Lord, that child had problems. She wouldn't say much 'bout her family, but I don't think they were very nice to her."

Poor white trash entered Deanna's mind, but neither of them was going to be unkind enough to say so. She knew how easy it was to label people. They are acceptable or not. You like them or you don't. What about the ones you weren't sure about? What happened if you changed your mind?

"How'd somebody like you come to meet Stacy in the first place?" Betts asked.

Deanna turned her attention to the older woman. It never occurred to her not to make a full disclosure. She realized that Betts inspired not only honesty, but trust. And Deanna *knew* that she wouldn't be unfairly judged. In a way, it was a relief to be able to speak openly.

"We met at a clinic. We were both scheduled to have abortions."

"Umph!" Betts murmured with a shake of her head.

"I'd made a bad mistake with someone I barely knew. I didn't want to have a child under those circumstances."

Betts reached out to pat her hand. "We all make mistakes, darlin'. What about Stacy?"

"She changed her mind. When I got out of recovery she was still in the pre-op room. She told me she wasn't sure what to do. She told me she had no place to go and she didn't want to return to—"

"Marcus," Betts muttered. "That no-good— Forgive me, Lord. That man is bad news. But Stacy felt beholden to him 'cause he took care of her when she first came to the city. He was good to her for a while. Then he changed."

"I brought Stacy home with me," Deanna said.

"Bless your heart," Betts cooed.

"I didn't want to be alone." Her voice dropped. "I was scared and confused, too. We needed each other."

"Then what happened?"

Deanna hesitated. "She stayed with me for a few weeks. One morning when I got up early to get ready for work, I walked into the bathroom and found Stacy crying. She had a kitchen knife in her hand." Betts's expression was wreathed in empathy. "I was afraid she meant to kill herself. So I grabbed for the knife, and it cut her on the forearm. It wasn't deep, but I think she panicked when she saw the blood."

"Oh, that poor child. God help her."

"She didn't want to see a doctor so I took care of the cut. And I stayed and talked with her the whole day. She left a few days later, leaving me a note saying that she was going to have the abortion after all. I never heard from her again and I didn't know she'd changed her mind again and had the baby."

"Jade," Betts said. "Well, I'm sure glad she changed her mind. That baby made a big difference in Stacy's life. Gave her someone to love."

Deanna fell silent.

"Oh, darlin'—I'm not saying what you did was bad."

"I know," Deanna said quietly. "I was just thinking how much braver Stacy was than me."

"Now don't be so hard on yourself. At least you

had some family you could turn to. Stacy had nobody. That's why she was so scared."

"I never told anyone about this except my sister, one good friend, and Stacy. Now you," Deanna said quietly.

Betts murmured a few comforting words. They both jumped when they suddenly heard a plaintive wail coming from the backyard. It was quickly repeated.

"Goodness gracious. Is that Mrs. Calhoun screaming like that?" Betts asked. She went to open the back door to listen.

"What's that?" Jade asked in a fearful voice, racing into the room.

"I don't know, honey," Deanna responded, getting up from the table and searching for her shoe with her toes.

"Betts? What's going on?" Patterson asked from the kitchen doorway.

"I thought I heard . . ." Betts began.

A female voice pierced the dark. "He's dead! He's dead! Help me, Jesus, please, somebody help me!"

The anguished sound tore through them all, but it was Patterson who responded first. He bolted for the back door, rushing past his stunned grandmother.

"Call 911," he ordered Betts, and was swallowed up in the night.

"My God," Betts moaned, heading for the telephone.

"Jade, stay here," Deanna said spontaneously.

Then she rushed out after Patterson.

Chapter Nine

Deanna immediately became disoriented. It was pitch-black outside. Then she caught a glimpse of Patterson as he neatly scaled the back fence into the yard beyond, where Mrs. Calhoun could be heard still crying hysterically, "He's dead, he's dead!"

Deanna stumbled over one of Betts's watering cans. She dragged a lawn chair over to the fence to stand on, scrambled awkwardly over, and dropped into the next yard. Light poured from Mrs. Calhoun's open back door. Deanna could hear the distant voices of neighbors who apparently heard the frightened cries and were now leaning out their windows to try to see what was happening.

She ran inside the house. A quick glance showed her that the occupants had just finished dinner. She followed voices into a hallway, where Patterson was kneeling beside a middle-aged man who lay on his back at the foot of a flight of stairs. Patterson pressed his fingers first to the man's wrist, then just under his jaw. He pulled up an eyelid and leaned close to check the man's pupils.

"Is he dead?" the woman asked anxiously.

"He's breathing," Patterson responded cautiously.

"Betts is calling for help," Deanna said.

Patterson continued his examination, not acknowledging her presence.

"Doris, is Ben on any medication?" Patterson asked. He began to loosen the belt on the man's pants, and opened the collar and top buttons of his shirt.

"Just his blood pressure and seizure medicine."

Deanna led the distraught woman to a chair, then watched in awe as Patterson carefully checked the man's vital signs and asked questions. He straightened out Ben Calhoun's body, tilting his head back until his mouth and chin were pointed toward the ceiling. He pulled his cell phone from a holder clipped to his waistband and tossed it to Deanna.

"I want you to call in an EMS request code. I'll tell you what to say."

Deanna, her hands trembling, followed his directions. In the meantime Patterson held Ben Calhoun's nose closed with his fingers and squeezed his jaw with his other hand until Ben's mouth opened.

"Tell them you're with Captain Patterson Temple of Engine Company 47 . . ."

Patterson began CPR, dictating additional information to Deanna in between breathing for the patient.

In less than a minute Deanna could hear a siren. She hurried to open the front door and rushed out to meet the emergency van. A three-person team quickly entered the house with their equipment. Patterson stepped back and let them take over assisting the unconscious man.

"Heart attack?" an EMS worker asked Patterson as one of them continued CPR until they could get an oxygen mask over Ben's face.

"Maybe combined with a seizure," Patterson added.

They radioed the patient's status ahead to the local hospital. Deanna gathered that Mr. Calhoun was stabilized, but his condition was serious.

Mrs. Calhoun soon calmed down enough to answer questions about her husband's medical condition and history. Deanna stood by, ready to help but feeling superfluous. While she murmured comforting words to the patient's wife, she was also experiencing a startling revelation about Patterson. He had been calm, focused, and methodical. She'd never given much thought to the work performed by firemen. They were people who simply put out fires, saving lives in an indirect way. Yet Deanna felt an unexpected pride in watching Patterson, whose experience and skill had possibly saved a man's life.

She felt nearly breathless with a realization that perhaps she'd been avoiding—or maybe had needed this night to confirm: Patterson Temple had exactly the qualities of strength, smarts, and sensitivity that she most admired.

Deanna glanced into the backseat and wasn't surprised to find that Jade had fallen asleep. She'd drifted off almost before Patterson's Jeep had pulled away from Betts's house. Deanna was feeling a little sleepy herself, perhaps in reaction to the adrenaline rush she'd had watching Patterson respond to the recent crisis.

"You were very good back there," she commented. "I'm impressed."

"By what?" He seemed genuinely puzzled.

"The way you helped Mr. Calhoun and his wife. If you hadn't been there, he might have died."

"That's my job."

"You make it sound so . . . ordinary. You deserve more credit than that, Patterson. I thought you were wonderful."

He was frankly surprised—and then pleased by Deanna's comment. He didn't need any praise, but he had to admit it felt good, especially coming from her. He chuckled quietly.

"Betts used to tell me that whatever good deeds people do, it's with the grace of God."

"In other words, don't get full of yourself."

"Exactly."

"Well, maybe it's fair to say you had some help. But you knew what to do and you did it very well. That takes training and smarts and courage."

"Thanks," he said simply.

"You really like what you do, don't you?"

"Yeah, I do. How can you tell?"

"It shows."

A companionable silence settled over them as Patterson maneuvered through the late-Sunday-afternoon traffic headed into Manhattan. Deanna felt relaxed and safe. He was no longer a stranger. In fact, the events of the afternoon had closed the gap considerably between them.

"You were right that visiting your grandmother was a good idea. I think Jade enjoyed herself today."

"What about you?"

Deanna smiled. "I like your grandmother. She's very sweet."

"I don't know if I'd call Betts sweet. She's bossy, but kind."

"And Mr. Stanley is so charming. I have to agree with Jade, though. Stanley Stanley?" Deanna chuckled.

"His full name is Stanley W. Stanley," Patterson clarified.

"That doesn't help much."

Another car cut sharply in front of the Jeep, and Patterson applied the brakes hastily. Deanna's body jerked against her seat belt. Automatically, she checked to make sure that Jade was secure in hers.

The little girl sat slumped like a rag doll, Oliver held loosely in her arm, her potted plant in a plastic bag next to her.

Patterson noticed Deanna's concern. "So how come you don't have any of your own?"

Deanna didn't pretend not to understand. He was talking about children. She could have had a baby. One that would now be exactly Jade's age. Her expression softened. Whenever she played with Jade, whenever they lay sprawled on the sofa watching a video or sharing their meals, Deanna would think about what might have been.

"What makes you think I don't?" she asked softly.

He snorted under his breath. "Women like you don't have kids without the whole package."

"You're right. I believe in the traditional arrangement. I never wanted to raise a baby alone."

"Didn't want all the hard work?"

"No. I think I was afraid of not doing a good job."

"You don't have to worry about that. From where I sit you're doing real good with Jade."

She felt a warm glow at his words, not just because of his compliment but because of Jade. Jade had such amazing, insightful, and funny takes on everything in her small world. She had shown Deanna that parenthood was not only a responsibility but a privilege. Every time the child reached for her, Deanna experienced feelings of pleasure and gladness. She'd never known anything like it.

"To be honest, Patterson," she answered, "I never seriously thought of having children before."

"You have Jade now." He stopped, then added casually, "So how come you're not married? Career thing get in the way?"

She looked to see if he was being sarcastic. She

decided he wasn't. His face was mostly in silhouette, but it was well defined and without any soft lines. Deanna liked that about him. Everything about him was strong.

"I'll answer that if I can ask you the same thing."

"Why I'm not married? I came close once, for a hot minute. It was before I got accepted into the fire department. I was back in New York after getting out of the service. It didn't work out."

"Have any kids?"

"I have a son," he answered pensively.

A month ago she might have held that against Patterson.

"You don't sound very happy about it."

He didn't answer for a while.

"I've never seen him."

Deanna stared out the window. She had to admit that it didn't shock her to learn that he had a child, but not ever to have seen his own son . . .

"Is that by choice?" she asked.

"I didn't know about him for a long time. I found out a year or so ago. When I did find out . . ." He left the sentence unfinished and then shrugged.

"What?" she prompted.

"It's too late. He's sixteen, maybe seventeen years old. He's not going to want me in his life."

"Aren't you curious?"

"Of course I am."

"Then why don't you do something about it?"

"Like what?" he asked testily. "Find him and say, 'Hi, I'm your daddy. Sorry I wasn't around your whole life'?"

"Yes," said Deanna sweetly.

"Maybe he doesn't care."

"First of all, you don't know that. You've faced

hard choices before, Patterson. You learned how from Betts. You don't strike me as the kind of man who's afraid of very much. You can do this. Find your son and let him know who you are."

Listening to her, Patterson didn't hear blame or accusation in her voice. What he did hear was her challenging him. He wasn't going to admit he was flat-out scared. So he remained silent for the rest of the ride. But he was also thinking about Deanna's advice.

Patterson pulled the Jeep to the curb in front of Deanna's building and turned off the engine. They both just sat there. He wasn't sure why he didn't get out of the car, help Deanna and Jade out, and go on about his business. But the moment felt anticlimactic, as if they both needed to say something more. He turned to look at her as she did exactly the same to him.

Deanna hesitated before she spoke. He had given her a gift when he'd complimented her earlier. She wanted to give him something in return. "Can I say something else?" she asked. He gestured to go ahead. "Sometimes things happen over which we don't have any control. It's not important what happened or didn't happen between you and your son's mother. When you trust other people, what you risk is that they might do something to hurt you. It would be a shame if you missed out on the rest of your son's life because of your pride, and a relationship that didn't work out."

He shook his head, resigned. "I don't think it's that easy."

"Maybe not, but don't give up." She began to gather her things. "I hope I didn't spoil the day with personal questions," she said sincerely.

"I started it."

"Don't look at it that way. I'm not trying to win points. I'm . . . I'd like to understand you."

He regarded her serious expression. "Why?"

She shifted nervously, not sure what she was admitting to. "I feel I've been unfair, and wrong about you."

"Does this mean I pass? I'm not the shiftless, low-life brother you thought I was?"

"No, you're not," Deanna admitted with a shake of her head. "And I don't think I'm the stereotype you thought I was, either. A bitch and a snob. The thing is, you've been very helpful to me and terrific with Jade. I want you to know I'm glad you've been there for both of us."

He felt a little uncomfortable receiving her praise. "Yeah, well . . . I did it because I wanted to."

"I know that."

Deanna turned to Jade and found her just waking up from her nap. Deanna got out of the car as Patterson helped Jade from the backseat. Jade stood on the curb rubbing her eyes and reached to hold Deanna's hand.

"Would you like to come up for a while?" Deanna asked Patterson spontaneously.

"I have to get to the firehouse," he said. "Maybe another time."

They stood awkwardly, looking at each other. He felt Jade tugging on his arm.

"Patterson, don't go."

He pulled playfully on her hair. "I start work in about twenty minutes. How 'bout a big hug?"

Jade threw her arms out, and he gave her a quick, affectionate squeeze before stepping back.

"You be good."

"You didn't hug Deanna," Jade pointed out.

Deanna and Patterson were both startled by the comment.

"That's because these are special hugs, just for you," he said.

"But Deanna is special too."

Patterson turned to Deanna with a curious smile as she stood waiting. "Yes. She is."

He took a step forward, and so did she.

"You game?" he said softly.

"I can take it if you can."

He raised a brow. "Another challenge?" He stepped even closer, his arms coming around her.

She gazed up at him with teasing amusement, but Patterson did not hug her. He kissed her. Instinctively, though taken by surprise, she responded. It was a very light, quick kiss with real warmth. They drew back. Neither said a word. And neither paid any attention to Jade's childish giggle.

Then Patterson returned to the Jeep and started the engine.

" 'Bye, Patterson," Jade called, waving as the car pulled away.

Deanna hadn't recovered enough to say anything at all.

Then she felt Jade lightly hitting her arm to get her attention.

"Deanna, look."

"What?"

"There's my daddy."

Deanna spotted two men lounging near a newsstand kiosk, staring at them. One was Marcus Lowell. The other was shorter and heavier, and looked much more menacing and disreputable. Deanna drew Jade protectively to her side, wondering not only how long Marcus had been there watching, but how he had found out where she lived.

He began walking toward her, his friend remaining behind. Smiling brightly at his daughter, Marcus spread his arms.

"Hey, Jade. It's Daddy. Ain't you gonna give me a kiss? Come on and say hi to Daddy."

"You're not supposed to be here," Deanna said, holding tightly to Jade.

"You can't tell me nothin' 'bout where I'm supposed to be," he said. "You told some fuckin' lie to the authorities so you could keep her away from me and get money from welfare. That Temple guy is bullshitting you 'bout him just being Stacy's friend. He tried to muscle in on my territory. Now he's going to do the same with you. I saw you lip-locked with him."

Deanna could feel Jade silently shaking. From the corner of her eye Deanna saw Julio, the doorman, approaching to check if everything was all right. She took advantage of the moment.

"Need any help, Ms. Lindsay?"

"Hi, Julio. Yes. Do me a favor and keep an eye on Jade while I finish my conversation here. Jade, go ahead with Julio. I'll meet you in the lobby in a few minutes."

Deanna watched Julio escort Jade away. Jade craned her neck, casting confused glances at her father. When she was inside Deanna turned back to Marcus.

"What are you doing here?" She glanced beyond him to the other man, who kept moving around nervously, as if he was on the lookout for something.

"I came to see my kid."

"Look, you want to see Jade and spend time with her, it has to go through her caseworker at ACS."

"Fuck that. I don't need nobody's permission. How come Stacy left the kid with you? Who the fuck are you?"

Deanna stood her ground, knowing that Jade was out of earshot and that Julio was keeping an eye on her through the revolving doors.

"I was a friend of Stacy's. She wanted me to take care of Jade if anything happened to her. Stacy didn't even mention you."

"That's 'cause she knew what I was gonna do if I ever got hold of her," Marcus threatened. "Bitch turned me in to the cops. After all I did for her. But she's dead and that's over. I ain't going back. You got this nice place to live. You got money. I'm trying to get myself together, but it's hard, man. Nobody wants to give me a break. See . . . this is why guys like me go out and do shit, 'cause nobody gives a fuck. I'm trying to do right."

She wasn't sure she believed him. "What did you do before you went to jail?"

"I was working."

"Doing what? Was it legal?"

He narrowed his eyes and took a menacing step forward. "You accusing me of somethin'?"

"No. I'm just trying to find out if you can take care of Jade. She's been through a lot. Right now she needs stability, and I don't think you can give her that. Do you even have a place to live?"

"Up in the Heights."

"Marcus. Hurry up, man!" His companion was showing signs of impatience as he paced ten feet away.

Marcus waved for him to shut up.

"Look, I'm a little short. I gotta have decent clothes for when I go looking for work. I can't go like this, right?"

"That's not my problem." Deanna doubted that Marcus had showed up to complain about his wardrobe. He certainly hadn't come to visit Jade. He'd barely spoken to her. He'd made no threats. Deanna considered the consequences of what she was about to do, but she reached inside her purse to withdraw her wallet nevertheless.

"Maybe I can help out," she murmured, looking through the billfold. She withdrew three twenty-dollar bills and held them out. "Here. That's all I have on me. You can consider it a helping hand if you like." She tried to speak firmly, even though she felt nervous about what she was doing.

He didn't hesitate to take the money. "That's all you got?"

She didn't doubt that Marcus's whole plan was to try and hit her up for cash. But if giving him the money meant that he would forget about Jade, then she would do it gladly.

"That's all you're getting," she said, heading toward her building.

"You trying to bribe me?" he called after her, grinning as he pocketed the money. "Trying to make sure I stay away from Jade? No can do," he said, backing toward his waiting crony. "Jade belongs to me, not you. Go get your own fucking kid."

Deanna was stiff and tense when she entered the lobby, but she forced herself to smile at Jade as if all was right in the world.

"Come on, sweetie, let's go upstairs."

"Where's my daddy? Did he go away?" Jade asked.

"Yes," Deanna responded with relief as they boarded the elevator.

"Is he coming back?"

"I don't know."

I hope not, she thought fervently.

Patterson sat trying to finish the statistical report for the week. In the background was the sound of the TV playing low in the lounge area, although he knew no one was watching. Two members of his engine company were comparing notes on their respective love lives. From the sound of it, neither was doing so hot. Another man was studying the manual for the next advanced-placement test. Another was sleeping. He was grateful for the quiet of the night. So far there'd been no calls, no alarms. But the silence also played havoc with his mind.

Patterson stared at the telephone again, as he'd been doing off and on since coming on duty at nine, a little more than three hours ago. It was after midnight in New York—but only after nine in California. Still early.

He suddenly bounced forward in his chair and from the top drawer of his desk removed a worn black address book. He leafed through the pages, found the number he wanted and, before he could talk himself out of it, dialed. The phone rang three times before a pleasant female voice answered.

"Hello?"

"Yeah, hello. This is Pat Temple calling from New York."

"Yes?"

There was enough caution in the tone to let Patterson know that this was a different woman from the last time he'd called. That had been close to a year ago.

"I'm calling for Phil. I'm a friend of his."

"Just a moment."

Patterson realized he didn't know exactly what he intended to tell his old service buddy. Having to wait for Phil to answer only made it worse. He was already a little nervous and ready to hang up.

"Yeah?"

"Phil . . . it's Pat, man."

"Heeyyyy, man! How you doing?"

"Not too bad. Yourself?"

"Can't complain. Man . . . when was the last time we spoke?"

"Sometime last year in the summer. You called to say you're getting married. I didn't get an invitation."

Phil laughed sheepishly. "Yeah, well . . . it didn't work out."

"So I figured. Who answered the phone?"

"That was Audrey."

"The latest?"

"And greatest."

Patterson laughed. "That's what you always say."

"What can I tell you? Gotta keep runnin' that play 'til I get it right." He laughed heartily.

"This the real deal, or you just kickin' it for a while?"

"Man, I'm just having fun! If we make it to the church, you're my best man. But don't hold your breath."

"Thanks for the warning."

"What about you? Eleanor bagged your ass yet?"

Patterson sat back and propped his heavy boot on the edge of the desk. He pushed to begin rocking gently. The question jarred him—the thought of him and Eleanor being a permanent couple had never entered his mind. It was a moot point now, he realized with relief.

"I'm too young," Patterson quipped, for want of a better answer.

"It's been a long time, my man. When you coming out for a visit? You know, I can hook you up. There's serious action out here. It's true what they say about California girls."

"Thanks, but I'm holding my own. Besides, I'm not looking for no girl . . ."

"Let me know if you change your mind."

"Listen . . . I called because I need to ask a question."

"I can't loan you no kinda money, man, so forget it."

Patterson grinned. "You don't want to go there. You still owe me ten big ones from some lame game two years ago."

"You know I'm good for it, if you want it back. No problem."

"That's not it." Patterson shifted in his chair. "Remember that time when we got to San Diego on leave? We hung out with some local guys, went to a few parties."

"Yeah, I remember. Man, that was what . . . almost twenty years ago. We was just young bloods. And we had a good time, as I recall."

"Right. Well, there was this girl . . ."

"Felicia," Phil intoned with exaggerated reverence. "She was something else. What about her? Don't tell me you trying to find her?"

"As a matter of fact, I am."

"Yeah? How come? You still got a jones for her?"

Nervously Patterson sat forward again, resting his elbows on the desk, and rubbing a hand across his forehead. So much hinged on Phil's answer.

"I need to get some information from her." There was a pause on the line.

"You ain't gonna tell me, are you?"

"Right now, there's nothing to tell, Phil."

"Well, sorry to disappoint you, but I lost touch with her brother years ago. You know, you never asked me before about where she was or anything."

"I know," Patterson said, caught between disappointment and resignation.

"Look, there's someone else I can call to check this out. When do you need to know?"

"Whenever," Patterson said, trying to downplay his own urgency. But time was being lost. His son was growing up.

"I'll start making some calls this week."

A loud, persistent buzzer suddenly sounded throughout the firehouse. Instantly there was activity in the crew room, and the start of the engine motor on the first level. Patterson was out of his chair.

"Phil, gotta go. We have a call coming in."

"Right. You'll hear from me."

Patterson hung up and raced for the other room. He grabbed the pole and effortlessly slid down to the apparatus room where the engine vehicle was already moving. He got into his bunker gear and stepped into his boots, reaching for his hood and helmet as he jogged to reach the open door of the truck. He hopped on as it turned onto the street, the siren already emitting a piercing blare.

Patterson was quickly in the moment, going through a mental checklist and reading the printout of information on their destination as he consulted with the chauffeur. Nevertheless, he couldn't completely block out not only his disappointment but what Betts and even Deanna had said about finding his son.

For a while he'd convinced himself that it didn't matter. What he didn't know couldn't hurt him. But the lack of information left an empty space in his life.

Having witnessed the transformation in Deanna, who had risen to the occasion in caring for Jade Lowell, someone else's child, Patterson now realized that if he didn't try to find his son, he would regret it for the rest of his life.

Chapter Ten

Weaving her way between the closely arranged tables of Plum Tomato, a quirky café ten blocks from her office, Deanna followed the hostess. She spotted Joy already seated, her menu open over her plate, scowling pensively.

"Sorry I'm late," Deanna said, squeezing into her chair and putting the blue-and-white shopping bag she carried under the table.

"I'm sitting here waiting for you and you went shopping?" Joy said indignantly.

"I'm only ten minutes late. And don't even try to tell me you were here that much longer, Joy. I can't remember when you were last on time," Deanna said, opening her menu.

"I can't take extra time for lunch today. I'm meeting this afternoon with the defendants in a case. We're trying to get them to settle."

Deanna sipped her water. "I have to get back myself. I'm so far behind in my work . . ."

"What did you buy at the Gap?"

"Oh, you've got to see this," Deanna said. She reached under the table for the bag. "They were having a sale." She pulled out a small pink T-shirt for Joy's inspection. "Isn't this adorable? And look at this."

Joy frowned at a diminutive denim jumper that buttoned down the front.

"You've got to be kidding, Dee. You can't wear that to work."

Deanna made a face at her. "Very funny. Jade doesn't have a single girl outfit. Everything is jeans and T-shirts. Worn and old. I took a quick look in the Oshkosh store on Fifth the other day. They have some great children's things too. I'll have to stop by there later."

Joy was speechless, watching Deanna carefully fold the clothes and put them back into the bag. She noticed that Deanna's lipstick had worn off and hadn't been touched up. Her nails lacked even a clear coat, let alone colored polish. This from a woman who always looked well groomed and elegant. The last clue that her friend had lost it was that she was wearing a pantsuit, something Deanna herself had admitted she only did when she was out of pantyhose.

"Didn't you buy Jade new shoes last week?"

Deanna began scanning the menu. "Not shoes. Sneakers. I noticed that she was pulling hers off every chance she got. I finally realized she'd outgrown them. "What are you having?"

"The chopped salad without olives." Joy fiddled with the salt and pepper shakers absentmindedly. "You've been spending a lot of money on that child, you know."

Deanna shrugged. "It's not all that much. And like I told you, Jade didn't have a lot of things to begin with. I never knew before how hard kids are on their clothes."

Joy smiled wryly. "I could have told you that. Boys are the worst, which is why I insist on less expensive clothing and better made. Kids also have very expensive tastes. But you know, when it's your kid you do what you have to do."

Deanna gazed openly at Joy. "I know Jade isn't my child. Don't forget I wasn't even sure I wanted to be responsible for her. Now that I am, I can't neglect her needs."

"I think you've done more than you have to, considering that any day now Jade's family is going to show up to claim her."

Deanna picked up the thread of their conversation after the waitress had taken their order. "Well, I got a call from the police department. Of course everyone knows now that Stacy was using the Lowell name, but she was never married to Jade's father."

"What do you know about him?" Joy asked.

"He's an ex-convict. Black, about thirty."

"You've met him?"

"Unfortunately, yes. First at Stacy's funeral, and then again just a few nights ago."

"What's he like? What's the story with him and Stacy?"

Deanna spread her cloth napkin across her lap. "He's a good-looking hustler. The other night he showed up at my building. I'm a little nervous about him knowing where I live."

"Maybe he just wanted to see Jade. She *is* his daughter."

"That's what I thought at first, but he barely noticed Jade."

"What did he want?"

"Money."

Joy narrowed her gaze. "You didn't give him anything, did you?" Deanna grimaced. "That wasn't smart, Dee. You know he's going to hit you up for more."

"I just wanted him to go away. It wasn't much. I could tell he didn't have any."

"Don't be naive. I'm sure he has lots of creative ways of getting cash when he needs it. And don't think he's not going to show up again. How in the world did Jade's mother get involved with him, anyway?"

"I think he picked her up when she first came to New York. Betts said Stacy didn't have the greatest taste in men. She was needy and always picking losers."

"Didn't she stay with you for a while?"

"Almost a month."

"Sounds like a TV movie. Unbelievable," Joy said dryly. "What about Richard? You haven't mentioned him recently. What does he think of Jade?"

"He's only met her twice. The first time, he took Jade and me out to dinner at McDonald's."

Joy nearly choked. "Richard at McDonald's? Get out!"

"He did it for me. Jade's not ready for Ruby Foo's or Café des Artistes." Deanna sighed. "Richard and I had a fight last week, but he sent me flowers to make up for it."

"That was classy of him. He gets ten points. What was the fight about?"

"Jade. In a way. He asked me to attend a gala dinner with him at MOMA. I asked the daughter of one of my neighbors to baby-sit, but I was so worried about leaving Jade that I couldn't enjoy myself. Richard was *not* pleased," Deanna said.

Deanna's thoughts drifted back to that night. Once at the museum's gala, the kind of event she normally looked forward to, she could only think of Jade's tear-streaked face as she'd stood at the door with the baby-sitter, watching Deanna walk away. Just as Stacy had once done, never to return.

Richard had been less than happy about her distraction.

"What's going on? You didn't even say hello to Meredith Hampton when she walked by a moment ago. That's the second person you've snubbed tonight."

"I'm not snubbing anybody," Deanna retorted, annoyed. Instantly contrite, she placed her hand on the sleeve of Richard's tux. "I . . . didn't realize it was Meredith until she'd already moved on. I just—maybe this wasn't a good idea tonight. You know, with Jade . . ."

Richard grunted with exasperation. "Dee, you knew about tonight long before the kid came to live with you. I seem to recall telling you that she would change things."

"And I told you it's only temporary."

"Look, I'm trying to understand, okay? But tonight is important for me. See that young guy over there? He started a company that's now worth about thirty million. I want to tag him as a new client."

"I know that."

"Then can you make a little bit of an effort?"

Deanna could feel the heat of humiliation flush her skin. It wasn't that Richard was wrong, exactly, but there was something about his chastisement that felt particularly insulting. As if she didn't know better. As if what she did reflected on him personally.

"You can take care of yourself, Richard. Jade is a six-year-old child, and the way I see it, she's the only one who has *any* excuse to throw a tantrum."

"Fine," Richard said tightly. "So, you want to leave now?"

She started to. By herself. Then, realizing that they were both indulging in an unnecessary fit of temper, she forced herself to calm down and stay.

What Deanna didn't tell Joy was what had happened when Richard drove her home. By then, they'd talked, with promises to make up for the spoiled evening.

"I guess I should have been more understanding," Richard admitted, "but do you realize that we haven't had any time together until tonight? And we weren't alone."

"Missed me?"

"If you have to ask . . ."

At the apartment Deanna was relieved to learn from the young baby-sitter that Jade had been well behaved and had gone to bed without a problem. Deanna was secretly gratified when the sitter said that Jade didn't want her to read a story because the ones that Deanna made up were funnier.

While Richard paid the sitter and escorted her to the door, Deanna peeked in on Jade. The sitter had told her that Jade had insisted on sleeping in Deanna's bed. Deanna was not only *not* surprised to find her there, snuggled with Oliver, but also had the oddest sensation that it was okay and right. That she and Jade were part of each other. By trusting the care of her daughter to Deanna, Stacy had inadvertently helped her resolve her feelings about having children of her own.

Deanna found Richard lounging on the sofa. He patted the cushions, and she stepped out of her shoes and went to sit in front of him, leaning back against his chest. Richard hooked his arm around her shoulders.

Deanna turned her face to welcome his kiss. Richard's mouth was demanding and urgent, rushing her from one sensation to the next. She wanted him to make love to her because she needed the closeness. But . . . it didn't feel right.

She was startled to find an image of Patterson Temple in her mind. As she'd seen him last, when he'd kissed her good-bye.

She pulled away with a soft gasp. "Richard . . . this isn't a good idea."

"Just for a little while, Dee," he crooned, his voice already hoarse with desire.

He captured her mouth again, more seductive and focused this time. Deanna found herself torn between the urge to give in and the need to make him stop. She wondered if Patterson knew anything about foreplay and affection. He was a man whose latent sexuality could dispel any resistance or hesitation. He was the kind of man who would overwhelm a woman with a seduction that might not be gentle, but would be powerful and enticing.

She pulled her mouth free. "Richard—" she said again, bracing her hand on his chest. "I can't."

"Why not?" he asked even as Jade's voice called out from the bedroom.

"Deanna?"

Deanna jumped, scrambling to pull herself out of Richard's arms, while trying to straighten the bodice of the formal dress.

"Jade? Honey, what are you doing up? You should be asleep." Jade appeared from the dark hallway. Deanna sat with her back to Richard, half shielding him from the little girl.

Jade's hair was a loose mane, and her eyes were squinting and blinking against both sleep and the glow of a living room lamp. She hesitated a moment when she saw Richard, then came right up to Deanna, who put a reassuring arm around her.

"I heard a noise," Jade explained in her soft, high voice. "I got scared."

"I'm sorry," Deanna said, patting Jade's back, kissing her forehead. "I . . . bumped into the table."

Jade peeked around Deanna at Richard, who had remained stretched out on the sofa, breathing deeply with his eyes closed.

"What's he doing? Is he sleeping?"

Deanna turned to Richard, her gaze apologetic. "No, he's not asleep." She stood up, discreetly shaking out the dress to drape around her appropriately. "Come on, sweetheart. You need to get back to sleep. You have school tomorrow." Deanna took Jade by the hand and attempted to lead her back to the bedroom.

Jade kept looking over her shoulder. "Is he going to spend the night, too?"

Richard sat up abruptly, swinging his feet to the floor and regarding Jade with a bemused twist of his mouth. He lifted his shoulders and shrugged. "There's no room for me," he said.

"You can sleep on the sofa," Jade offered innocently.

Richard couldn't help grinning. He shook his head and stood up, catching Deanna's gaze to let her know it was okay. "Thanks, but I think you have the best spot."

Deanna escorted Jade back to bed. She explained that it was much too late for a story, but promised to tell her two the next night. She was taken aback when the little girl reached up to hug her, her small body warm and loving against her chest.

Deanna returned the embrace on an indescribable

wave of emotion. She kissed Jade's cheek and tucked her under the covers.

"Are you coming to sleep now?" Jade asked, her eyelids already closing.

"In a minute. I have to say good-bye to Richard."

In the living room Deanna was not surprised to find Richard back in his jacket and ready to leave. She thought he'd be angry. Instead, he expressed humor and an air of resignation.

Deanna spread her hands helplessly. "Richard, what can I say?"

"It's okay," he forestalled her. "I should have known that children and pets are great at grabbing the spotlight."

"It's not like that," Deanna said.

"I know that, too. But what about me? What about *us*?" he asked seriously. "How much longer is this supposed to go on?"

Deanna was not about to ask Richard if he meant how long before they would make love again, or how long before Jade left. The answer to either question seemed fraught with uncertainty. She had no intention of trying to figure it out at that moment.

"I don't know," Deanna said honestly.

"I hope it's soon, Dee. I can see you've got your hands full. Maybe we should just put a hold on things for a while." He kissed her forehead and left.

Deanna knew that Richard had not been threatening her, or giving her an ultimatum. But she also knew that he was right. Something had to give.

The next day she'd received his flowers.

"No man ever sent me flowers to apologize when he was wrong," Joy observed.

Deanna let Joy believe the flowers were for Richard's less-than-understanding attitude about Jade.

"Richard is a decent man. He's the flower-sending kind," Deanna explained.

"I'd hate to think that Richard was so thoughtful because he's white," Joy said. "What does he know that the brothers don't?"

"Maybe we've set our sights too high," Deanna suggested. "How many black men are there with M.B.A., Ph.D., LL.D. or M.D. after their names who aren't married, gay, or chronic womanizers?"

"There's no such thing as aiming too high. Why would I want some man who's less educated, doesn't make nearly as much money as I do, doesn't own a tux, and has never heard of Bill T. Jones?"

Deanna laughed, both amused and saddened by Joy's observation. There was a certain truth in what she said. But Deanna knew that finding a do-right black man was hard enough without adding qualifiers like money, status, and advanced degrees. She herself had been accused of sidestepping the issue by going with a white man. She was finding out, however, that dating a man of a different race didn't solve anything.

Skin color was a totally false indicator of a man's real worth.

Deanna smiled absently at the receptionist as she hurried to her office. She was late getting back from lunch.

" 'Scuse me, Ms. Lindsay," the receptionist said.

Deanna slowed down and turned back. "Yes, Gloria?"

"Did you get the envelope that came this morning from the news division?"

Deanna thought for a moment. "I don't remember seeing it."

"One of your staff people said she'd give it to you. She was just coming back from the ladies' room."

"Do you know who?" Deanna asked.

"Young woman with dark hair. She picked up something here yesterday, too."

Deanna nodded. "Maybe my assistant has it on his desk."

"Maybe," Gloria said, none too convincingly. "I don't want to mind anybody's business, but she's always asking if there's anything for you."

"Is there any particular reason why you're mentioning it now?"

"So I don't have to give her anything else that comes for you without your say-so. I don't want anybody coming back to me saying it's my fault if something didn't get where it was supposed to."

Deanna easily read between the lines. "I agree. You shouldn't get caught in the middle. Consider this a direct request. From now on, don't give any mail or packages addressed to me to anyone except me or my assistant, Stephen Adler."

"Thanks." Gloria nodded.

Deanna stopped at Stephen's desk on her way to her office. "Did someone bring you an envelope from the reception area yesterday or today?"

Stephen turned away from his computer screen. "Nope. I would have remembered. I log in all the packages."

"One was delivered from News. Can you track it down? Then draft a memo from me to Reception. Mail and special deliveries are NOT to be given to anyone but you. If there are any questions, they're to call me directly. I'll sign the memo when I get back. I'll be in the studio office."

Stephen frowned. "You have a meeting I don't know about?"

"Matt and Peter."

"Your boss, and your boss's boss? The big brass."

"That's right," she responded, putting her lunchtime purchases in her office and taking off her coat. She smiled brightly at Stephen as she headed for the studio offices. "Maybe we're being nominated for an Emmy."

The last time she'd visited the network's executive offices, on the eighteenth floor, it was to explain new information procedures. The eighteenth floor was where all the offices of the station's head honchos were located, suites that included private lavatories, a four-star dining room, and a fully equipped fitness center. It was a place of power where the uninvited did not stand a chance of getting past the reception area. The studios where Deanna usually had her meetings were in another part of the same building. Even the rich and newsworthy who passed through the halls on their way to makeup and finally in front of the cameras did not wield the power of the executive suites.

Matt Wolff came out to the reception area, pleased to see Deanna, and escorted her into his office. Gesturing toward the seating area with windows that overlooked the New York city skyline, he requested that she sit down.

She sank into the plush chair. "I thought Peter was joining us."

"I decided it wasn't necessary."

Matt closed his door and took a seat facing her.

"Did you want to see me so you don't forget what I look like?" Deanna teased.

"Hey, I would never forget what you look like.

You're prettier than the crew, and we couldn't do our job without you."

"Thanks for the compliment," Deanna smiled. "I'll take as many as I can get."

"Usually you don't need them."

Deanna watched him closely. "Is there a problem, Matt?"

"I have to tell you, Deanna, I'm a little concerned that maybe you're not really focused on the job. I don't want any executive producer to get substandard work from you or your department."

"You make it sound like there have been a lot of mistakes."

"More than there should be," he confirmed. "Are there any problems in your department? Maybe I can help."

Deanna realized that this was her second warning. Telling him her suspicions about Nancy Kramer would be admitting she couldn't handle her staff. She shook her head. "Thanks for your concern. There's nothing to discuss from my end. Can you give me some examples of what you've been getting from the library in response to your research questions?"

Deanna listened closely as Matt outlined some of the problems he'd encountered. She was astonished to hear the details. Clearly Nancy had done more than take it upon herself to fulfill Matt's needs; Deanna now suspected that Nancy was deliberately attempting to sidestep Deanna's authority and raise questions about her credibility. But Deanna had to keep that awareness to herself. Right now she had no proof of Nancy's agenda, only her gut instinct that something was amiss.

"I've instituted a review of procedures that should

solve the discrepancies we've had in releasing projects that are still in draft stage."

She outlined some of the changes she had in mind. She also realized that it would probably be a very good idea to begin to document Nancy's actions . . . for the record. Just in case. Most important, she assured Matt that the information center would be on the ball in the future.

He walked her to the door. "That's good to know. Don't worry. This discussion won't leave this room."

She was glad to hear it, but Matt's discretion wasn't what Deanna was worried about.

Deanna had always considered herself to be a fair supervisor. She believed that the way to get the best work out of her staff was to treat them as professionals, delegate responsibility, and avoid micro-managing their activities. Except when a member of her staff acted too independently or when her own job came under fire, as seemed to be happening now.

Nancy had come to her with strong credentials and several years' experience. Her ability to multitask was precisely why Deanna thought she'd be a valuable addition. True, Nancy's previous place of employment had not been as busy or demanding as the station's information center, but it should have been a simple matter of training Nancy and then giving her time to rise to the level of performance expected. But Deanna had not counted on the possibility that Nancy had an attitude problem. Or a hidden agenda.

Deanna recalled recent comments from the other staff members. Although they'd made no outright complaints, Ruth and Stephen in particular had shown a hesitancy and caution when talking about Nancy. Deanna now began to add up the little incidents and things that didn't seem right, which had raised warning flags in her mind. They were the sort of things she felt but couldn't prove, and which needed to be watched. What if Nancy's goal was sabotage? What if that sabotage was motivated by personal ambition? Or by racism?

Deanna still had to be careful. Nancy was too smart to make blatant attacks. But her daily work was something Deanna could closely monitor and redirect. So far, nothing Nancy had done was a hanging offense. But she certainly warranted watching.

Deanna also wondered, how was she to watch her own back? For the moment she had to give Nancy the benefit of the doubt. But not more than once.

Returning to the information center, she went directly to the conference room. She called Nancy inside and, as Matt had done, quietly closed the door.

"I want you to cover the reference desk for the next few days," Deanna instructed. "As you know, Ruth has been forced to take personal time away, and I need to have someone with your experience to handle the reference requests."

"Of course." Nancy nodded, always pleasant and self-effacing.

Deanna looked at her pointedly. "However, any questions from the news division are to come directly to me. Call me on my cell phone if I'm out of the office."

"There's no need to bother you. I can handle research for the news team."

"This request is not open for discussion, Nancy. I've given you specific instructions. I expect them to be followed."

Nancy seemed mildly offended. "I know that. I always make sure I do the work."

"Your dedication is appreciated," Deanna observed

carefully, "but let me make myself clear. I'm in charge. I don't want you to forget that."

She dismissed Nancy and started back to her office. Passing the reference desk, she heard Marianne call out, "Stephen just asked if I'd seen you."

Deanna frowned. "Problems?"

Marianne shrugged. "Not here."

Deanna picked up her pace. What could have gone wrong in the forty-five minutes she'd been occupied with Matt and then Nancy?

Stephen was on the phone when she approached his desk, and when he saw her he quickly hung up.

"I just called Matt Wolff's office, but he said you'd already left. You got a call from the Hayden School."

Deanna's heart seemed to stop. "That's Jade's school . . . What happened? Is she all right?"

"They didn't say. Just told me to tell you to get over there as soon as you can."

Deanna rushed into her office to get her purse. Already she was imagining the worst.

"I'll call the guard in the lobby and ask him to flag down a cab," Stephen offered, picking up the phone and punching in numbers.

"Thanks," she said, emerging with her coat over her arm. "Tell Marianne I had an emergency and she's to cover the office. I've assigned Nancy to reference. And I'd appreciate it if you could stay with her until after the six o'clock broadcast begins. I'll call you later to see how things are going."

"I hope it's nothing serious, Deanna," Stephen said.

"Me too," she replied, heading for the elevator.

A cab was waiting for her at the curb when she rushed out of the building. After giving the driver the address of Jade's school, she called the assistant principal on her cell phone.

"Is Jade all right? What happened?" she asked.

"I didn't mean to alarm you, Ms. Lindsay. Jade had a minor mishap. She's okay. It's school policy to call parents whenever any child gets hurt."

"Hurt?"

"Not seriously. I'll explain when you get here. Jade will be in my office."

School was ending for the day when Deanna arrived. Children were rushing out in a boisterous horde, their loud voices filling the air. She maneuvered as quickly as she could through the milling kids and made her way to the office. The secretary pointed to an open door.

"She's in there."

Deanna spotted Jade sitting in a chair just inside the door. "Jade, honey . . ."

She bent over to scrutinize the child. Jade looked forlorn, her face marked by dried tears. There was a cut on her lip, and she had scrape marks on her chin, cheek, and forehead. The scrunchie from her ponytail was gone, and her hair fanned out from her head. Her eyes were still awash with tears and, seeing Deanna, she looked like she would begin to cry again.

"What happened?" Deanna asked, horrified, holding Jade's chin and turning her face to examine the scrapes.

"I had a fight," Jade muttered. "See . . ."

She opened her mouth and tilted her face toward Deanna. There was a tooth missing on the bottom row.

Deanna gasped softly. "Oh, sweetheart . . ."

"I'm glad you're here," came a voice from behind her.

Deanna stood as the assistant principal, Rosemary Battle, returned to her office. "What fight did she get into? Did you see her face?" Deanna asked, incredulous and angry.

Ms. Battle looked uncomfortable. "We do everything we can to prevent fights, Ms. Lindsay, but sometimes they happen. The schoolyard aides broke up the fight as quickly as possible. Jade will heal. And so will the other child." She beckoned to Jade. "Why don't you wait outside with the secretary for just a minute, okay?"

Jade obediently left the office.

"Sit down, please." Mrs. Battle gestured toward a chair in front of the desk.

Deanna sat, impatient for an explanation. "Jade lost a tooth, for God's sake. She could have been seriously hurt."

"Ms. Lindsay, I understand that you're upset. And, of course, as her guardian, you should be. But parents understand that this happens. Accidents happen. Fortunately, it wasn't serious."

Rosemary Battle took a small wad of tissue out of her desk drawer and passed it to Deanna, who unfolded it. She found a tiny white tooth on the bloodstained center. She wrapped it up again and put it into her purse.

She was incensed over the assistant principal's comment about parents and didn't believe for an instant that a birth mother could be any more upset than she was. But that was not the issue here. And Deanna knew how to pick her battles.

The phone call from the school had taken a year off her life. Jade's bruised face had pulled at her heart and made her fiercely protective. Was she overreacting?

"You can see it's a baby tooth," Mrs. Battle reassured her. "Jade's teacher said it was a little loose to begin with."

"There are also scratches on her face," Deanna said, keeping her voice level. "I want her to see a doctor to make sure there are no other injuries."

"I did a superficial once-over, and Jade seems fine. I believe you've seen the worst of her injuries."

"What started the fight?" Deanna asked. "Jade is not an aggressive child."

"This is not the first trouble Jade has had. There have been a few minor incidents since her first day here."

"Why wasn't I told before?"

"Children shove one another all the time. They chase each other around the schoolyard, or get into arguments over school materials, or whatever. As an educator I see it as part of their socialization."

"Mrs. Battle, 'incident' does not sound like a little shoving match."

"Jade is a little . . . different," Mrs. Battle tried again. "Unfortunately, that has made her the target of some of her classmates."

"You're telling me Jade is being harassed because she's biracial? And that you didn't think it was important enough to discuss with me? Jade should not be hurt in school because other children are intolerant."

"I agree, Ms. Lindsay. By the same token, one of the things she'll no doubt have to learn for herself is how to deal with her peers. Neither you nor any school can shield her from that."

Deanna stared at her hands. She felt tired. Overwhelmed. And scared. "I know."

"Maybe you should have a talk with her."

"I have. I'll try again."

"And again, if you have to. Would it help you to know that Jade is doing really well here? She has friends. She's quick in class and generally well behaved. We can't monitor the children one hundred percent of the time, but we do our best. Jade is surprisingly well adjusted, considering all that she's gone through. You should be proud of that."

"I *am* proud of her."

"Jade held her own. I don't think it's necessary to suspend either child in this case. I think I can assure you that in a day or two both will have forgotten it. And, of course, I'll keep an eye on the situation now that we know about it."

Deanna stood up to leave. "I'm sorry if I came in full of fire."

"Oh, don't apologize. You have a right to be protective of her. Under the circumstances she *is* your child. Do you know that Jade calls you her mother?"

Patterson watched from the rig's window as Eddie took up a position in the street, his job to stop traffic as the truck turned ninety degrees in order to back into the apparatus floor. Patterson nodded in approval. Though not thoroughly seasoned, Eddie was doing a good job of keeping his eye on the angle of the truck while monitoring pedestrian and vehicular traffic.

"I think Billy's gonna have to call it a day, Captain," said Kevin, the chauffeur driving the rig. "He really pulled his knee taking out that heater. I can't believe he got messed up on a stupid thing like that."

"It could have been worse. Make sure he's signed off the rest of this tour," Patterson ordered. He jumped out of the truck as it coasted to a stop.

"When we're off, check the roster, will you, and see who we can reschedule for the rest of Billy's shift."

"Sure thing."

Before the truck had come to a complete stop, most of the men had already disembarked and were stripping off their heavy gear. While unhooking the closures on his coat, Patterson headed for the dispatch office to record the results of the run, a fire in a basement wall behind a hot water heater. He felt a heavy tap on his shoulder.

"Hey, Captain. He's here again," Gary said.

Patterson placed his helmet on the desk and faced the house watch attendant. "Who's here?"

"Remember a couple of weeks ago I told you some kid was asking about you? He's outside."

Patterson frowned. "You sure he wants to see me?"

Gary unhooked his heavy rubberized coat and shrugged out of it. "I thought he was family or something like that. You got a kid brother?"

Patterson chortled. "No, I don't have a . . ." He stopped abruptly, making the connection. "Where did you say he was?"

"When the rig was coming in, he was standing to the left."

"I didn't see him," Patterson said, pushing past and out the office. "That's the driver's side—"

The bay door was still open and he hurried outside. No one. Patterson turned to Gary, who had followed him out. "What did he look like? I mean, what did he have on?"

"Jeans and orange hiking boots. A windbreaker, dark color. And a cap. Raiders, I think."

Patterson went to the middle of the street, standing so that he could see the entire length of the block in both directions. He spotted a retreating figure heading east. He began jogging, hampered by his heavy boots.

"Hey!" Patterson called out. "Wait a minute. You. In the cap."

The tall, thin teenager turned and stared. Stopping dead in his tracks, Patterson stared right back. His throat felt like it was closing off air to his lungs. He let his eyes take in everything. His height—not quite as tall as himself; his clothing—typical of a teen but with taste and style. His attitude—nervous but open. His features—

"Jesus." Patterson didn't have a single doubt that he was looking at his son.

His heart was pounding in his chest. It was one thing to wonder what it would be like to actually see his son face-to-face, another to know once and for all that the boy was real. Patterson was afraid to speak, afraid to move. It didn't help that the boy was waiting for him to do something. Or that the look in his son's eyes wasn't exactly warm and welcoming.

"You've been asking about me," Patterson finally said.

The boy shifted from foot to foot. "Yeah, that's right."

Patterson swallowed. He'd always imagined his son as a small boy with a little boy's voice and mannerisms. Standing before him was a grown male on the verge of adulthood, his voice already deepening, his face no longer holding any trace of the small boy he'd been.

Trying to absorb every detail, Patterson took a cautious step closer. He noticed the shape of the mouth and chin, a faded scar at the corner of one eye, the dark gaze behind which the boy concealed his feelings. Patterson had learned how to do that himself, many years ago. After his mother had died. After finding out that a woman he'd known for only a few weeks had neglected to tell him she'd gotten pregnant with his child some fifteen years earlier. He'd felt used and betrayed. Angry. Confused. Just the way his son was apparently feeling now.

"Do you know who I am?"

The teen swallowed, his Adam's apple bobbing. He licked his lips and nodded, averting his gaze. "Yeah, I know who you are."

Patterson began to sweat under his gear. "Why don't you tell me, then? Who am I?"

"You're my father," he said. "But you don't know anything about me."

Patterson heard the underlying accusation. He wasn't surprised, but he didn't know what to do about it.

"You're right. I don't. Anything I say to you right now is going to sound lame. I should have known about you, but I didn't. I swear to God, I didn't. So, now what do we do?"

The boy shook his head. "I don't know . . . I gotta go . . ." He turned to walk away.

"Wait. Why did you want to see me?"

The boy shrugged, retreating a step back. "I just wanted to see you, that's all."

"Why?" Patterson asked again, unable to keep the urgency from his voice. "I was waiting for you to come back," Patterson said quickly, taking liberties with the truth. "One of my men told me you'd been around, asking for me." The boy said nothing, but he didn't leave either. "What's your name?"

"Drew."

A thin rivulet of perspiration trickled down the side of Patterson's face to his chin. "Drew—what?"

"Cannon."

Jesus . . . Jesus, Patterson kept repeating to himself. He closed his eyes, overcome with emotion, paralyzed by fear and shame. "Cannon . . ."

Drew shrugged and turned his face away. Patterson suspected he was fighting back tears, and he wasn't going to say anything that would make them come and embarrass the boy. He wanted to call Drew his son. He didn't know if he had that right. What happened next might determine if he ever would.

"It took a lot of guts to come looking for me, Drew. I wish I'd tried to find you when I heard that I had a grown son. I didn't know what I could say to you. I've been scared as hell that you wouldn't want to see me. Maybe you wouldn't even—"

"I gotta go. I'm supposed to be somewhere."

"Drew . . ." Patterson called after him as the teen started walking away. After ten feet or so he stopped. "I'm glad you made the first move, man. Do you think . . . can we meet again sometime? Maybe on one of my days off? We can talk."

"I don't know."

"So you were only curious? Was seeing me enough?"

"I . . . don't know."

"It's not enough for me," Patterson said, frustrated. He wasn't prepared for this. It had happened so unexpectedly. All the missed years that could never be made up. "Wait, don't leave yet." He opened his coat, his sweat-soaked shirt sticking to his body. He forced his hand into his trouser pocket and pulled out several business cards. "Here." He handed one to the boy.

Drew stared at it for a moment before finally taking it.

"That's the firehouse number." Patterson took it back and flipped the card over. "You have a pen on you?"

Drew pulled one out of the side pocket of his knapsack and handed it to Patterson.

"I'm putting my home number on the back. And my cell phone." He glanced at Drew. "Does your . . . mother know you've been looking for me?"

"Not yet."

"Are you going to tell her?"

"Maybe," he said. He took the card back again and put it into his pocket.

"What do you think is going to happen when she finds out?"

"She'll probably get mad 'cause I did it without telling her. But she'll probably be scared, too."

"What does she have to be scared about?" Patterson asked.

"That I might like you and want to spend time with you. If you'd let me."

Patterson swallowed hard and flexed his jaw to hold his emotions in check. He nodded. "I'd let you. So what are you going to do?"

The boy shrugged. "I have to think about it."

Patterson remained where he was, watching the tall teen walk away, his gait confident, his posture erect. He tried to remember everything about the few minutes he'd just spent in his son's company, knowing full well it might be the first and last time they'd ever meet.

Betts hummed along to the gentle strumming of Patterson's guitar as she folded a dishcloth around the handle of the oven door. She swept her hand once more over the counter and felt nothing but a smooth, clean surface, free of crumbs and food residue. She checked the foil seal over the two glass dishes of food that she'd packed for Patterson to take with him when he went home. After turning out the light, she walked into the small living room where her grandson was sitting on the ottoman, leaning over his guitar, absorbed in the fingering of the piece he was playing.

Betts sat in her E-Zee Boy lounger just behind him and fanned herself with the evening paper. She closed her eyes and listened until he strummed the last chord of her favorite hymn.

"I love that piece, Pat. You sure play better than Mr. Stanley does on the church organ. But don't you go tellin' him I said so."

He didn't answer, instead staring pensively into space. He plucked again on the strings, but there was no melody in the random notes.

"I know he's on your mind and you want to see him again. Do you think he'll call?"

Patterson shrugged. "I don't know."

"What if he doesn't?"

"I don't know that either, Betts."

"Well, you should, Pat. I didn't raise you to give up at the first sign of difficulty, and Lord knows there's plenty of it in our lives. I told you, you have to understand that child is scared, and he's angry. You know, come to think of it, he reminds me of Jade just after her mother was killed. Kids don't understand how things go wrong in grown-ups' lives. They just want to feel safe and be loved. If you want to get to know your son, you need to give him a little time to get used to who you are. And you have to roll up your sleeves and do some of the hard work."

Patterson set the guitar aside, leaning it against the coffee table. He faced his grandmother with his forearms braced on his knees.

"Was I a lot of work?"

"You sure were," she said with a huff. "Thought you were going to send me to an early grave. It was when you got to be your own son's age that I worried the most. You know, there's so much going on out there in the street, it would have killed me if you'd gotten mixed up with the wrong crowd."

"I don't think there was much chance of that. I never wanted to disappoint you."

"Darlin', your Betts loves you more than life itself. You're my baby. Drew, that's a good name. Does he look like you?"

He nodded. "You can tell he's my son. I think he walks like me, too."

"Lord have mercy," she murmured.

"I didn't want to do it this way, Betts. I thought I'd meet someone, fall in love, we'd get married and have kids. We'd raise them together and—I didn't want to be like some other black guys who don't care."

"Hush now, darlin'. Sometimes God has something else in mind for us. You got to trust in Him."

He smiled at his grandmother. "You trust in Him enough for both of us."

"The boy'll call. You mark my words. He come looking for you 'cause he wanted to know his daddy. That's a good sign, you know."

"I hope so."

"I used to think that you and Eleanor were going to make a go of it together—"

"We've broken off. I'm sorry."

"You don't have to be sorry on my account. You didn't have a say in raising this boy, but that don't mean you can't have other children." She leaned back in the recliner, a mischievous grin tickling her lips. "To tell the truth, Pat, I like that other young woman."

He frowned at her. "Who said I'd like someone like her?"

"The first thing you got to do is stop thinking that Deanna is better than you. And forget all this business about where she went to school and who her people are. You've got to listen to your heart."

"Betts . . ." he began patiently.

"Don't 'Betts' me."

"I don't think *she* thinks I'm good enough for her."

"That's 'cause you probably acting like you're not. Let me tell you something, Patterson Temple. Any woman would be damned lucky to get you. Forgive me, Lord," she said, rolling her eyes to the ceiling and placing a hand over her heart.

Patterson laughed quietly at his grandmother's staunch support.

"There is only one question that matters," Betts said firmly. "Do you like her or not?"

Patterson realized he couldn't answer. At least not with the choices Betts had given him. There was a third choice.

Maybe.

Chapter Eleven

Patterson heard the phone ringing the moment he entered the vestibule of his converted brownstone. He dug out his keys, juggling his dry cleaning and a bag of groceries. He worked the double lock and had the door open on the fourth ring, just as the answering machine picked up. He dumped his bundles in a heap onto the leather sofa in the media room and stretched to reach the cordless on the chrome-and-glass end table.

"Yeah," Patterson said into the receiver when the answering machine cut off.

There was no response, but he could tell that the line was open. He listened intently.

"Hello?" Finally, tentatively, he said, "Drew?"

After a few seconds the line was disconnected. Patterson clutched the phone, muttering an oath. Meeting his son had been the single most incredible fifteen minutes of his life. Since then he'd been wondering if Drew would reach out again. He sighed in frustration and replaced the receiver in its cradle.

For the hundredth time Patterson wondered if it had been a mistake not to have asked Drew where he was staying. He understood instinctively that the boy wasn't ready to trust him, but that didn't make the waiting any easier.

He walked into his bedroom with the dry cleaning and, without removing the protective plastic, hung it all in his closet. Then he retrieved the groceries he'd left on the sofa and carried them upstairs to the kitchen.

He checked the time. He had a rehearsal with his band, 4-Alarm, in half an hour, but suddenly he didn't want to leave. Just in case his son called again.

Patterson put the groceries away and took out a can of soda, which he carried back downstairs with him. In the media room, where he spent most of his time, was a big-screen TV, a desk with his computer, audio racks filled with professional-quality equipment, and hundreds of CD's, mostly blues and jazz.

On small metal stands were two guitars, an acoustic Martin and a Yamaha that had been converted to electric.

And there was his portable phone.

He sat down in a chair and propped his feet on the matching ottoman. Sighing deeply, he scrubbed both hands roughly up and down his face. There wasn't a thing he could do.

Drew Cannon . . .

He had a son. He was a father.

"Man," Patterson whispered to himself. He took a long, chilling gulp from his soda.

Until Drew Cannon, aged seventeen, had materialized outside the firehouse, he existed only in Patterson's mind, as a phantom, without size or shape . . . or a face. But now he was not only flesh and blood; even more, Drew Cannon, Patterson realized in awe, was irrevocably a part of him.

Patterson recalled when he'd first met Drew's mother. Felicia had been beautiful, flirtatious, and fun. On leave from the navy for several weeks, Patterson knew that when he left San Diego, he would go his way and she'd go hers. He thought he'd taken all the proper precautions for a short-term affair. Felicia had said she was on the Pill. He hadn't known until more than fifteen years later that she'd nevertheless become pregnant. He'd never wanted to fit the profile of the irresponsible black man. He'd seen too much of it when he was growing up. Betts had always cautioned him to do the right thing, and he'd always understood what she meant. He still sometimes believed it had been his fault, that he'd failed a test of manhood.

He knew that Betts thought that Deanna was a good person, capable of loyalty and faithfulness. Someone who believed in tradition. She set standards for herself, so he could hardly fault her for wanting the same in a man.

But Deanna Lindsay was definitely out of his league.

As Deanna finished smoothing the coverlet on her bed, placing the two pillows against the headboard, she realized she was standing on something.

"Jade? I think I found your other sock," she said, bending to pick it up. "Are you getting dressed?"

She followed the sound of a kitchen chair scraping across the vinyl floor, stumbling over one very small sneaker just inside the living room.

Evidence of Jade's presence was everywhere. Books and toys and clothing. What wasn't in a wicker basket Deanna had purchased to use for Jade's things was on or under the TV cart. Anything breakable had been removed to a higher shelf.

Deanna saw the matching sneaker under an end

table and dropped the one she held next to it, so that the child could find them both later.

"Jade, what are you doing?" Deanna entered the kitchen and stopped short.

"I'm making breakfast," the little girl said brightly. She held a heavy container of milk poised over a bowl of cereal.

She was partially dressed, in a long-sleeved cotton T-shirt and yellow panties, the partner sock to the one Deanna had found in her bedroom adorning one foot. She had pulled a chair from the dining table into the small kitchen and used it to reach the cabinet where the cereal was kept. The refrigerator door stood open and the flatware drawer hung at an odd angle.

"What did I say about leaving the fridge door open like this?" Deanna shut the door, closed the silverware drawer, and took the milk container from Jade in several fluid movements.

"I can do it," Jade said as Deanna finished pouring milk on her cereal and returned the container to the refrigerator.

"I know you can. I'm just helping a little." She gave Jade the sock. "Put this on."

"Okay," Jade said, sitting on the floor.

"Didn't I tell you to fill the plastic measuring cup with cereal first and *then* empty it into the bowl?"

"I forgot," Jade said, standing up. She carefully lifted the bowl and carried it to the dining table.

"I was going to make French toast with bacon."

Deanna put two slices of raisin bread in the toaster for herself and began microwaving a cup of water to make tea. She tore off a paper towel and walked to the table, where she put it under Jade's cereal bowl as a place mat.

Jade's eyes lit up. "Can I have French toast, too?"

Deanna grinned at her elfin expression, a hole in her smile because of the missing tooth.

"Finish your cereal. I'll make French toast tomorrow."

"I like when you make that," Jade said, spooning cereal into her mouth. "My mommy never made it for me."

"Don't talk with your mouth full," Deanna said automatically, getting butter for her toast and a teabag from a canister on the counter, then joining the little girl at the table. As Deanna ate her breakfast, she fielded endless questions and "Can I have" requests.

When Jade had first come to stay with her, Deanna had been reluctant to deny her anything. Since then it had gotten easier to say no and not only to threaten consequences for bad behavior but also to follow through on them. Deanna had to admit she enjoyed the chance to shop for lovely little outfits for Jade. She thought she was being a concerned guardian. Carla and Joy, however, accused her of trying to make Jade into her own image. Carla, in particular, questioned many of her decisions.

"You got her *what*?" her sister had asked incredulously when Deanna told her she'd bought Jade two Barbie dolls. "They're so retro. So . . . politically incorrect."

"They're toys," Deanna said. "I got them for a reason."

"I hope not as a model of what Jade should try to be when she grows up."

"Why not? In case you never noticed, Barbie is not a baby doll. She's a grown-up woman with all kinds of careers. There's even a Barbie in a wheelchair."

"That's awful," Carla scoffed.

"That's real. There are little girls in wheelchairs, you know. Jade told me her mother promised to get her a Barbie doll for her birthday. She turned six in December. Apparently Stacy never got around to it."

"You could have bought her something else."

"Carla, the doll Jade wanted had blond hair and looked like her mother. I also got her one that looks like me."

"Yeah, and I bet she liked the white doll better."

"Why not? It's familiar to her. She got into a fight at school last week because one of the kids called her black. She told me about it that night and was very upset. She doesn't want to be black. Somehow she knows it's hard."

"Well, it's not your business to teach her otherwise."

"I don't agree with you. I think I need to at least show her that there's nothing wrong with being black. Having two dolls exactly the same except for the skin color is a good start. When Jade carries around the white doll she can see for herself that she doesn't look like that doll."

"No one looks like Barbie. Besides, not looking like the white doll doesn't mean she thinks she looks like the black one."

"She may not, but that's okay. For now I want her to understand she's a little of both, and that she's special. I also want her to see that both dolls are equally beautiful."

Now, recalling the conversation with Carla, Deanna watched Jade absently brush a floppy lock of hair from her face. She had a milk mustache, and to Deanna she looked like an adorable Charlie Chaplin. She finished her cereal and a small belch escaped her. She covered her mouth and looked shamefacedly at Deanna.

Deanna raised her brows and waited.

"'Scuse me. Am I going to live here always?"

The question came out of nowhere, and it produced in Deanna the ambivalence she'd been feeling as she, too, wondered about Jade's future. It also forced her to think about what it had been like so far, having Jade live with her.

Hard. Tiring. Delightful.

What would it be like without her?

Deanna shrugged her shoulders. "I don't know. If you continue to eat everything in sight, you'll eat us both out of house and home. Then I won't be able to afford to keep you."

"I have some money," Jade offered brightly.

"Where did you get money? Do you have a job?" Deanna asked. Jade giggled, shaking her head. "Do you have a money tree?"

"No," Jade said, laughing at Deanna's silly ideas.

"Oh, I know . . . you found a trunk under your bed filled with money."

"The tooth fairy left it for me. I found it under my pillow."

"The tooth fairy never gave *me* money when my tooth came out."

"Maybe you were a bad girl," Jade suggested solemnly.

The telephone rang as Deanna laughed. "That's probably true. Maybe I'll keep you and you can take care of *me*."

"I don't mind," Jade agreed.

"Thank you," Deanna said, answering the phone.

"Wow! Whatever you had for breakfast, I want some. You sound happy."

It took only a moment for her to recognize the voice, and when she did Deanna felt a quick and curious sensation snap her to attention.

"Patterson? Hello," she said, unconsciously playing with her hair, as if he could see her undressed, uncombed state through the phone line.

"Is it too early to be calling?"

"You know, somehow I don't think that would stop you. I've been up for more than an hour, thanks to Jade. I was teasing her and we were laughing."

"Ummm. I don't know what could be so funny this early on Saturday morning," he murmured.

"You're hanging out with the wrong folks," Deanna said.

"You're right."

"Who's that?" Jade asked, coming to lean on Deanna's lap.

"It's Patterson," Deanna said, partially covering the mouthpiece.

"Can I talk to him?"

"You have to go and finish getting dressed. But I'll tell him you said hello, okay?"

"Okay," Jade agreed, turning obediently to do as she was told.

"Jade says hello."

"Thanks," Patterson murmured. "Sounds like you two have gotten used to each other."

"I think so. We've had our ups and downs. I really should congratulate my mother for raising three of us without selling us all."

Patterson laughed in his booming, full-chested way. "Betts used to say when I was a kid I could drive a saint to drink."

"How is she?"

"She's good."

"And Mr. Stanley?"

"Trying to keep up with her. But hey . . . I didn't call to bend your ear about my family. I wondered if you had any plans today with Jade. I know this is short notice . . ."

"I have to do marketing, and there's a program at the Children's Museum. Why?"

"I have something for Jade."

"Really?" Deanna asked, curious. "Oh, my God—Patterson, *please* don't tell me you got Jade a kitten or a puppy."

"What will you give me not to?" he teased.

"My undying gratitude. And I won't kill you."

"I like the first one. Tell you what—why don't you and Jade meet me around noon and find out for yourself?"

"Can't you just tell me what it is?"

"No."

"What if *I* say no?'

"Jade will miss out."

Deanna gnawed on her lip. "You *promise* this isn't anything that breathes and needs to be fed?"

"I swear."

"All right. I trust you. Where shall we meet you?"

Deanna sat on the edge of the park bench, poised to spring forward as Jade struggled to find her balance on the wobbling two-wheel bike. Pacing just a little behind her was Patterson, ready to help if she veered dangerously to the left or right. Deanna could hear his instructions, and she admired not only his patience but also his ability to inspire in Jade absolute confidence and trust.

He was beginning to work his way on her as well.

"Don't turn the handlebars too much, Jade. Try to

keep that front wheel pointed straight ahead. That's it. You got it," Patterson encouraged.

"Deanna, look at me," Jade called out. "I'm riding by myself."

"Yes, I see, sweetie. You're doing great!" Deanna applauded.

Patterson began to slow down, falling behind until Jade was moving ahead on her own. He watched, following her progress, glad to see she could manage without his calling out corrections and warnings. Deciding that she was fine, he made his way to the bench to join Deanna.

He couldn't see her expression behind her sunglasses, but when they'd met up at the park on West End Avenue, she'd seemed pleased to see him. Her smile had been warm and welcoming. Maybe Betts was right after all, he thought, allowing himself to relax.

Watching Patterson's approach, Deanna marveled at how different things were between them from a month ago. Then they'd thought they had nothing in common. Now, because of Jade, they were getting to know each other. And she liked what she was learning.

"You've made Jade really happy. I wish you'd let me reimburse you for the bike."

"And I wish you'd forget it. I got it from a super whose granddaughter had outgrown it."

"Thank you, anyway. I'll have to make sure Jade tells you, too."

"She looks like she's having a good time. That's enough thanks."

"Should one of us stay with her, just in case?"

"She'll be okay," he said, sitting next to her. He leaned forward to brace his elbows on his knees, keeping his eye on Jade. She was riding in a wide, erratic circle, following a paved path around a concrete water fountain.

"How many kids have you taught to ride?" Deanna pushed her sunglasses up her nose, realizing immediately what she'd said.

Patterson's expression seemed wistful, even a little sad. "A few," he remarked with his usual stoicism, which made Deanna feel as if he could handle anything. "Kids in the neighborhood near the firehouse," he clarified. "They come to us to fix their bikes, and we end up teaching them how to ride. A lot of times their parents don't even know how. Don't care. Aren't around. You name it."

"You sound . . . I don't know, maybe annoyed."

"I can't do much about what other people do. I'm annoyed at myself."

"Why? You and your men are going out of your way to help those kids. I think that's something to be proud of."

He stared into the distance. "I wish I could have done it for my own kid."

"You would have if things were different."

He seemed genuinely surprised by her comment. "How do you know that?"

"I just do. Besides, didn't you say you didn't know you had a child until recently?"

"I saw him," Patterson announced.

"What?"

"I said, I saw him."

"You mean your son?"

"He came to the firehouse looking for me. I was as close to him as I am to you right now and . . . he's my son."

"Patterson! That's wonderful! Oh, I'm so happy for you," she said, reaching out to touch his arm.

Patterson was prepared for derision, not understanding. His gaze roamed her face. He wished she would take off the dark glasses so he could see her eyes. He wanted to *see* if the empathy he thought he heard was real.

"There's not much to get excited about. That was it. I haven't heard from him since."

"Well, I'm sure you will. What's his name?"

"Drew Cannon," Patterson said. "His mother didn't even give him my name." Patterson sat up and took a deep breath as if to shake off his disappointment. No matter what happened from now on, he would have to deal with it. "Maybe he just wanted to get in my face and see if I was real. Maybe he wanted to see if I would react . . . if I care."

"Of course you do," Deanna said with conviction. "You do, don't you?"

"Yeah. I care."

"Then it will work out. I'm sure of it. It may take a little time, that's all."

"Watch me, Deanna! Watch . . ." Jade cried, excited.

Deanna turned her attention to Jade, who was less wobbly now.

"I see you, sweetheart."

She wondered if when Patterson looked at Jade, or any of the other kids he knew, he wished that he could have seen Drew at their age.

Watching Jade's energy and her liveliness made Deanna herself think about how wonderful it would be to watch Jade grow, see her become a bright and engaging young woman. They could be together, like a real family. Patterson's son was real, and she sympathized with his frustrations and was glad he wasn't indifferent to the boy.

Jade stopped to get a drink at the water fountain. The bicycle lay on the ground.

"I think you're doing a great job with her," Patterson said quietly.

"You think so? I sometimes worry that I'm not doing enough. I'm not patient, or understanding, or kind. Maybe I should be more . . ."

"More like a mother?"

She let out a long sigh. "I don't really know what that means. It's scary to think how much kids depend on you."

"So does that mean you don't want any kids of your own?"

Deanna didn't respond right away. Instead, she watched as Jade wiped her wet hands down the front of her T-shirt and then pulled the bike into an upright position by its handlebars. She got back on and tried to figure out how to get it moving and put both feet on the pedals at the same time. After several false starts, she got herself going again, steering drunkenly in a circle. Deanna removed her dark glasses to really look at Patterson.

In that moment she knew that they were both feeling the same ambivalence about raising a child, being a parent, and whether or not they could do a good job. To have or not to have kids was no longer academic, abstract, or philosophical. She had Jade. He had a son.

"I had an abortion seven years ago, Patterson," Deanna confessed. "That's how I first met Stacy. We were both getting abortions the same day, but she changed her mind and had Jade."

"Why are you telling me?" Patterson asked.

"I don't know. I guess to remind you that we all make mistakes. I don't want you to beat up on yourself because of what happened with your son. If you'd known about him, maybe you would have acted differently. I think I did the right thing for myself at the time. I didn't mean to get pregnant."

"That was then. This is now."

"The answer to your question is . . . I guess I haven't met the man I'd want to have kids with."

"Look, that was personal, what you just told me. I should mind my own business. I appreciate that you were honest," he said solemnly.

They heard a crash and turned. Jade lay on the ground with one leg caught under the overturned bike.

"Ooowww," she wailed.

Deanna jumped to her feet, but Patterson grabbed her arm.

"Wait a minute."

"She's hurt . . ."

"She's all right," he insisted calmly.

Jade wasn't crying. Instead, she pulled her leg free and sat next to the bike, tugging up the leg of her jeans to examine her scraped knee. She twisted up an arm and found another bruise on her elbow. She stood up, and kicked the seat of her bicycle as hard as she could in frustration before righting the bike and getting on again.

Patterson went to her. "Remember what I said about using your feet to push off, Jade."

Deanna's cell phone began to ring. She dug it out of her bag and answered, "Hello?"

"Hi, Ms. Lindsay. This is Maria Sanchez from the news department at the station. I'm sorry to bother you, but Mr. Wolff says he'd like you to come in to the Information Center."

"There's already someone scheduled to be there. What's happened?"

"There's a report in from the wire service that a commercial plane from Paris may have been hijacked, with several high-ranking U.S. officials onboard. The station has preempted some regular programming for a special report and continuous live coverage. We're going to need some background information and graphics."

Deanna frowned, glancing at her watch. "What am I going to do with Jade?" she murmured absently.

"What should I tell Mr. Wolff?" the assistant asked.

"Tell him I'll be there within the hour. I have to take care of some personal arrangements first. In the meantime, I'll call the library and try to give the assistant on duty some leads on what you need. What airline is involved? And who did you say is on the plane?"

Deanna committed the information to memory. After she disconnected, she speed-dialed the reference desk. Succinctly, she instructed Marianne on how to expedite the research. She decided against phoning Nancy to come in as well. When she ended the call, she sat contemplating her options. Her mother lived in New Jersey. So did Carla. She would lose a lot of time trying to get Jade to one or the other. It was a little after one in the afternoon on a Saturday. *No* one was going to be available to babysit. Should she bring Jade to the station? In desperation, she dialed Joy's number, but got the answering machine. She wasn't any more successful in trying to reach her aunt Celia, actually a friend of her mother's whom Deanna had known since she was a little girl.

"Problem?" Patterson asked, returning to the bench.

"There's been a development in Europe, and the network has to be ready to put out extra news reports tonight. I'm being called in. I'll have to take Jade with me." She stood. "Jade . . . come here, please."

"Wouldn't it be better for you to leave her with someone while you go to your office?"

"No one seems to be around."

"I'm here. Leave her with me."

"I can't do that."

"Why not? I'm offering."

She made an impatient gesture. "I've imposed on you too much already. I appreciate your help, but I don't want you to get the idea that I can't take care of my own business. Anyway, you probably had plans for today."

"I'm making the offer for Jade. Why make her hang around your office with nothing to do? Ask her if she wants to go."

"If we hadn't seen you today and I'd gotten the call, I'd still have had to bring her with me. I have no idea how long I'll have to stay at the station."

Patterson stared at her. "Yes or no?"

She hesitated. He was sincere. "What will you do all day?"

Patterson glanced around at Jade, who was watching several older kids on their bikes as they took turns showing off for each other. "She's having fun with the bike. It's nice out, so we'll probably stay here for a while."

"All right." Deanna beckoned Jade over and explained the situation to her.

"I can stay with Patterson?" Jade cried out with excitement.

"Just you and me," he agreed.

"Thank you, Deanna." Jade threw her arms around her before running back to her bike.

"I *really* appreciate this, Patterson."

"I know you do," he said. "You're going to owe me."

"Big time?"

"Yeah. Big time."

Deanna knew that Patterson was mostly teasing. She gave her apartment keys to him, along with her cell phone and office numbers. As she was leaving, Jade got off the bike long enough to give her another quick hug around the waist.

" 'Bye!" Jade waved Deanna on her way.

" 'Bye," Patterson called, imitating her.

Deanna laughed and hurried off.

Once she arrived at work, Deanna had absolutely no time to think about Jade and Patterson. For more than two hours she frantically processed requests for maps, photographs, bios, and information about past hijackings, terrorist acts, and measures to prevent both. Faxes were sent and news department runners dispatched to get books and other materials to be used as props on the air.

By six o'clock things had calmed down. As a safety net, Deanna provided other visual aids to cover any number of possible outcomes to the situation. By eight the hijacking had been aborted, the passengers and crew released unharmed.

The broadcast went to live, on-the-scene coverage,

and Deanna called Patterson to say she was on her way home.

Jade came running to the door to greet her. She practically climbed onto Deanna, trying to get her arms to reach around her neck. Even though she was exhausted, Deanna bent to lift Jade. Jade wrapped her legs around Deanna's waist, holding on as Deanna walked them both into the living room.

Patterson had remained in the living room. For the moment, Jade had Deanna's undivided attention, and he could openly watch the woman who was occupying more and more of his waking thoughts. Her eyes were bright with interest and affection as she listened to Jade's excited report on the afternoon's adventures, and he wished she would look at him the same way.

Betts had told him that he and Deanna were very much alike, with the same values and principles. But that still didn't mean there could be more between them than Jade. He was finding that he wanted something more to bring them together.

Deanna sat on the edge of a club chair in her living room with Jade straddling her lap. She couldn't remember when anything so simple as a hug had given her such warm pleasure. She'd only been able to nod a hello to Patterson before Jade had climbed onto her lap, hugging and pressing against her, as if trying to become a part of her.

"Jade, it's time to go to bed. You can tell me all about what you did in the morning. I'll come tuck you in in a little bit. Okay?"

Reluctantly, Jade grabbed Oliver and headed to her room, leaving Deanna and Patterson alone.

"How goes it?" he asked.

"Details later on the eleven o'clock news," she quipped.

"I've been watching some of it."

"We supply all the background information, but then it's processed by writers, producers, the anchors, and news directors. They shape the raw data into a story."

He crossed his arms over his chest and regarded Deanna with a speculative look. "You're not a typical librarian, are you?"

She grinned. "You're thinking of the woman you remember from your school library."

He grinned back, slowly checking her out. "You're not anything like Mrs. Hathaway."

"Should I try to figure out if that's a compliment?"

"Figure away. I'm not going to tell." Abruptly Patterson shifted. "I'm leaving. You need to chill out, get something to eat. I took Jade to Mickey D's. She wasn't much interested in my cooking."

He headed to the door. "The doorman is letting Jade keep her bike in a storage room."

"I hope she wasn't any trouble." Deanna followed him. At the door, they stopped. "I'm sorry we took up all of your Saturday."

"I'm not complaining. The night's young. My band, 4-Alarm, is playing later at the Running Board uptown."

"Do you perform often?" she asked, genuinely interested.

"Once or twice a month." He opened the door. "Jade told me you make up stories for her."

"It's fun. I can tell her anything, the sillier the better. She likes to laugh."

"I'd like to hear one sometime."

"I'll ask Jade if it's okay. She gets first dibs on all my original work." He smiled at that.

"Maybe you should put them down on paper. Get them printed or something."

"Maybe . . ."

He was standing outside the door. For a moment all they did was look at each other. It was as if they hadn't really done that before—taken the time to notice that they were coming to like each other. Maybe even more than *like.*

Deanna was going to thank him again and Patterson was prepared to tell her she was welcome. He'd enjoyed Jade's company. But something else got communicated, and when Deanna leaned forward to lightly kiss his cheek, Patterson met her halfway to make it easy.

It seemed to take a long time to do something so simple. They were close enough that he slipped his arm around her waist and squeezed lightly as it became a loose hug, their cheeks pressed together briefly. Everything that he had imagined about Deanna was apparently true. That if she trusted someone, she held nothing back.

He couldn't pass up a chance to find out if she would welcome more from him than just comfortable friendship and a sympathetic ear. He wanted to find out how much his own feelings about her had changed. When the moment was right, Patterson brushed his mouth against hers. It was quick and light like that first time several Sundays ago. They stepped apart. Patterson continued on to the elevator.

Nothing else was said between them, and no other acknowledgment made of the kiss. But it changed everything.

* * *

When he arrived at the firehouse the next morning, Patterson parked the Jeep and turned off the engine. He placed the official sticker on the dashboard that gave him permission, as a fireman, to park in restricted areas of the community. Just as he unlocked the door, his cellular rang.

"Yeah?"

"Hi . . . this is Drew."

Caught off guard, Patterson needed several seconds to regroup. "Hey. It's good to hear from you, man."

"Thanks. Ah . . . I was wondering . . . if we could get together again?"

Patterson slumped in the seat and closed his eyes, so grateful he felt weak. Thank God. "Of course we can," he said smoothly. "Just name the time and place."

Chapter Twelve

Patterson couldn't recall much of what he and Drew said as they walked toward Central Park. The park was neutral ground that wouldn't make Drew feel emotionally cornered.

It was a warm day in April, a prelude to the coming summer and the end of the school year. A day Patterson saw as the start of something new.

They stopped at a street vendor's cart. "You want a soda?" Patterson asked, passing Drew a hot salted pretzel.

"Sure."

"Maybe next time we can have real food and sit down somewhere," Patterson suggested. They began to walk aimlessly along the path into the park, just off the corner of West Eighty-first Street.

"I can't stay long. I got some time off school because of some tests. I go back to Virginia on Sunday."

Patterson digested the explanation. "Does your mother know where you are right now?"

"Sort of. I told her I was going to spend school break with a friend of mine. He lives in Westchester."

Patterson had to accept that Drew apparently hadn't told his mother about what else he was doing. Drew was seventeen years old, trying to deal with a situation that was not of his making. As they crossed the southbound road in the park and began walking north around the Great Lawn, Patterson decided not to try and second-guess him.

After a while, they stopped to sit on a bench and finish the pretzels. For a few minutes they didn't talk. Patterson hadn't had a lot of kind thoughts about Felicia Cannon since he'd found out about Drew. But whatever her reasons for not telling him about the boy, he could find no evidence that Drew had not been wanted and well cared for.

He and Felicia had both been young, ready, willing and able. As it later turned out, it had gotten them both into trouble. Patterson glanced at Drew again. No, not trouble. She had given him a son. Patterson honestly felt she'd done right by Drew.

Patterson wondered if Drew felt as nervous as he did. He couldn't tell just by looking at him. Patterson was trying to play it cool himself and not stare at the boy too often. Looking at him was like looking into a mirror.

Patterson tore off a piece of the warm pretzel and popped it into his mouth. "I'm really glad you called, man. I thought maybe . . ." He stole another glance at his son. "Maybe I wasn't going to hear from you again." When their gazes met, the teen looked quickly away. Patterson felt a little awkward himself.

"Yeah? I thought maybe you didn't want me to come around."

That was so far from the truth that Patterson didn't know what to say.

"I'd like a chance to get to know you, and have you know me. If you want to."

"Yeah, that's cool," Drew murmured.

Patterson grinned. He squinted across the wide expanse of the Great Lawn, particularly noting all the men with young children, toddlers, babies. A few of the guys he knew liked to brag about how many kids they had, as if the number validated them as men. But Patterson had to admit he didn't hear a lot about what they did with or for their kids. He'd never wanted to be that kind of man.

He'd always wanted to be a dad who was involved in his kids' lives, maybe because he'd never had that from his own father. He could picture himself wheeling a stroller, or carrying a kid on his shoulders—or teaching his son how to ride a bike like he had Jade. That's what he missed. Not the having-the-baby part—anybody could do that—but the being-a-father part. He liked to think he would have been pretty good at it. He looked at Drew again. Maybe he still had a chance.

"Tell me about yourself. Where do you live? What grade are you in? You know . . . basically I want your whole life story." Patterson was trying to joke, and he was rewarded with a quiet laugh from Drew.

"Wow. It'll take me all day to go over everything."

Patterson tapped him playfully on the arm. "Tell me what you can. Or don't say anything, if you like. I'm just really glad to see you."

"Thanks." Drew munched on the pretzel. "We live in Oakland, but I was born in San Diego."

That was where Felicia had been living when he'd met her, while on shore leave. Patterson worded his next question carefully. "Do you have sisters? Brothers?"

"Two sisters."

"So you have a stepfather?"

"Yeah, James. He's an executive with Dell, and Mom works at the university. I call him Dad, but . . . we both know he's not really my father."

Patterson's gaze was bright with admiration and relief. "You don't have to explain. He's the only dad you know."

"It was Mom's fault."

"What?" Patterson asked, confused.

"The reason I didn't know anything about you. Mom never told me. I heard her and my dad . . . James talking once. It was a couple of years ago and Dad . . . James . . ."

Patterson rubbed Drew's shoulders. "Call him Dad if you want."

"My dad said something like, it wasn't right what she did, not telling my real father that I existed. He told her I had a right to know and you had a right to know. And then she started crying."

"How did you find out who I was?"

"I asked her. I told her what I'd heard." He shrugged and looked away. "She started crying again, and . . . and . . ."

"I know this is hard. Believe me, Drew, it's hard for me to hear, too."

"No, you don't understand. I was mad at you for a long time. I thought you just didn't want me. And when Mom told me you never even knew about me, I told her I had to find you."

"Thanks."

Patterson was unprepared for a sudden rush of emotions. It was a relief and a vindication to hear out loud that the way things had happened wasn't entirely his fault. But more than that, the present was important, not the past. Patterson really wanted to be a part of his son's life. He couldn't wait to tell Betts about seeing Drew again.

He also wanted to tell Deanna.

It wasn't that he needed her approval—or anyone

else's, for that matter—but Patterson felt the need to show that he could be accountable. More than that, he was ready for the responsibility.

"I found out only a couple years ago that I had a son," Patterson confessed.

"How come you didn't do anything about it?"

"You mean like try to find you? I wasn't sure I believed it at first. I ran into an old navy buddy who told me your mother had a baby. He knew your uncle—your mother's brother. It was through him that I'd met your uncle and mother in the first place. But he couldn't tell me where your mother was living. So, when you showed up at the firehouse looking for me, I couldn't believe it. How did you track me down?"

"I used the telephone book. Mom remembered you were born in New York. So I let my fingers do the walking."

Patterson laughed at his son's ingenuity. He finished his soda and stood up, then crushed the can and tossed it with a perfect wrist action into a trash can.

"Good shot," Drew said, following suit.

Patterson clamped his hand on Drew's shoulder. "So how do you think your mother will feel when she finds out we made contact?"

"It's hard to say. Maybe she'll think I'll want to come and live with you or something." He looked furtively at his father.

"Is that what you want?"

"I don't know."

"How about we take things one step at a time? You have school . . . a life that hasn't involved me. But if you want, I could be part of it now. Just a little part so that your mother isn't hurt—so she knows we can both share you. This isn't either/or," Patterson assured him. "Come on. Let's walk."

They meandered slowly around the field, asking a lot of questions of each other. Drew was very curious about Patterson's job as a fireman. He seemed impressed with the complexity of the job, and the inherent danger. He thought it was cool that Patterson was a captain.

But to Patterson's way of thinking none of that held a candle to the fact that his son was a junior at a prep school in Virginia. Close enough to visit, he thought. Drew wanted to go into computers. Patterson advised him to let him know when his future company went public with its stock because he intended to buy into a solid investment.

All too soon they were on the path back to Central Park West, near the American Museum of Natural History. Drew was planning to hop on the subway and head for Grand Central, then take the train to Westchester. They stood a little awkwardly by the subway entrance, not quite knowing how to say good-bye.

"Maybe I could show you around the firehouse someday, if you're interested," Patterson suggested. "I'll call you." He wrote down the phone numbers that Drew dictated to him.

"Yeah, I'm interested. I have a few more days before heading back to school," Drew admitted.

"You should meet your great-grandmother, Betts. She raised me."

"Great-grandmother," Drew repeated with a shake of his head.

"She's not as old as she sounds. She could probably still whup my butt if I got out of line." They both laughed. "Hey, maybe you can give me some pointers on my computer. I haven't had the time to get into HTML or XTML."

"Sure, they're easy," Drew declared.

Patterson stuck out his hand. When Drew took it, it was with the automatic blood ritual that seemed to transcend generations of black males. "I'm really glad you called." But it went a step further when they came together for a brief embrace, their joined hands pressed between their bodies as they clasped each other's arms.

Betts swung open her arms and pulled Patterson's head and shoulders to her.

"Oh, Pat! I'm so happy for you, darlin'. Lord knows, I been prayin' for this day to come. Thank you, *Jesus.* When you going to bring him here so I can meet my great-grandchild? Lord, I never thought I'd live to see the day."

Patterson waited until Betts's enthusiasm died down. "I don't want to push him. Drew is caught between a rock and a hard place. I know he wants to have a relationship with me, but he doesn't want to hurt his mother."

"I'm glad to hear it. Don't you worry none. She'll come around. She's got no choice. That boy wants to know his daddy, and ain't nobody going to stop him."

Betts shook her head again at the wonder of it all. She got up from the table, patting his shoulder on her way to the counter, and began cutting two wedges of pie, which she slipped onto dessert plates.

"You tell that woman yet?"

"What woman?"

She stood with her hands on her hips. "Pat, you know who I'm talkin' about."

"Deanna," Patterson supplied. "Yeah, she knows about Drew. I told her."

"What did she say?"

"She said Drew is lucky to have me as a father."

Betts gasped. "She said that about you?"

"She sure did." Patterson nodded, inordinately pleased.

"Well, she's right. I knew I liked her. She can't cook worth a dime, but she'll learn."

Patterson kept his expression neutral until Betts handed him a plate with a huge slice of her homemade lemon pie. "What's on your mind, Betts?"

"There ain't a thing on my mind other than seein' you happy."

"Don't worry about my happiness. You always say, 'All things in their time.' Now I believe it."

"That's right," she said. "And 'God helps those who help themselves.' Now, I didn't raise no fool, so don't you go actin' like one. You know very well what I'm talking about . . ." She sat down and began to eat her own pie. "Lord knows, if I'd waited for Mr. Stanley to get movin' we'd both be in the grave."

Patterson paused with his fork halfway to his mouth. He looked steadily at his grandmother, well aware of her complacent, self-satisfied expression. "Meaning?"

"Well, I was going to wait until after church on Sunday, but I guess I can say something to my own grandchild. I asked Mr. Stanley, and he said yes. Your old Betts is getting married again, darlin'."

"I should be back by two o'clock," Deanna told Stephen as she left her office and he got up from his desk. "I'm not going to stay at the seminar the whole afternoon."

"Fine. If anyone calls for you I'll let the voice mail take messages," Stephen said. He fell quickly into step next to her. "I'll walk out with you. I have to go over to Shipping."

Nancy glanced up from her computer screen and watched Deanna and Stephen walk toward the reception desk and the elevators. Uncontrollable resentment rose swiftly in her with the thought that came to her daily: she should be in charge of the library.

She reluctantly returned her attention to the research she was conducting for the public relations department, scowling at the pages of mundane facts and figures. This was a waste of her time, and it infuriated her to no end that not only wasn't she appreciated but she also had to take orders from Deanna Lindsay. Someone who obviously had gotten where she was through affirmative action. Impatiently, Nancy finished the search, not bothering to check some of the links on the Internet that might have yielded more specific answers to the inquiry. She E-mailed the page attachment to PR as it was.

Ruth returned to the desk from the stacks, carrying several bound journals. "Nancy, can you manage the desk by yourself for a few minutes?" she asked. "I have to run to the ladies' room."

"Sure," Nancy said, not even looking at Ruth.

Ruth placed the journals on the countertop. "I pulled these for the daytime division. Someone might come for them before I get back."

Nancy perked up the minute Ruth was out of sight. Leaving the reference desk, she quickly went to Stephen's desk, where she immediately opened the lower right-hand drawer. She'd learned that this was where Deanna's assistant kept a folder marked "Priority." She also knew that it often held interesting information and important names.

She scanned the most recent documents, committing to memory the details she wanted before returning the file to its proper place. As she stood up she noticed that Deanna's office door was open. Again, Nancy saw an opportunity. She calculated how much time she had left before Ruth would return. She wasn't worried about Stephen, knowing that Shipping was across the street in the studio building. There was certainly enough time to take a look through Deanna's personal agenda, which she had conveniently left open on her screen.

Boldly, Nancy sat on the edge of Deanna's chair and clicked out of the address directory and into the datebook. She enlarged the view to show a full month of appointments and deadlines and studied the information she saw there. In less than a minute she had restored the screen to the address files.

Nancy slipped out of the office and returned to the reference desk, already knowing how some of the information she'd read could be of use to her. She nearly collided with Ruth as they crossed paths outside of Deanna's office.

"Oh! I wondered where you'd gone to," Ruth said. "I told you I'd be right back. You were supposed to stay at the desk."

"I had to look something up," Nancy said easily as she returned to her chair and began making shorthand notes to herself on what she'd found on Deanna's calendar.

"What were you looking for in Deanna's office?" Ruth asked carefully.

"I needed the . . . the . . . publicity outlet guide for New York," Nancy improvised smoothly.

Ruth frowned as she also returned to the reference desk. She looked through the select reference titles that were kept at hand because of their frequent use.

"That book wouldn't be in Deanna's office." She removed a spiral-bound book with a red cover. It was hard to miss with even a casual glance. She held it out to Nancy. "Is this what you want?"

Nancy accepted the book with a shake of her head. "I could have sworn I saw Deanna with it earlier in the week."

"Maybe," Ruth murmured as she reached to pick up the ringing telephone. "But it still wouldn't have been in her office."

Deanna wasn't sure why she thought she might get a call from Patterson. Or why she'd been waiting for one.

She'd been trying for the better part of the week to figure out what had happened between them when he was leaving her apartment, when they had suddenly kissed.

She'd felt something. Not just surprise, but a rush. Not just a nice warmth, but pleasure.

Had Patterson felt the same thing? If he had, would he tell her?

Deanna didn't think so.

He was a careful man. He didn't suffer fools and he didn't like being taken for one. They had held each other off, hiding behind the armor of their different backgrounds. They had circled around each other like enemies to keep one another at bay. And then they had kissed.

But had anything really changed?

Deanna knew with a certainty that she wanted to find out.

When her phone rang, she was hopeful. But it wasn't Patterson. It was Joy.

"Hey, girl. I wondered if I was ever going to hear from you. You missed your manicure appointment again."

"Getting my nails done is the last thing on my mind these days. I need to talk to you about a cleaning service."

Joy howled with laughter. "Don't tell me you can't keep your apartment together because of one little six-year-old child."

"I'm glad you find this so funny. Do I laugh when you haven't had a date in months?"

"All right, you've made your point. So what's going on?"

"Are you busy Friday night?"

"Didn't you just finish reminding me I haven't gone out with a man in months? Nothing has changed. What do you have in mind? And I'm not interested in a blind date."

"There's a blues club I want to go to called the Running Board."

"Who's performing?"

"A group called 4-Alarm."

"Never heard of them," Joy intoned. "Why don't we go to a place with some class? Like the Carlyle."

"Tell you what. We go to the Running Board and I'll treat for dinner. I want to make the last set."

"Why there? I never even knew you liked blues."

"Maybe I want to learn. This is one of the few times I can arrange to get out sans child."

Joy sighed. "I like blues, but it's so sad, Dee. If there's one thing I don't need more of right now, it's blues."

"You might meet someone."

"I doubt it, but what the hell. I don't have any other plans."

The Running Board was *not* a cute little bistro or café, with interesting people and an upscale menu, Deanna observed as she and Joy entered. It was a joint. A dive whose sole function was to bring together people who loved listening to down-home blues with those who loved to play it.

There was no atmosphere, unless one counted bare brick walls, cement floors, and teeny-weeny round tables with butcher paper for tablecloths. Judging from the people jammed knee to knee, the die-hard music lovers were nonetheless out in full force for the second set of the evening.

Deanna didn't know if she was *that* much of a music lover, but she remembered the way she'd felt listening to Patterson play his guitar. More than the surprise of his obvious talent was the realization that Patterson was a soulful, introspective man who didn't show that side of himself very often. He had gotten her attention. She was curious to learn more about both the man and his music.

"I don't like this table," Joy complained after they had settled into their seats and ordered drinks. But already the lights were dimming and a scattering of applause broke out.

"Why? What's wrong with this table?" Deanna asked.

"It's too close to the front. We're going to be too obvious if we have to sneak out in the middle."

"Will you stop complaining?"

"I'm telling you, Dee, if they stink I'm walking out and leaving you right here."

"Be quiet," Deanna hissed. The lights faded completely.

"Settle back, everybody. You're in time for our last set of the evening, and the group is all warmed up and waiting for you. We have a returning favorite with us. These four musicians auditioned for the club on a dare—and they've been here ever since. Let's give it up for 4-Alarm!"

Even before the disembodied voice of the master of ceremonies had finished, clapping and whistling began. Deanna sat tensely in her chair. The applause became enthusiastic and sustained.

The stage lights came slowly up to show the four musicians in place. A drummer. A keyboard player. Someone on horn. And Patterson on guitar.

Deanna didn't know what she'd expected, but from the moment the group appeared on the stage, she couldn't take her eyes off Patterson. When the welcome applause died away, there was just music. And it was good. Listening to him play his guitar was like sharing a kiss again.

He wasn't playing the basic acoustic guitar she'd first heard at Betts's, but an electric guitar that amplified the most incredible soul-wrenching chords and notes Deanna had ever heard. Joy was right. She knew nothing about blues. But she could feel *everything* that this music meant to Patterson.

A smile curved Deanna's lips and stayed there as she listened. The keyboard player was also the vocalist. His voice was rough and broken, the words squeezed out of him, weaving in and out of Patterson's melody. Patterson concentrated on his instrument and his fellow musicians. Despite the fact that he was performing in front of a live audience, he and the others could just as easily have been alone and playing for themselves.

Sometimes Patterson closed his eyes, his expression changing with his own inner connection to what was being played. His hand curved around the neck of his guitar, his fingers stretching the strings to produce a high-pitched sound.

Deanna lost herself in the music.

Like Deanna, the audience was silent, a tribute to the artistry of the musicians. Joy said nothing, but at least she hadn't walked out.

Each musician took a turn playing a solo. When it was Patterson's turn, his improvisations and riffs on the original composition had the audience clapping and calling out their approval. His body rocked and contorted as if he were wrestling with something alive.

"Do you know any of them?" Joy whispered to Deanna after several numbers had been played.

"The guitarist."

"Ummm. Cute," Joy assessed. "You've been holding out on me, Dee. You never said you knew a musician."

"I didn't know that I did."

"Excuse me?" Joy questioned.

"Ssshhh. I'll tell you later."

Deanna wasn't sure she wanted Joy to know too much yet about Patterson. She still hadn't recovered from their kiss a week before.

The emcee's voice interrupted her reverie.

"4-Alarm, ladies and gentlemen. They're gonna take five, and be right back."

The room exploded with more applause, and the house lights came up. Deanna followed the musicians with her gaze until they disappeared behind a curtain.

"They're not bad," Joy observed. "I love 'Hoochie Coochie Man.' I think B.B. King has a version of that. How do you know the guitarist?"

"I heard about him from somewhere," Deanna hedged.

She was uncomfortable not only with Joy's questions but also with her own reluctance to explain. She didn't want to be interrogated, which is exactly what Joy would do if she sensed there was more to the story. Belatedly, Deanna wondered if it wouldn't have been better to come to the club by herself.

Thankfully, Joy got onto another subject until the musicians returned for the rest of their set.

Patterson retrieved his guitar and glanced up absently, looking out over the crowd. Sometimes there were folks in the audience he knew. Eleanor used to come in the beginning. Other guys from the firehouse. Betts had never been. Too late at night, too noisy and smoky for her.

So when Patterson caught sight of Deanna, he had to stop and blink to make sure she wasn't an apparition. He smoothly continued getting into place, his mind reeling with the realization that she'd actually come to hear him play. He'd been thinking about her. Seeing her made him feel as if he'd been caught at something, exposed. Seeing her reminded him of that totally unplanned moment between them that he sometimes regretted. Except that it had felt so good. That was why he couldn't forget it.

He shook the thought away and turned his attention back to the stage and the opening notes of "Motherless Child."

"Oh, I love this one, too," Joy whispered. "You know, there's someone you have to listen to sometime . . . Etta James. She's fabulous."

Deanna thought Patterson was fabulous.

The group played for another twenty minutes and finished with a lively and funny song called "But I Was Cool." The vocalist had the audience laughing and stomping their feet. The applause that came at the end was prolonged and well deserved.

"Okay, so I was wrong," Joy said.

"Did you enjoy it?"

"Yeah, I did. They sure didn't sound like amateurs."

The musicians acknowledged the audience with nods and waves, then wandered among the tables to be greeted by friends and acquaintances. Before leaving the stage, Patterson looked directly at Deanna and made a brief gesture. She was slow to move, wondering what the acknowledgment meant and feeling suddenly shy.

Patterson could concentrate only on Deanna's presence. Her steady gaze told him she liked what she'd heard that evening, but he hoped he saw something else there as well.

"Hey, Pat," Oscar, one of his fellow band members, called out. "We're going to Jimmy's to get something to eat. Unless you got other plans."

"I'll pass," Patterson said, still watching Deanna.

He returned to the stage and methodically began to put away his instrument. He helped Oscar disconnect the cables from the amplifier and store them. The club was emptying out. He sneaked a look and saw that Deanna was still there, still looking at him.

"Dee, I think the guitarist is trying to get your attention," Joy said. "Is there something going on you want to tell me about?"

"No . . . not a thing."

"Then how do you explain—"

"Joy Harding. What are you doing here?"

Joy turned to face a trio of men, then gasped in recognition. "Brett Abbott! Oh, my God! I can't believe this!"

Distracted by the exuberant greeting, Deanna watched as Joy and a handsome, stocky man in casual clothes engulfed each other in a laughing, cheerful hug. It was obvious that they not only knew each other, but that their connection went back many years. After several minutes of excited conversation, Joy turned to Deanna.

"Oh, Dee. This is a friend of mine from law school."

Deanna could see from the sudden glow in Joy's eyes that this either was a significant old friendship or had the potential to become a significant new one. More amazingly, she could see that Joy could probably have her pick of the three men, if their expressions of interest were any indication.

"Brett wants us to join him and his friends for drinks," Joy said.

Deanna could see that Joy wanted to very much. But she hesitated. "Why don't you go ahead?"

"I can't just leave you here."

"I can get a cab."

"I'll see that Deanna gets home."

Everyone turned to look at Patterson.

"I—" was as far as Deanna got.

"Hey, great set, man," one of the three men interjected, shaking Patterson's hand.

"Patterson Temple," he introduced himself.

Joy gasped and studied Patterson more closely. "I've heard about you. You're the fireman."

Deanna felt her heart sink. She looked briefly into Patterson's expressionless face. When she recalled what she'd first said about Patterson to Joy, it seemed fitting that her own words . . . her own attitude . . . had come back to haunt her.

"You probably want to go with your friends," he said stiffly, taking a step back.

"You're welcome to join us," Brett invited.

"Thanks, but I have to start a six a.m. shift in the morning," he answered before Brett was pulled into an animated discussion with Joy and his companions.

Patterson glanced at Deanna. "Maybe you should go," he said just to her.

"No. They're Joy's friends," Deanna said, returning his gaze.

"I can't leave Dee. We came together," Joy told Brett with regret.

"Joy, I don't mind," Deanna assured her.

"Are you sure?"

"I could make you feel guilty and say you owe me," Deanna said, causing the three men to laugh. "I have a baby-sitter at home who's expecting me before midnight," she added.

"You have kids?" one of the men asked.

"Well, a little girl."

"It's a long story," Joy added.

Deanna turned and lightly touched Patterson's arm. "I'll accept your offer of a ride if it's still on the table," she said boldly, taking a chance.

"Sure."

Patterson had agreed, yet Deanna sensed his reticence and knew he'd picked up on Joy's reference to his day job. That was her fault, Deanna knew. She had to find a way to apologize.

Joy and Deanna said good-bye, with promises to

talk in the next few days. Then Deanna was left standing alone with Patterson. He was silent. Waiting. Deanna plunged in.

"I'm sorry you got caught up in that. And I'm sorry about what Joy said . . ."

"All she said was the truth. I'm a fireman. What else did you say about me?"

Deanna sighed. "When I first met you, I brushed you off. Pretty much the same way you did me, isn't that right?"

He crossed his arms over his chest. "That's right. Because you acted like what I did wasn't good enough."

"And you made me sound like a snob and a bitch. Yet you didn't know anything about me."

"It's probably true that we didn't have much use for each other at the start."

"I think that's a fair statement," Deanna agreed.

"What about now?"

"I think it's also fair to say something has changed. If I didn't think so, I wouldn't have come tonight. If you didn't think so, you wouldn't have kissed me last week. That's why I didn't want to go with Joy. Because of what happened between us last week."

Patterson had to give Deanna points for laying everything out in the open. She certainly wasn't afraid to confront the situation head-on. He began to relax.

"The truth is, I'm glad you didn't go with them."

Deanna averted her gaze briefly, startled by his honesty. She was feeling a sudden breathlessness and an odd awareness of Patterson that was purely physical.

"We can fight about it outside," he said. "The club is closing and we're going to get kicked out."

While heading for the parking lot where he'd left his Jeep, he asked quietly, "Why did you come?"

"I was curious," she admitted. "When I first heard you play at Betts's, I guess I was surprised. I hadn't expected—you're very talented."

"Thanks." He didn't want to say what looking up and seeing her in the audience had meant to him. Especially not after last weekend. He wasn't ready to be *that* open, that vulnerable.

There were a few moments of silence. Deanna felt an anticipation that had her slightly on edge. In the dark of the car she couldn't see Patterson's expression. She couldn't tell what he might be feeling or thinking.

The trip back to her apartment was short. Patterson parked around the corner from her building and escorted her inside.

His hand at the small of her back guided her into the elevator, and he stood in such a way as to allow him to openly stare at her. He felt an awareness he'd never known before with a woman. He realized that he desired her, but he wanted more than passion or the brief high that sex would give. She was right, of course. Something had changed between them, and the kiss was only part of it. Nothing could have convinced him that he would ever see anything in a woman like her. Just as important, that she would ever take him seriously. So what did it mean that she had not only come to the club but had also admitted that she'd been thinking of him?

Where did that leave them now?

The elevator ride felt like forever. When the door opened Deanna stumbled briefly, distracted by his closeness and the silent appeal in his dark eyes. At her apartment she reached in her bag for her keys and turned to thank him, to tell him good night, all the while secretly wishing they had more time. On the other side of the door were the baby-sitter and a sleeping Jade. Everything had to be said here and now.

Nothing was said.

She looked into his face. She knew and he knew. She felt him search for her hand. Their fingers touched and entwined. Deanna tilted her face upward, closing her eyes. Patterson bent forward, his mouth opening to cover hers. If she had had any ambivalence before, it all vaporized with the contact of his lips. She didn't bother to wonder what he was thinking. It seemed to Deanna that their mouths and tongues and warm breath pretty much said it all.

Patterson's kiss enthralled her. She was mesmerized by the feel and the taste of him. She was breathless with the racing of her heart. It was amazing. It was wonderful.

Patterson dropped her hand and drew her into his arms. Deanna stood on tiptoe to bring herself closer. She could hear the quiet rushing of his own breath, and she encouraged him to deepen the kiss, which was already making her senses spin.

She knew that this could lead to something that wasn't possible. Not tonight.

It was by mutual agreement that their mouths separated. They drew back in surprise to gaze with heated shock at each other.

"This is dangerous," Deanna declared softly.

"Very dangerous," Patterson agreed.

"I didn't expect . . ."

"Me either."

Each took a minute step back, not so much embarrassed as flustered.

"Maybe we should . . ."

"Think about this?" he asked.

She was surprised. "What's there to think about?"

Patterson tilted his head back and stared at the ceiling for a moment, and then back at her soft expression.

"I'm a little afraid of you," he said.

It was the last thing she would have expected him to say.

"Good night," he whispered, then abruptly turned toward the elevator.

Deanna had no rebuttal for his declaration, but she knew exactly what he meant.

Chapter Thirteen

Deanna grabbed for the phone on the first ring. She'd learned from trial and error that if Jade was sleeping and the phone rang twice, it would awaken her. And if she herself had any opportunity to sleep in on Saturday or Sunday mornings she was inclined to take it.

"Hello," she whispered, her voice hoarse and drowsy with sleep.

"Are you sick or something? You sound awful."

Not sick, Deanna mused to herself. Just worn-out. In need of a little R and R. A good massage. She was a bit overwrought with the management of one energetic child, a busy research facility, a renegade employee, and romantic fantasies. She knew she had probably overlooked one or two other things on the list, including a major decision on what to do about Nancy, but she was too tired to figure that out.

Realistically, after having spoken to Ruth, Deanna realized there were only two possibilities. Nancy herself had proved once too often that she no longer deserved the benefit of the doubt. But all that could wait until the coming week.

Deanna stretched her legs and tried to roll onto her back. She stopped when she felt a warm weight against her thigh and knew that Jade had once again come into bed with her sometime in the night.

"I was sleeping, Joy," she said softly into the phone. "It's one of the few private moments I get."

"Well, I'm sorry I woke you up, but I wanted to talk about last night."

Immediately Deanna thought of Patterson. Their kiss. She called it the "Oh, my God" kiss, because it had been so powerful. Disoriented by Joy's statement and her own drowsiness, she was wary of talking. "What about last night?"

"Did I ever tell you about Brett?"

"Joy, I don't remember. What about Brett?" Deanna yawned. She tried to shift away from Jade and the child accommodated her by turning over in the opposite direction.

"We were in law school together. He was a good guy. Smart and fun to hang around with, but there was never anything romantic. As a matter of fact, he was so unattached that there was a rumor he was gay."

"So the revelation is that he's not?"

"Right. And he's become something else! I don't mean professionally, although he is doing quite well. I mean just himself. He's cute and funny and smart and . . . he confessed that he used to have a terrible crush on me, but that I always treated him like he was a brother. Which is true. I never knew he liked me that way."

Deanna yawned again. "And now?"

"Well . . . who knows? The thing is, he made it clear he wants to see me again. And there's more."

"Ummm," Deanna murmured, struggling not to drift off to sleep again.

"Remember the two other guys he was with? They're both doing very well, too. Corporate something-

or-others with fabulous golden parachutes and loads of stock options."

"Jackpot," Deanna murmured.

Joy laughed. "I can't believe it. They're all so accomplished—and I think they're all interested in me!"

"Can you stand the pressure?"

"I'm sorry you didn't come with us, Dee. They were curious about you, but I told them you were spoken for, at least for the time being."

The comment caused Deanna's eyes to pop open. Now she was fully awake. She didn't know if Joy was referring to Richard or Patterson, but Patterson was at the top of *her* list.

"I'm glad you had such a great time," she said, steering the conversation back to Joy.

"It was fun. Honestly, I can't remember when I've felt so smart and sexy. I'm so glad you dragged me along to that club. I certainly never would have gone there without you."

"You're welcome. Anytime."

Joy laughed again. "If I work this right I may not need 'anytime.' I could have a steady and a couple of spares. Okay. Now I want to hear about what happened with you and that musician after I left. Patterson the fireman."

Deanna felt tension rolling over her. She remembered it wasn't all that long ago that she and Patterson had been hissing at each other. Now they'd shared kisses that had electrified her. And confused her. And shattered a whole bunch of preconceptions.

"Joy, the way I look at it, you owe me for last night. So, do me a favor and don't ask me about Patterson. At least, not yet."

*　*　*

Mentally, Patterson forced himself into the zone—an inner space that made it possible for him to rise above the physical dangers of the fire and smoke, to fight through the suffocating heat that transformed his suit into a sauna. He was drenched in sweat, and his heart pounded from an adrenaline rush. It took all his concentration to push past the fear and get the job done.

Every time he and his company responded to an alarm he wondered if it would be his last. There was always a chance of being seriously injured or killed. He and his men *never* talked about the possibilities. It was as if doing so would jinx them—cause it to happen for real. He recognized that his work created a fundamental fear. It simply came with the territory. It taught him to be careful.

Even with the best preparation, and constant exercise and drill, he knew nothing was guaranteed. Besides, he figured a little fear was a good thing. It stopped them all from taking unnecessary risks.

Intent on the safety of his men, and in charge of the inside team, he scanned the immediate area. This fire had been almost entirely contained in two apartments. The apartment where he stood now had been pretty much gutted. Everything was blackened, steam heat rising from the soaked contents. It was some hours yet before dawn, and the darkness made the burnt-out rooms seem particularly claustrophobic.

Patterson tapped his hook against what used to be the TV, then walked past a glass-and-chrome coffee table. One end of the sofa remained untouched by the flames, and cockeyed pictures, their glass shattered, hung on walls that were now blistered and peeling.

Patterson assessed the ceiling, then the walls, alert

for the telltale signs of still-smoldering fires. He began to tap along the walls. He pointed out a particular area to his men, the so-called Can and Iron team that was responsible for clearing obstructions.

"Danny," he said to the "Iron," "check that out. Be careful with the halogen. There are probably gas and water lines back there." He adjusted the face mask of his SCBA oxygen supply and checked the time. Five minutes before he would receive a warning vibration from the unit that his oxygen was low.

"Gas and water have both been capped off by the super," said Danny. "I checked coming in."

"All right. Then let's go through and make sure there's nothing still going."

Beneath his heavy boots the floor was awash with a mushy mixture of burnt debris and water. Patterson clumped through the mess, taking the lead into the other rooms. Another truck company had also been called to the alarm, and its Roof and OV team had already ventilated the fire floor before the hose came in. Here, in the apartment below where the fire had started, there was enough clearance to examine the damage and evaluate potential danger spots. Shafts of light coming from the helmets of both the truck and Patterson's engine company shot back and forth through the darkened, smoke-filled rooms like blurry laser beams. Visibility was poor.

"Captain? You should see this."

Beckoning to two of his men, Patterson followed Eddie's hand signals and voice to the bathroom. What he saw made him even more wary. One wall had buckled, and plaster had cracked around the protrusion. Patterson checked it out carefully. He didn't believe there was fire, but it could still be dangerous.

"Billy, get into that wall and find out where the stress is coming from," Patterson ordered.

He stood back in the tiny space to allow his men room to work, watching Billy and Danny use ax and hook to create a break. Immediately a rush of water spurted through the seam and quickly grew bigger, the force of it spraying the four men.

"Shit . . ." C.B. muttered.

Patterson squinted, letting his gaze travel the line of the bubble until it reached the seam of the ceiling. He shot out his arm, grabbing the nearest man.

"Hold it, *hold it*!"

No sooner had Patterson shouted the warning than there was a loud groan, followed almost immediately by a cracking from the floor above.

A great bellowing, earsplitting explosion brought displaced soot and ash, and what remained of the contents of the upstairs bathroom, cascading down on them. They made a desperate stumbling move to get out of the way, but they weren't fast enough.

The impact shoved Danny and C.B. into the bathtub, which was filled with gunk and murky water. The upstairs tub hurling down nearly crushed Patterson, who, along with Eddie, was knocked to the floor. They were buried in a swoosh of water, plaster, and tiles.

Then the roar of destruction died, and it was suddenly silent.

Patterson lay at an awkward angle, Eddie sprawled on top of his legs, debris over the rest of him. Stunned and dazed and unable to catch his breath, he struggled to yank off his nonfunctioning SCBA. He gasped, but the air filling his lungs was full of noxious smoke and dust. A searing pain in the side of his neck made him clench his teeth in agony. The back of his head was jammed against his helmet and his left knee felt as if it had been ripped apart.

"Captain Temple?" He heard his name being called from a distance, but his throat burned too much to answer.

"Back . . . here . . . bathroom," C.B. tried to shout for assistance to the men from the trunk company, who had entered through the front door of the apartment, carrying more equipment. He leaned over the rim of the bathtub. "Captain? You okay?" He pulled himself up.

"Yeah." Patterson coughed, feeling his own warm blood trickling into his collar. He tried to lift his arms. "Help . . . help me . . . up," he croaked.

C.B. moved to Patterson's head and shoulders. Patterson tried unsuccessfully to conceal a groan as C.B. slid him out from beneath the avalanche.

"I . . . want a head count," Patterson ordered, struggling to breathe.

"All here," C.B. assured him, "but Danny's unconscious."

Deanna knew there was no putting off her decision. Nevertheless, she kept reviewing the information she had been receiving for months about Nancy, including discussions with Matt Wolff. It all added up to the conclusion that Nancy Kramer would have to be released.

Deanna called Stephen on the intercom. "Nancy should be at Reference. Have Marianne take over and tell Nancy I want to see her. I want you here as well."

"Will do."

"Oh, and Stephen, did you call Security this morning?"

"It's taken care of."

"Fine. Then let's get started."

When Nancy arrived at her office, Deanna was reviewing a number of official documents. Stephen entered just behind her. Deanna asked him to close the door.

"Is something wrong?" Nancy asked.

"Let me get right to the point, Nancy," Deanna said. "I've had several discussions with Human Resources and told them of my decision to release you from your responsibilities in the Information Center. You're terminated as of today."

Deanna saw that Nancy looked not so much shocked as deeply affronted. "You're firing me?"

"Your record will indicate that you failed to pass the probationary period of your employment. You're being released for unsatisfactory job performance."

"I was never told about any probation," Nancy said, her indignation rising.

"According to your records, and your initials, you received an employee's handbook at orientation."

"That's right."

"You should have read it. I'll have to ask you to return all company keys. I'll also want your I.D. You have fifteen minutes to clear your personal belongings from your desk."

"This is ridiculous. You can't do this to me! I work very hard. I do more than my share of work. I've covered for you all the time you've taken off . . ."

"Nancy, this is not up for debate. You now have only twelve minutes to get your things. If you feel you haven't been treated fairly, you can take it up with Human Resources."

"Well, don't think I won't. And don't think I won't tell them about how you leave work to take care of personal business. It's outrageous. I could do a better job."

Deanna smiled kindly. "Perhaps you'll get a chance to do just that at your next place of employment."

Stephen left with Nancy, escorting her to her desk, where someone from Security stood by watching as she gathered her things. Deanna made final notes in Nancy's file records and reflected on the turbulent couple of months that had made today's actions necessary.

She heard Stephen's phone ring and prayed that it was something that didn't require her attention. She was already juggling a number of crises. There were only two calls that she would take without hesitation. One would be from Jade's school . . . and the other from Patterson. But so far he hadn't called.

It had only been three days since she'd been with him, yet if Patterson had experienced *anything* like the mind-altering feelings she had, Deanna guessed that he was probably just as dazed. She couldn't decide whether or not she should place any significance on his silence.

"Deanna, Matt Wolff is on the line," Stephen yelled out. "Can you take it?"

"Put him through."

As she picked up her phone, Deanna reached for a pad and pen. "Hi, Matt."

"How did it go?"

"Nancy was escorted out of the building a few minutes ago."

"I think you gave her every opportunity to get with the program."

"I know, but I do feel that as a manager I should

have been able to turn the situation around. Maybe if I'd worked more closely with her."

"I can speak for Peter and myself when I say that you did everything required of you. The rest was always up to Nancy. It's over . . ."

"I wouldn't put it past her to try and bring legal action," Deanna suggested.

"We're prepared, and it's no longer your problem. Look, I called for another reason. I need your help. We have two breaking news items and I'll need some quick information."

"Sure. What's going on?"

"Okay, we have a report that one of the mayor's press secretaries may have been involved in a sophisticated pyramid scheme while he was working on Wall Street prior to being tapped by City Hall. Can you find out if there's any history on a financial house called Howell Wyatt and Day? And see what else comes up for this guy."

"I'll run a database search."

"Great. The second report is about a fire that broke out sometime after midnight a few blocks north of Lincoln Center. There were some injuries and a possible fatality. We have a team at the scene now, but I need to know how many firemen have been hurt or died so far this year while responding to alarms."

At the mere mention of a fire emergency Deanna felt a surge of apprehension. The Upper West Side was Patterson's territory.

"Do you know if any of the *firemen* were killed?"

"We know, for sure, that two of the injured were firemen. All casualties have been moved to the hospital."

"Which hospital?" Deanna asked hoarsely.

"Hey—I'm supposed to ask the questions."

"I just want to make sure I understand the facts," she said.

"I don't think they mentioned which hospital, but let me check," he said, putting her on hold.

Every screaming siren she'd ever heard and ignored, every late-night news replay of the day's events that she'd seen on company monitors and her home TV, conjured up the horrors of men fighting back the power of fire and heat and sweeping destruction. And sometimes losing. Deanna began a mental mantra. Maybe he wasn't hurt. Maybe it wasn't Patterson's engine company that had answered the call.

The possibility that he could be injured or even killed had never before entered her mind. Why should it? She'd always seen Patterson as invincible, in control and in charge. It was only now that Deanna realized how dangerous his work really was.

"Looks like they've been taken to Roosevelt Hospital," Matt finally said. "There's one confirmed death. The body's on the way to the morgue."

"The morgue . . ."

Deanna nearly stopped breathing. That was where she and Patterson had first met. She couldn't let herself believe that was where it would end.

When she got off the phone, she sat, thoughtful and scared, as she imagined the worst. She had to find out for herself whether or not Patterson's engine was involved in the alarm. She called the firehouse, but got no answer. That meant the entire crew was out on a run.

She quickly pulled herself together. She had to respond to Matt's needs first. She ran a thorough search on the databases on the Wall Street story, while she ordered Stephen to call the NYFD PR office for background information on recent injuries or fatalities. In the meantime Marianne located additional information in the archives. As soon as the news research crisis was under control, Deanna turned to another priority. She *had* to find out about Patterson.

"It's not serious, Betts. I swear I'm not lying," Patterson tried to assure her over the phone in a voice made raspy from smoke. He grimaced as he moved his shoulders to a more comfortable position against the pillows.

"Patterson Temple, you are *not* okay if they had to carry you off to a hospital. Now, I'm going to talk to Mr. Stanley and have him bring me to you."

Patterson had to chuckle, though it hurt throughout his chest. "Old woman, Mr. Stanley hasn't been to Manhattan in fifteen years. He shouldn't even be behind the wheel of a car."

"I just want to see you for myself."

Wearily, Patterson dropped his head back on the pillows. "I'm okay."

They'd given him something to ease the pain when his dislocated shoulder was realigned. He'd taken a dozen stitches to the gash between his neck and shoulder. The medication was starting to make him drowsy.

"I'm getting out in the morning," he said. "By the time you and Mr. Stanley get ready to leave Brooklyn, I'll be home."

Patterson listened patiently while Betts continued to voice her skepticism and concern. Department officials had checked in on him. Some of his men had stopped by briefly. But it wasn't the same thing as—he didn't know what.

"And who is going to take care of you when you get home?" Betts demanded of him.

"I don't need anybody to take care of me. What I need is—" Patterson stopped.

Deanna was standing in the doorway.

"What?" Betts prompted.

Patterson swallowed, blinking to make sure he was seeing right and then trying to read the expression on Deanna's face as she took a few steps toward his bed.

"Look, I tell you what," he said into the phone. "You make me some of your baked honey ham and potato salad, and I'll be out to Brooklyn in a heartbeat."

Betts laughed, clearly relieved. "Lord, child. I'll also make you some of that apple cake you like."

"Betts," Patterson rasped, "you're my girl. I'll see you in a day or two."

Deanna looked him over. A thick gauze pad was visible at the top of his hospital gown near his shoulder and neck. A dark bruise marred his cheek and the corner of his jaw, which was a little swollen. His left wrist and hand were wrapped in a gauze bandage, but didn't appear to be broken. His left knee was swathed in thick wads of cotton, propped on a few pillows, and surrounded by ice packs.

He was alive, thank God.

"Hi," she said with a tentative smile.

"Deanna—"

She'd never heard Patterson say her name quite that way before. It was all the signal she needed to go to him and take the hand he offered. His engulfed her smaller one, his grip strong and possessive.

"What are you doing here?" His rough voice was filled with wonder.

"I heard about what happened."

"From where?"

"I'm in the news business, remember? I came because . . . I wanted to see for myself that . . . you know . . . that . . ."

"I'm fine."

"You don't sound fine."

He tried to clear his raw throat. "You don't think I sound sexy?"

"You're too old for your voice to change. But I like it."

He squeezed her hand. "I know I look pretty beat up. I'll clean up in a few days."

They were still holding hands when she remembered the bundle she'd brought with her. "These are for you." She handed him a bouquet. "This doesn't mean we're engaged."

He laughed softly, accepting the gift. "You brought me flowers. I'll be damned. The woman brought me flowers."

"I know it's corny, but I wanted to bring something." She perched on the edge of the bed.

Patterson's good hand embraced the back of her neck and pulled her face close to his.

"You're here. That's enough," he whispered as his mouth closed over hers.

The flowers were crushed between them.

She tilted her head so that their lips fit together perfectly.

When their kiss ended, they stared at each other, moonstruck.

"I'm glad you came," he whispered.

She examined the damage to his face and felt a wave of intense sympathy. "Did you lose any of your men?"

"No. One of the building's tenants."

"The report said there were injuries. Who else besides you?"

"Danny. He had a concussion and the wind knocked out of him. They're holding him for observation, like me. We'll both go home tomorrow."

Deanna gently touched the bruise on his cheek. "I make a really good chicken soup."

"It ain't soul food, but I'll take what I can get." He grasped her hand and raised it to his lips.

"When I heard about the fire I was afraid something had happened to you."

"Deanna . . ."

"Look, if I'm all wrong about what's going on, just tell me."

Patterson moved the flowers to the nightstand, which was already crowded with health-care items and a telephone. "I was going to say that I never thought you and me could get it on."

"I thought you were arrogant."

Patterson rested his head against the pillows and regarded her through tired eyes. "You were a little high and mighty yourself, you know."

"We still don't have a lot in common."

"So—" He took her hand again. "Here we are. Nothing has changed. I'm still a fireman. I'm still a brother who's out of your league."

"Maybe I'm out of *your* league," Deanna mused.

The corner of his mouth lifted, and he leaned forward to brush his mouth across hers with a slow, warm sensuality that made her want more.

"I don't know where this is going," he rasped.

"Neither do I. Maybe it's just a passing thing."

"You mean like getting the flu or something?"

She laughed. "Something like that."

"Let's put it to the test. Would you go out with me if I asked you?"

"You mean, on a date?"

"That's right."

Of course, that was the next reasonable step, Deanna realized. But she hadn't pictured Patterson making a formal offer. She wanted to smile, but didn't want him to think she found his idea amusing. She found it surprising and charming.

"I don't know. Why don't you ask me?" she suggested.

Patterson drew in a deep breath. "I'd like to go out with you. I thought dinner or a movie. Maybe both. Anything you want." It wasn't very pretty—

Deanna smiled. "I get the picture. Thank you, Patterson. I'd like that."

"All right!" he murmured victoriously, with a slight incline of his head. "I'm doing this right now. I can't have you thinking I'm not housebroke yet."

Deanna chortled skeptically. "As if you've never asked a woman out before."

"Not anyone like you," he admitted.

"I take that as a compliment. I wouldn't have said yes if I didn't mean it."

"I know. I take *that* as a compliment." Patterson slid his arm around her waist. "Come here," he whispered and drew Deanna to him.

He kissed her with erotic intensity, as if he were trying to meld them together. Deanna leaned into him, giving herself up to the euphoria of the moment, aware of the steady wave of heat that rolled over her. The kiss was heady, intoxicating. It filled her with a mindless and unexpected joy.

Patterson rode the wave of gentle passion with her until his breathing was labored and Deanna rested limp and warm against his chest. He wasn't feeling any pain now. He forced himself to end the kiss, knowing he'd achieved his goal.

"I don't think this is what your doctor had in mind when he told you to take it easy and rest," she murmured.

"Works for me." He grinned wickedly.

Chapter Fourteen

Deanna stood outside Jade's school, facing the entrance. Around her was a buzz of conversation as small groups of parents, nannies, or older siblings waited for the after-school classes from kindergarten through third grade to let out. They chatted among themselves with an easy familiarity born of the routine of dropping kids off each morning and picking them up every afternoon. For almost two months Deanna had been witness to at least the morning rituals without once being a part of them. She knew none of the women or the handful of men who were gathered and, in truth, had never before felt she had much in common with them.

Coming for Jade at her after-school program also never presented an opportunity to form relationships. There was a rotating cast of characters who were difficult to remember, when all she was concerned about was picking Jade up, and getting home so that there was time for dinner, bath, and bedtime stories.

The adults standing around were mommies and daddies. She was simply a guardian, a stand-in—terms that now seemed cold and legal to Deanna, and didn't come close to defining the relationship she and Jade shared. Still the connection, Deanna knew, was tenuous. She and Jade were living in a kind of limbo. Joy had told her to respond to Jade as if she was an aunt, or a big sister. But that was not accurate either. Perhaps at the beginning . . . but not now.

The gathering had increased until there were easily a hundred people standing around the entrance. There were even a number of cars and taxis waiting to drive children home for the start of the weekend. Deanna looked up and down the street, but she didn't see Patterson's Jeep. The thought of him coming to pick her and Jade up from the school gave her an odd sense of belonging. A sense that she—they—were part of each other, were part of a family. It was a warm and comforting thought.

But she was only playing a temporary role. The ticking of her "biological clock" suddenly had not only new meaning but one that was twofold. If she *wanted* to have her own child, there was still time to do so, although the very idea was new, and overwhelming. The second awareness, which she'd been warned about from the beginning, was that Jade was not her child and would never be. Sooner or later ACS would have to make a decision about Jade's future. Deanna was already beginning to dread the inevitability of it. That was overwhelming too.

"Thank goodness it's Friday."

Deanna turned to smile at a dark-haired woman, about her own age and dressed very casually. In her high heels, Deanna was a few inches taller.

"Yes." She nodded pleasantly.

"Of course, it's not like we parents get any rest. Tomorrow my son has violin lessons and a soccer game in the afternoon. Then there's a sleepover with one of his friends, thank goodness. Otherwise my husband and I would have no time alone," the woman chuckled wryly. "I'm sure you know what it's like."

Deanna continued to smile but didn't comment. The center doors opened with a male staff member standing to supervise the exodus of children.

"What grade is your child in?" the woman asked.

"She's in first grade. Mrs. Talbot's class."

"Oh, really! So is my son," the woman said as the first half dozen children filed out of the building. "What's her name?"

"Jade Lowell . . ." she said automatically, and turned her attention back to the flurry of activity as more kids were dismissed. She didn't see Jade in the crowd.

"Jade—I think my son mentioned her. She's new. Joined the class back in March?"

"That's right."

"I'm surprised we haven't met before. Were you at parent-teacher night last month?"

"No, I missed it. I had to work late. I spoke to the teacher at another time."

"You should bring her to the soccer game tomorrow. There are girls on the teams now, and you'll meet some of the other parents."

"Thanks, but Jade is going away for the weekend. I'm taking her to Penn Station to meet up with my sister and nephews."

Deanna held up Jade's turtle knapsack, which was packed with clothing and favorite toys for her stay with Carla's family.

"Oh, how nice. I hope you have something fun planned for yourself while she's away."

"Oh, I do." Deanna smiled, thinking of the arrangements she and Patterson had made.

* * *

"Pull up there," Marcus ordered HoJo as the silver Camry cruised slowly down the street.

"Man, you not going to find her in that crowd. What if you get caught?"

"So what? They can't do nothing to me. I'm her daddy."

"Look, there's that woman. The one taking care of your kid."

"I can handle her," Marcus said confidently, spotting Deanna as she stood talking to another woman.

HoJo made an impatient sound as he maneuvered his car around the traffic of kids and adults. "What good's it gonna do? What do you get out of the kid?"

Marcus smirked. "Big bucks. Stacy used my name, so I use Jade to get what I can. You know how much money the city gives out if you have a kid to take care of? Sweet deal, if you work it right. I'm telling you, I know all these people who get a shitload of money to take care of kids. That Lindsay woman don't even need it. She one of them high-ass bitches work midtown and make a lot of money."

HoJo parked near a fire hydrant, across the street from the school building. They sat watching the activity through the windows.

"She ain't gonna let you just take the kid, Marcus."

"Look, I don't need the bitch's permission to do a damn thing, understand? She want Jade, she can help me out, know what I'm saying? Just like she did the last time."

"She could call the cops, or them welfare people."

"She won't. She's gonna be scared the city'll take the kid 'cause she don't watch her."

"How you know that?" HoJo asked.

Marcus opened the car door, preparing to get out.

"Man . . . you know how many foster homes I been in? That shit used to happen to me all the time."

Deanna still couldn't see Jade. Although the press of children was thinning out somewhat, there were still a lot of kids and parents meeting up and slowly going their respective ways.

"There's my son now. Over here, Brian." The woman next to Deanna called out and waved.

A small boy appeared. His knapsack straps had slid to his upper arms, pulling his jacket off his shoulders. He held a sheet of drawing paper in his hand.

Deanna listened to their exchange, noting that despite the woman's seemingly casual questions and comments, her great pride and love for her son were obvious.

"Brian, this is Jade's mother," the woman said, her hand on her son's shoulder.

Brian blinked as Deanna smiled. "She's not Jade's mother."

Deanna froze inside.

"What are you talking about?" the woman asked.

"Jade said her mother is dead."

"Are you sure?" the woman murmured, regarding Deanna with suspicion.

"Jade's mother passed away in March. I'm her guardian," she explained.

"Oh . . . poor thing," the woman said awkwardly. "I'm so sorry. I thought you were her mother."

"That's okay. It was a perfectly natural mistake," Deanna said, even though she could sense the woman's withdrawal and embarrassment at her own presumption.

"Well, we have to go. Nice talking to you," the woman said abruptly.

"Same here."

Bemused, Deanna quickly dismissed the parent and child from her thoughts and walked toward the entrance. There were only a few dozen children and adults left now. At last she spotted Jade in her new denim jacket with the Tasmanian Devil embroidered on the back. Deanna was about to call to her when she realized that Jade was talking to a man who had squatted down in front of her. Apprehensive, Deanna rushed forward, bumping into a woman who had backed into her path with a stroller. She ignored the apology and kept moving.

The man was standing now, trying to urge the little girl to go with him.

"Jade," Deanna called out. " 'Scuse me . . . excuse me, please," she said, forcing her way through.

Jade was holding back, not rejecting him completely but not willing to accompany him either.

Deanna finally got close enough to recognize Marcus Lowell. "Jade!" she called out, finally drawing their attention.

Breathless and anxious, Deanna grabbed Jade away from Marcus. "What are you doing here?" Deanna demanded angrily.

"He said he has a present for me," Jade explained to Deanna.

"Honey, don't you remember me telling you *not* to go anywhere with anyone unless I know about it?"

"Yes," Jade said contritely. "But he's my daddy."

"Hear that?" Marcus said arrogantly. "I got more right to see her than you do."

Deanna took Jade's hand, not wanting to cause a commotion in the middle of the street.

"If you intend to exercise your rights as a father, then you can do it through family court. I'm responsible for Jade, not you. Until the court tells me otherwise, I have to insist that you stay away from her. You're confusing her."

"Hey . . . the only person that's confused is you, bitch!"

His tone of voice and the bad language caused Jade to stare wide-eyed at Deanna. Deanna rubbed the little girl's shoulder. If Jade didn't understand what the word meant, it was clear that she at least understood her father's threatening tone.

"Come on. I'm taking you with me." Marcus took hold of the child's shoulder, attempting to pull her away from Deanna.

Jade whimpered in confusion.

"Marcus, you can't do this."

"Maybe you got a little money you can spare," Marcus bit out.

"Wh . . . what?" Deanna asked, holding firmly onto Jade.

"I need some money."

Deanna thought quickly. "I'm not giving you any more money just to make you go away."

"Fucking bitch!"

"Marcus, let go! She doesn't want to come with you."

Even before the words were out of her mouth, Marcus had pulled Jade away from Deanna. She gave a frightened scream.

"No! *Mommy*!" Jade cried.

The parents, staff, and children who remained suddenly grew quiet as they listened to the argument.

"Come *on*," Marcus ordered, playing a tug-of-war with his daughter.

"Let her go, Marcus," said a deep male voice.

A hand gently shoved Deanna aside and Patterson

pushed past her to confront Marcus. She was relieved to see him but afraid of an escalating altercation between the two men.

"You buggin' on something?" Patterson asked in a tone of ridicule. "Why you want to carry on in front of all these people? This how you want your daughter to see you?"

"Stay out of my business, Temple. I ain't like Stacy. You can't get over on me."

"I'm not about to try, but Jade's not going anywhere with you. Let her go. Jade, go on back to Deanna," Patterson said calmly to the child.

A small gathering of people stood a safe distance from Patterson and Marcus. Someone asked if Patterson needed any help, should the police be called, but he gestured to indicate he had the situation under control.

"Deanna, take Jade and get in my car. Behind you . . ."

Jade hesitated, her eyes filled with fear.

"Come here, sweetie," Deanna crooned, opening her arms to the little girl.

"Don't you move!" Marcus bellowed at the child.

Jade hurried to Deanna, burying her face against her.

A horn blew across the street, and the driver shouted out the window to Marcus. Deanna glanced briefly at him but noticed only that he was wearing a bright yellow windbreaker with what looked like a word running down the right sleeve. She looked around, saw Patterson's Jeep Cherokee, and led Jade to it. They got into the backseat, and Deanna put her arms around the little girl, whispering reassurances and stroking her hair. She was horrified at what Jade had witnessed.

"I'm scared," the child whimpered.

"Don't be scared, honey. You haven't done anything wrong."

"He's mad at me 'cause I didn't go with him."

"I think he's just upset, but Patterson is going to talk to him."

Anxiously, Deanna watched out the window as the face-off continued.

Marcus tried to go around Patterson. Patterson stood his ground, blocking the way, which seemed to enrage Marcus even more. Deanna felt a thudding anxiety in her chest as he got right in Patterson's face, trying to force a confrontation. Despite the size and weight difference between them, Marcus tried to push Patterson into a fight. Patterson easily held him off.

Deanna bit her lip and turned away. After a few moments she hazarded another glance in time to see Marcus strut angrily to the silver Camry waiting at the curb. Deanna shielded Jade as the car screeched past them, continuing at the corner across the intersection. In another few moments, Patterson got into the driver's seat.

"You two okay?" he asked. He glanced at Deanna in the rearview mirror.

"We're fine."

"Where did he go?" Jade asked, her voice muffled against Deanna's chest.

"He went home," Patterson improvised. "He was . . . sorry he yelled at you."

Jade lifted her head to peek out the window. "Is he coming back?"

Over the top of her head Deanna and Patterson exchanged glances. They weren't sure of the answer to that question.

"I don't think so. Right now, we're going to Penn Station to meet Carla. You're going to have a fun weekend with her and her sons at their place in New Jersey," Deanna reassured Jade.

Patterson started the engine. "Stay back there with her," he instructed Deanna.

By the time they reached the entrance to Penn Station at Thirty-third Street and Seventh Avenue, Jade had recovered her spirits, and was talking excitedly about her trip.

"I'll stay with the car," Patterson told Deanna when they'd all gotten out of the Jeep.

"Are you all right?" she asked him. He'd been silent on the ride downtown.

"I'm good."

Seeing the strain on his face, Deanna was not convinced. He'd been out of the hospital for only a few days. He was moving his head stiffly, and she realized he must have pulled the stitches on his upper shoulder and neck while tussling with Marcus.

Patterson touched Jade's hair. "You have fun now."

"I will," Jade promised.

He reached into his pocket and withdrew a folded bill. "Here, take this. You might see something you want to buy."

"Thank you," Jade said in awe. She took the five-dollar bill, but looked up at Deanna to make sure it was okay.

"Wow, you're rich," Deanna said. "Here . . . let's put this money in the pocket with what you got from the tooth fairy and zipper it closed. Don't lose it." She smiled at Patterson. "You didn't have to do that."

"It's all right. See you later," he said to Jade.

After Jade had hugged and kissed him, Deanna took her hand and led her into the station.

Deanna was glad that Jade would be out of the city, out of reach of her father. It bothered her that he always seemed to know where to find Jade. She knew she would have to tell Marilyn Phillips, Jade's caseworker, about Marcus's attempts to see his daughter. That was the troubling part to Deanna. He *did* have more rights to Jade than she did.

"Dee! Over here . . ."

Deanna scanned the crowd of travelers standing around the electronic information board and spotted Carla waving. Holding Jade's hand, she made her way to her sister and nephews.

"Hi, Carla! Hey, you guys. I haven't seen you in so long . . ." Deanna got hugs and kisses from Tyler and Cody, ages eleven and nine. Both wore team baseball caps and identical T-shirts. "Goodness, Carla . . . they're getting so big."

"Tell me about it. You can't believe the amount of food the two of them eat," Carla added as she and Deanna exchanged kisses.

Although the two sisters looked a lot alike, Carla was an inch or so shorter and twenty pounds heavier than Deanna. She wore her hair short like Deanna's, and glasses like her oldest son's. Carla turned to Jade, who stood a little apart watching them all shyly.

"Hi, Jade. I'm Deanna's sister, Carla."

Deanna drew Jade forward and introduced her to the two boys. Immediately they engaged in conversation, and whatever insecurities the little girl may have had about meeting strangers were quickly gone.

Deanna turned back to her sister. Carla raised her brows and spoke in a low voice. "Girl, you weren't kidding when you said she was fair. I swear, when I saw you I thought you were with a white child."

"I know. A lot of people assume I'm her nanny."

"Humpf. I hope you set them straight."

Deanna smiled as Tyler gave Jade a Tootsie Roll

from a stash in his pocket. "She doesn't need explaining, Carla. I know that the way Jade looks is sometimes going to influence how people accept her. You know how folks can be. She's already gotten into trouble with a few kids at school."

"I'm not surprised," Carla commented dryly. "How's she doing?"

"She's learning to protect herself, but I don't want her to become a bully."

"Ummm huh." Carla watched the three children. The boys were examining Jade's turtle backpack.

"What about her family?"

"Right now there's only her father, and he's no bargain. I don't think he really wants Jade, but he's being . . . difficult."

"If you need some advice, you should talk to Glenn. Child advocacy law isn't his field, but he might know someone in family court."

"Joy has been helping a lot, but thanks for reminding me about Glenn's connections."

"Does Jade know she's coming home with me after they all see the ice show and we have dinner?"

"Oh, yes. She's looking forward to it."

Deanna pointed out the knapsack that held Jade's overnight things. Barely visible was the head of Oliver on one side of the top opening, and on the other side the twin heads, one white and one brown, of the Barbie dolls.

"I don't know why you think those Barbie dolls are going to work with that child."

"I have to start somewhere. She'll have to figure out her own identity sooner or later, but she can't do that unless she understands what identity means."

Carla nodded, thoughtfully watching the three

children. "It'll be interesting to see how the boys react to her."

"I know. That's one of the reasons why I'm glad you wanted to have her over to your place. Now, she doesn't like eggs . . ."

"Listen to you, sounding just like a mommy. What a hoot."

Deanna felt a bit foolish. "I'm used to Jade's habits, is all I'm saying."

"I know. I just think it's funny, considering you never showed much interest in having kids. Don't worry about your little Jade. We're gonna have a good time."

"Thanks for taking her, Carla."

"Now, what is it you said you're doing this weekend?"

"I need some time to . . . to take care of . . . things."

"Oh, you mean you're spending time with Richard, right? What's going on with you two?"

"Nothing, but I'll tell you about *that* later. Look, I have to go. If Jade gets antsy and wants to come back home, call me. But I don't think that will happen."

"Well, what are you going to do if this situation goes on for another month or more? You can't keep that child forever, you know?"

Deanna's first response was to ask, "Why not?" Recently she'd been giving thought to how to make more space available in her apartment, what summer camp to enroll Jade in, and taking her to Disney World for her next birthday. There were more answers to Carla's question than she wanted to consider just then. "I haven't had time to think about it. Look, I have to go. Thanks, Carla. I appreciate that you could take her."

"No problem. Enjoy your weekend. I'll call Sunday

and let you know what train she and Glenn will take on Monday morning. Don't worry, she'll still have time to get to school."

They hugged again.

"Give Glenn my love." Deanna bent to hug Jade and say good-bye. "Have a good time, sweetie."

When Deanna finally appeared at the station entrance, appreciation and apprehension swept over Patterson. She was wearing a plain knit sheath with matching coat. Purple was a good color on her, and the dress was neither too short nor too tight. There was something confident and stylish about Deanna that made her stand out from other women. But his perception also seemed to be colored by how he felt about her now. It made all the difference.

Patterson wasn't sure if he could trust what he was feeling. He was beginning to experience a strong sense that she was the woman he was meant to be with. The thought of how she might feel still made him nervous.

He was leaning against the passenger door but stood straight as she approached. He watched her eyes, trying to read her expression. From her distracted look, he knew her thoughts weren't on him but on Jade.

He planted a light kiss on her mouth, briefly savoring her soft lips and faint perfume.

He pulled back. "How did it go?"

"Jade's going to be fine."

"You think she'll get homesick?"

Deanna considered the question. His referring to Jade's coming home with her made her feel good and helped to allay some of her own doubts. "I don't think so," she replied.

"Are you going to worry about her?" he asked.

"Not while she's with my sister, but . . . I'm concerned about Marcus."

Patterson stood back and opened the car door. Deanna got in. "I want to talk to you about that."

He headed west, then north on Eighth Avenue, taking his time in the Friday-afternoon rush-hour traffic. Deanna didn't know where they were going, and she didn't ask. It was just comfortable being with him, without any of the ducking and weaving that had begun their relationship.

"Has he come around before?" Patterson asked.

"Not at the school. Jade has never said anything about seeing him there."

"You've seen him somewhere else?"

"Outside my building. The Sunday evening after Jade and I had dinner with you and your grandmother."

"Why didn't you tell me?"

"I didn't see a reason to. I mean, I wondered how he found out where I lived, but he wasn't threatening."

"What did he want?"

Deanna shifted in her seat. "He said he wanted to see Jade."

"Did you believe him?"

"Marcus doesn't really seem all that interested in Jade. And . . . he said he needed money."

He glanced sharply at her. "You didn't give him any, did you?"

"Well . . ."

"Marcus set you up. He knows if he plays you right, he can come back for more."

"I felt sorry for him," Deanna said. "I only gave him sixty dollars."

"He's a con artist and a liar."

"Maybe, but I can't forget that he's also Jade's father."

"So what do you think he really wants?"

"I don't know. I don't think he would do anything to hurt Jade, really. But . . . whatever he's up to is for his good, not hers."

Patterson reached out and patted her thigh. Deanna took comfort in the gesture, but knew that there was little they could do about Marcus. Of course she intended to call Jade's caseworker at ACS. But no one had said Marcus didn't have a right to see his own child.

"I don't like it that he shows up at her school and makes an ass of himself in front of Jade," Patterson said tightly.

"I don't either, but what can I do?"

"Maybe you need to go to family court."

Deanna was silent for a moment. "I don't think I should do that."

"Why? Are you afraid of what he'll do to you?"

"No. I'm afraid of how it will make Jade feel."

"All right. I can understand that. But you tell me if he shows up like that again, at either Jade's school *or* your place."

"What will you do if he does?"

"Kick his ass," Patterson mumbled angrily.

Deanna knew she should be shocked, but she found herself grinning instead. She believed Patterson would do it, and Marcus would probably deserve it. But it still bothered her, because no matter what, Marcus was Jade's father.

By the time they'd arrived uptown, they'd dispensed with Marcus Lowell as the topic of conversation. They parked near Columbia University, and he escorted her to a Thai restaurant, one of her favorite cuisines. His too, as it turned out. She smiled at him, pleased and surprised. For different reasons she knew that any place more formal on a first date would have made them both uncomfortable. The informality set the tone for the rest of the evening.

They both loved the *Tom Kha gai,* chicken with coconut soup, but Patterson was a pork man and Deanna wanted shrimp. They shared the main dishes. Afterward Deanna let him talk her into ice cream at Tom and Jerry's. What she enjoyed most was that Patterson held her hand. Not just to lead her across a street or to help her out of her chair, either. He reached for her hand for the pure pleasure of the contact. So simple a gesture, so fundamental to couples, and yet she couldn't recall that she and Richard had ever been so demonstrative in public. Deanna was stunned to learn that Patterson could be so possessive and expressive of his feelings. And so utterly romantic. Holding his hand made her feel very special because she suspected that he was not normally given to such displays.

They had never discussed what the evening would be like, and Deanna sensed that he was pretty much making it up as they went along. That was the charm of it. The evening was just right.

So when Patterson drove her home just after midnight, she was not surprised. She'd begun anticipating the eventual end to the evening, especially after they exchanged licks of each other's ice cream cones.

It was also no surprise when Patterson drew her close in the elevator, after the only other occupant got off on the third floor. There was just enough time for them to kiss with a warm sweetness, a tender and seductive combination. It was no surprise that when they reached her apartment Patterson took her keys and unlocked the door. Still standing in the hall, he slipped his arms around Deanna's waist and embraced her again. Their kiss this time was deeper, more intense. Deanna had no doubt that they both wanted more.

So she was totally surprised when Patterson, groaning deep in his throat, reluctantly pulled back and handed her the keys.

"Good night," he whispered. "I had a good time."

"Don't you want to come in?" she tried to sound casual, not sure what to make of his withdrawal. She was prepared. She wanted him to stay.

"Yeah . . . but not tonight."

Deanna was confused and showed it.

"We've got time," he said smoothly. "I'm not going anywhere. I don't want you to think I don't know how to act."

"You don't have to worry. That's not a problem at all."

"Good." He nodded, almost shyly. "Got any plans for tomorrow?"

"Make me an offer I can't refuse."

"I'll pick you up around ten. Let's start with a late breakfast."

"I'll see you then. Good night, Patterson. I had a good time, too."

He headed for the elevator.

"Patterson?" He turned to her once more. "You're not just slumming, are you?"

He burst out laughing. "You're pretty expensive real estate for that."

The elevator arrived. He waved.

"Patterson?"

He held the door open. "Yeah?"

"Are you still afraid of me?"

The corners of his eyes crinkled. "Absolutely," he said, stepping into the elevator and letting the door close.

Deanna slowly began to grin.

Chapter Fifteen

When the music stopped and the last notes faded, Deanna joined the audience in enthusiastic applause. Around her, people rose to their feet, a sign of respect for the four musicians. True to what she'd witnessed the first time she'd heard Patterson and his band, the quartet seemed modestly unaffected by the rousing reception they were receiving.

Deanna felt enough pride for them all. She was also feeling other things as she watched Patterson interact with the audience. Quite simply, he was an amazing man.

The young woman in charge of community events came forward to stand next to the group as they began packing up their instruments. She leaned forward to speak into the microphone.

"Thank you all for coming to this afternoon's program. The appearance by 4-Alarm is the third in our spring and summer music series at Barnes and Noble, and we're very glad to have them. We hope they'll agree to come back again."

Slowly the crowd began to drift out. Deanna remained seated while Patterson and the other band members talked among themselves, reviewing the performance. She'd met them all, and found them to be surprisingly shy men. Patterson had laughed and told her they'd fall out if they knew she'd said so.

"These guys don't know from shy," he chortled. "They just don't want to make fools of themselves around you."

That remark made Deanna feel that perhaps Patterson's band members had some preconceived ideas about the kind of person she was. Whatever that impression was, it kept them from being themselves around her. But hadn't she done the exact same thing with Patterson?

Her complete turnabout regarding him was sobering. It still preoccupied Deanna that she cared a great deal for a man who didn't at all match her long-held vision of the man of her dreams. Had she unconsciously maintained an idealized image, a composite of traits that, when she put them together, made up the perfect man?

More than any other man she'd ever known, Patterson not only earned her admiration and respect, he made her feel the power of being a woman. She felt an attraction for him that was electrifying and physical. Deanna had no doubts that he was responding to her in the same way. However, unlike his earlier penchant for going toe to toe with her, he now seemed overly polite. Careful. He had never shown himself to be reticent about anything, so she was puzzled about what he was thinking and feeling now.

Outside the bookstore, she patiently waited until the members of 4-Alarm finished making arrangements for their next rehearsal and joked about needing an agent before they went their separate ways.

"4-Alarm is getting to be very popular," Deanna said, as she and Patterson walked to his Jeep, which was parked around the corner.

"Looks like it," he said thoughtfully.

"You may have to quit your day job to go on the road with the band," she teased.

"I don't think so." He chuckled quietly. He unlocked the car and held the passenger door open for her before putting his guitar case in the back and getting into the driver's seat.

After snapping on her seat belt, Deanna swiveled to face him. "What if you could really make it as a musician?"

Patterson waited until they were in traffic before finally responding. "I don't play music because I want to become famous or expect to make a living from it. I do it because I like to. The guys and me . . . we like the sounds we make together. We understand each other's groove, know what I'm saying? If other folks want to listen in, and like what they hear, then that's cool."

"How about cutting a demo CD?"

"Nope."

She was surprised. "Afraid of failing?" she asked softly.

"I'm happy being a fireman," he said simply.

"Patterson, you need to get over that. I know you like being a fireman. That doesn't mean you can't be other things too."

He drove for a block or so in thought. "You know what'd I'd like to be good at? Being a father to my son. I want his love and respect. I want to have a place in his life, and I'd like him to be part of mine. I want him to be proud to have me as his father."

"Oh, Patterson," Deanna said, deeply moved by his confession. She rested her hand on his thigh. "You told me you finally got together with him last month. Isn't it working out?"

"I got a letter from him."

"That's good."

"I'd like you to do a couple of things for me."

"Sure. What?"

"I want you to read the letter."

She tried to interpret his tone. "Are you sure? Maybe it's too special to show to anyone."

He reached for her hand, grabbing it and holding on tightly. "You're not just anyone," he murmured.

Surprise shot through Deanna as she registered Patterson's words. She wasn't sure, however, if that was a confession that she was just different, or that she was special. She hesitated to guess what he meant, but squeezed his hand back.

They were headed east through Prospect Park and away from the Slope, which she knew was not the direction back to Manhattan. She didn't ask, but she suspected Patterson was taking her to his house. She'd only been there once, when they were on their way to the Brooklyn Museum for an evening reception she had been invited to. She'd asked Patterson to go with her. He'd been indecisive about what to wear, and she'd found that amusing. But despite her assurances that casual was fine, he'd insisted on changing again.

Deanna had been truly surprised by where Patterson lived. His block was a combination of rundown and neglected buildings, and a half dozen or so that were being renovated. Patterson's four-story dwelling fell into a third category of work that had been completed. The building had the classic details of the late 1880 architectural style unique to New York City. She was charmed to find decorative planters at the top steps to the salon floor, filled with ferns, English ivy, and impatiens. She had a feeling it was Betts's handiwork. The two lower floors that he'd made into his own place were another surprise. But at that first visit he had not taken the time to show her around, rushing them in and out of the house as if he wasn't willing to share his sanctuary with her.

Now things were different.

In the past few weeks they had reached a comfort level that seemed to have left their differences behind them. Their energies were no longer focused on trying to do each other in, but on forming an alliance that made them more than friends . . . but less than lovers.

The term went through Deanna's mind, and she caught her breath, feeling a wave of disorientation at the idea of Patterson making love to her. She wanted him to. The boldness of her admission was no longer confusing to her. She'd tried to have a conversation with Joy about this change in herself without giving up any secrets. What if there was this man who wasn't on her eligibility short list but who appeared in her fantasies? Who made her daydream? Who was in every way desirable . . . perfect?

When Patterson escorted her into his house this time, she had the sense that he was revealing yet another part of himself. She was coming to know him layer by layer, as he became more and more willing to share.

The two floors of his duplex were nicely organized and beautifully decorated. Patterson favored earth tones in brown, tan, and black, and Afrocentric patterns and motifs. But the black thing wasn't overdone, and there was a tasteful blending of contemporary furniture in leather, chrome, and glass. Several large plants in floor pots added warmth: peace lilies and ficus benjamenia.

"Where did you say Jade is?" he asked as he closed the door.

"At a play date with her best friend from school."

"When do you have to pick her up?" Patterson walked down a staircase to the ground level with Deanna close behind him.

She checked her watch. It was almost three o'clock. "I said I'd pick her up about six-thirty or seven."

"Good. We have time."

On the lower level was a combination TV, office, game room. Complicated audio equipment was arranged against one wall, and she saw what seemed to be hundreds of CD's, several expensive-looking headphone sets, and two guitar cases leaning against the side of the computer tower.

Deanna caught a glimpse of a second room, where she could see free weights and Nautilus equipment, a press bench and a NordicTrack. There was a third room. The door was open but the lights were out. She guessed that was the bedroom . . . and felt a slow tension coil within her.

He took a letter from the desk and held it out to her. "This is from Drew."

They sat together on a black leather love seat. Deanna unfolded the two pages and read the salutation. Stopped. Looked at Patterson for a swift second, and started again.

"Dear Dad . . ."

Patterson had been beside himself when he'd gotten the letter marked with the return address of Drew's school. He'd come as close to tears as he'd ever been since he was about thirteen years old, all because his son had addressed him as "Dad." The letter had been filled with awkward phrases and simplistic sentences about school, news of Drew's varsity teams and his friends. He talked about going home to California when school let out in another two weeks, and having a summer job in a dot-com start-up company where he'd get a chance to design Web sites.

What the letter had not said was when they would see each other again. Or if Drew even wanted to.

Patterson had told Betts about the letter, and she had been sympathetic, but also pragmatic.

"Pat, remember he's only a boy. He's got a family that he loves. That don't mean he won't come to love you, too. You're his daddy."

Everything Betts had said made sense. Patterson knew she didn't understand the terrible fear he'd been living with since receiving the letter. And yet, the only other person he thought to discuss it with was Deanna. He knew she would appreciate his anxiety, because he had witnessed her own over Jade.

Deanna finished the letter and felt two things. Empathy for Patterson, and something far more complex. A full awareness of how having children changed a person. She was beginning to understand that raising a child was one of the most significant legacies a person could leave. The full impact of what she would miss if she ever lost Jade hit Deanna like a splash of cold water.

She carefully folded the letter before giving it back to him.

"What do you think?" he asked. "Is he telling me he's not interested in getting to know me? He doesn't have the time? What should I do?"

Deanna felt genuinely pleased and flattered that he would value her opinion. She had no doubt that he didn't let his vulnerable side show very often.

"Drew is only telling you he already has plans for

the summer and he has to return home to California. That doesn't mean he doesn't want to get to know you. That's why he wrote the letter. That's why he called you Dad.

"If I'm also reading between the lines correctly, he has his mother's permission to come East at some point, and is hoping you'll extend an invitation. He needs you to ask him to come, Patterson. He wants to make sure *you* still want to see him. Call, write, E-mail. Tell Drew you'll be waiting for him."

Patterson listened intently, nodding occasionally and feeling a huge relief that Deanna saw much more in his son's letter than he had. His own disappointment at having to wait to see Drew again had colored his reading of it.

"What I think," Deanna reflected, "is he doesn't want to hurt you or his other family. Don't make him choose sides, Patterson. He shouldn't have to."

"I won't," he murmured, relieved. "You know, I'm not the only one trying to figure out how to be a good parent. I've been watching you and Jade. She called you Mommy."

Deanna blinked at him. "What?"

"Jade called you Mommy. Remember the day outside the school when Marcus showed up? She called out for you."

"You heard that, too?" He nodded. "It was natural that she'd call to her mother for help."

"She was asking *you* to help her. You are her mommy."

Deanna couldn't look at him. She'd been remembering that moment. Jade had not called her Mommy since then. There was a special bond between them, one she cherished more than she'd ever imagined. But it was a huge leap from that to believing that

Jade could accept her as her mother. She glanced at Patterson, finding it strange that he would remember and mention it now. Had he guessed how she felt?

"She took me by surprise. I thought she was calling out for Stacy. I'm ashamed to say so, but I was a little . . . envious." She found his gaze understanding. "I felt that way again as I was reading that letter from your son. You're so lucky. I hope you know that."

Patterson smiled at Deanna. He slid an arm around her waist to draw her to him. "Now I do," he said.

Deanna let him hug her. She wanted whatever comfort he was willing to give. She needed to feel his solid, reassuring strength. She drew on the fact that they had somehow miraculously landed on common ground. It was sweet and satisfying and surprising. And she didn't want to lose it.

Patterson was feeling exactly the same way.

"I wanted you to realize the same things you just told me," he whispered against her ear. "I can tell that you love Jade."

"I do," she confessed softly.

"You think somebody's going to come along and take her away."

She nodded against his chest, her eyes closed. If she had been alone, she would have cried. "Yes."

"Deanna, if you want to keep her, if you think you can raise Jade, then say so."

"To whom?"

"Anyone who will listen. Don't give up. You just told *me* not to."

"Patterson, there's a huge difference. Drew is your natural son."

"Yeah, but I know I have to earn the right to be called his father. Giving a little sperm doesn't cut it."

Deanna couldn't help chuckling.

"Can I ask you something?" he said. "Are you sorry that you had that abortion?"

"No, I'm not. What I am sorry about is that I may not get a second chance to do it right. I never wanted to before. Now . . . I think I do."

Patterson caressed her for a moment, then drew back to regard her intently. "Me, too."

He placed his hand on her cheek and lifted her face. His kiss was sweet and gentle, as if he feared breaking the tenuous understanding they'd found together. But he wanted more as well.

Their lips began a sensual foreplay that instantly released the need that had been simmering between them all day. Longer. Patterson knew he'd been holding himself in check, not willing to risk rejection from Deanna. His lips became more demanding with each kiss, until she opened her mouth so that their tongues could meet and dance.

They both began to relax, to trust what was happening.

He ended the kiss, glad to see that she looked exactly like he felt. Dazed. Breathless. Hot.

"When I was a young blood, this was easy. The sofa, the floor would do fine. But you're not that kind of woman. I've been thinking about you and me. Maybe . . ."

She touched his mouth with her fingertips, stroked his face, his surprisingly soft beard. "Is this what you want?"

"It's been on my mind," he whispered, kissing her with erotic slowness.

"I thought you'd never ask," she whispered.

They didn't rush. Like teenagers, they were locked in each other's arms, awkwardly kissing and petting.

They seemed unwilling to stop long enough to make it to Patterson's bedroom, as if they were afraid the interruption might bring them to their senses. Patterson's kisses alone made Deanna soft and wet with longing. It was the growing need for something more satisfying that finally got them off the sofa and into the bedroom.

Patterson didn't bother to put on the light. He knew what he was doing and exactly what he wanted. He kissed her with growing urgency as his hands explored her body through her clothing. Deanna found the gliding of his hands and the pressing together of their bodies stimulating and erotic. She pulled his polo shirt free of his slacks and buried her hands beneath it, finding his torso bare and hard, his skin warm. This first intimacy made her want more.

They began to undress, their need to touch each other getting in the way. He yanked off the shirt and tossed it aside. He did the same with Deanna's sweater, and quickly dispensed with her bra. He didn't do what she expected him to—cover her rounded breasts with his large hands and squeeze them. Instead he put his hands around her rib cage, and used only his thumbs to stroke the undersides of her breasts with feathery caresses. Deanna moaned, never before having realized how sensitive she was there. She slid her hands down Patterson's smooth back as he rotated his hips and hardening penis against her. She grew dizzy thinking about what they could do together.

The rest of their clothing came off in a final rush of desire. Deanna was not surprised that Patterson had a king-size bed. He was a man who needed a lot of space. There was something incredibly stimulating about being totally naked with him on top of her as his weight and heat and erection pressed her into the mattress. She felt an almost desperate need to join with him in complete primal intimacy. They'd held each other at arm's length for so long . . .

Deanna was not shy about exploring his body, enjoying the flexing of his muscles where she touched or caressed him. Sheathing his erection with her hand, she built his arousal with gentle but firm movements until she felt the rush of his breath against her neck and heard him moan deep in his throat. His kisses consumed her, his mouth hungry and wet, plundering hers. His hands took bold liberties and his fingers sought all the secret places that set her nerves on fire. Deanna opened herself to him and surrendered all control. The sexual tension drove them both to the brink of madness.

"Pa . . . Patterson," Deanna moaned, short of breath and almost unable to speak. "Wait . . ."

He knew what she wanted.

"I got it," he whispered.

He rolled away for a moment, opening the drawer on the night table. She was reassured that Patterson was taking precautions for them both. Now she wanted him to hurry.

They needed no lengthy preliminary exploration, no prolonged foreplay. There was no time for her to warn him that if he continued to stroke her between her legs she was going to break. And she did. He shifted, then slid into her still-contracting canal, drawing another gentle moan from her. But her murmurs only drove him on. He began plunging into her, deeply, rhythmically, her arms locked around his back and shoulders. Her legs, wrapped around his hips, held him in place. Her hand stroked his nape, then slid down to massage and squeeze his flanks. The spiraling of sensation pulsed through her loins. She gasped and cried out, sure that the pleasure was going to kill her. He kissed her deeply, adding to her feeling of being on fire.

It was a different kind of experience for Patterson, to be with a woman who could give as good as she got. What he wanted to give her was simply everything he had. He went the extra distance, pouring his heart and soul into showing her that this was the moment of a lifetime.

He wanted it to last longer, but he felt the eddies of pleasure tightening his scrotum, making his heart race and his mind spin, pitching him over into bliss. He held on to Deanna, squeezing her against him. She was whispering to him. Caring words. Encouragement. Praise.

He wanted to stay like this, holding on to her. Even after the last of his climax had dissipated and he had slid wet and limp from her body, he stroked her thighs, her breasts. He was relieved to find that her proper, world-class upbringing didn't extend to the way she made love.

Neither spoke for a while afterward. They lay curled together, touching each other with gentle reverence and awe. The weeks of anticipation hadn't prepared Patterson for the discovery that what he was feeling for Deanna made this moment all the more powerful. And pulled the rug right out from under him. A month ago no one could have convinced him that their relationship would *ever* come to this.

"I've been cheated," Patterson said in a sated voice.

"Disappointed?" Deanna kissed his chest, her lips pressed against his heartbeat.

"God, no. But this feels like . . . like the way I

always thought it was supposed to be. Like it should never end."

"It would kill you."

"Then kill me," he muttered, his hand lightly gliding up and down her back.

Deanna felt languid and satisfied. As much as she'd wanted him to take her to bed, to make love to her, part of her had wondered if he would see her as any easy score. She, too, wished it would last forever.

Patterson trailed his hand down her rib cage and stomach, making her catch her breath and utter small sounds in her throat. He began to kiss her again, slowly at first, but deeper and deeper as passion flared again between them.

"Patterson . . . I . . . I really . . . have to go," Deanna managed to get out, even though her only movement was to make it easier for him to explore between her legs with his tender strokes.

"Me, too," he murmured, making no attempt to stop. He didn't see any point in putting off for later what was so good right now.

Deanna's entire staff was crowded around the television in the conference room. "There it is," Ruth said.

The screen showed an image of the president in a debate when he was an up-and-coming politician. What was more important, however, was that his opponent was a man who now had international ties to terrorism. It was a never-before-seen picture that the reference desk had managed to dig up. The image had been playing on news shows across the country all day.

The department broke out into cheers and applause as the Information Center was given air credit for unearthing the photograph.

"Very nice, everyone," Deanna said. "I'm pleased with the effort that went into this."

"Does this mean we can have Friday off with pay?" Stephen asked to accompanying laughter.

"Not a chance."

"But we should celebrate," Marianne offered.

"I could bring in some brownies on Friday," Ruth volunteered. "Everyone was very understanding about filling in for me when I was out because of my husband's stroke, and I certainly appreciate it."

"We're just glad that he's making a full recovery, Ruth," Deanna spoke for everyone, turning off the TV. They all headed back to their various positions and responsibilities.

"I know there were some important projects that came in to be researched," Ruth said, walking with Deanna back to the reference desk.

"It was taken care of, Ruth. We all made sure it got done."

"There was one request in particular," Ruth persisted. "It was from the director of the news division and I should have gotten it right to you personally."

"Do you mean the material on the attorney general's office for the director?" Deanna asked her smoothly. Ruth nodded.

Deanna knew Ruth was hinting at Nancy Kramer's role in completing the assignment that hadn't been intended for her. Ruth might feel it reflected on her, but Deanna was the one who ultimately had to bear responsibility for her staff and their work.

"Ruth, it's over. The director eventually got what he wanted," she said carefully. "The most important concern right now is making sure that whoever is chosen to replace Nancy understands the position and its limitations better, and can fit in and work with everyone here."

"Well, almost anyone would be an improvement," Ruth confessed.

Deanna realized that her staff felt as much relief as she did that the Nancy Chronicles, as she'd come to think of it, had had a satisfactory ending.

The telephone was ringing in her office when she returned, but she called out to Stephen. "If that's Peter's secretary, tell her the budget will be ready in the morning."

"It's Patterson Temple."

"Oh," Deanna said, quickly closing her door and reaching for her line with unseemly haste. She knew she should be more circumspect, but she couldn't manage it when she was so pleased to hear from him. He wasn't in the habit of calling her during working hours. She wasn't sure yet if that was because he didn't want to interrupt her, was too reticent about discussing anything personal over the phone, or was trying to torture her.

"This is Deanna," she answered the call.

"Okay, that's your official library voice. I'll call back later."

"No! Now is fine," she said quickly.

"I'm not interrupting your work?"

"Not at all."

"Good. How are you?" he crooned.

"Glad to hear from you," Deanna admitted. She didn't see any point in being demure.

"About last weekend . . ."

"Yes?"

"It was pretty awesome. Tuesday morning wasn't bad, either."

"It was nice that I didn't have to go into my office that morning."

"Ummm. I'm glad you didn't have that presentation at Pratt until noon . . ."

"And you were just getting off a tour . . ."

"And Jade was in school," Patterson added. "Any more of those mornings coming up?"

She laughed, delighted and relieved. She sat on the edge of her desk with her legs crossed. She wiggled her foot out of her shoe and let it hang by her toes as she swung it back and forth. "I'll see what I can arrange. You sound like a teenager."

"Feel like one, too. And . . ." He inhaled deeply. "I'm feeling a little hesitant."

"Tell me about it," she encouraged.

"I want to see you again."

"I've been thinking about you, too. I wondered if you were going to call or should I call . . ."

"I don't want you to think that if we get together it's only to rock and roll, know what I'm saying?"

Deanna shook her head ruefully at his choice of words. It was more charming than crude. And honest. The fact of the matter was, making love with Patterson was a singularly heart-stopping experience. There was a virility to the way he took charge that made her feel safe. She liked that he knew not only what he was doing but also what she liked having done to her.

"I know our working hours are different. So what's the answer?" she said.

"How about I take you to lunch?"

"Seriously?"

"Don't you think I know how to do stuff like that? I'm not a caveman."

"That's not what I meant and you know it. I thought you started work at nine this morning."

"I got relieved to attend some sort of induction program. I'm representing the city. But it'll be over by noon. I could pick you up by twelve-thirty, if you're free."

"I am free and it's a lovely idea."

When Deanna got off the phone, however, her excitement at the chance to see Patterson was tempered by a slight case of unease. Was there really enough between them for a true relationship? What was a relationship to be built on? And where could it lead?

And yet she had to admit that when they were alone together, in bed with their guard down and their clothes off, the only thing that mattered was what they said to each other. What they felt for each other. And the recognition that neither of them was taking their attraction lightly.

She had told no one about Patterson. Not because she was hiding anything but because she knew some of her friends wouldn't understand why she had a thing going with a New York City fireman.

Deanna opened her office door and then returned to her desk to look over her calendar. The first thing she did was mark the next time she would have a day off. Memorial Day Monday. She wanted to do something special with Jade. And she was trying to find an opportunity to spend time with Patterson. In bed or out, she was willing to take what she could get.

She reminisced about the Tuesday morning Patterson had mentioned. They'd spoken the night before and discovered that they both would have the morning free. When Deanna had returned from taking Jade to school, she found Patterson waiting in the lobby of her building. His eyes seemed to smolder with meaning and purpose. Their restraint disappeared as soon as they entered her apartment. She melted into his arms the moment the door was locked.

When he kissed her, she'd responded as if it was mouth-to-mouth resuscitation and she couldn't get enough. The slow, seductive dance of their tongues created an immediate pooling of desire in her groin and made her weak with anticipation. She realized she'd been foolish to think either of them wanted to spend their few hours together talking or watching TV.

Now, she was looking forward to having lunch with him. When the lobby security called, it was only a little after twelve.

"Ms. Lindsay, there's a man—"

"Thanks. I'm expecting a visitor. Send him to the Information Center."

In the several minutes it would take him to get the elevator to the ninth floor, Deanna fluffed her hair, reapplied her lipstick, and brushed her teeth in the ladies' room. She was glad she'd worn a dress today. She wanted Patterson to see her legs.

"You have a visitor," Stephen said coyly.

Deanna left her office to meet Patterson near the reference desk. But it wasn't Patterson who was waiting for her. It was Richard.

She stopped in her tracks and stared at him. She hadn't seen or heard from Richard in nearly two months. She realized that she also hadn't given him any thought. That alone made it clear that their relationship had been a lovely affair, nothing more. The last person she wanted to see right now was Richard.

He was dressed impeccably in executive attire and

looked very handsome and urbane. He maintained a polite demeanor, but she could see the longing in his eyes, and it surprised her. She was over it. She'd thought he would be, too.

"Hello," Richard said smoothly. "It's good to see you."

"Hi. What are you doing here?"

"I wanted to see you, of course."

"Now?" she frowned. "Couldn't you have called?"

He raised his brows. "You don't sound very happy to see me."

"I'm surprised, Richard. The last time we saw each other didn't leave me with the impression that you understood what I was going through."

"I probably didn't," he admitted. "That's why I'm here now."

She held her breath. "Yes?" Deanna whispered, with trepidation.

He glanced around, and then back to her. "Is there somewhere we can talk privately?"

"Not really. You know what my office is like. And this is not a good time."

"I only need a few minutes," Richard persisted.

It was hard to turn him down. He was being calm, pleasant, even attentive. His blue eyes and seductive voice were compelling. There was no privacy in the library. It was too open, and there were too many pairs of ears.

"Let's go to the reception area," Deanna suggested, hoping to encourage him to leave.

That part of the office was rather spacious, and besides the front desk there were two small banks of club chairs and reading tables. Deanna didn't want to sit down. She stood far enough away from Gloria to allow them to talk, but she did nothing to make Richard comfortable.

"I'm sorry. We'll have to talk here."

He kept his cool.

"All right. Look, I've been thinking about us. I know we've had some misunderstandings, but I think we can work them out, Deanna. I know that keeping that little girl, the daughter of your friend, is important to you. If that's what you want, fine. I'll learn to deal with it. You and I really had something good going. Let's not throw it away."

Deanna showed no sign of how she felt about Richard's recital. She was surprised, of course. She shook her head.

"It's too late, Richard. You can't start and stop relationships like turning the hot water tap on and off. I think you made yourself very clear when I told you I really wanted to be Jade's guardian."

"Come on, Deanna. What do you mean it's too late?"

"I mean that whatever I felt for you is gone. You weren't around to keep my feelings alive. Quite honestly, I didn't have the time to chase you down and make you see that Jade was no threat to our relationship."

"Deanna . . ." Richard stepped forward and took hold of her arms. "I'm sorry. Really. Maybe I did feel that Jade was going to come between us. Maybe I wasn't willing to share you. But I don't want to lose you, either. You want to know something? You're the only woman I've ever known that I asked for a second chance. Do you understand what I'm saying?"

"You can have your second chance . . . but it can't be with me." She continued to hold his gaze, trying to make him see that she meant it. When the message finally sank in, his disappointment was palpable. He pulled her a few inches closer.

"Are you sure?" he asked solemnly.

Deanna never had a chance to respond. A bell dinged, announcing the arrival of the elevator. She glanced up. Patterson stood just outside the reception area. He was formally attired in dress uniform. He held a hat under his arm . . . and a small bouquet of flowers in his hand. The look in his eyes made Deanna realize that Richard was still holding her closer than he should be, closer than she should have allowed. She twisted free to face Patterson.

"Deanna—" Richard tried to gain her attention.

"Patterson—" Deanna began, feeling guilty, frustrated, and annoyed.

"Sorry, wrong floor," he said stiffly.

He seemed to consider the flowers for a moment and then stepped forward to give them to the receptionist. Without another glance in Deanna's direction, he headed back to the elevators.

"Patterson, wait a minute," she called, more urgently this time as the elevator door closed firmly behind him.

Stunned, Deanna stared at the elevator. She couldn't believe that in a flash, a chasm had been created between her and Patterson.

Deanna and Joy waved at Jade as she circled back on her bicycle. She was trying not to get too far ahead as the adults followed behind her on foot.

"Well, one thing for sure . . . he's acting just like every other man when it comes to being jealous," Joy said calmly. "I guess you should be glad. That means your fireman really likes you, Dee."

Deanna gave her an impatient glare. "He's not my

fireman and it's not that simple. Richard isn't just another man. Patterson saw me practically in the arms of a *white* man. I know that pushed his buttons. Patterson isn't like every other man, either. He's a more complicated black man than you can imagine."

"Well, he needs to get over it. He sounds like too much work. You've known him for less than three months, only been to bed with him a couple of times, and he has the nerve to think he can make a claim?"

Deanna wanted to say yes, for reasons that she didn't want to explain to Joy. "Not a claim, but now's the time when we do that courtship dance and figure out if this is for real, or just a fling."

"What do you want?" Joy asked.

"I'm not sure yet, but I thought it was worth getting to know one another. See how things work out."

"Is that based on his personality . . . or his performance in bed?"

Deanna sucked her teeth. "You know I don't do that. There was only one time in my life when I let lust get in the way of my good sense, and we know what *that* got me. For me there has to be more than sex involved because that's not going to last."

"So, then, the fact that he's only a fireman . . . as you so readily dismissed him when you first told me about him . . . is irrelevant?"

"I'm getting over that. Patterson is incredibly smart and brave and—"

"Yeah, yeah, yeah . . . but can he handle himself in mixed company? What's he like at a dinner party with maybe the director of the Studio Museum on one side and Ismael Reed on the other? And don't tell me you haven't thought about that."

"Patterson is good with people, period."

"Except for when he flies off the handle and jumps

to unfair conclusions. Did he call and ask you about Richard?"

Deanna slowly shook her head, the memory of the incident in the reception area making her feel dispirited. "I haven't called him, either. And I won't. He should have waited and given me a chance to say something. I wasn't going to go chasing after him. He didn't see what he thought he was seeing."

"Yes, he did, Deanna. Look, from his perspective the bottom line was you were with another man. You're probably right that Richard's being white made Patterson go ballistic. You know that's the third rail for black men. If you care about him that much, maybe you should bite the bullet and just call him. Try to explain."

"I don't have time for that," Deanna insisted. "There's something more important I have to take care of right now. This business with Patterson will have to wait."

"Huh-huh," Joy cautioned. "Not too long. He sounds like a very proud man. He may not wait."

"Well, I don't have a choice. Right now Jade is the priority. I got a letter yesterday from ACS. The authorities have found Stacy's family in Reno, Nevada."

"Really? What did they say when they found out about Jade? Are they coming to get her?"

"They're not interested," Deanna informed Joy with more relief than she would ever admit to.

"Oh . . . Do you think it's because Jade's father is black?"

"Who knows? I just see their decision as one more problem out of the way. If Stacy didn't want to have anything to do with them, I'm glad they don't care about Jade."

"Deanna, I think you should try to get permanent custody of Jade," Joy said firmly. "You're kidding yourself if you think you would ever be willing to give her up."

"I know." Deanna sighed. "But it's not going to be that easy. ACS has scheduled a hearing early in June to determine custody."

"There's only you, and you're already taking care of her."

"There's also Marcus Lowell. He has more rights than I do. He's her father."

Chapter Sixteen

As the taxi sped across the bridge to Brooklyn, Deanna recalled all the times she'd made this trip with Patterson and Jade. Their time together had become almost routine. Time that had allowed her and Patterson to get to know one another. Time enough to know that something good was going on. She remembered their conversations, and the revelations they'd both made of their hopes and fears. She thought they had finally come to like and trust each other. It might have led to something more. Except for the minor detail of Patterson's having walked in on her with another man. He had drawn the worst possible conclusion.

Which was why Deanna now found herself traveling alone to Brooklyn. To try and find out what had gone wrong. Her pride told her she might be making a mistake, making a fool of herself. Her heart told her that Patterson was worth it. She also kept remembering something that Joy had told her—that Patterson did not strike her as the kind of man who would wait indefinitely. Because she feared that Joy might be right, Deanna was willing to hold her pride in check rather than risk losing the man she was falling in love with. That didn't mean she wasn't still annoyed with him for not giving her—them—the benefit of the doubt.

And Deanna didn't have a plan B if plan A didn't work. It was three o'clock on a Sunday afternoon. She'd left Jade with a sitter, claiming an important errand and promising to be back in a few hours.

The taxi drove up the block toward Patterson's brownstone, and Deanna scanned the street for his Jeep. She saw it parked on the side opposite his house. She instructed the driver to return for her in half an hour, and paid him for the trip out. As she approached the brownstone, Deanna could feel her anxiety mounting. Her determination was fueled by her staunch belief that, before Richard's reappearance at the wrong place and the wrong time, something significant had been developing between her and Patterson.

She rang the bell, and waited. She heard no footsteps and so was startled when the door opened after a while. Her heart felt as if it were skipping beats. Silently, she faced Patterson across the threshold. She tried to read his expression, and was uncertain when he seemed surprised and less than pleased to see her.

He must have been asleep. His eyes seemed slightly clouded and dazed. He stood bare-chested in a pair of sweatpants that hung low on his hips, as if he'd pulled them on to answer the door. Deanna's first objective had been to see him face-to-face. That, she realized now, may have been the easiest part.

Patterson couldn't have spoken if his life depended on it.

The very last thing he would have expected was for Deanna to show up on his doorstep. He could tell by her furrowed brow and dangerous glare that her bad mood matched his. But he had no idea why she should be mad. He watched warily as she stepped right up to the door and stared him down.

"Are you going to invite me in or close the door in my face?" she asked.

"Why did you come here?"

Deanna felt her stomach churn at his flat, indifferent tone. "Don't pretend you don't know, Patterson. We have a few things to get straight between us, and I'm not leaving until we both understand what's going on, what went wrong, and what we're going to do about it."

His jaw flexed. "What if I don't care?"

"Then say so and I'll leave," she challenged him bluntly. And held her breath.

Slowly Patterson pulled the door further open and stepped aside. He couldn't get over the fact that she was here. He'd never seen her so angry. He'd never seen her so fearless.

Deanna marched in, her entire body trembling with tension. She clenched a fist and clamped her jaw to control it. She tried to gather her wits before turning and facing Patterson again.

"This isn't going to change anything," he said.

Deanna narrowed her gaze on him. "Maybe not. But at least I didn't run away. At least I'm willing to find out if there is something more between us than curiosity and lust. At least I want to figure out what went wrong."

He walked past her into the media room and began to pace. "It seemed pretty clear to me. Was I *supposed* to catch you like that?" he scoffed. "You don't look at a man the way I saw you look at him if it doesn't mean something. You don't let a man hold you the way he did unless he has a right to."

Deanna stepped into his path, forcing him to stop and face her. She put her hand on his chest to keep him there. His skin was firm and very warm.

"It's because Richard is white."

"I got there just in time to see what I was up against. Hell, I can't compete with a man who is *everything* I'm not."

"You don't have to and I haven't asked you to. Whatever you think was happening is in your head. There is no competition between you and Richard.

"Richard broke off with me months ago, when I told him I wanted to care for Jade. When you saw him, he'd just showed up at my office without warning to tell me he'd changed his mind. But I haven't. Not about Jade." Deanna took a step closer and held Patterson's gaze. "And not about you."

Patterson knew she had him.

Deanna had effectively put the ball in his court. There was only one shot he could take . . . and he didn't know if he could risk it. It had been easy enough to sign off on the end of his affair with Eleanor because she was not the woman he wanted. He knew that even before he met Deanna. But she had become his gold standard.

Patterson wasn't sure what he had to offer her when there was someone like that white guy who had the same things she had: class, status, and good breeding. Real family history. Power. He didn't think his background could hold up under close scrutiny.

"Maybe it's just as well that this happened," he said to her. "It'll probably happen again. It just reminds me how different we really are. Like your friend who only saw me as a fireman."

"You're right. I *am* a bit of a snob. I *am* selective. Because *I'm* worth it. I chose you because *you're* worth it. We chose each other, Patterson. Our background has nothing to do with that. You didn't risk any more than I did. I still think the risk is worth it."

Patterson stepped away from her but could still feel the gentle press of her fingertips on his chest. He could still see the flashing challenge in her dark eyes. He felt powerless to tell her what it had really been like to walk off the elevator and see her with that other man. It had knocked the wind out of him.

"I don't think I'm wrong in how I feel about you, Patterson. But I need to know you're not going to hold my past against me. I need to know you're willing to fight for me . . . with me."

He knew that Deanna was right. Either he had faith in them or he didn't. They couldn't build a relationship on half measures.

He found himself moving, walking toward her, holding her gaze because in Deanna's bright eyes he saw encouragement. And hope. Her bravery astonished and humbled him. Patterson silently swept her into his arms, feeling the way her slender body curved to fit against him. No resistance. No hesitation.

He kissed her with deep satisfaction and a relief that rocked him like a sudden cool breeze rushing through his body. He kissed her like a hungry man who had gone too long without nourishment. Patterson kissed her to say he was sorry, because the words would not come naturally to his lips.

And they simply held each other, because that seemed the most natural remedy.

"Listen to me . . ." Patterson began. He pulled back so he could see her. His fingers restlessly rubbed her back. "I'm probably *that close* to being in love with you. There has never been anyone I could say that about."

"Is *that* what you're afraid of?" she asked, incredulous. "That I might break your heart? What about *my* heart? I'm here because I'm willing to take a chance."

This was a first for Patterson. Meeting a woman who just put it out there. Deanna had a self-image that didn't allow for being faint of heart. He'd known when he opened his door and saw the fire in her eyes that he'd made a few mistakes with her. The first had been not to take her seriously enough. The second was to doubt her sincerity. There was no place for them to go if he couldn't believe himself worthy of her.

That was his problem, not hers.

The next afternoon, Deanna was on the uptown bus on her way to pick up Jade, when her cell phone rang.

She hoped it wasn't her office, calling her back for some news emergency. She hoped it wasn't Jade's after-school program with a report of yet another crisis.

"Hello," she said as quietly as possible, aware of the incongruity of taking personal calls in a public place.

"Yeah . . . you know who this is?"

For a moment she didn't. The voice was aggressive and cocky. She hesitated, frowning. "Is . . . this Marcus?"

"Right," he drawled out.

Deanna was incredulous. A thread of apprehension tightened in her stomach. "How did you get this number?"

"From Jade." He sounded both amused and triumphant.

Deanna's apprehension became dread. She sprang forward on the edge of her seat, drawing the attention of several nearby passengers.

She stood up and pushed her way through to the exit door, where the shallow bay of stairs provided a few more feet of space. She didn't know whether to get off or stay on. She couldn't think. "Jade? When did you see her? You're not supposed to come near her."

Now passengers were openly staring at her.

"Ain't nobody gonna tell me what I can do. I told you that. No point in going to that school to look for her. She ain't there."

"No—" Deanna gasped softly. It felt as if her heart had jumped into her throat and lodged there. She was suddenly hot and faint. Perspiration prickled her skin.

"I got her. Just for a little visit."

"No! You can't do this," she raised her voice. People were craning their necks to see her.

"Hey, I'm doin' it."

"Oh, my God," Deanna murmured, her voice quivering. She felt a hand touch her shoulder. She spun around and found an older woman staring at her with concern.

"Are you all right, dear?"

Deanna's attempt at a reassuring smile failed. She nodded weakly. "I'm . . . fine."

She frantically pressed the stop signal and stumbled off the bus, needing air.

"You freakin' out, right?" Marcus chuckled.

"What do you want? Where did you take her?"

"You can have her back. Maybe tomorrow. But I want something for her."

"Money."

"Smart lady."

"You'd blackmail me with your own daughter? How could you? What kind of man are you?" She was on the verge of tears.

"Hey, careful what you say to me, bitch. This ain't blackmail. You forget Jade is my kid. I didn't kidnap her, either. She came with me on her own. All I'm saying is, you give me some money, I give her back.

No big deal. Don't call no cops. This just between you and me."

Deanna covered her mouth, preventing a sob from escaping. "Wh . . . where is she?"

"She's okay. She's with me and HoJo. My girl is watching her."

"What do you want me to do?"

He laughed again. "Let me think about it. I'll get back to you."

"When?"

He disconnected.

Deanna, standing huddled against the side of a building, broke down and cried. She got over it quickly. Then she got mad.

But she didn't call the police. She had to trust her instincts that as immoral as Marcus Lowell was, he wouldn't physically hurt Jade. Unless, perhaps, he was cornered by the cops. If it came to it, Deanna would give him anything he wanted to make sure Jade was returned to her safely.

She had to do something. She composed herself with a deep breath and tried to think. Her options seemed precious few. She could wait it out, trust that Marcus would call her back soon. She could call Joy—who would tell her to call the police. Ditto her mother, Carla, and any other rational human being. Instead, she called Patterson.

His cell phone was turned off and she got the voice mail. She tried him at home with the same results. She called the firehouse, but the phone just rang and rang. Glancing around in frustration, she saw that rush-hour traffic was stalled, as usual. There would be no point in catching a cab. She headed for the subway instead.

Deanna was breathless when she reached the firehouse, and devastated when she found the red bay door closed.

Frantically, she paced back and forth, wondering what to do next. The police came to mind again. She decided no. *Not yet . . .*

Then she spotted what looked like a buzzer between a dark frosted window of the firehouse and the closed door. She pressed it, holding it for several seconds. She could hear it ringing inside. In another moment, a narrow side door opened and a fireman in navy blue slacks and a T-shirt stepped partially out.

"Yeah, can I help you?"

"I . . . I was hoping to see Pa . . . Captain Temple, if he's here."

The man looked her curiously up and down. "Yeah, he's here. He expecting you?"

"No, but I know him and . . . this is important."

"Well, you'll have to wait here. I'll go get him. What's your name?"

"Tell him it's Deanna."

Patterson was trying to read the latest edition of his professional newsletter, but he couldn't concentrate. He was in a foul mood. The sound of the TV in the crew lounge and the idle chatter of his men repeatedly broke into his thoughts.

They were about Deanna.

He had a clearly defined image of her as he'd last seen her—saying good-bye, gazing up at him with frustration, followed by tender understanding, which he knew he didn't deserve.

"Stay," he had pleaded with uncustomary shyness. "I feel like I should say something more to you."

"You should," Deanna agreed, "but not now. I have to get back to Jade. And you have a lot to think about, Patterson. It takes two people to have a relationship. I'm willing if you are."

He'd watched as Deanna got into a waiting taxi. Then he'd stood alone in his media room, fingering his guitar and knowing he might have blown it with the only woman he'd ever really wanted.

He would have to earn her respect again.

Patterson got up restlessly and attempted to regain his focus by reading the dozens of official notices posted on a bulletin board.

"Captain, there's someone downstairs to see you," Gary announced, appearing at the doorway of the lounge.

"Black teenager, about seventeen?"

"Nope. A beautiful lady . . . and I'm not going to guess how old she is," Gary joked.

Patterson rushed past Gary and took the stairs two at a time. He opened the public door and pushed out of it. Deanna stood waiting for him.

She looked scared out of her wits.

Patterson's emotions shifted from nervous to fearful. He took hold of her arms.

"What happened?" he demanded. "Is it Jade?"

Deanna tried to speak, but only nodded.

"Where is she?"

"Marcus has her. I was on my way to get her . . . and he called, and . . ."

"Why?" Patterson was confused.

"He wants money. He'll give her back, but he wants money first."

In his rage Patterson inadvertently gripped her arms tighter. "He's trying to blackmail you?"

"He said he needs some money, that's all. And he told me not to call the police."

Patterson mulled it over. "No," he agreed, "you can't do that. Not yet. What else did he say?"

"He said he'll call me later. He has my cell phone number. He could only have gotten it from Jade. Patterson, I . . ."

"Okay, okay," he soothed, putting an arm around her as she tried not to cry. "Come inside."

He led the way. The apparatus room was dark, the space taken up almost entirely by the parked rig. He ignored Gary's curious expression and sat with Deanna in two chairs right outside the room, which gave them a little more privacy.

"When did he call? Tell me exactly what he said to you," Patterson demanded.

Deanna told him everything she could remember, including Marcus's information that he lived in the Heights, and that he was with his friend HoJo.

"Hollis Jones," Patterson muttered.

"You know him?"

"Just a dumb punk. One of Marcus's flunkies. Can't think for himself. You said Marcus told you he was staying in the Heights? Could be Washington Heights. Or Morningside."

"What about Crown Heights in Brooklyn?"

"No, I don't think so. He seems to be operating in Manhattan since he got out of jail. He's probably crashing with a friend."

"A girlfriend," Deanna added excitedly. "He said his girl was watching Jade."

"Good," Patterson nodded.

"But there's no way to know," Deanna said. "Shouldn't we be doing something?"

He took her hand. "Marcus isn't crazy enough to hurt Jade. He only wants what he can trade her for."

"That's cruel of him."

"I agree," Patterson said dryly. "The first think I have to do is see if I can find out where he's living."

"How?"

"I have a couple of friends I can call." He got up to head for the office.

"Patterson, I'll give him the money. It's not important to me. I just don't want anything . . ."

He turned back and squatted down in front of her chair, laying his hand against her cheek. "It's not going to come to that. Marcus is not that smart. He's left himself open, and I'm going to figure out where and how."

"I'm really afraid."

"You're braver than you think. I won't let anything happen to Jade. I promise. Can you trust me?"

She nodded without a moment's hesitation.

Patterson went into action with the same thoroughness he employed to run his command at the engine company. He devised a plan and executed each step carefully. The first thing he did was to claim a personal emergency and call in someone to replace him for the remaining three hours of his tour. The second was to call two fellow firemen, Oscar from 4-Alarm and Victor, a buddy from the NYFD training academy. Both were available and agreed to help, understanding that what they might be doing was not in their training manual.

Third, Patterson called Officer Keisha Findlay, whom Deanna had seen outside of Bellevue the day he'd met Deanna. He asked her to do him a favor and run a check with Marcus's parole officer for his last known address. While he waited for that information, Patterson returned to Deanna.

"Look, I can't let you stay here. I'm going to leave

to check out a few things, and a fire call could come in at any time. You'd be in the way." He escorted her back outside.

"What are you going to do?" Deanna asked anxiously.

"Put together a cavalry," he said. "Do you have a driver's license?"

"Yes, I do."

He dug his keys out of his pocket and gave them to her. "My Jeep is parked down the block. Take it and go home."

"No. I . . ."

"I need you to be where I can find you."

"Can't I come with you? What are you going to do?"

"I don't know yet. I'm waiting for some information from a friend of mine. We don't know what Marcus is going to do. He could bring Jade back and ask for the money from you in person. Jade could try to call you. As soon as I know anything I'll call."

Patterson walked Deanna to his car, watching as she adjusted the seat and the viewing mirrors. She looked at him through the window.

"You'll call me?"

"As soon as I know anything."

Bracing his hands on the window frame, he leaned in and kissed her. He had given her all the verbal assurances he could without knowing whether he could pull them off. And he was going to do his damnedest not to disappoint her.

The three men got out of the 4x4. With the careful scrutiny of trackers scoping out enemy territory, they scanned the street, direction of traffic, number of pedestrians and residential units. Out of habit Patterson checked for hydrants, street lights, and alarm boxes.

"That's the address over there," said Oscar, the vocalist in 4-Alarm, nodding.

The building was fairly new, of red brick construction. No visible fire escapes, Patterson noted.

"Do you know what apartment?" Victor, Patterson's academy buddy, asked.

"Keisha couldn't get that for me. The apartment isn't in Marcus's name, anyway, so that makes it harder. Could be rented to this girlfriend he mentioned."

"The building isn't that big. Seven stories . . . maybe forty-eight units in all," Oscar calculated.

"So what do you want to do, Pat? Knock on every door and see who's behind each one?" Victor questioned.

"That's the easiest thing. Let's think this through. We can't start at the top. If Marcus is on a lower floor he might be alerted. So we'll work the other way around. Keisha faxed me a mug shot of Marcus." Patterson unfolded several sheets of paper from his shirt pocket and distributed them to his friends. "So you'll know what he looks like. There's also one of HoJo, a.k.a. Hollis Jones. One of us should stay at the front door, while the other two go floor to floor. Just in case Marcus tries to slip by."

Patterson frowned as he studied the front of the building. "There's probably a back door. What about that?"

"Technically, we know that has to remain accessible because of the possibility of fire, and for deliveries. But it can be blocked up until we're through."

"Okay, let's do it," Patterson agreed. "We're going to need a reason to tell folks they have to leave the building. This is where you guys have to decide how far you're willing to go. I say we wear our department jackets, show our badges, and act official as hell. Baffle them with bullshit."

Victor and Oscar laughed.

"No problem. I can do authority," Oscar said in his rough baritone voice.

"This could backfire," Patterson warned.

"I think we have justification if we need it," Victor countered. "The cops do it all the time and call it undercover and surveillance. And I know a few folks in high places if we need help later."

"What if nobody moves?" Oscar asked.

Victor rubbed his chin. "Let's just make an official announcement that there's a dangerous gas leak, or something like that. We can use the horn and talk loud. We'll say we have to evacuate the building for everyone's safety."

"I like that idea. No panic and no one gets hurt," Patterson said. "Marcus might head for the roof, but I'm betting he won't think of that. It would mean jumping to the next building to get away. I doubt he'd try that with Jade."

"What else?" Victor asked.

The three men looked at each other.

"If anyone questions what's going on, say there was a report and we have to check it out in case there's potential for a fire," Patterson instructed. "And another thing—if *anything* goes wrong, it's my fault, my responsibility. Agreed?"

Victor shrugged. "Fine with me. I love you, man, but I ain't gonna hang with you."

They all laughed nervously.

Chapter Seventeen

She didn't like this place.

She was hungry and she wanted to go home to Deanna.

She didn't know these people, and she didn't want to stay with her father.

She sat in a corner of the sofa, very still, trying not to draw attention to herself. She held on to her school backpack, but that lady in the kitchen had already gone through her things and taken the bracelet Deanna had given her. Every now and then the woman would look at her as if daring her to do something wrong. The woman had yelled when her father brought her here. Told her to sit and not to move. She'd done as she was told, but now she had to go to the bathroom.

She leaned back against the cushions. She was getting sleepy, but she was afraid to go to sleep.

She wished Deanna would come and get her.

She jumped when there was shouting in the hall. There were men yelling and they kept getting louder and louder.

Marcus came out of the bedroom. "What the fuck is going on?" he boomed. "Who's making all that noise?"

"Don't ask me," the woman said, turning the frying fish in the pan. She wiped her hands on a dish towel and threw it on the back burner of the stove.

Jade slid off the sofa. She couldn't wait any longer. "Can I go to the bathroom?" she asked in a small voice.

No one answered her.

Marcus walked back and forth. "Something's going on." He went to the door and opened it. There were men in the third-floor hallway, going from apartment to apartment, telling people to get out of the building.

Jade stood squeezing her legs together. Deanna might get mad at her if she had an accident. She hurried into the bathroom without permission and closed the door.

HoJo came hurrying into the apartment from the hall. "There's some shit goin' on in the building. Maybe a fire or something."

"You see any smoke?"

"Nothing, man. But I did see a couple of firemen."

"Firemen?" Marcus asked suspiciously.

At that moment a smoke detector went off somewhere in the building. Marcus opened the door again. He stepped into the hall. People were milling about, asking each other what was happening, where was the fire.

It didn't smell like no fire to Marcus.

What he smelled was a trick. He leaned over the stairwell banister. One floor below, a couple of men in uniforms were ordering people to leave the building. Marcus went back into the apartment and closed the door.

"Baby, we better get the hell out of here," his girlfriend said, fearful, already starting to gather her things.

Marcus marched through the living room to the windows. He opened one and looked out. It was dusk and the streetlights were on. People were already coming out of the building onto the sidewalk, plus a lot of people who were just curious were gathering. But there were no fire trucks. No official red NYFD cars. No firemen in front of the building. Just one man, directing people to the other side of the street.

"There ain't no fire. Something's going on," he scoffed.

"What we gonna do, man?" HoJo asked.

"I'm not burning in this place, Marcus," the woman said. "See, I *knew* there was going to be trouble if you brought that kid here."

"This is fucking up my plans," Marcus fumed. "I told that bitch I'd come to her and get the money. That's all she had to do and she could have had the kid back, if she wanted her. I bet she called the cops . . ."

He put on his shoes, got a jacket and a few other small possessions.

"Forget the money, Marcus. It ain't worth it. Let's get *out*. I don't know what I'm going to tell my aunt if her place burns down . . ."

"We can't leave the building with those men in the hall. That guy that knew Stacy is slick. He's a fireman. It could be him out there." He glanced around. "Where's Jade?"

"I don't know. Maybe in the bathroom. Leave her there. They'll find her," his girlfriend said.

"Marcus, she'll tell them what we did," HoJo complained.

"We ain't done nothing. She was visiting, that's all. I'm her daddy. We'll say we couldn't find her . . . she was hiding or something . . ."

"You can stay here if you want. I'm leaving," the woman declared.

"Okay, okay. Look, you go first. You gotta find a

way to get their attention so me and HoJo can sneak by them. There's only two of them."

"Naw, man. There's this big dude in front, too."

"Shit. Okay, we do this. If they stop us, we tell them the kid is stuck in the apartment. If they want her, they can go get her."

"They could hold you and still come get her," the woman said. "Just make up your mind already."

"Okay . . . go!" Marcus told her.

Smoke and the pungent smell of burning fabric were filling the kitchen.

"Fuck!" Marcus screamed at the woman. "You left something burning on the goddamn stove!"

He went into the kitchen and found the dish towel on the stove already engulfed in flames. He tried to toss it in the sink, but he burned his fingers and the towel landed on the table. A spark flew and caught on the hallway carpet leading to the apartment door. The cloth became cinders, but not before the fire spread to a shirt on the back of a chair and some papers on the dining room table.

"I'm getting out!" The woman ran out of the apartment, leaving the door open.

"Marcus, what we gonna do, man?" HoJo held up his arms against the heat and the quickly growing flames leaping from one surface to another in the tiny apartment.

"Forget this shit." Marcus grabbed his coat and without another word rushed out of the apartment, slamming the door behind him.

Fire caught the bottom of a jacket hanging inside the open closet door . . . and then another. Flames erupted through the closet and roared outward, licking along the walls and around the door frame.

HoJo knew this was bad. He tried to grab the outside

door handle, but jerked back because of the heat. He knew that somehow he was going to be blamed for this. When things went wrong, Marcus always told him it was his fault. But if they never found the kid, then nobody would ever know. He would just walk away.

HoJo looked around frantically for something to use on the burning-hot door handle. He dashed back to the living room, found Jade's hooded sweatshirt on the coffee table. He grabbed it up and wrapped it around his hand.

"Wait!" He heard a cry. He glanced over his shoulder.

The bathroom door was open. Jade stood there, paralyzed, staring at the fire, which was gaining momentum and quickly spreading in the kitchen on the far side of the apartment. She squinted against the smoke and flames. Hunching her small shoulders, she began to shake with fear and confusion. Her father and his girlfriend were gone. But the other man was still there, standing in the front door.

"Don't leave me!" Jade wailed, running toward him. She screamed. A wall of heat from something burning on the floor forced her back.

HoJo, fumbling to get out, grabbed the burning handle, pulling the door shut behind him. It slam-locked.

Pandemonium set in.

The evacuation of the first floor and a half went smoothly. No one asked questions; they just hurried past Patterson and Victor as they directed the tenants out. Residents from the upper floors, however, were coming down faster than they could screen, and Patterson thought it better to let everyone pass, as long as they were leaving the building. Oscar was out front and hopefully would spot Marcus or HoJo if either made it past him and Victor. But Patterson didn't care about either of them. He was looking to see if Jade was among those fleeing the building.

People were already beginning to sense that this wasn't a deadly emergency after all. Until someone yelled, "Fire." At first Patterson thought it was a prank warning, making their own theatrics frighteningly real. Then he realized it was no longer a game. He and Victor had been trained to detect the chemical odors of burning materials, and there was no doubt now that something was actually burning somewhere.

Patterson was forced to switch his focus, to consider the real deal. They kept going, the need to get everyone out of the building taking on the momentum of a serious crisis. On the second floor they found themselves hampered by the suddenly crowded hallways.

"Pat, this is getting out of hand," Victor shouted over the din.

"Something's wrong," Patterson agreed. "There's a bad situation somewhere in the building. We have to call in an alarm after all. We better check to see where it's coming from. And we've got to find Jade."

Just then the very person Patterson was looking for came running down the stairs from the third floor.

"That's him, that's Marcus," he said, getting Victor's attention. Patterson planted himself in the corner of the hallway and took the impact of Marcus, who tried to barrel past him. He grabbed Marcus's shoulders, jerking him around. "Where's Jade?"

"I don't know what you're talking about, man." Marcus struggled to get free. "Get the fuck off! The place is on fire!"

Patterson slammed him against the wall. "*Where?*"

Marcus pointed. "Up there. Ain't nothing happen to her, man. Let me go."

"Which apartment?"

"*Up there!* 3-E," he shouted.

Patterson released him. Marcus escaped down the stairs, but Victor grabbed his arm. "Don't you want to hold him? I thought he was the guy you're looking for."

"Let him go. I don't want Marcus, I want Jade. Come on, we have to find her."

Halfway up the stairs Patterson found himself violently shoved against the wall as a husky man stumbled past. He recovered his footing as he recognized Hollis Jones but continued up to the third floor. Several people were screaming now. He knew before he'd reached the top step that there was, indeed, a real fire raging in one of the units.

And he could hear a child screaming.

"Oh, Jesus." Patterson rushed down the hall to an apartment where smoke crept out from beneath the door. 3-E. The screaming was even louder. "*Jade!*" he bellowed. He reached for the handle of the metal door but knew it would be too hot to touch. Wildly he kicked at the door, hoping that it wasn't shut all the way, or that it was unlocked.

"Pat, that's not going to work. I'll call in an alarm."

"Right. Check if Oscar has a can with him," Patterson called after Victor, who was already halfway down the stairs. "And some rope! I'm going to the roof. *Hurry!*" Patterson said, breathing heavily. His heart twisted painfully at the sounds coming from beyond the door. "Jade, can you hear me? It's Patterson. *Listen to me!* Get to the bathroom and close the door. *Go to the bathroom!*" Suddenly the crying stopped, but Patterson didn't take time to think about what that meant.

He headed for the staircase and ran up the next three flights to the roof door. It was locked, but in the stairwell was a little closet, inside of which was an encased fire ax. It wouldn't do a thing on metal doors in the building, including this one, but Patterson used the back of it like a hammer and swung vigorously at the doorknob of the roof exit until it bent and came loose. He threw his shoulder against the door several times until it gave way, and he rushed out. It was almost dark, and only one light burned over the doorway.

Patterson figured out which direction was the front of the building and ran to lean over the parapet. There was a crowd on the street below. Smoke was coming out of two windows on the third floor. That was it. Not knowing what the situation was like inside the apartment where Jade was locked, Patterson couldn't risk that smoke inhalation of flames wouldn't reach her before real emergency help could get there. The very idea made him crazed.

"Come on, Victor . . . hurry up, man," he muttered to himself.

A moment later Victor came through the door. He had a long coil of heavy rope slung over his shoulder. He also had a small fire extinguisher.

Patterson reached for the rope, looking around for a way to anchor it. "Where's Oscar?"

"He's on his way up. He called in an alarm. He saw Marcus but didn't bother stopping him when you didn't come down. I told him about the little girl, and he figured she was more important."

"He figured right," Patterson said.

He tied a length of the rope around his waist and

created a foot stirrup from the short end. He tossed the rest to Victor, heading for the edge of the roof over the front of the building. Oscar arrived, out of breath, and filled them in on what was going on below.

"Oscar, I need you and Victor to secure that end to something or to hold it. I'm going to rappel down to the third floor and go in through a window."

"Wait a few more minutes, Pat. I can hear the truck arriving now."

Patterson stood at the edge, calculating where to position himself. "Jade doesn't have a few minutes. Right here. Come on, lower me down. I'll yell when to stop."

"You want the can?" Victor asked, extending the extinguisher.

"Naw, I can't hold it and the rope too."

Patterson had rappelled down the sides of buildings dozens of times before. But it had always been a drill. He'd never had to actually do it in an emergency with jury-rigged equipment, and go over a roof with no safety below him. He had no idea if the rope would hold. He wasn't wearing the right gear. But there was no other option.

As soon as he put his full weight on the line, he lost control. He'd made the mistake of using his left foot in the loop, and he could feel the strain in the knee he'd injured less than a month ago. He had no gloves and the rope began to burn his hands and to chafe through his clothing to his skin. With no way to balance himself, his body swung and twisted on the slow descent. With his peripheral vision he could see an engine company vehicle stop in the street below, parallel to the building. Another was turning the corner and heading for the site. Their emergency high-beam searchlights went on, throwing Patterson into a spotlight.

He used his free hand to try to avoid slamming into the side of the building.

When he got to just above the third floor, he shouted to Oscar and Victor. One of them yelled something to him about help, but he couldn't hear the words and didn't take the time to have it repeated. Patterson hoped it meant that help was on the way to 3-E. Flames had not yet reached what appeared to be a living room, but black smoke was billowing out through a window blasted out by the built-up heat inside the apartment. A bedroom window next to it was similarly open, but it didn't have as much smoke, being further away from the source. He knew the bathroom window would be a tight fit, but he hoped that Jade had gone there like he'd told her to, to close herself off from the fire.

He shouted for a little more rope, and dropped another foot, close enough to kick at the frosted glass. He had to kick it several times before it broke.

Below, the tillar rig was rotating a ladder into place, extending it to reach the third floor windows, in front of which Patterson dangled precariously.

Patterson reached out to grab the edge of the broken window frame, and pulled himself closer. He put his right leg inside, and wiggled to a sitting position across an opening encircled by jagged shards of glass. But he was still half out of the window.

He didn't see her. "Jade? Jade?" he called into the small room. Smoke was just beginning to squeeze under the door.

He heard coughing. He wasn't completely sure it was coming from the bathroom. Then he heard sobbing and his name.

"Patterson! I'm scared!"

His relief was overwhelming. She wasn't unconscious from smoke inhalation. But his relief was short-lived. They weren't out of the woods yet.

"Don't be scared. I'm going to get you out. Come over here to me . . . to the window. Stand on the toilet seat so I can reach you. That's it . . . good girl! I got you." He was able to wrap his arm around her waist and drag her up so he could get a stronger hold on her. "Put your arms around my neck real tight."

A fireman was beginning to climb the ladder at a forty-five-degree angle to reach them. From near the apartment door he could hear the sounds of an inside team at work on gaining entrance. An outside team already had a roof man with Oscar and Victor, and he could hear shouts from above.

He wasn't going to be able to hold his position much longer. With Jade in his arms, the strain on the rope was that much greater, and he had no balance at all. The best he could do was to stay put and wait until the rescue came to them. But flames were now at the bathroom door and the heat was becoming intense. He tried to shift so that his back would take the brunt of it. He whispered for Jade to press her face against his chest so she wouldn't breathe in any more of the smoke, but Patterson could feel it drawing into his own lungs.

"See, someone's coming to get us, Jade."

"Okay," she mumbled in a shaky voice.

Finally, a pair of black-covered hands reached out to take Jade from Patterson's arms. Quickly the fireman began the trip down again, taking her to safety. The gathered crowd in the street broke out in applause.

Patterson got out of the foot loop and maneuvered himself onto the top of the ladder. The rope remained wound around his waist and torso, but was released from above. When he was firmly planted on the familiar apparatus, he worked quickly to disentangle himself from the safety line.

Finally, he began the descent back to the ground.

Deanna was a nervous wreck, and there was nothing she could do except imagine the worst.

She was sorry she'd let Patterson talk her into returning home. She didn't know what she could have done to help if she'd insisted on going with him. He had been right about one thing. Marcus had called again.

He wanted to come and get the money from her. First—no meeting place, no secret drop-off point, no *cops*—then she could have Jade back.

Deanna had had a better idea. He must bring Jade with him when he came to get the money.

No deal. Then—he would think about it. Call her back. That had been hours ago. When the phone had rung, it had been her mother. Without launching into hysterical detail about the crisis, Deanna had put Faith off. It was now almost nine-thirty at night and the phone remained depressingly silent.

Desperate, she'd tried calling Patterson on his cellular several times. She always got his voice mail. She paced and paced, then finally sat on the sofa. Her body was wound tight with tension and raw nerves. Her stomach was a knot of stress.

She hadn't bargained for this.

She didn't know that along with the responsibility for Stacy's daughter would come this overwhelming awareness of how much she'd come to love the child. Deanna couldn't imagine anything more agonizing than the possibility of anything happening to Jade . . . or of losing her.

She wanted to keep her. She was going to do whatever it took to make her guardianship permanent. And Deanna *knew* she could do it because Patterson would not let anything happen to Jade.

At a little after ten the phone rang. She clutched the receiver and held her breath.

"She's okay. I got her," Patterson said.

"Are you sure?" Deanna asked in a small, frightened voice.

"I swear, she's fine," Patterson assured her.

"Your voice sounds strange. Are you okay?"

He tried to clear his throat. "Yeah. I'd let you talk to Jade, but she's being checked out by EMS."

"EMS? What happened? I've been going out of my mind. Where are you? I'm on my way . . ."

"Deanna, by the time you get here . . ."

"*Patterson,*" she began in a weak voice. "Please."

He kept it short and sweet.

"She's not hurt. Justly badly shaken up . . . and covered in soot. She wanted to know why you weren't there. I took the blame for that."

"But I have to go to her, Patterson," Deanna declared. "I need to see for myself that she's okay."

"She might be on the way to the hospital for further observation."

"Did they check you out, too? Are you hurt?"

"Just a few bruises."

"I don't know if I should believe you," Deanna complained. "I'm on my way."

"There are a lot of emergency vehicles and workers. Lots of cops. If you can't get through, just tell someone that Jade is your daughter."

That Jade was her daughter.

Chapter Eighteen

Jade was covered from head to feet in black soot. Her green eyes eerily bright in her dark face, she was lying on a gurney in the back of an EMS van, an oxygen mask over her small face. Deanna's heart felt as if it had stopped until she could see for herself that Jade was mostly tired and hungry. She took the child in her arms, cuddling and rocking her, and whispering that she'd been so brave.

Deanna caught a glimpse of Patterson near a second emergency vehicle, but although he was as filthy as Jade, he didn't show any signs of injury either. Though Jade was her first priority, she was just as concerned about Patterson. He was in discussion with a group of official-looking men, but when he saw her he excused himself and joined her.

"Patterson . . ." She reached out to touch him.

"Don't worry about me," he said, taking her arm and escorting her back to Jade's ambulance.

"Your voice . . . your hands," she murmured, noting the blisters and raw abrasions.

"It's not serious. You need to go with Jade. Make sure she's okay. I'll find you in a while."

At the hospital an hour later, Deanna appeared to be lounging in the visitor's chair at the side of the bed, but she was fully awake and alert as she stared at the small girl in the bed. For the dozenth time she sat forward and leaned over Jade.

A single wall light illuminated the child's face as she slept. Deanna smiled tenderly and carefully brushed her hand against Jade's cheek. There was still a hint of soot sprinkled through her golden hair, but she had otherwise been washed free of the residue of black smoke.

Jade had complained that her throat hurt, which seemed to be the only physical evidence of her ordeal. But the doctors warned that there might be nightmares, and even posttraumatic shock syndrome. Otherwise, she'd suffered only minor smoke inhalation and fright. Deanna had been given permission to stay the night, not only to satisfy herself that Jade was okay but also because she was not inclined to let Jade out of her sight.

A Mylar balloon was tied to the metal side rail of Jade's bed, and Oliver's fluffy ears stuck out from beneath the blanket. Jade had been allowed to wear one of her own nightgowns that Deanna had brought from home. But at first none of that was enough to reassure the child that the hospital stay was only a precaution. She wanted to go home with Deanna.

Deanna sat back again, yawning. She pulled her stocking feet into the chair and tried to get comfortable, covering herself with the extra blanket a nurse had been kind enough to provide.

There was a soft knock on the hospital room door. Deanna craned her neck to see who it was, hoping that Patterson would appear.

"Just checkin' to see how she's doin'," the night nurse said in a lilting Caribbean accent. She read several monitors at the head of Jade's bed.

"She's been sleeping peacefully," Deanna said.

"That's good, you know. She probably won't recall what happened."

"What about her throat? She complained that it was hurting after the doctor left."

"It's not serious. She'll be fine in a few days. You been here all the time?" she asked Deanna as she was about to leave again.

"I'm staying the night. I want to be here when she wakes up, and I can take her home."

"She's a pretty child," the nurse observed.

"Thank you."

The nurse left, but a moment later Deanna felt a hand on her shoulder. She jumped and looked up to find Patterson standing over her.

"Patterson!" she exclaimed. She scrambled out of the chair to greet him, reaching out to him. "Patterson, I'm—"

He pressed his fingers to her lips and motioned for her to be quiet, then led her from the room. Out in the hallway he replaced his hand with his lips, drawing her gently against him as she circled her arms around his waist.

She melted against him, responding with gentle ardor. His damaged hand pressed against the back of her head. His fingers massaged her scalp as he held her face tilted at the perfect angle for his kiss.

"You can go into the visitor's lounge, you know," the night nurse said, laughing softly as she passed them.

Deanna was a little embarrassed by her public display, but Patterson wasn't. She shook her head. "I don't want to leave Jade."

He ran his hands up and down her back, enjoying her weight against his chest and thighs. "I can wait."

Deanna thoroughly scrutinized his face. She

touched his jaw, felt his soft mustache and beard. "I wondered what happened to you."

"I had some explaining to do to the authorities. About the fire. What I was doing there to begin with."

"Do you know who set it?"

"I have a pretty good idea. They're taking care of it."

"What happened to Marcus? Did you see him?"

Patterson hedged. "He slipped away before I could get hold of him. I was more concerned about Jade. The police know all about Marcus. They'll probably pick him and HoJo up before morning."

"Thank goodness," Deanna murmured, resting her forehead against his chest. She felt him kiss the top of her head.

"It's not over yet," he said.

"What do you mean?"

"The police want to take Jade."

"But why?"

Patterson sighed, thinking how to explain. "Mostly it's because she's officially a ward of the state, even though you're her guardian. The way they see it, she could have been hurt, maybe even killed last night. They want to know how come she ended up in the hands of a felon."

"But, it's not as if I was careless, or even knew it was going to happen."

"I understand that. But you're dealing with city politics. The agencies come under the gun all the time for not taking better care of kids in foster care. You don't want to know how many die each year while they're with people who are supposed to be watching out for them."

"Then why didn't they take Jade?"

"You're still going to hear from them. I told them Jade already lost her mother. It would be a shame if she lost another person who loves her. She needs you."

Deanna averted her gaze. "Maybe I need her more." She hugged him. "I love you, Patterson Temple."

The words finally sank in, but Patterson wanted to be sure of what Deanna was saying.

" 'Thank you' would have been enough," he teased hoarsely.

"Would it?"

"No."

Deanna looked at him. "So what is it going to take for you to believe I mean it?"

He touched her mouth, stared into her eyes. "Mind saying it again?"

She kissed him instead.

It was enough.

Deanna led Jade by the hand down the long official corridor. She was looking for Room 319 and the chambers of Judge Simone Horton, who was to preside over the hearing requested by the ACS. The purpose of the hearing was to establish the custody and long-term care of Jade Taylor Lowell. It was also to hear a petition on behalf of Deanna Lindsay, who had applied for the right to adopt Jade.

She was aware that arriving ten minutes late might not help her case or give the judge a good impression of her. Marilyn Phillips had told her to be prompt, as if she didn't already have enough to make her anxious. Deanna finally located the room and, as she expected, found the door closed.

"Where are we going?" Jade asked.

"Remember, I told you we're going to a special meeting?"

"How come?"

"Because we have to talk with Marilyn Phillips and a very important judge."

As Deanna reached for the door handle, Jade held back, pulling on her hand. "Jade, we're late. What's the matter?"

"Deanna, do you have to go to jail?"

Deanna stared at Jade. "Where did you get that idea?"

"That's what the judge did to my daddy. I don't want you to go," Jade said fearfully.

Deanna hugged her, forgetting about the time. Forgetting about the proceeding . . . and the outcome. "Jade, I promise you I'm not going to jail."

"You won't leave me?"

The one thing Deanna had been fighting since she'd gotten up that morning was the urge to indulge in a desperate and prolonged fit of crying. Jade's heartbreaking plea just about did her in. If being censored for inadequately caring for Jade weren't a real possibility, she might have found Jade's fear of her going to jail endearingly funny. She smiled brightly. "I'm not going anywhere," she said, skating around the truth.

Marilyn Phillips was standing at the front of the chamber and addressing the small gathering when Deanna and Jade entered. Everyone turned to look at her.

"I apologize for being late," Deanna said, quickly ushering Jade into a row of chairs at the back.

"Ms. Lindsay, would you mind coming forward with Jade?" Judge Horton directed.

Deanna's stomach churned. She glanced at all the

expectant faces around her for some indication as to what would happen next. Marilyn Phillips and Ida Levine appeared more confident than Deanna felt. Joy was looking officious and not giving anything away. Faith Lindsay was sitting in the front row, her expression watchful. Deanna knew that Patterson was finishing his last tour and would be late. Betts was not present.

At the front of the room the judge leaned forward and smiled down at Jade.

"Good morning."

"Hi," Jade murmured, sidling closer to Deanna.

"Jade, I'd like you to go into that next room with this man"—she pointed to a court officer—"while I have a talk with Ms. Lindsay. Can you do that for me?"

Jade hesitated, glancing at Deanna. "Please don't put Deanna in jail."

Deanna groaned and closed her eyes. Subdued laughter rippled through the small room.

The judge looked down at some papers and adjusted her glasses to hide her amusement. "Jade, I want you to know that you don't have to worry about that at all. I'm not going to send Deanna away."

Jade was escorted out by the judge's clerk, and Deanna found herself standing alone in front of the judge.

"Sit down, Ms. Lindsay. Mrs. Phillips was just giving her official evaluation as to Jade's development and adjustment to her mother's death over the past three months."

Deanna sat down next to her mother and was taken completely by surprise when Faith briefly squeezed her hands. Joy gave her an encouraging pat on the shoulder.

As she listened to Marilyn Phillips's comments, Deanna felt some of her anxiety lift. Marilyn had given her high praise. After Marilyn sat down, the judge read from another report.

"As was stated in official documents, the family of the deceased, Stacy Lowell, has been located. However, after a complete briefing about Ms. Lowell's life for the past eight years, during which time the family has had no contact with her, the family has indicated no desire to assume any responsibility for Ms. Lowell's daughter. They have further agreed to sign documents stating they permanently relinquish any claim to Jade and will not interfere in her placement with another caretaker."

The judge looked up once more when the door opened.

"I'm sorry I'm late, everybody."

Deanna heard Betts's slightly winded voice behind her, but she didn't turn around.

"I can only go as fast as these ol' legs will move me."

"And you are?" the judge asked patiently.

"I'm Mrs. Bettina Butler, Your Honor. I'm a friend of Deanna's . . . and I just adore Jade."

Laughter broke out again.

"Who's that?" Faith whispered to Deanna.

It occurred to Deanna that her mother didn't know half of what had gone on in the past twelve weeks. "That's the woman who used to baby-sit Jade—she's almost like a surrogate grandmother. She's Patterson's grandmother."

"And who's Patterson?"

Deanna grinned. "He's the man I'm in love with."

"What!" Faith exclaimed, drawing the judge's attention.

"Ssshhh," Deanna cautioned her mother. "I'll tell you later."

"Let's see if we can finish this proceeding sometime today," the judge said, continuing with her recitation. "Second, there is the question of the parental rights of Jade's natural father, Marcus Lowell. Mr. Lowell has recently been released from jail . . ."

The judge was interrupted by the court clerk, who handed her a folder. She took a moment to peruse the top sheet.

"However, I have just been handed a police report stating that Mr. Lowell is once again in police custody for a variety of crimes, including the suspected kidnapping of his own daughter."

"Lord, have mercy," Betts sighed from the back of the room.

"It has been recommended, and will likely be upheld by state court, that Mr. Lowell be denied parental custody and all future contact with his daughter." She put the papers down. "That leaves me with the decision as to what to do with Jade."

"Your Honor," Joy called out, standing up. "I represent Deanna Lindsay in a petition to request permanent custody of Jade. You've heard from Jade's caseworker that Deanna has not only done a wonderful job of taking care of Jade, but she has also come to love Jade very much."

"It's true, Your Honor. She even told me so." Betts spoke up again.

"Who *is* that woman?" Faith demanded of Deanna, sotto voce.

"Isn't she wonderful?" Deanna said.

"Yes, I have the petition," the judge said. "I see

no problem with it, but of course it's subject to a state review and judgment. A final decision will most likely be made by the end of June."

"I object!" Faith said, jumping to her feet. "It's ridiculous to keep a six-year-old child waiting that long to find out where she's going to live and who's going to care for her."

The judge sighed. "I take it you're a friend of Ms. Lindsay and you love Jade, too?"

"I'm Deanna's mother," Faith demurred, preening at the implied compliment that she was not old enough to be Deanna's mother. "And I've watched that child blossom in her care."

"I can certainly attest to that, Judge Horton," Mrs. Levine said.

"Me, too," a deep male voice chimed in.

Now Deanna did turn around. It was Patterson, who quietly entered the chamber and took a seat next to Betts. He looked quasi-formal in slacks and a sports jacket, and so handsome that Deanna felt pride and joy bring a smile to her lips. He winked at her, and her smile broadened.

"Okay, I get the picture," Judge Horton said with a chuckle. She closed the folder and turned to Faith. "Mrs. Lindsay . . . everyone . . . I appreciate your obvious concern and support for Ms. Lindsay and Jade. It's admirable. You all feel that Jade should stay with Ms. Lindsay, and you support her petition. I'm inclined to agree."

A collective sigh swept the room.

"As I said, however, there is still the state court's decision to be heard. But until then, I am ordering that Jade Taylor Lowell remain in the care of her court-appointed guardian, Deanna Lindsay, with the recommendation that Ms. Lindsay be granted permanent guardianship through adoption."

Outside the judge's chambers laughter, hugs, and kisses were abundant. Jade, in particular, loved the attention she was getting, and Deanna enjoyed seeing her so happy.

Marilyn Phillips and Ida Levine were genuinely pleased with the way the hearing had gone.

"This is one of our happier outcomes," Mrs. Levine confessed.

She and Marilyn offered congratulations all around before returning to their offices. Marilyn had already indicated that she would continue as Jade's caseworker until the state decision was handed down. Joy hugged Deanna, promising to share all her notes on how to raise a child in ten easy lessons. She even gave Patterson a surprise peck on the cheek, leaving him dumbfounded.

Faith, with her usual presumption, introduced herself to Patterson, studying him closely.

"Deanna never told me about you."

"Well, she never told me about you, either."

"I'm not surprised," Faith said dryly. "Did I hear right? She told me she's in love with you."

Patterson did an admirable job of keeping his cool. "I'm in love with her, too. Do I have your permission to court her?"

Faith broke out in surprised and delighted laughter. She patted his arm. "Oh, I like you."

Deanna bent and kissed Betts's soft cheek. "Thanks for coming today. It means so much to me and Jade."

"Well, I told Pat that even if he had to carry me on his back, I wasn't goin' to miss this hearing. I want to see that child in a good home, and I know you can give her one."

"And I promise I'll learn to cook."

Betts laughed and turned her attention to Jade, who wanted to know if she could wear the necklace that Betts had on. Betts promptly took it off and, winding it into a double strand, placed it over her head.

Over the noise and exuberance Deanna and Patterson exchanged a look. They walked toward each other slowly, stopping within a mere foot of one another.

"Still afraid of me?" Deanna asked softly.

He grinned, reaching for her hand. Boldly he leaned close to kiss her on the lips. Behind them, Jade giggled.

"I'm getting over it," he admitted.

"I think we should do something about it."

He arched a brow. "When?"

"Whenever."

"Tonight?"

"I'll arrange for a baby-sitter."

He stepped closer and kissed her again.

"And then what?" Patterson asked, enjoying the sparring.

"And then I'm all yours."

"Ms. Lindsay, before you leave, the judge needs to have you sign something," the clerk called out from the chamber door.

"Coming," Deanna said. She smiled warmly at Patterson, released his hand, and hurried away down the hall.

Patterson watched her walk away, still feeling a bit dazed at how things had developed and where they